A Different Reflection

For Irene

A Different
Reflection

Enjoy

Jane L Gibson

Jane L Gibson

Matador
9 Priory Business Park,
Wistow Road, Kibworth Beauchamp,
Leicestershire. LE8 0RX
Tel: (+44) 116 279 2299
Fax: (+44) 116 279 2277
Email: books@troubador.co.uk
Web: www.troubador.co.uk/matador

ISBN 978 1784622 503

British Library Cataloguing in Publication Data.
A catalogue record for this book is available from the British Library.

Printed and bound by CPI Group (UK) Ltd, Croydon, CR0 4YY
Typeset in Bembo by Troubador Publishing Ltd, Leicester, UK

Matador is an imprint of Troubador Publishing Ltd

MIX
Paper from
responsible sources
FSC® C013604

For Thomas and Ryan
Always believe that you can achieve anything, follow your
dreams and make your wishes come true!

Introduction

My journey to work most mornings on the London tube can be somewhat busy, rushed and hot. I am however distracted from the bustling stations by the many posters showing the new, upcoming and already running shows on at the West End. They help me recall my childhood, and in particular that clever way in which a child's mind can create a whole other world of fantasy from a well-told story. My mother always made sure that she read a fairy tale to me every bedtime, or when I was sick. I found that I had the ability, like most children, of having a very creative imagination, enabling me to conjure up the most vivid images of the wicked witch, the fairy godmother, the damsel in distress and of course the well-documented Prince Charming. I am sure that even today there is not a little girl under the age of ten who would not want to be carried away on horseback by Prince Charming, in a wonderful land filled with romance and magic.

I had the understanding that fairy tales were something that we accepted in our childhood as make-believe. I have however come to realise that magic and fairy tales do indeed exist, and I can confirm this as I have experienced it first-hand. Maybe after reading my story you may find a spark of belief lost in our adulthood; that out there, in our ever-evolving world, there can be the magic and excitement that we experienced as a child, and you can believe in the reality that fairy tales do indeed still occur to this day.

Chapter One

My usual Monday morning trip to work consisted of a very crowded tube ride eight stations long, then a ten-minute walk to my office. I had a very fulfilling job as a journalist and writer for a well-known magazine, which enabled me to interview interesting people and travel a little. This pleased me, as I would never choose to be stuck behind a desk on a full-time basis. During my time as a journalist for my current employer, I met my fiancé, Mr John Cardel, a very successful businessman that I had interviewed some eighteen months ago. It was slightly surprising when he proposed so soon, but we had been engaged now for about ten months, and as our lives were very busy, due to our professional schedules, I could not see us marrying in the very near future. A long engagement was our plan; we had no reason to rush into becoming husband and wife. Just being together was enough for us, for now.

John could be very trying sometimes; his job was stressful and he tended to have a short fuse, which was completely the opposite of myself – calm, relaxed and content (most of the time) – but we seemed to be happy with our situation. We did have slight disagreements, however, on where we should live once married. I did not want to be held ransom to the confines of London city centre living; as much as I loved London, working here was enough for me. John would be happy to have the largest state-of-the-art apartment overlooking the city, but – call me old-fashioned or romantic – I would prefer an old, large house that had been lived in, with a garden and definitely not within a stone's throw of London city centre, but hopefully within commuting distance! Wishful thinking – the cost for property here was phenomenal.

Monday was fairly uneventful, and on the way home I stopped at the newsagents to buy my favourite magazine (other than the one that I worked for, of course) and a lottery ticket. It was always nice to dream of what we would like to buy in the fortunate circumstance of winning. There would be no John for dinner tonight; he had a business meeting over dinner and a late return home planned, and to be honest I am glad of the respite from niceties. Work had thrown a new challenge at me – finding unusual, heart-warming stories that were true. In London, there should be plenty – but whether they were true or not was another matter! I wanted to explore something different, not the usual recovery after illness (which by definition is still remarkable), or the winner of the lottery, or successful businessperson that came from nowhere. I wanted something that would be inspiring and a change from the everyday, miraculous, feel-good stories. So I intended to do some research at home, with a glass of wine in hand.

When I arrived at work the next morning, we had a general meeting on which items were prioritised for the next month's issue. I knew I had six weeks maximum to get this new feature underway, so research was my main priority at the moment, but after a couple of hours on Google last night, it was not looking very promising.

"So Kat, any luck with your research? I know that this has just been handed to you, but any thoughts?" my editor called across the conference table.

To make you aware, all of my friends, family and colleagues – even John – called me Kat, short for Katharina. Long story, but my mother used to love the names of princesses from any country – usually ones that were significant in fairy tales – so I inherited a couple of them! It didn't really bother me that they shortened my given name – it was after all a mouthful and slightly old-fashioned – but I did like my name, even though I didn't hear it very often.

"Not yet Angela, but I am going to sink my teeth into it and hope I have something for you within the next week or two!" I confidently replied. I certainly wasn't one to back down from a challenge or new venture.

"Great, well keep digging – there has to be something different out there worth writing about!" she calmly concluded as the meeting came to an end.

I walked back to my desk and slumped into my chair as a coffee appeared in front of me. "Hey, want to talk about it?" Claire, my lovely assistant and friend (whom unfortunately I share with two other journalists), asked me.

"No, it's fine Claire. Starting a new project is always a little frustrating until a spark of inspiration starts bubbling!" I replied.

"Well, you always come up with something amazing, so I'm not worried!" she stated as she sipped her coffee.

"Thanks, I'm just a little tired. John came home at one in the morning and I didn't go to bed until eleven, he woke me up and I couldn't sleep! Tuesday morning blues, that's all it is!" I laughed after yawning, then took a large gulp of my strong coffee.

Claire placed a hand on my shoulder and muttered, "I bet he woke you up!" She laughed and winked at me, then went back to her desk.

I shook my head at her, smiled and then turned my computer back on. One thing that we did have here was a wealth of knowledge on our database, so I was going to continue my research. Claire had already returned with piles of things to plough through, and so for the next four days I tried to pick up on something that I could expand on, and turn into the story it ought to be. By the time Friday arrived, I was glad it was the weekend. Even though I had a list of possibilities, nothing was particularly inspiring me at this point, which was extremely frustrating.

John and I were meeting with friends of his for dinner tonight, and I welcomed the fact that I need not cook. However, the company we were holding was not the most stimulating at times – Charles and Helen are nice enough, but so very straight-laced. It's a hard task to sit smiling continually whilst wanting to fall asleep during conversation, but Charles and John are work colleagues and enjoy each other's company. Helen is a full-time mum, and although one day I would love to have children, I do not find a whole evening's conversation regarding their child's first potty success, snotty-nosed cold or small achievement at playgroup the most stimulating conversation, or the most exciting way to spend a Friday night.

Tonight, though, I found myself interested in one thing that Charles had to say. John asked him:

"So, how is the house hunting going?"

"Oh, don't ask. It is not as easy as I expected it to be!" Charles replied.

"I didn't know that you were planning on moving home!" I stated with surprise.

"Well we want a garden for the children, and plenty of space, including a spare room for guests to stay. It's not as easy as you might imagine near London!" Helen confirmed. "Oh Charles, tell them about the house we went to see on Wednesday!" She then excitedly said, "It was so strange!"

"How so?" I asked curiously. And so my intrigue began.

"God yes, it was so strange. A beautiful old stately-looking home, with about eight acres of land, ten bedrooms – a little bit run-down, but doable if the price was right! In fact, that's what attracted us in the first place – the price seemed lower than it should be, which made me think that something must be wrong with it. Anyway, we pulled up outside after driving up the long driveway and we both said 'Wow'. On first impression; it was amazing! Definitely old – it must have been over two hundred years – but amazing to look at!" he said, with slight disappointment.

"Well it sounds perfect Charles. You can afford it anyway!" John then said as he sat back in his chair.

"Ah, but wait!" Charles then replied. I waited in

anticipation. "We went up the elaborate front steps to meet the agent and entered the main door. Jesus, John, it was like walking back in time; marble floors, marble stairs, chandeliers, old portraits and furniture and lots of mirrors. It was a little creepy, if I'm being honest, but with an open mind we followed along and looked around and then, bam, there it was – the problem!" he finished as he punched his own hand.

"What?" John asked inquisitively.

"A clause in the deeds and ownership of the house – named George!" Charles finished. John looked at them, then at me, then back at Charles.

"George?" John asked. "Who for the love of God is George?" Charles laughed.

"George is the old butler of the house, I think. He has been granted the right to live in the house and to have the freedom to roam within it until he should so depart this world! The original owners signed rights of the property over to him with the clause that he can stay there! Oh, and get this – there is nothing that can be done about it!" he finished.

"But surely if the house is empty, he would not want to stay there any longer – particularly if he's not working there. God, how old is he?" I asked.

"I wouldn't like to put an age on him! Trust me, we asked all of the questions, Kat, but believe me when I say that old George is a spritely chap and doesn't look like he is going anywhere anytime soon! He lives in an apartment attached to the place. He said that, as he feels that he lives there, it is his duty to continue the upkeep as much as he is able, but he chooses to stay there because

6

– and these were his words – 'How can one leave a place that they have been all their life, with people they love, with memories they treasure, in a place that they call home?' God, it was like something from a movie!" Charles took a swig of his wine.

"The sad thing is, as much as George seems like a nice man, how can we possibly live there with the children? He's a stranger and he's entitled to roam around anywhere he should choose! It's very strange; I think that they will struggle to sell or rent it at all," Helen confirmed.

"I'm sorry, I can't understand why, if he is so happy there and has the right to live there, he is trying to sell it, or rent it, or whatever he intends to do?" I asked.

"Well, that's the other thing. It is marketed on the low side, but the purchase is leasehold for ninety-nine years, so it goes back to George's family eventually anyway!" Charles took another gulp of his wine. "I cannot think of anything worse – spending a large amount of money and then having to share the house with someone else, with stipulations on renovation because George likes it the way it is. I think he needs the cash to look after it and he's probably a lonely old fool! We walked away confused at the situation, but decided that it was not for us!" Charles finished.

"Well, sounds too complicated to me. I say good riddance and keep looking!" John answered.

I sat for a while contemplating the whole story. The more I thought about it, the more I found it a touching story, and I wanted to find out more. Whilst John and Charles moved their conversation to sport, I looked to Helen and leaned across the table to speak in a quieter voice.

"Helen, do you think that you could let me have the name of the property agent marketing this strange house? I'm doing a new feature for the magazine and I think that this could have the grounds for a good story!" I smiled at her.

"Oh sure," she replied as she dipped into her purse for a pen and paper. "In fact, I think that I have one of his business cards in here. I will write the name of the house on the back!" she excitedly chirped as she pulled a purple card from her purse and scribbled 'Northfield' on the back. As she passed the card to me, I had a good feeling about it, and looked at the name she had so neatly written. "Ooh, how exciting. Wouldn't it be great if you did write a story on this? I definitely think there is a story there!" she stated, then leaned closer and whispered, "I actually think that I felt sorry for George, but don't tell Charles. He just looked so lonely." I nodded in reply and placed the card carefully into my bag. I felt as though I should treat it with respect; it could be my next – no, *the* next big story for the magazine. It would be my first line of enquiry on Monday morning.

The weekend passed relatively insignificantly; it was nice to chill a little bit, with no pressure. John had to work from home on Sunday; when I awoke, I found him already hard at work. When we decided to take a stroll around Regent's Park in the early evening, I was glad of the fresh air. We dined and shared wine at The Open Air Theatre, which was showing the re-imagined play of *The Winter's Tale*, which John had purchased tickets for, as he knew my love of stories – particularly ones involving princesses! When we arrived home I felt perfectly content with the evening, and ready for my week at work.

When Monday morning arrived, I was quick to call the property agents from the card that Helen had passed to me. Mr Justin Temperley of Madison Cleaver; it sounded very exclusive indeed. I punched the number into my phone and when the receptionist answered I asked for him. She in turn wished to know what my call was regarding, and when I mentioned Northfield, she almost sounded surprised that I had said the word. After holding for only a few seconds a young, enthusiastic male answered.

"Hello, Justin Temperley speaking, how may I help you?" he politely asked.

"Hello, Katharina Stuart from *Resolute* magazine," I replied.

"Oh, hello Katharina, how can I help you?" he asked again, with surprise in his voice.

"I was calling about a property you are agents for, and was recently told about – Northfield? My friends recently went to view it. I am doing an article for the magazine about unusual true stories and I am led to believe there is an old butler that still resides there. I would really like to meet him; if he is in agreement, I would like to do a piece on him!" I replied.

"Ah!" Justin answered, sounding disappointed that I was not a prospective buyer. "And what exactly is it that you require from me?" he then asked.

"Well, actually Justin, I wondered if you could put me in touch with him, or take me there to meet him? If anything, the piece may rouse some interest from potential and possible buyers," I then stated, sounding very sure. There was silence for a few seconds and I sat with my eyes closed and fingers crossed, hoping to hear the words that I needed to hear.

"Very well Miss Stuart, I will give Mr Grey a call and see what he says. Is this the best number to get you on?" he asked. I punched the air in excitement.

"Yes, absolutely. Thank you so much, Justin. I look forward to speaking with you soon," I replied.

"I will call you as soon as I have been in touch with him," he then said.

"Claire!" I called as I hung up. "I think that I may have that story!" I happily announced. She came bouncing across to my desk to find out the details.

"Brilliant, what is it, can you tell me?" she curiously asked. I sat with her and briefly explained the situation. "Poor old chap, rattling around there; I bet he is really lonely. I do think it will be interesting, though; I bet he has some real tales to tell from working there! So what do you need from me?" she then asked.

"I need as much information as you can find on Northfield. How old it is, who built it, who has lived there, what happened to previous owners, and any exciting events that have taken place there!"

In the meantime, I started to do some research of my own on the building itself. From plans, it did look spectacular; as I became engrossed in the information I was gathering, I was taken by surprise when my phone rang. It was Mr Justin Temperley.

"Katharina, hello there, it's Justin from Madison Cleaver!" he stated.

"Yes, hello Justin, I'm hoping that this is good news?" I winced as I crossed my fingers again.

"Well, it took a bit of persuading, but he is happy to see you. He has insisted though that it must be at two o'clock on Wednesday."

"Fantastic. Thank you for your help, Justin. Should a story be printed from the outcome of this meeting with Mr Grey, I will be sure to mention you in the piece," I replied as I stood with excitement.

"I should hope so!" he said with sarcasm. "Good luck with him. I will say that he isn't the most forthcoming of gentlemen!" Justin then finished, before ringing off.

"Yes!" I happily exclaimed as I walked to get another coffee. I passed Claire's desk. "Book me out for the afternoon on Wednesday, I have a meeting in place!" I informed her.

She smiled. "I told you not to worry!" she said confidently as she tapped away on her computer.

Tuesday was spent researching and doing more researching. The more I looked back at the history of Northfield, the more captivating it became. There were pictures and drawings of the building itself dating back to over two hundred years before, including plans of the house and gardens. Unfortunately there was not very much to find on the people who had lived there or anything that had taken place there. It was fast becoming a fascination; surely there must be something in its long history to uncover? However, it was quickly becoming apparent that we did not know how old this house actually was – definitely a question for George who, after working there, would hopefully have some knowledge of its past. I had a fairly good feeling about this and couldn't wait for tomorrow. Roll on Wednesday.

Chapter Two

When lunchtime on Wednesday arrived, to say that I was relieved was an understatement. Although I had a couple of other leads that I had followed up, they were not intriguing me as much as Northfield and George. I had been given the use of one of the cars from work. The drive out there seemed long, mainly due to the heavy traffic, but the mileage was not high.

I completely understood what Charles and Helen had meant; just the driveway itself was impressive. As I passed through the tall iron gates that were open and travelled the length of the driveway, the house slowly came into view. It was magnificent; almost a picture book mansion from a film. Yes, a little run-down, but more impressive than I had been expecting! I had an even better feeling about this now; the facade was a good start and the pictures would make an impressive feature page. More questions sprang to mind as I pulled up near the elaborate stairs to the front entrance. I nervously reached for my bag, which held already researched paperwork, my notepad and Dictaphone.

I stood and looked at the front of the building before climbing the stairs. I rang the old bell and waited patiently. A few seconds later, the door slowly opened and a very charming-looking older gentleman stood there. He looked at me and then smiled.

"Miss Stuart, I presume?" he said in a very kind manner, as he gestured for me to come in.

"Why yes. George, I presume? It's very nice to meet you!" I then replied, as I reached my hand to shake his. He looked at it briefly and took it in his, then proceeded to bend and kiss the back of it delicately.

"The pleasure is all mine!" he replied. I felt like I had stepped back in time; then, for a moment, I looked around the hallway in which we stood and I stopped breathing.

Staring at the intricate features of the ornate ceiling, chandeliers, furniture and incredible staircase before me, I quietly whispered to myself, "Oh wow!" Then I was brought back to reality with the loud noise of the door closing, which George had pushed forcefully. I had caught its closure in the large mirror before me and quickly turned to face George.

"Yes, it is impressive, isn't it?" he remarked at my state of awe.

"It's amazing. I had no idea that places like this still existed. Well, places like this that are still being run as a home, and not as a public attraction!" I replied.

"Oh goodness no, I do not want to share it with half the population of the country!" he smiled. "Shall we?" He gestured toward an open doorway to his left.

"Yes of course, I do not wish to take up too much of your time!" I replied, as I walked into the most stunning day room. It was luxurious in its decor and rich in colour, and had antiques that I am sure many collectors would die for. "I think that I am going to be shocked into silence with every room I should walk into, George!" I remarked as I looked around, noting again another large mirror either side of the fireplace.

"I forget its splendour sometimes, Miss Stuart. After living here for so long, I think that I take it for granted!" he replied as he again gestured for me to sit.

"Please, do call me Kat!" I replied as I sat and took out my notebook.

"Kat? Did your parents not like you very much?" he then asked sincerely. I laughed and shook my head.

"No, not at all!" I replied, then tried to explain, "It has become a nickname – a shortened version of my name that most people tend to call me."

"What is your given name?" he asked.

"Katharina!" I replied. "It's a little old-fashioned, I know; I seem to have inherited the shortened version for the ease of my friends!" I explained.

"Katharina. Such a beautiful name, it should be spoken every day!" he said warmly. "I should prefer to call you by your full name, if that is acceptable?" he asked.

"Katharina is good. I do actually like my name. My mother had very romantic notions toward names, but that's another story! Anyway, enough about me!" I quickly ended that explanation as I shook my head. He smiled.

"So, Katharina. You would like to do an interview with me because...?" he questioned.

"Ah, well, friends of my fiancé came to look around a couple of weeks ago and mentioned that you lived here alone, and I was intrigued that you didn't want to leave. I thought it may be a heart-warming story to find out why!" I explained. He looked at me and then stood to pour some tea that was waiting on the table.

"Tea?" he asked.

"Yes, with milk please," I answered. As he poured, he began.

"This house has a long story, Katharina, and I am not sure how much time that you have, but I can certainly start by telling you the history of the house and how it came to be here," he then replied.

"Great!" I replied. "It was not easy trying to find any history on the house in the library at all, other than plans or drawings," I informed him.

"Hmmm, I believe that is the case!" he then said. "It is a good job that some people are still living, who have all the knowledge up here!" He finished as he tapped the side of his head. I smiled. He took a sip from his tea and then continued:

"Well, once upon a time... It was the year 1696, during the reign of William III. It was quite an eventful year for this house. It had just been finished in the spring by the original owner, Mr Charles Montagu Montgomery. He made his fortune by inheriting his father's fortune as a Noble, but then he proceeded to squander it away with gambling and drinking. The house was a statement of his new position, but he had no common sense. By the time the year 1702 had arrived, he was well-known for his debts and Northfield was sold to the highest bidder," he explained. He took a sip from his tea whilst I scribbled notes.

"Who was to buy the house from him?" I asked. George smiled.

"That would have been Mr Howard James Aldersley and his wife Mary Anne. Very nice people, but very unfortunate in circumstance," he said, slightly dismayed.

"How so?" I asked curiously. He sat and looked deep into his cup and carried on again.

"They purchased the house and brought it back to life. By the summer of 1705, Northfield was well respected and many balls for nobility and gentry had been held here. For many years, it thrived. Then, tragedy struck." He shook his head. "In 1709, poor Mary, who was with child, had complications and died along with her unborn child. It was more pain than Howard could bear, and for a long time he lived here in solitude, trying to cope with his grief. It was only when his wife's sister Margaret came in 1711 to come to the aid of her brother-in-law that his life started to regain purpose. Margaret stayed here for nearly a year before she managed to get any useful occupation out of Howard. She too had lost her dearest sister and together they became united in living a life without her." He smiled again, took a sip of his tea and then looked to me. "Am I going too quickly for you?" he asked. I quickly put down my cup and saucer.

"No, not at all George, I am completely spellbound by your story. Please do carry on!" I replied as I put pencil back to paper. George looked toward the mirror that was opposite him and then looked at me and carried on.

"Margaret fell in love with Howard, as he did her, and in 1715 they married and once again Northfield became a place of social gatherings. Many happy years continued and when Margaret found that she was with child in 1720, Howard – although nervous – was elated at the possibility of an heir." He stood to place his teacup on the table.

"Gosh, I cannot imagine how troubled Howard must have been after losing his first wife to pregnancy. Did she survive?" I asked with hope.

"Oh yes, she was very well indeed throughout her pregnancy, and the birth by all accounts was not complicated at all," George said as he stood by the fireplace, then he turned to me. "A son was born – Master James Henry Aldersley, 3rd September 1720, a day of celebration at Northfield. The staff were delighted at the new arrival, and at the good fortune that had found the Aldersleys." He then walked toward me. "Perhaps, Katharina, I should show you a portrait or two so that you know of whom I speak."

"Why yes, I would love to," I replied as I stood and took my Dictaphone – it was easier to record than write whilst walking. "Do you mind if I record everything you say?" I asked George.

"If you find it at all interesting, then no, I do not mind at all. That is why you are here is it not?" he asked. I smiled and nodded and we walked along through two grand rooms before coming upon a large elongated room, upon which every wall had a portrait of some description. Yet again, though, there were mirrors to be found in every room. As I stopped and looked into one of them, I had to ask:

"Was one of the previous owners very vain? I find it slightly unnerving to have so many mirrors to catch images of myself!" I asked. George came and stood beside me.

"Why, what do you see?" he asked, as he stared into the mirror with me.

"I see you and myself!" I replied. George looked disappointed; he sighed heavily.

"Hmmm, maybe for now. There is something special to be seen when gazing in a mirror!" George then said as he walked away. I looked at myself and thought his remark was slightly obscure, then turned to catch up with him. I found him muttering to himself as he walked along. Maybe he wasn't as sane as I had first thought. As he realised that I was beside him, he stopped. "So I think it best that we start at this end of the room, with the first portrait of where it all began," he happily said. "This strange-looking fellow would be Edward Montgomery, who authorised the building of Northfield before his death in 1690. He never saw Northfield finished, but insisted to his son that he finish it and live here. He was the last of their family. His mother had died some ten years prior," George confirmed. I looked at the painting.

"He's a slightly aggressive-looking person, isn't he?" I stated as I looked at the person in the portrait.

"He was, I am told, a very headstrong man. He never backed away from anything he saw fit," George replied. We moved along; "This would be his son, Charles Montagu Montgomery," he then said. "Before you say anything, this portrait, I believe, was done a year or two before his addiction to alcohol and gambling. Otherwise we may have had a portrait with him asleep or intoxicated!" George raised his eyebrows and I laughed, moving along with him.

"This is a beautiful portrait," I then stated as I stared at the graceful and angelic looking woman in the painting. George sighed and then clasped his hands together as if in prayer.

"Ah yes, this would be the very lovely Mary Anne Aldersley." He smiled.

"She looks no more than twenty-one or two in this painting!" I said.

"She was twenty years of age and it was the year of her wedding to Howard. How very heavy-hearted it makes me feel to know that only eight years or thereabouts after this portrait, she was to lose her life to something we find is so controllable today," he said, slightly pained. I touched George's arm.

"Yes, it is despairing, but she also had great love in her short life – many of us do not have the opportunity to experience," I stated with slight regret. If I think of my relationship with John and how much of our lives are focused on our careers, I cannot imagine him being so grief-stricken at my loss for too long a time. George gestured for me to move on.

"This is Howard James Aldersley, whom I consider to be the 'main master' of this house. He turned it around from being complete ruin, even after tragedy," George happily stated.

"He looks very gentlemanly and very kind!" I replied.

"That he was; a very kind and fair man!" George then stated as a matter of fact.

"You express the sentiment as if you knew him!" I exclaimed to George. He looked at me with surprise and shook his head.

"Only what I have heard in stories past!" he confirmed. I nodded in agreement. "This is Margaret Elizabeth Aldersley, Howard's second wife. She was very beautiful, like her sister, but the elder of the two, and

Howard's saviour I believe!" George then said as I stared at her.

"She is very beautiful, but very petite," I said with surprise. "Her hands look like that of a small child, unless the artist himself was not too good at perspective!" I queried as I looked at George. He laughed heartily:

"No, the artist was quite experienced; it was well-documented that she was only a small lady, but had a heart the size of an elephant!" he said as he finished laughing.

As we walked to the next portrait, of a young boy with dark, long, floppy hair, I smiled. "Don't tell me – James Henry Alderlsey?" I asked, hoping that I was correct.

"Yes indeed. A very spritely four-year-old boy; he did not really have the patience for sitting for a portrait, but, at the order of his father, was made to do so!" George said, with his arms folded across his chest like a proud father.

"He does look somewhat resentful at the request. He looks like a typical boy of that age and was desperate to be exploring and playing, I suspect!" I replied.

"Oh, quite the adventurer, I don't think that there has ever been a child with as much energy as young James. Stories that have been told lead me to believe he was quite the handful!" George remarked.

"Well, handful or not – and resentful or not – he still does have a slight angelic look about him, I think," I smiled at the portrait just as the clock chimed four. "Goodness, George, I've already taken up two hours of your time, and I haven't even asked anything about you!"

I said, feeling slightly bad at the fact that I had been so engrossed in the story that he had started telling.

"It has been quite the trip down memory lane!" he replied in a light-hearted manner. He paused briefly and then, just as I was about to ask him if I could call on him again, he did the asking for me: "I have found your company a refreshing change, Katharina. Maybe you would like to visit again soon?" he asked.

"I would like that very much George, if you have no reservations about me continuing with your story?" I replied, as we started to walk back toward the day room.

"Maybe Friday?" he then enquired.

"Yes, I can fit an appointment in on Friday; I would like that!" I nodded, knowing that my schedule for the rest of the week was pretty free. I had planned on being in the office.

"Maybe rather than just an appointment, you could stay for dinner? I still have some skills – cooking being one of them!" he suggested. I smiled.

"Alright, it's a date!" I happily replied. "Friday at what time?" I enquired.

"Let's say four, then you can ask me any more questions before dinner," he answered.

I packed my belongings into my bag and George held my coat for me whilst I placed my arms into the sleeves, and then headed out of the door and down the stairs to my car. "Oh darn, I've left my keys on the table," I called to George, as I sat my bag on the bonnet. He held up his hand.

"No problem, I will get them," he replied as he turned to walk back indoors. I started to walk back toward the main door, and as I got nearer I could hear George talking. "You need to stop being so sceptical. How do you know she's only been here once!" I moved nearer to the day room and listened closely. "Anyway, your company is getting a little tiresome at times. Just remember it's not only you – I am stuck like this too!" he then said.

I started to question his sanity again; schizophrenia sprang to mind. I coughed loud enough for him to hear and walked in. "Everything alright, George? I thought that I heard you talking!" I asked him. He turned quickly toward me.

"Katharina! Yes, sorry, I'm just mad at myself. Forgot for a second what I came for – think it's an age thing! Ah! Here we are!" he then said as he grabbed the keys and came and placed them in my hand.

"Thank you. I just came to give you a business card. Should you need to change our appointment, my number is on there," I informed him.

"Lovely!" He nodded as he accepted it from me.

"So Friday at four then!" I confirmed as I skipped back down the stairs.

"Indeed!" he replied. "Lovely to meet you!" he called.

"Likewise!" I shouted back as I hopped into the car and started the engine.

I could see him waving in my rear view mirror, so I wound my window down and extended a waving arm out of it. "Well that was interesting!" I commented to myself. I drove back to the office thinking about what he had told me. It certainly sounded like the truth and I had to confess that I was looking forward to seeing him again on Friday. I found him quite charming – not difficult, as Justin Temperley had suggested. On my arrival back at the office, I wanted to type up my notes whilst they were fresh in my head. Besides, most of the office worked on until seven on a Wednesday. Claire was inquisitive and wanted to know how the interview had gone. She jokingly said that I had a new admirer in the form of an old gentleman. I knew, though, that if she met George, she would see that he seemed to be a very charming, kind and endearing man, who unfortunately, I suspected, was a little bit lonely.

Chapter Three

I t was a long day at work on Thursday, and a frustrating one again with regards to research. Everything that George had told me about the previous owners of Northfield led to very little reference from the library, or online. By the time I arrived home, I was somewhat deflated. My enthusiasm for the story was there, but I couldn't get my teeth into it any further without other documented history to follow up.

I dropped my bag by the island in the kitchen and immediately went to the fridge. A glass of rosé had the ability to give an immediate 'pick me up' at times like these. John arrived home about thirty minutes after me; his day, by all accounts, had not been much better. We both had a glass of wine, and then John moved into the office whilst he continued working on an important business deal. I proceeded to buy Chinese food; I was not in the frame of mind for cooking!

I slept well, woke early and showered, changed and had breakfast. I took it upon myself to take a bottle of wine for the dinner tonight, so I placed one in my bag whilst I was thinking about it. When John walked into the kitchen, looking like he hadn't slept very much, I poured him a coffee and then reminded him of my dinner date.

"So I could be a little late back tonight. Don't forget I have a business dinner!" I reminded him.

"Ah yes. With the mad, lonely old man, at the big creepy old house!" he sarcastically replied. He took a sip from his coffee and then looked at me. "I can't say that I'm happy about this, but I trust your judgement on the situation. Let me know when you're on your way back. I also have to stay on at work tonight for a meeting, so I may not get back until late either," he confirmed.

"Alright, I will. Please don't worry; he is honestly harmless!" I tried to reassure him. He simply nodded in agreement with my statement, grabbed his things, quickly kissed me on the cheek and then made his exit to work.

My tube ride into work was, as usual, hot, busy and crowded and resulted in me getting a slight headache, but I was nevertheless slightly distracted by the theatre posters, which always made me think of a colourful, magical and alternative life to my own. I made sure that during the day I gathered together all the pictures, drawings and research I had accumulated to date. I wanted to check that what I had was correct in reference, and I knew that George would have knowledge on this. By the time it got to two o'clock, I had a brief meeting with Angela, my editor, on what I was working on, and to let her know where I was going.

"Well there's one thing, Kat, if this George does turn out to be slightly mad and he locks you up in the house with him for eternity, we will still have a story to write about!" she laughed.

"Very funny, you're starting to sound like John!" I remarked.

"No, seriously just be careful, you never know. I'm sure he will be a wealth of knowledge and I agree it does sound like there is a story there. I know had it been my story Kat, I'd be doing exactly the same thing!" she replied. I smiled.

"Well, I will let you know how it has gone after the weekend!" I then told her.

"Yep, Monday morning's meeting should be interesting!" she smiled. "Off you go then!" she then stated as she flicked her hand toward the door in a gesture for me to leave.

As there were no spare cars available at work today, and it was the weekend approaching, Angela had authorised the use of a cab there and back, which was easier than trying to get public transport out there. As the cab arrived at Northfield and I reached forward to pay, I was happy to see that George had appeared and was walking down the stairs toward me. He opened my door.

"Katharina, I am so very pleased to see you again!" he happily exclaimed. He reached out a hand for me as I stepped from the cab.

"Thank you George. It's not always the easiest getting out of one of these cabs!" I laughed, trying to juggle my bags.

"Indeed. I was expecting you to be in the car. I could have come and picked you up!" he kindly replied.

"Oh that's not necessary George," I quickly said. "You do not want to be driving in London traffic on a Friday afternoon! Besides, I would have driven myself had there been a car available from work. It really is no trouble," I replied. He gestured for me to walk up the stairs with him. "Before I forget, I brought a bottle of wine for dinner. I wasn't sure if you liked wine, it might need to breathe a little while though!" I remarked at the expensive bottle of red wine that I had taken.

"How very kind. I do like wine, and red is my favourite. Maybe we should go to the kitchen first before we continue, then I can take out the cork?" he suggested. I nodded and let George lead the way down the corridor and into the biggest kitchen that I had ever seen. It was old-fashioned in its looks, but it was easy to imagine this being a busy working kitchen in years past.

"Wow, what an amazing space for cooking!" I remarked. George stopped and then looked at me.

"Yes, well back in the days it was a kitchen that produced the finest food. I find it a little too big for me, so I tend to use the small back kitchen attached to my apartment," he smiled as he then continued through another door and into a humble dwelling off the back of the main house that was well lived in, but very cosy. I smiled.

"This looks very homely, George!" I told him.

"Yes, I love it here. As you can imagine, it is a little more manageable than the rest of the house!" he laughed. He reached for the bottle opener and then, with the cork out, suggested that we continue where we had left off. He checked the oven and then gestured for me to walk back to the main house with him.

"It must have been amazing in its day. I mean, it is amazing now, but when it was full of people bustling around working here, and a family here, and it was thriving... I would really have liked to see it like that!" I commented. George smiled.

"Houses like this love to be full of life and love and laughter, so it is a little sad that only I live here at the moment. It is one of the reasons that I wanted to try and sell the space to someone whom would enjoy it as it is. Unfortunately people these days seem to love this new modern way of living and this is far too old and outdated for them!" he sadly replied.

"Well if it's any consolation, George, I love it as it is. I think it's an amazing house and I think it should be left as it is. I would love to see the rest of it!" I replied with excitement. George smiled.

"Well, let me show you then! Maybe I am wrong in my assumption that everyone has moved on from places like this. I mean, you are a beautiful young woman and you like it; there is possibly hope for me yet?" he then stated as I blushed at his comment.

He proceeded to show me the other reception rooms and the bedrooms. Oh, my goodness, I had never seen such intricate four-poster beds, with luxurious fabrics and paintings and furniture; the floorboards throughout were polished and had that lovely woody, waxy polished smell. I loved everything about it: its splendour, its age and detail, and, most of all, its warm feeling that drew you in and made you wish you lived there. Or, at least, that is how I felt. George, I then realised, was watching me.

"I would love to know what you were thinking just now!" he then said. I smiled.

"I love it, everything about it, and how it makes me feel when I am here. If I had the money, George, I would buy it myself, it's just perfect. Well, perfect for me!" I happily stated. He gave me the warmest smile and then gestured for us to continue.

After looking at every other room, we arrived at the library. It was magnificent and had a character of its own; it was not huge in size, but was well stocked with books from years past. The colourful spines all neatly side by side were a sight to see, and as with all libraries I closed my eyes and took a deep breath, to inhale the smell. I asked George if he should mind if I looked at a book or two and he was more than happy that I was so interested.

"You know, I am going to go and get us both a glass of the wine that you so kindly brought," he suddenly stated. "You help yourself and look at any books you so wish, I will be back promptly!" he then finished as he left the room. I was in my element; I loved books – particularly old books – and that smell of the old printed pages and the leather spines was blissful. I looked at the many books on the shelves and then saw a whole section that were Scott's Waverley novels and the works of Lord Byron, and then it continued with books of poetry, tales, and then fairy tales. I stopped immediately. The works of Charles Perrault; *Little Red Riding Hood*, *Puss in Boots*, *Cinderella*, *Sleeping Beauty*, and then The Grimm Brothers, Hans Christian Handersen, Carlo Lorenzini, and Charles Ludwidge Dodgson (Lewis Carroll). I smiled the biggest grin; here were all of my most loved and favourite fairy tales, and it looked like they were first editions too. I carefully pulled *Sleeping Beauty* off the shelf and took a deep breath before opening the front cover. It was an exquisite, old, beautiful leather-bound book, with a small but pretty font. I started to read the first pages and walked back and forth in front of the huge mirror that covered a large part of the only spare wall. I carefully turned the pages and continued reading and walking and fell into the spell of make-believe and memories of my mother reading it to me. As I smiled at the pages and continued to pace, I turned and stopped to face the mirror whilst still reading. I do not know what caught my eye, but I looked up from the book at my reflection and found that it was not me staring back but a young, dishevelled man, with his hands clasped firmly on his hips, as if slightly annoyed with me!

I dropped the book as George suddenly appeared and took me by surprise. "Here we are!" he said in a spritely tone. As the book hit the floor, I turned with a sharp jolt and George looked at me with worry. He placed the glasses on the round table nearby. "Are you alright, Katharina?" he asked. I turned back to the mirror; the only thing I saw was my reflection. I turned back to George, who was now beside me.

"I looked in the mirror, but I did not see me!" I replied.

"What did you see?" he asked. I paused for a minute and then replied.

"I know that I saw a young man, with dark, slightly dishevelled hair. I must have had too long a day!" I replied, feeling slightly foolish. George put his arm around me and moved me toward the table, looking over his shoulder at the mirror. He replied:

"Sometimes we see things that are necessary, but not completely logical!" he said as he placed a glass in my hand. "Maybe this will help?" he then said, as he pointed to the wine. I looked at it and then took a long hard gulp. I looked at him.

"That is much better!" I replied as I turned to the mirror. "I think I have been brought up with too much belief in fairy tales and happy endings, and now I am seeing things!" I said as I walked over and picked up the book I had so carelessly dropped. "This was always one of my favourites," I then said as I showed it to George.

"Ah, and a good choice it is!" he replied, looking at the book. "There is much to be said about so-called fairy tales and magic!" he then said. As I looked at him, slightly vexed, he then looked at his watch. "Dinner will only be ten minutes. Let us head back to the kitchen; you can ask me more questions there," he finished as he walked toward the door, but not before putting the book back on the shelf.

The small kitchen in George's apartment was filled with the aroma of chicken and tarragon and I immediately felt hungry. He asked that I take a seat and enjoy the wine that he had refilled my glass with upon entering the kitchen. He put on a dark blue apron and then proceeded to start busying around the kitchen.

"Anything that I can do to help?" I asked as I watched.

"No, that will not be necessary Katharina, but please go ahead and ask me any questions that you should wish to ask whilst I finish dinner," he happily replied. I excused myself and got up to retrieve my bag from the reception hallway. As I turned to walk back, I caught my reflection in the large mirror and stopped for a second. *Have I been working too hard? Am I going crazy?* I asked myself these questions whilst looking at my reflection and then shook my head and returned to George.

He was happy in his kitchen and decided to carry on from where he had left off. "So, we finished at the mischievous Master James, I recall from last time?" George prompted.

"Yes, 'quite a handful' were your words, I believe!" I joked.

"He was that! For a number of years he would disappear for hours on end and cause his parents no end of worry!" George shook his head. "He would be happily tucked away in one of his corners or hiding places, usually with a book of some description, about exploration, pirates, building and architecture or animals; unfortunately, usually the dissection of them and how they work!" He laughed like a proud grandparent.

"Boys, eh?" I asked as I took a sip of my wine. "He was an only child?" I then queried.

"Yes indeed; not wanting to ask too much, Howard did not want to put his wife at risk after a successful pregnancy. They chose to stop at one child. Howard loved James so much, they were inseparable!" George replied as we moved to the table.

George cooked the most amazing meal. We laughed and talked about Northfield and the building itself, including the gardens, and as we ate and drank wine, I found myself having the most relaxing and enjoyable time. As we finished the last drop of wine from the bottle, George suggested we return to the portrait gallery and carry on, which was what I wanted to do as I was fascinated by the whole history and ambience of this place.

We moved along to the next two portraits. "Wow,

that's a very sorrowful looking boy!" I said as we stopped and looked at the sad young boy on one of the paintings in front of us, all in black and with heartache in his eyes.

"This was Master James on his sixteenth birthday – the day he became a man!" George sighed. "Unfortunately, two months earlier his father became very ill and took to his bed for two weeks before dying. He initially contracted influenza and then it progressed into pneumonia. Poor Margaret was inconsolable, and James had become heir to the estate overnight and had become the head of the house! He was devastated at the loss of his father and unfortunately in the days that followed it was to take its toll," George said sadly.

"I am sure at that age it was a very hard duty to uphold whilst trying to grieve and console his mother at the same time," I replied.

"Hmmm, Howard was indeed missed by all. He was a very sound employer and friend," he replied. "This is why I am glad that they had a family portrait done whilst James was fourteen. Happier memories are good to reflect on sometimes; it reminds us of why we should go on living our lives." George smiled as he looked at the painting alongside the one of James; all of them, smiling, an inseparable family. "A little like having a photograph to cherish!" he then said. I smiled at the portrait and tried to understand how tough it must have been for a sixteen-year-old boy to have so much responsibility. George gestured for us to move on and we passed another large mirror which he glanced in briefly as I smiled at him.

The next painting was, as portraits go, breathtaking. It was of a very handsome well-built man, with sapphire blue eyes and dark long hair that was swept back. He was well dressed and held himself very well indeed. I stopped and stared for a long time when George spoke:

"You like this portrait?" he asked. I turned to him.

"Well, as a woman, you would have to have no pulse not to like that one!" I laughed as I replied honestly and openly, with the courage of wine.

"Yes, well… Master James became quite the 'magnet' for young women, very much to his mother's disapproval!" he replied, with his arms crossed across his chest. I gawped at him in surprise.

"Wait a minute, this is the same person as the sorrowful sixteen-year-old?" I asked as I walked back to the previous painting, looked at it and then returned back to George. "He looks so different, so well… how can I say it… so well lived and sure of himself!" I finished.

"Oh yes, he lived well. Drinking – or drowning his sorrows – gatherings, gambling, girls… he was only twenty-five at the time of this portrait, and as the years passed it only got worse. His mother did not try to stop him any longer; she hated watching him live the way he was. She wanted him to find love – real, true love, as she had – but she knew his behaviour was to avoid disappointment or loss the way she had suffered." He sighed. "It was a truly sad and heart breaking time for all who had watched him grow from a small boy, to see what he had become. However, everyone tried to support him the best that they could," he then finished.

"So there was no marriage? Is that why she was so negative?" I asked.

"Oh Katharina, marriage would have been ideal,

according to his mother; the problem with Master James was that he did not want to settle down. After the loss of his father and having to run the estate, he became isolated from society for quite a time. After some time, though, he could not bear to see his mother so upset on a daily basis with her loneliness. With him needing to attend social meetings and gatherings, he started to surround himself with more and more people at events where he felt important and needed," George explained.

"So he thought being surrounded by many people would stop him from becoming lonely?" I queried. George nodded as he looked at the painting.

"He started to realise that he was popular with the female species – usually rich, beautiful women – and he used it to his advantage!" George replied.

"Reckless, I would say, and self-destructive! I take it he only attached himself to these women for the night, or as long as they entertained him?" I then asked.

"Nice way of putting it, Katharina! Yes, that's exactly what he did. He had the notion in his thick head that if he did not get close to any single woman, then she could not break his heart. Marriage was not anywhere near the top of his list, I assure you!" he said with anger and regret.

"I find it very sad that he felt that way. After seeing his mother so upset, I can imagine it would make you very protective of yourself, but to deny that kind of love and affection and commitment with someone… it's a far worse torture to endure, and extremely sad!" I answered, as George looked at me.

"Do you believe that love and commitment of that

magnitude are available to everyone?" he questioned. I smiled.

"Oh George, absolutely!" I stated with conviction. "I am a huge believer in the 'happily ever after' story of love and affection on that scale. It's what I have always wanted!" I replied as I stared at the portrait.

"You do not have that now? You are engaged, are you not?" he asked. I looked at the ring on my finger.

"Yes, I am engaged, but there is another story entirely!" I replied with doubt.

"Your fiancé is not a romantic, then?" George asked as he looked directly into my eyes. I smiled and touched his shoulder.

"Unfortunately he is not! Unlike some of us, George," I sighed and moved along, then continued, "I thrive on stories of love that has lasted against all odds. A love worth dying for, and certainly worth fighting to live every day to experience!" I finished as I turned and looked at him. I shrugged and smiled again. "I cannot believe I just told you that!" I then quickly followed it up with.

"Well, do not give up hope, Katharina; after all, I find it is always acceptable and possible to believe in fairy tales!" George smiled at me and walked toward me.

"I always live in the hope of being promised a love like that!" I laughed lightly. "So what happened to James?" I then asked. George sighed.

"You really want to know?" he asked.

"Hell yes, I am completely wrapped up in his story now. I really want to know whether he found happiness!" I confirmed.

"Well, I think that maybe you should ask that on your next visit! It is getting very late and I do not want you travelling alone very late at night," he smiled as he guided me toward the door. I looked at my watch: it was 9.45pm.

"Gosh, I didn't even realise that so much time had passed. I have had such a lovely evening, George!" I was quick to reply.

"Let me call you a cab," he suggested as we walked back to his apartment and I packed my belongings. "Would you like to call again?" he then asked.

"I would really like that, if you are sure. I feel like I am taking up so much of your time though."

"Time, Katharina, is one thing that I have plenty of!" he laughed. "I find your company refreshing; as long as you don't mind spending time with an old fool like me, I would be honoured if you would pay me another visit!" he remarked.

"Please don't be so harsh on yourself. I find you an interesting, generous and very likeable person, George; I love your stories and your company, and better still I love your cooking!" I smiled as I replied. "I would have loved to have lived in a house like this; it really is my dream one day!" I replied.

"Maybe I could fulfil that wish for one day and night?" he replied.

"How so?" I asked curiously.

"Why don't you come and stay here, for one whole day and one night? You can have one of the original master rooms and imagine that you are lady of the house for a day and night," he suggested. "If your fiancé approves, of course!"

"I think that you will find I dictate my own decisions and choices!" I replied as I thought for a minute. "Alright, George; one day, one night – one life experience I will never forget. I would love to – on one condition!" I replied.

"Which is?" he asked with anticipation.

"We will both cook, and… I would like one dance in that huge ballroom!" I said forcefully as I smiled. George laughed.

"Well that seems like a fantastic deal for me!" he joked.

"When do you request my company?" I asked.

"I can do Monday, Tuesday, Wednesday or next weekend!" George quickly answered. I looked at my planner.

"How about Tuesday? I am quite liking the idea of this, and Tuesday means that I do not have to wait too long," I asked.

"Tuesday it is. I feel very fortunate that you have accepted my invitation. Shall we say nine o'clock? I am so glad that we met; you are a breath of fresh air in my otherwise very boring life!" he then stated.

"Thank you George; likewise!" I announced in return. The cab outside sounded its horn.

I turned and walked toward the main door, which he opened, and as I turned back to shake his hand, he once again held it gently, kissed the back of it and bid me goodnight. I waved as I got into the cab and text John to say I was leaving as we pulled away down the long driveway. I couldn't wait to tell him all about it.

Chapter Four

"Like hell you are!" John shouted at me. "Are you completely out of your mind? You have no idea who this guy is and what he is capable of!" he angrily said.

"John, for goodness' sake, he's ancient. What do you possibly think is going to happen to me? He has been nothing but charming and insisted that I check with you first! He's hardly likely to do that if he's intending on holding me hostage, is he?" I answered back with annoyance.

I had not expected John to be so upset about me staying for one night at Northfield. To add insult to injury, I was really looking forward to it! He looked at the disappointment in my face and then carried on:

"Look, I know you can look after yourself – it's the reason I bought you self-defence classes – but I just think it's a little odd! A young woman staying with an 'ancient' bloke? I would be mad not to worry!" he then said as he kissed me on the forehead. I sighed.

"I know, and I appreciate you worrying, but I have a really good feeling about this story, this house and George. It just feels right, and I know I can make a great story out of this. I don't expect you to understand my reasons, but I really want to do this. I will have my phone and you know where I am!" I replied, trying to pull my best sympathetic doe-eyes at him.

He shrugged and grunted at me as he walked to the bathroom. "Sweet Jesus, Kat, I know you – and I know that you will not be happy if I try and talk you out of this!" he called back to me. He had pushed the bathroom door nearly closed and so I punched the air with excitement that he was coming around. "It does not mean that I am happy about it though!" he then said. I slowly danced around the room whilst he was brushing his teeth. I was so excited. I thought about the grandeur of Northfield and the fact that I was going to be spending a night and a whole day there! I was going to make sure that this was enjoyed to the maximum.

The weekend couldn't have dragged more significantly, and by the time Monday morning arrived, I almost ran to the tube station. I knew that there was a brief meeting this morning, so there would definitely be the question asked of how my evening with George had gone. I hoped that Angela, my editor, could see a great story, and along with my enthusiasm, let me stay on Tuesday night. It was alright getting John to agree, but I had to convince Angela it was worth pursuing.

As expected, the meeting swayed my way, and I gave them a brief rundown on what had happened to date. I was surprised at the response from most of the team, including the men. I expected some negative feedback, but everyone seemed to like the idea and the women were, like me, intrigued with George. "It's good to get some background, but we need to know his story Kat!" Angela confirmed.

"Yes, well hopefully I will get to that tomorrow – and tomorrow night!" I replied.

"Well just in case you need a quick getaway, take one of the cars," Angela then said.

"You can take mine – I'm in all week, I've got a deadline coming up, so I can take the tube to work!" Martin, one of our journalists, suddenly announced.

"Great, that's sorted then!" Angela finished as she closed the meeting.

I walked back to my desk to find a steaming cup of coffee waiting for me. Claire had collated all the appropriate data for me and it sat neatly stacked in a pile on my desk. "So did she say yes?" she suddenly asked as she appeared at my side. I nodded as I picked up the mug of coffee.

"Ooooh, this is so exciting!" she replied, as she clapped her hands with the eagerness of a small child.

"Well, I'm just hoping that I don't find myself with a boring, non-printable story at the end of this!" I casually replied.

"Well, I hardly think that's going to happen! Even I'm intrigued and wish I could come with you!" she happily pointed out.

The day was steady. I thought about the best way to approach my overnight visit, then made sure that I wrote down some appropriate questions to ask. George had a very clever knack of completely enticing you into his stories so that you forgot what you asked in the first place! I needed to try and focus, especially as I was to be there for a long length of time. After all the planning, I was glad to be on the way home. Driving through London in the early evening traffic was not so great, but as I had been given the use of a car it was bearable.

I arrived back to an empty apartment – John was always working all hours at the moment – so I used the opportunity to get things packed before he changed his mind. I decided I would take a favourite tea dress (purchased solely to attend a recent wedding) for dinner tomorrow evening. I would perhaps be a little over-dressed, but if I was staying at Northfield I was certainly going to make the most of it. I sat on the end of my bed and thought about what life would have been like back then, in such a grand house. I always felt that we were never as romantic these days as back in those times, and George's many stories certainly confirmed a lot of that.

I had just finished packing when John arrived home. I could tell that his day hadn't gone all too well, but I tried to ignore the negative signs. I started an evening meal as he finished up on his computer. Once we had sat down to eat, I asked him about his day.

"I take it you haven't had a good day?" I asked hesitantly.

"One of the worst! Things are not going to plan with this new deal, and it means I am going to have to work longer hours tomorrow night!" he snapped in return. I looked down at my plate.

"Probably best that I am away tomorrow night then?" I reminded him. He took a bite of food and then looked at me.

"Ah, I forgot – yes, you and the lonely old fool! I still don't think that I'm happy about this, Kat," he said, slightly aggravated.

"Well it's all arranged now, and I am going!" I insisted.

"It had better be worth it!" John then snapped again.

"I mean, you are going to look fairly silly if there isn't really a story there!" he then laughed. I slammed my fork down onto my plate.

"Well, thanks for that vote of confidence!" I remarked. I suddenly wasn't very hungry and took my plate to the kitchen.

"Yeah, but come on, Kat, it is all a bit strange, you not knowing him that well and staying. People will talk!" he smugly commented.

"Well let them!" I snapped back. I walked to our bedroom and closed the door. I stood and looked out of the window at the grey sky that was accumulating above; it remarkably reflected my mood. I decided to take a hot bath, get into my pyjamas and read.

By the time John came to bed, I had nodded off whilst reading. I was only aware of him being there when he took the book from out of my hand that had fallen onto my chest. I briefly woke.

"I don't want to fight with you, Kat. Just be careful!" he whispered in my ear as he snuggled up behind me.

"Hmmmm!" I lazily replied, too tired to restart our argument.

I seemed to have the most vivid dreams and the one that woke me at 3am was no exception. I sat up in bed and looked at the clock. Great, another early wakeup call! I stumbled to the bathroom and, whilst washing my hands, looked at myself in the mirror. *Mirrors – I must put that on my list of questions for George. Why are there so many mirrors?* I stumbled back to bed in my half state of slumber and went back to sleep; it was raining outside, again, but the sound was soothing, and before I knew it the alarm had kicked in at 6.30am. I woke to find that I had knots in my stomach – not the horrid type, but the excited and slightly nervous type, like a first date! I showered and changed into some casual clothes and then went for coffee. John had already woken and I could hear him in the kitchen.

"Got to dash babe!" he said as I appeared. He kissed me on the cheek and grabbed his keys after putting a slice of toast into his mouth. It was all a little quick.

"Alright! See you tomorrow night!" I replied. He stopped at the door before exiting, put down his briefcase and removed the toast from his mouth.

"Promise me you'll be careful?" he said as he walked back and gave me another kiss.

"Of course. I'm looking forward to finding out more!" I replied honestly. "I hope that your day is better than yesterday!" I finished as he turned and replaced the toast back in his mouth. He raised his hand in the air in acknowledgement, then left. As the door slammed shut, I sighed, *Hope it goes well!* I sarcastically mimed to myself. I decided to have some coffee – a good cure for anything. I would let the rush of early business traffic make its way through and then I would set off. This gave me time for a very leisurely breakfast and time to look at the paper, which was a novelty for me.

As I pulled out of the underground garage, I had butterflies in my stomach again. I really wanted this to work, and I knew it had to be good to convince Angela to print it, but there was always that small thought at the back of my mind that it may be a non-runner. The traffic wasn't too bad, the weather was dull and cloudy and looked like rain, but I had plenty of time to re-run the questions in my head for George before I got there. As I neared Northfield, on the quiet roads away from London city centre, my phone rang. I answered it. "Hello?"

"Kat, it's Claire. I just wanted to wish you luck. I am actually slightly envious of that fact that you get to spend the night in a beautiful old house!" she commented, with a hint of frustration.

"Ah, thanks Claire. I am nearly there now, so fingers crossed!" I replied.

"Well, keep your phone on just in case. Ring me anytime!" she replied.

"I will. It's really nice that you called. I am quite excited now!" I replied honestly.

"I bet you are! I would be. If it does turn out that he is an old pervert, though, don't be afraid to use your self-defence. Just don't kill the guy – that would make the wrong kind of story!" she joked as I laughed. We said goodbye as I reached the main gates.

As I parked the car and started to open the door, George appeared with a larger smile than normal; he almost skipped along to my car. I stepped out and smiled. "Good morning, George!" I said as I went to the boot to get my overnight bag.

"Good morning, please allow me!" He reached in and retrieved my bag and other things.

"It's not a particularly nice day, George!" I commented on the accumulating grey clouds.

"Typical British weather, I think!" He smiled and gestured for me to walk ahead of him up the front steps.

On entering the amazing house I stopped and

glanced around again as I shrugged my coat off and placed it on a nearby chair. It made me smile again, just to see the splendour of it all. George closed the door and I turned to face him. "Are you sure that you are alright with me staying, George?"

"Absolutely! In my not-busy schedule, it is my sheer delight to spend some time with you, Katharina!" He was so sincere and seemed good-hearted. "Let me show you to your room!" He gestured toward the stairs and walked along side me with my bags.

"I still cannot believe how beautiful this house is!" I pointed out. "I am really looking forward to being here!"

"Well that is good news. The place could do with some cheering up!" he laughed as we walked past the big mirror at the top of the first stairway.

We walked along a corridor that I remembered briefly from the tour that George had given me on a previous visit. We stopped at a door about halfway along. He turned a large door handle and pushed the door open, which creaked as I walked in. It was a large room with a four-poster bed; it was very lavish and filled with paintings, and furniture that was of a more feminine style. In the corner stood a dressing table, and as I walked to it, it felt like I had stepped back in time. There was a beautiful hairbrush and mirror inlaid with fine, intricate silver. Old perfume bottles stood, still half-filled, alongside a jewellery box. I lifted the lid to find the most beautiful bright blue inlay, and around the outside of the inner lid was what looked to be mother of pearl. Oddly, there was still jewellery inside.

"I didn't have the heart to remove it!" George

suddenly said. "It belonged to Margaret. It feels like parts of her are still around here; she did so much. I like to keep reminders of people past!" He seemed so sad.

"I can understand that, George. I think it's a very sweet sentiment," I smiled.

"Feel free to wear anything within it!" he then remarked. "So, do you find the room to your liking?"

"It's more than I could have imagined myself staying in this time last week!" I laughed. "It's amazing, I love it."

"Good!" he quickly replied. "The bathroom is two doors down. I will go and put the kettle on, if you want to unpack! Come down to my kitchen when you are ready."

It took me a few minutes just to take in the whole room after George left. I strolled around the edges, looking at the paintings and another large mirror. The fireplace was a beautiful cream marble and had logs sat within it, ready for lighting. The walls were decorated with a subtle, pale-green paper with darker green trailing leaves and pretty little pink flowers. It felt delicate to the touch and looked hand painted. As I returned to the bed and sat at the foot of it, I took a deep breath and imagined Margaret in this room. It intrigued me to think of who had been here before me.

Not having much to unpack, as I was only staying the night, I laid my dress on the bed and placed my shoes on the floor. I straightened the creases from travelling and then took out my wash bag. I could take that to the bathroom later. On removing my notepad with its questions, I headed down to the kitchen to find George.

As usual, he was busy in the kitchen; he was just finishing making us a coffee, so I sat at the table.

"I suppose it will be strange for you to have someone staying here for the night! How long is it since anyone else occupied the house?" I asked curiously as he handed me my coffee mug.

"Ah, now let's see. I think that the last people to be here were the Wainwrights." He questioned himself for a second. "Yes, that's right. They lived here for about eighteen months, going on eight years ago now!" He sat at the table opposite me as I nearly choked on my coffee.

"Eight years? You haven't had any company here since then?" I was shocked. I thought it was a recent vacation that had prompted George to want new owners or tenants. He nodded.

"I don't mind. I get to stay in a beautiful house and can do whatever I choose!" he laughed as he sipped his coffee.

"But eight years? Gosh, I think I would be lonely, George. Why did the Wainwrights only stay for eighteen months? That wasn't a long stay – and, more importantly, why would they want to leave?"

"Well, I think you would have to ask them that. It had something to do with their twelve-year-old daughter and her wanting to be nearer her friends, I believe!" he stated. I had the feeling he knew the real reason, though. I scribbled that down in my notebook, something to follow up.

"Did they move back to London?" I asked.

"Yes, I think that Mr Wainwright works at Hendersely Brothers Solicitors in Knightsbridge."

"Ooh that is a huge company, with big cases!" I replied, feeling the need to ask Mr Wainwright about George. I smiled, not wanting to give the game away, lest George stop being so open.

"So, Katharina, shall we stroll back to the house and continue?" he asked.

"Yes that would be great, thank you. I am intrigued to learn more about our young Master James Aldersley and what became of him!" I picked up my notebook as we headed out of the kitchen.

"Well, I am happy to indulge, but only if you tell me something about yourself in return!" he asked hopefully.

"I assure you, there is nothing exciting about my life!" I was quick to reply.

"Maybe not to you, but it is far more exciting than mine of that I am sure!" he smiled.

We walked back to the gallery of portraits and stood in front of the handsome James Aldersley. At twenty-five he was absolutely gorgeous and I stood for a minute as I soaked up the idea of him, in this house, and thought of how the women of that day would most definitely be swooning. God, as a woman of the here and now, I was struggling not to!

"You look intrigued, Katharina?" George suddenly announced as he snapped me back into the land of reality. I shrugged.

"I find I am slightly breathtaken at how handsome he was!" I confided.

"Well, that is what most women thought of him. Handsome, secure financially, young and willing to give them what they desired!" he winked at me. I know that I blushed. "Should I continue where I finished?" he then asked.

"Oh, please do!" I replied, with pen in hand, and he began.

Chapter Five

"Our young Master James had most women eating out of the palm of his hand by this age. It wasn't a pretty thing for his mother to see, and as he grew up, he distanced himself even further from thoughts of a long-term relationship." George declared this with sadness.

"His mother had no influence over him at all? How did he treat his responsibilities here?" I asked.

"I cannot fault his duty as the man of the house. This place was thriving; he had invested money, extended the house and maintained it in a way that was beyond his years. His mother, I know, was proud of him for that part of his life. He took care of all the staff and was a fair employer, making sure that everyone – even with the smallest job – were happy here. But it wasn't enough! He needed to feel wanted for a short space of time, but nothing more!" he explained.

I carried on scribbling notes in my pad, wanting to ask more questions, but also wanting to hear more from George. "It must have been upsetting not only for his mother, then, but for everyone around him that he shared a relationship with. I feel sorry for whoever was personally attached to him as his valet – if he had one? It must have been heart-breaking to watch him change!" I sadly replied as George nodded.

"Indeed it was!" he then replied, before looking at me. "Shall I show you some of the plans in the library, showing the designs and work he did here?" he then asked.

"I'd love to, George. How interesting; I would like to see what his ability and talent was for designing." It would be fascinating to look at original plans from works carried out here. George gestured for me to walk out of the door first. As we did, I looked at the large ornate mirror that we passed. "Can I ask a question, George?"

"Of course, anything!"

"What is with all the mirrors in this house? I know that James Aldersley was a 'magnet' to women, as you so eloquently put it, but I cannot see him being someone who wanted to look upon himself so frequently."

"What makes you think that?"

"I get the impression that he probably wasn't very proud of his behaviour, particularly with women, but I don't think he probably could help it either. He had dealt with huge distress, and that must have been tough. I would not however think that he would have wanted to look at himself daily, so frequently – it just doesn't fit!" I stated.

"You're very observant, and no, it wasn't James Aldersley that had all of the mirrors in this house put up. That happened after his time here, but that is another story – for later, maybe," he concluded. That wasn't quite the explanation I was expecting, but I was glad that I had assessed James correctly.

We arrived at the library and George proceeded to go to a high shelf at the back of the room, where he pulled papers bound in ribbon down from. He passed them to me so that he could climb back down the ladder, then walked to the round highly polished table and untied the ribbon. "He was a very talented young man with lots of vision and scope, which I think he definitely inherited from his father!" he smiled as he unfolded the first plan.

"Wow, look at the work that has gone into these drawings!" They were amazing to look at. "Did he draw these too?" I asked curiously.

"No, no; his talent was great, but he had an architect draw these up. I do have small sketches here that he did to show what he was trying to achieve!" George pulled some smaller pieces of paper to the front and handed them to me. I had shivers down my spine. It was a little eerie – James Aldersley had hand-drawn these many years ago. I lifted them to my nose and inhaled; there was something satisfying about the smell of old paper and ink. When I opened my eyes, George was staring at me.

"Sorry!" I quickly exclaimed. I put them on the table and flicked through them with great interest.

"Don't be sorry; history is intoxicating, isn't it?" he smiled. I returned the smile. George wasn't about to make me feel foolish.

We stood for a long time, going over the workings and notes from a time when James Aldersley seemed completely in control of what he wanted, and George explained where and when all the works had taken place. He then pulled a large, leather-bound book from the shelf and suggested that we sit on the luxurious chaise longue, which looked a relaxing place to read.

"This became what I call the house bible; anything

that happened here – socially, with staff, works carried out – were all noted in here by Margaret at that time. She kept records of everything done from the moment she married Howard. It is interesting reading. If you promise to look after this, maybe you could borrow it for your work?" he then offered.

"Really? I don't know what to say, it looks so interesting! I am sure that there will be items in here that I can use in my piece about the house. But we still do not seem to have revolved much around yourself, George, and how you came to be here!" I pointed out.

"Well I think it is about time that you told me a little about yourself, Katharina!" he requested.

"There's not much to tell, really."

"How about how you came to have such an interesting name?" he asked.

"Ah yes, my name. It always seems to cause interest, usually of the 'how old-fashioned is that' kind! You really want to know?" I enquired.

"Absolutely! Please do go on!" he insisted. He placed the book down alongside him, glanced in the mirror opposite and then gestured for me to continue.

"Alright. My mother, since she was a little girl, loved – and I mean *loved* – fairy tales of any type, from any country – particularly ones with happy endings. She read so many of them that when I was born she had names bouncing around her head for what I should be called, all of them linked in some way to her favourite stories. Honestly, I think that I could have ended up with about ten names if my dad hadn't put a limit on a first and middle name!" I laughed.

"So your full name would be?" George asked.

"Katharina Josephine Stuart!" I replied, waiting for his reaction. He smiled. "Please don't laugh, I know it is a mouthful, and I am absolutely sure that my mother was born in completely the wrong era, but even those two names were a hard decision."

"She chose very wisely. I like it. It suits you and your personality!" he kindly remarked.

"Thank you. She was, when all was said and done, a true romantic at heart. Unfortunately my father wasn't and when I was three he took off and left us for someone else! It broke my mother's heart, and I know that she never fully recovered."

"I am sorry!" George said as he placed a hand on mine. "So do you not see your father?"

"I never really wanted to as I grew older. Besides, he started a whole new life – a very successful career, and with a new family – and we were not part of that. He never really contacted us once he left, so when I learned he had died about six years ago, it's sad to say that I didn't even feel any sorrow. For me, he had died a long time before; he was never really in my life. My mother was my mother and father and she did an okay job!" I smiled.

"I think it's fair to say that she did better than okay!" he remarked.

"Thank you, that's sweet."

"So does she live in London?" George then asked. I swallowed hard.

"Not any more. She died two years ago. Cancer," I replied.

"Oh Katharina, I am so sorry. I shouldn't be prying!" he quickly replied. I placed my other hand on top of his.

"George, it's fine, really. It's nice to talk about her – I very rarely get the chance to these days! Anyway, my love of fairy tales and my name are all credit to my mum. She taught me to fight for what I wanted and also to never settle for anything less than true love that was reciprocated tenfold!"

"She was a very smart woman, and I agree whole-heartedly!" he smiled.

"That is why I find James so fascinating; that he had such a connection with both his parents, particularly his father. I have never experienced anything like that with my dad – that respect and love and need to be with him, and feeling so empty without him. Maybe that's a blessing?" I stated.

"Maybe. Let's not dwell on the sad things, though. You have your whole life to look forward to, and you are engaged yourself and so have prospects of your own family!" he then reminded me. I sighed.

"Yes, but that is another story entirely. I love John, I really do, but he proposed just about a year after my mum had died. At that point I was truly missing her and so lonely; it made me so sad still to know she wasn't there." I shrugged. "I wonder sometimes if I was hasty in saying yes to his proposal, and just needed the connection of something close that was missing."

"You think you have made a mistake? Under the circumstances, I think that you needed the emotional support!" George added.

"Emotional support? Yes, that is exactly what it was

that I needed." I shook my head. "I don't know, in the last six months we seem to have grown apart a little. Work schedules don't really help!" I replied as I looked at him, then realised I was pouring my heart out to a total stranger! "Gosh, I'm sorry. I can't believe I just told you all that!" I surprised myself.

"No need to apologise. Sometimes it's easier to talk to a stranger. I find that we tend to tell the truth!" he replied as he patted my hand. "I have an idea – let us go outside and get some fresh air. I can show you the grounds before the weather changes for the worse!"

"Brilliant idea, I think the fresh air would be a good break," I replied as I stood.

George almost jumped up. In the entrance there was a door that lead to the biggest cloakroom I think I have ever seen. He retrieved his coat as I put mine on and then we went out of the front door. It was decidedly cool, and the dampness in the air gave the promise of rain. Even in the shadows of the clouds, the garden was pleasant and it was easy to see how amazing it would be in full bloom. I asked how often it was tended, as George was not getting any younger, and wasn't surprised to find that he had a team of gardeners that kept it looking so tidy and well maintained. There were outbuildings, old stables and a garage that surprisingly held three cars – a fairly new Range Rover, an old but loved Porsche and a vintage Aston Martin. George explained that he had purchased them over the years and that he still did love to get out and drive. It amused me to think of him behind the wheel. As we walked back toward the house, the first large drops of rain started to fall. A very heavy downpour was imminent and so we hurried back to avoid the soaking. We had just managed to get back indoors as the heavens opened, and we took our coats off and shook off the heavy drops that had caught us all too quickly. I had that distinct feeling that someone was watching me, and I knew it wasn't George – he was in the cloakroom asking me for my coat. I quickly turned and glanced around the entrance and toward the mirror, which caught my eye. There was nothing out of the ordinary, but I walked toward it nonetheless and placed my hand on it. It surprised me to find that it wasn't cold to the touch, as I had imagined a mirror to be, but that it was warm. I quickly took my hand off it as George appeared at the side of me. "Everything alright?" he softly asked.

"Fine, I just had the strangest feeling!" I replied. George looked in the mirror at me and then asked me for my coat, which I gave to him without moving my gaze from my reflection. I suddenly realised what a mess I looked. Wet strands of hair clung to my face and so I quickly tousled my hair and then turned to George.

"Lunch?" he asked.

"Yes please, I am hungry now!" I replied as we strolled along to his kitchen.

We prepared lunch together and chatted about everyday things for a short time until my phone beeped. A text – not from John, as I would have expected, but Claire. 'Hope it's going well!' it simply stated. I quickly replied with one word; 'Remarkably'. We laughed, ate the sandwiches we had made, talked more and decided what we would have for dinner, with the added emphasis that I would help cook! I felt like I had known George for years; he was an easy person to like and I felt really relaxed around him.

The afternoon carried on in the day room, with me expressing that I could understand why he would want to share the splendour of the house with someone else, but also that I couldn't understand why he would want to have anyone here at all. My argument wasn't very convincing; if I was in George's shoes, I wasn't sure what I would do either. He explained the expense and time it took to look after such a house, and that although he had money and it wasn't the sole reason for wanting new occupants, he missed the house being filled with voices and love and laughter. He talked about all of the old gatherings here, like balls and dinners; he captivated me with his stories. He had a way of storytelling that almost transported you back there; like he had been there himself. As I sat engrossed in the magical tale he was telling of a grand and colourful ball held for James' mother's birthday, he suddenly jumped up.

"I must show you something – being a woman I am sure that you will appreciate them!" he quickly said as he grabbed my hand. He was quick to pull me up the grand staircase, down the corridor, past my bedroom and into the largest bedroom in the northeast corner of the house. It was nearly bigger than the entire apartment that I shared with John. George released my hand and walked across to the ornate wardrobe that stood in the corner. "This is what I am talking about!" he said as he released the catch on the doors and let them swing open. I felt my mouth almost drop to the floor, and I slowly walked toward it.

There they were… the most delicate, beautiful and colourful gowns of silk and lace and petticoats. The boning of the bodices, and laces for fastening up, with the masses of material it made them heavy to the touch… "Oh my goodness, George, these are beautiful. It's hard to believe they are still so intact!" I said as I touched them one by one: pink silk, cornflower blue, green, gold and a dark crimson. They were exquisite. "They should be in a museum, George, for everyone to see!" I proclaimed, still stunned.

"There are these too!" he then remarked as he opened the dresser to the side of the wardrobe, revealing long gloves and fans made of what looked to be ostrich feathers, dyed in shades that matched the gowns. As he pulled open the bottom drawer, he revealed five pairs of shoes – each one to match a gown – alongside small purses of pearl and lace. "You like them?" he asked.

"I'm speechless, they are so, so beautiful; I feel honoured that you have shown them to me," I told him as I gently touched the fine silk and lace.

"Margaret had impeccable taste. She had the crimson one made for her birthday ball; a sign of her passion and love that she missed with Howard. Alas, she never wore it."

"Why ever not? It is such a shame that she did not wear such perfection!" I replied as George lifted it out of the wardrobe for me to inspect it further.

"She decided it was maybe the wrong sign to everyone else. Reds of any shade were depicted as someone desperate to attract attention!" he remarked. "She opted for the blue; I imagine it mirrored her feelings on the inside."

I sighed heavily. "I feel like I knew her. You are so good at telling stories, George. If I didn't know any better, I would think you had been there!" I replied.

George placed the dress back into the wardrobe and closed the doors. He smiled, gestured for me to exit the room and then he looked around the whole room, smiled and closed the door behind him.

George was quiet on the walk back down the staircase, and I had the distinct feeling that the fate of Margaret and her loneliness played heavily on his mind. Maybe it made him think of his loneliness? I linked my arm with his and looked at him. "She will be happy again now, George, as she is reunited with the love of her life!" I remarked. He smiled and patted my hand in recognition of my words, but he did not reply. Once we returned to the day room, as it had been near on three hours since lunchtime, George made more tea and I looked more closely around the room in which we sat. It was filled with intricate ornaments, beautifully handcrafted antique furniture, and fabrics that I knew could not be replicated today hanging at the windows. The old shutters still existed, and as I sat at the window seat and looked out across the garden, I had my own visions of how amazing this house must have been. I had not really noticed that George had returned until he passed me a cup and saucer.

"Lost in thought, Katharina?" he asked. I sighed.

"It was such a different time then, everything was different; business, family, acquaintances, social ethics, love, chivalry... I find it very hard to understand where everything went so wrong today. I mean, everything then seemed to mean so much more!" George nodded at my words.

"I think there is some truth in that, Katharina; I do think people take too much for granted these days. Although, I think in years past some people took too much for granted too, like young master James!" he then stated as he took a sip of tea.

"Yes, you must finish the tale of James. Quite the handsome fiend he seems to be shaping up to be!" I remarked. George took a sip of his tea as he looked in the mirror opposite.

"Fiend? Maybe too strong a word. Bloody fool seems more appropriate!" He smiled.

"What did he do?" I asked. "Well, besides the gambling, the using of women and the lack of respect for himself and what his mother required of him!"

"Indeed. Unfortunately his mother was heartbroken for a second time when he had his thirtieth birthday. He was now classed as a philanderer and there had still been no marriage. One woman however was to change his whole life forever on that birthday, until such a time that he could learn a little respect!" he concluded as he stood and walked toward the mirror. I almost thought that he was mumbling to himself under his breath, and it made me slightly uneasy again.

"A woman made him come to his senses?" I asked. He turned and faced me.

"Well, she taught him a lesson!" he replied. He shook his head and then gestured for me to join him.

I placed my cup on the table and walked toward George, who smiled warmly at me. "As an old man, I find that I cannot wait for long lengths of time between meals. Shall we go and prepare dinner, then we can change and eat not too late?" he asked.

"Sure, if that's what you would like. I am happy with that," I replied as we left the room, but not before I picked up the tray with the beautiful porcelain teapot and the cups, saucers, milk jug and sugar bowl. As we walked, I pried. "So in what way did this woman teach James a lesson? It wasn't gruesome, was it?" I asked, slightly hesitantly. He laughed.

"It may have been kinder, but no, nothing gruesome. Let us make dinner and then we'll have something to discuss whilst we eat!" he replied.

"Alright, it's a deal, George. But then I must learn something about you. That is, after all, what my story was supposed to be about," I confirmed, thinking about what my editor had said, but being somewhat obsessed with James Aldersley.

Making dinner with George was fun. We talked and swayed along to music on the radio, mainly Radio Two and 'golden oldies'. Once dinner was in the oven, I looked at my watch; it was now a quarter past five. Time was flying, and my stay would be over here faster than I could imagine, so I needed to keep focused. George had already given me one glass of wine whilst making dinner, so I told myself to be responsible, as I was working.

"I am going to shower and change for dinner, George, if that is alright?" I enquired.

"Absolutely, me too. It is not very often I get to have dinner with a beautiful young woman. It is certainly a night for me to remember!" he remarked. I smiled at his humour.

"I will see you in about half an hour, George!" I replied as I turned and took my wine with me to my room to change.

Chapter Six

I closed my bedroom door behind me, tasted my wine (a large mouthful) and then placed it on the dresser before throwing myself on the large, four-poster bed. I closed my eyes and reached out my arms; I couldn't even reach the edges, this bed was so big! It was soft, with heavy fabric, and I couldn't wait to wrap myself up in it later that night. I clambered back to my feet and walked toward the window, unfastening my earrings; the rain had not relented since it started and it was getting heavier. It was dark and cloudy, and as the rain lashed on the old leaded windows, I shivered. I drew the heavy, long curtains to close out the cold. On grabbing my wash bag, I ventured out into the hallway, and walked two doors down to where George had explained the bathroom was. Even though I had been given a brief tour, it was hard to remember exactly what lay behind each door. I was relieved to find that I had chosen the correct one, and walked into the vast space that was the bathroom.

It was decorated in an old style, with the bath in the middle of the floor, but it thankfully had taps and plumbing. I looked toward it and sighed, wishing I had the time to wallow in warm, foamy bubbles in the deep roll-top bath, but half an hour by any girl's standards was not going to allow that! So I turned to the large shower that was built into one of the recesses and turned it on. I undressed and stepped into the warm and refreshing spray. The large fluffy towels were enormous and almost trailed along the floor, but the feel and smell was divine. I walked across to the mirror, stood and looked at myself, then attempted to put minimum make-up on. It wasn't like I was venturing out on the town, so I didn't need much make up. I thought I would try and look flawless in complexion with very little, as I somehow felt that George would appreciate that more. I slipped on my robe and hung the large towel once I was finished and ventured back to my room. As the rain had wet my hair earlier and it did not look too good, I had washed it quickly. With hairdryer in hand, I quickly tousled it as I dried it, leaving a length of natural waves. Tonight I would clip it up to suit my tea dress.

Once ready, I quickly reached for my phone. I found no missed calls or texts from John but, knowing he was busy, I sent a text anyway, saying: 'All is going really well. The story is as interesting as I thought. Find out more about George tonight over dinner. This place is amazing! Don't work too hard – Kat x'. I was in all honesty slightly annoyed that I had not heard from him, so I decided that I would leave my phone in my room to charge. I slipped my nude-coloured heels on, checked my hair, which I had now neatly pinned up, applied some light lip gloss and left my room.

Returning down the grand staircase gave me shivers, thinking of the balls in past years and the people that must have attended. I had visions of the dresses and laughter and conversation, but was then brought back to earth with a large flash of lightning that lit the slightly dark entrance hall. I scurried quickly down to George's apartment and knocked as I entered. I couldn't help but smile as George turned to me, dressed in a suit. It looked somewhat dated, but I liked it. It was dark grey in heavy tweed; he had a cravat that was pinned and a crisp white high-necked shirt. He bowed at my presence and then smiled back. "Why Katharina, you look delightful!" he stated.

I curtseyed in return, then placed my empty glass on the counter and replied: "George, you look very handsome!"

"Why thank you. One does like to make an effort!" he joked. "Shall we?" He gestured for us to leave his apartment and return to the main house. Surprised, I turned and exited. I had thought that we would be eating in his humble apartment, but he had apparently decided differently!

We walked back through the kitchen. As my heels clicked along the stone floor, he continued: "I decided that if we are to let you have a taste of this house correctly, then we should eat in the dining room!" he confirmed.

"Oh, really? I don't want you going to any trouble, George!" I replied as we walked across to a door that showed a subtle glow through the frame. He pushed the door open to a roaring fire in the fireplace and the long dining table that I remembered seeing before on my tour. It was set with an intricate lace cover and place settings for two, at one end of the table, opposite each other. I smiled. "Oh George, this is beautiful!"

"Yes, it is a room that I like very much. Before we go

in, though, I am going to make you keep your promise – I hope that you will grant me one dance in the ballroom!" he suggested.

"Absolutely, I would love to. I'm not the best dancer, George, and your toes may suffer, but yes. I am so excited!" I replied as I clapped my hands together in anticipation. It was something that I had seen many times in stories, fairy tales and movies: the grand ballroom, where so much tension, pleasure, passion and connection happened. I linked arms with him and we walked across to the ballroom door which was open. The lights in the ballroom were on; they were subtle and reflected the painted ceiling and the gold ornate carvings along the walls, which were imbedded with gilt mirrors designed to reflect the many dancers at such a function. I stood and turned, taking in the whole room, and smiled.

George walked across to an old gramophone and placed the needle gently onto the turning record he had chosen. Immediately after the lovely crackling sound, a whole orchestra burst into life and he walked back across to me with his hand outstretched. "May I have the honour of this dance?" he asked. I nodded and then we took our positions in the middle of the floor. George held himself so well, standing as he took in the beat of the music before gracefully leading me around the whole ballroom floor. We moved easily and turned; he led with such elegance that I fluidly followed. As the music came to an end and he continued to keep spinning, I threw my head back and laughed. It was a sheer delight, and I felt for the first time in ages so very, very happy. The music had stopped but the player still crackled, and then George stood me steady and released me from the confident hold that he had. "Thank you. I had forgotten how much I enjoyed dancing!" he sadly stated, as if he had missed it for so very long.

"The pleasure was all mine. I feel like a princess in a fairy tale in the most elaborate room!" I replied. He turned and walked to lift the needle from continuing the crackling and then walked back to me and held out his arm.

"Shall we dine?" he then asked.

"Let's!" I simply replied, as we walked back to the dining room.

"Please, be seated and I will pour you some wine!" he then instructed as he gently guided me to my seat and pulled back my chair. I nodded in acceptance at his request and gently brushed my dress neatly down, once sat, as George placed a linen napkin in my lap. "Red wine?" he asked.

"That would be lovely, thank you!"

"I shall return promptly with dinner," he then stated as he disappeared back out of the room.

I took a sip of the wine and then glanced around the room at the ornate features. The mirrors reflected the glow of the fire, and as I sat and gazed at the leaping flames, George returned with plates in hand. He placed my plate down first and then his own before sitting. I lifted my glass: "A toast I think; to new and interesting friends, who are delightful company!" I spoke with sincerity. By all accounts, I would rather sit and talk to George over dinner than many of John's work colleagues and friends.

"Indeed. New and interesting and beautiful new friends!" he then replied as we held up our glasses, chinked them just once and took a sip.

"This looks really good, George!" I then stated as I looked at the dinner in front of me.

"Well, it was not just my fair hands that made what we are about to eat!"

"Shall we?" I asked, realising how hungry I now was.

Dinner was delicious. George had followed it with a chocolate tart that would give Gordon Ramsey a run for his money. By the time we had finished, a few glasses of wine later, I was contently full. I needed to make sure that I did not lose sight of why I was here, although I felt that I could escape here for a long time. "George, I really must ask you about *you*! I still have a story to write and I know less about you than I do about James Aldersely," I then remarked.

George sighed and sat back in his chair, took a sip from his glass and then replied, "But to know about me, you have to know everything about James!"

"Well, again you intrigue me! Do you want to tell me about you?" I asked, wondering if he wasn't willing to divulge anything to me about himself.

"It's complicated and, I assure you, hard to believe. Although you may think that I am a story – and of that I can assure you, Katharina – I am not sure how successful it will be for you!"

"Can I be the judge of that?" I asked, hoping that he wasn't going to now say nothing at all about how he came to be living here.

"You really want to know?"

"Yes I do. I think!"

"Can you be open-minded? More importantly, can you think long and hard before you make a decision as to whether this is a story that has truth? I can tell you it is hard to believe, and I know that I have tried many times before!" George explained as he leaned forward and placed his glass back on the table.

"I like to think that I never judge anything until I have all the facts, and then I can assimilate them into some form of understanding, George!" I confirmed. He smiled, closed his eyes, took a deep breath, then opened them and looked toward the large mirror at the end of the table before replying:

"Very well! Just remember that you asked me for the truth!" he stated. I nodded and started to feel a little uneasy; that I may not like what I was about to hear. He refilled our glasses, turned to the fire and then began.

"It was now 1750, a year that changed everything. James had many acquaintances scattered across the country, and one thing he did like to do was travel. He would ride for days and stay with other single friends, with whom he would embark on nights of passion, drinking and gambling. In March of that year, he took it upon himself to visit a business acquaintance named Henry Cavendish, another handsome young man of only twenty-five years. He lived in a small village called Haworth, in Yorkshire. He had a sizeable estate and the same way of life as that of James, so they seemed well suited. His friend Henry threw a lavish ball, to which he invited many single suitors for both James and himself, but all the while with no intention of any serious connection other than of that sole night. One very beautiful young lady, by the name of Alice Elizabeth Ainsworth, was asked to attend this ball. She was only twenty-two and had the elegance and beauty that could, it was said, stop a man in his tracks."

"Let me guess; James wanted her immediately?" I quickly interrupted.

"He made it no secret that she had attracted him immensely. He spent that night with her and subsequently the following week whilst he stayed with Henry. By all accounts, they were inseparable: picnics, gatherings and dinner at Henry's estate. However, when it came to James leaving to return home, he broke the news to her that she would not be joining him."

"I bet that went down well?" I joked.

"The argument that followed did not make his departure easy. James was furious at her behaviour – she had declared her love for him. He had simply wanted a companion with no further involvement; she did not take the news well. She called him a liar, a scoundrel with malicious intent to women, and made it clear that just because he was leaving, it would not be the end of the matter. However, James left and returned home, and simply put it down to experience."

"So I'm guessing that she didn't leave it at that then?" I asked intently.

"Oh no!" he replied as he took a sip of his wine, whilst I gulped a large mouthful of mine, wondering what the young woman had done for revenge.

"News travelled fast about James' behaviour. His friend Henry had tried to eradicate all rumours, but

Alice seemed to be well connected and she fast had people, particularly women, whispering in his presence. He was angry and frustrated and as women avoided him more, he drank more. Then, in August – the month before his birthday – everything seemed to settle and James became a little less anxious as life appeared to return to normal. He carried on his duties here, drank slightly less and started to attend social functions again."

"I take it that his philandering ways re-appeared then?" I asked with annoyance. He may have been good-looking, but his treatment of women seemed more reminiscent of men's behaviour today, not back then.

"I am not painting a very good picture of him, Katharina, but you did ask for the truth. I know that his heart is good, and can be again!" he sighed as he re-filled our wine glasses.

"You said 'is good' and 'can be'... I think we are getting past and present tenses mixed up here, George. This was a long time ago!" I reminded him. He held his finger up to me.

"Ah, yes, a long time ago it was, but please let me finish," he asked. I nodded in agreement.

"You cannot stop now; I want to know what happened to that scoundrel too!" I said.

"The lovely Margaret wanted to mark the thirtieth birthday of her only son. With the absence of her beloved Howard, she held a ball here at Northfield, to which she invited all the acquaintances and families that they knew. Of course, there were many girls that attended that James had seemingly had intimate liaisons with, so it was not the most comfortable of situations. His dear mother had the intention of finding him a wife once and for all, should he like it or not."

"Oooh, I cannot see them lining up if they knew his ways though?" I cringed.

"Well, he conversed, I think, with every person that attended as he made his way through a large amount of wine, but nothing prepared him for the one thing he least expected…"

"What?" I asked. "Someone shot him with a pistol? I bet there were a few who wanted to!" I quickly asked. George shook his head.

"Alice!" he simply stated as he stood and walked to the roaring fire.

"Oh dear! A big scene at his birthday ball, and in front of all his friends." I grimaced.

"Oh, you have no idea! She arrived in the darkest shade of red that I think I have ever seen, but the stories were true; she was beautiful and flawless but full of hate and anger."

"Gosh, I would have loved to have seen the look on his face!" I smirked.

George then walked to the table, put his glass down and then took mine and set it down beside his. He crouched in front of me and took my hands in his. "The next part is the hard to believe part!'" he sincerely said. The look in his eye told me I needed to be prepared for something big, I swallowed hard.

"Go on," I replied.

"She waited until the ball was all but ended, and then appeared alone in the middle of the ballroom, where

Henry and his mother were. Alice was no ordinary girl. She had watched James since he left her in Yorkshire, and waited for the right moment to get her revenge over her broken heart. In fairness to her, she did truly love him, I believe."

"You say she was no ordinary girl… what exactly did she do?" I hesitantly asked. George squeezed my hands.

"I have a good feeling about you, Katharina. You know your love of fairy tales and stories that your mother used to read to you as a child?" he asked.

"Yes? I don't see how that is relevant?"

"What would you say if I told you that most of those stories were written based on truth?" He gazed into my eyes, looking for an answer.

"I would say that a 'fairy tale' is exactly what they are – make-believe tales." I laughed lightly. "Why, George? Are you telling me that they are real?"

"I said that some are based on truths. Not everything is always as it appears, Katharina," he then replied. I released my hands from his and took another sip of wine.

"Please do go on, I am at a loss as to where this story is leading," I replied. He pulled a chair up close to me and we sat with our knees inches apart.

"Alice declared that she was a witch," he then said, matter-of-factly. I had unfortunately just taken a sip of wine and nearly choked.

"I'm sorry, a witch? Like the wicked witch of the west? You are joking, right?" I asked rhetorically.

"I never joke about this!" he replied sternly. I stopped laughing. "She had waited until she could punish him vengefully, and in front of the one woman who loved him so much… Margaret! She was not going to let him suffer lightly!" he remarked. I tapped my hands onto my thighs, thinking that I would humour George, who I was now starting to think was slightly deranged.

"Alright, so what did she do then?" I asked, trying to sound serious.

"She cast a spell – one which would see him suffer for many, many years – and he still does!" he remarked.

"Wait, you are saying he is still *alive*?" I quizzed.

"In a manner of speaking!"

"How so? We are talking over 250 years here, George. Have you done the math?" I asked. He grunted and shook his head.

"Always this part that gets the questions!" he remarked.

"How many people have you told about this? Is this why the Wainwrights left? I mean, it is hard to take in, George, without you sounding like you need institutionalising!" I replied sarcastically.

"You promised that you would listen to the whole story and then assimilate and let me know your thoughts!" he suddenly snapped. I stopped and held my hand up.

"I did. I apologise. Please do finish and then I will let you know what I think!" I laughed lightly, trying to sound convincing.

"Alice conjured up the most vengeful of spells. She wanted James to suffer and learn from his behaviour. The spell she cast upon him was to torture him slowly over many years, whilst she sat and watched with delight."

"You haven't told me what she did though, George," I asked, now a little irritated.

"She banished him to live a life watching from the outside looking in!" he said as he walked to one of the large mirrors. "He is captive within the mirrors that you have so frequently remarked upon; bound to watch life pass him by, like looking through a window, but never being able to pass through it," he said as he touched the mirror. Now he had my attention; I too had thought a couple of times that I had seen something. I stood and walked toward him.

"You are telling me that the thirty-year-old James Aldersley, the man in the portrait in the long hall, from 1750, is trapped inside this mirror?" I repeated.

"That's exactly what I am saying. Good summary, Katharina!" he remarked as I stepped back.

"So he can see us?" I asked, feeling a little uneasy, as now George was sounding like he was a little bit more insane, but the hairs on the back of my neck stood up.

"Oh he can see us alright, and I him. I have had to put up with his sorry sight in this form for 264 years now!" he replied as he turned to me.

"You can see him? Can you talk to him? Wait, why am I even asking these questions? This is insane! Brilliant, but insane!" I laughed as I went back to get my glass.

"She's not going anywhere!" George then said. "Give her a minute, I feel more questions..."

"You're talking to him now?" I asked, frustrated.

"There we go!" George remarked. "Yes, he's a little angry at me for trying to explain his sorry situation!" George said. "What he has to remember is that I have had to share it with him!" he then stated. I stood still.

"What?" I asked. George sighed and returned to his chair and re-filled his glass again.

"Alice cast the spell that night. All in the name of love! She wanted him to think about what he had done to her and other women in his past for as long as she saw fit. She thought it was about time that he had the opportunity to assess his life completely, and the best way to do that was to isolate him from anyone in this world."

"But he's not dead?" I asked.

"No, not dead, just… stuck! Alice gave him the opportunity to rectify himself, by saying that the spell would be broken if he could make a woman fall in love with him through his words alone, which would be spoken to her through the mirror. Someone pure of heart, who would want to know him completely and would fall in love with him without his touch! That woman has to declare her love openly and truthfully to free him and me. Or if that didn't happen in fifty years, she said that she would come back and break the spell herself, as he would have learnt his lesson well. However, witches being witches and all… unfortunately, ten years after she cast this spell, she was caught in a witch hunt and burnt at the stake, so that put an end to that!"

"He can never get out?" I asked, trying to believe a word he was saying.

"Oh, he can if he can stop being so pig-headed and feeling sorry for himself and actually try. God knows I have tried!" he remarked as he gulped down his wine.

"How do you fit into this, George?" I then asked.

"That valet that you spoke of before… the one that would have been disappointed watching him change, so

78

dramatically, and be saddened… that was me. As Alice cast the spell and his mother tried not to collapse at the loss of her son, I felt duty-bound to ask that he have someone familiar to be able to converse with. She happily obliged – with me! So we are now both stuck like this, at the age we were back then, with no hope of life carrying on normally until he can get his act together!" George gestured toward the mirror.

"How does he eat, drink and sleep?" I asked, thinking that I could stop George and his 'tale' from being so believable.

"Oh, Alice was clever. Everything that we see reflected that is not living – as in people, or animals – he has the mirror image on his side of the mirror! He can eat the same foods, read the same books, have the same objects, but everywhere that we see a mirror it is like a window to him back to this world! So he watches everything passing along in front of him, with little or no hope!" George shook his head. I gulped my wine down.

"How is any woman supposed to be able to listen to his words if they cannot see or hear him?" I asked. George sat up promptly.

"Ah, good question Katharina. I believe that the spell is impenetrable to most, and only those pure of heart, and willing to believe, can see. They have to be believers of all things possible and then they too will be able to see him and indeed converse with him!" he stated.

"Like children and ghosts?" I asked.

"Well, twelve-year-old Maria Wainwright definitely saw him and conversed with him many times, much to her parents' disapproval. They thought the house was haunted and that she was going mad! She was too young and too naïve; trying to get her to stay in hope of something progressing didn't happen, unfortunately!"

I sighed and looked into the mirror to which I returned. I placed my hand upon it. "Even if I wanted to believe your story, George, it really does sound like a tall tale with no truth." I sighed, starting to think that my so-called front page story was an old man intent on being a big believer of fairy tales himself.

"But you have seen him!" George then replied. "You have felt his gaze!"

"The mirrors feel warm to the touch, unlike most!" I then remarked. My head was spinning from a story that was leading nowhere fast, and from the amount of wine that George had obviously supplied to help his courage to tell the story and mine to accept it.

The thunder had now started. With the flashing lightning and the rain that had still not relented, I had the sudden urge to retire to bed. I could tell from George's face that he most probably expected me to run, but one thing I had learnt was that there was no harm to be had from him. I held my hands up in defeat. "George, I like you and this has been an interesting evening, but can I please take all of this in and speak with you tomorrow, at breakfast? I seem to have a headache accumulating and feel the need to sleep!" I stated.

"Of course. Thank you for not bolting out of the door! I will see you in the morning!" he replied as I walked from the room, but not before taking off my heels, which were now making me feel slightly precarious.

I walked up the staircase and every mirror that I now came upon I stared at intently. It was an unnerving thought that someone could be watching me, a bit like in the movies, where the FBI or police have interview rooms with two-way mirrors. I wanted to see him – if he even existed! I shook my head – what on earth was I thinking? This was ridiculous. All I could think about now was how much John was going to love this, which made me frown.

I entered my room and took the liberty of undressing behind the screen, just in case, as there was one large mirror in my room. By the time I slipped under the heavy blankets, my eyes were nearly closed. I had no idea that listening to stories could be so tiresome…

Chapter Seven

I knew that I had not slept too long when I awoke with a start, but the banging thunder, which I was sure was right above the house, was enough to wake anyone from the dead. I jumped up just as the lightning snapped again, and the lamp that I had left on at the side of my bed flickered and then went out. I sat up. The room suddenly seemed very large, bathed in only glowing embers from the fire that had been lit without me realising. Feeling thirsty from the wine that I had drunk too much of, I decided to go to the bathroom and get some water. I stumbled to the edge of the bed and reached out for the dressing table, which had my phone charging upon it. *Apps are fast becoming a favourite piece of technology*, I thought, as I turned on the torch.

I stubbed my toe on the doorjamb not once but twice and bent to rub it; then, losing my sense of direction for a second, I turned the wrong way. As I started down the corridor and saw my reflection in the mirror at the end of the hallway, the beam of light illuminating my face, I stopped and tutted, then turned the right way. I walked about three steps and then the hair on the back of my neck stood on end again, so I stopped. God, I was going to give myself a heart attack if I kept carrying on this way, I had far too many thoughts of fairy tales running through my mind! "For goodness' sake," I muttered to myself and I turned and shined the phone light at the mirror I had just turned away from. No sooner had I raised the light and shined it directly at that mirror did my heart start racing. It was not me looking back at myself, but the figure of a man with his hand to his eyes, cursing about the bright light in his!

I turned quickly and screamed, hearing someone tell me to 'wait', but I tried to tell myself I was dreaming and walked away in the darkness. Mumbling to myself all the way down the corridor, I neared what I thought was the bathroom. Another mirror was on the wall beside me, and something caught my eye and moved when I stopped. I froze for a second, then swallowed hard and turned and looked toward it in the dark and slowly lifted my still-lit phone. There he was again, slightly dishevelled, wearing a loose white shirt and a very worried look about his face.

"Hi," he said simply as he raised one hand and waved to me. It took me about three seconds to absorb what was in front of me, then as the hallway spun and I felt myself passing out, I distinctly remember him saying, "Not quite the effect I was hoping for!" then I hit the floor.

I could hear voices. As I tried to process what had happened, I listened; I knew George's voice, but not the other.

"Hi – that's all you could think of to say?"

"Well, she took me by surprise, not to say blinded me with that light!"

"What were you trying to do? Scare the living daylights out of her?"

"Well I don't know, George! I think you were doing a fine job of sending her running during dinner with your story telling!"

"Well it was the truth, and nothing is ever going to change with your attitude. Eventually this house will fall into disrepair and we are going to be in serious trouble!"

"It wasn't exactly my choice to be left like this!"

"Nor mine, but your lack of respect for women in general is what got us into this mess in the first place! Maybe Katharina was correct and Alice should have shot you with a pistol – it certainly would have saved a long lifetime of misery for both of us!"

"Well thank you for that, George! I still cannot believe that she agreed to stay the night anyway, after you enlightened her. I was simply intrigued by her strength of character and choice to remain here, so I was watching her out of curiosity."

"Well, now that you seem to have caused her to faint, she may have second thoughts about staying!"

"She is quite beautiful, is she not?"

"Will you focus for one moment boy?"

"I was merely observing, George!"

"Well, stop observing and think about what you are going to say when she wakes up, because quite clearly she can see and hear you!"

I groaned lightly as I fought to open my eyes and was then blinded by light as the electricity came back on.

"Oh this should be interesting!" I heard a voice say.

"Are you alright, Katharina? I think you had quite a shock then!" George asked me. I blinked a couple of times, looked at him and then at the mirror to my side, only to see the same young dishevelled man still staring at me. I quickly scooted up closely to George, who laughed lightly. "It really is alright, you have nothing to fear, it is only James that you see before you!" I stood after looking at George and realising that he was encouraging me to take a good look. Then I continued to stare for some time at the man in front of me. He looked agitated and placed his hands on his hips with frustration. "Give her a moment, James!"

"Well say something, please; it is highly frustrating not knowing what you think!" The man in the mirror then said to me. I took a step closer, as did he, and touched the mirror. Even though he was dishevelled and his hair was long, there was no mistaking those blue, alluring eyes. I gasped, stepped back and then ran down the hallway and toward the staircase. "You see – I didn't even really say anything George and she's going!" I heard him exclaim with annoyance.

"Great, another chance lost. Katharina, wait!" I heard George shout after me.

I raced down the staircase and across the entrance into the long hall that held the many portraits I had looked at with George. After turning on the lights and rushing up to the portrait of James Aldersley, aged twenty-five years, I stood there and tried to calm my breathing. Not taking my eyes off the picture, and as George caught up with me and stopped at my side, gasping, I asked the only question that popped into my head. "What kind of trickery is this?"

George, still gasping, replied between breaths. "No trickery. I swear that I was telling you the truth,

Katharina!" he replied as he bent over and held his knees. I reached out and rubbed his back.

"Are you alright?" I asked him. He held his hand up whilst he caught his breath to acknowledge that he was alright.

"He'll be fine, it's just far too many years of doing not an awful lot!" The voice from before suddenly said. I looked to the mirror further along from the portrait and reluctantly went over to it to find a very nervous-looking James Aldersley. "You promise you will not scream or faint at the sight of me this time?" he asked.

I shook my head and stared at him, then the portrait, then back again. "I cannot believe that this is true," I then said as I found my voice.

"Well I am standing right here!" James replied as he looked at himself. He then ran his fingers through his hair and straightened himself up a little bit. "I do apologise about my appearance, though; I wasn't expecting that you would see me so quickly!"

"You have been stuck within these walls for 264 years?" I asked.

"Unfortunately, yes, but I have had the privilege of having George for company," he replied as he looked to him, realising that he had now straightened up again and caught his breath.

I turned and looked at George, who gave me a very pleading look, silently begging me to believe him. I laughed, then shook my head. "Well you're not boring, I'll give you that!" I sarcastically replied, and then walked across to a chair, sat in view of the mirror and portrait and sighed heavily. "Oh sweet Mary and Joseph, my mother always told me there was magic in the world. I thought she was just keeping my childhood fantasies alive." I placed my head in my hands and growled. "Well unless I want locking up in an asylum for the mentally unbalanced, I cannot really be printing this story, can I? No one in their right mind will believe me – particularly my editor. Then there's the creepy strange people that may try camping out here or breaking in, which in the grand scheme of things is not going to help you two at all!" I announced as I looked up to find both of them looking at each other. "What?" I asked them.

"You mean, you're not going to run? And you believe us?" George asked hopefully.

"Well, unless this is the work of Steven Spielberg, or a reality television programme, the evidence is kind of staring me in the face, isn't it?" I replied.

"Steven who? And what programme?" James asked. Both George and I found ourselves laughing uncontrollably at James' remark; he had obviously not been too bothered about keeping up with many relevant things of today. "What's so funny?" he asked with irritation as I tried to stop laughing.

"I need coffee!" I announced as I stood and walked out to the hall. I thought about the magnitude of what they had told me. Everything that I had believed as a child, that I had convinced myself was fantasy and fairy tale, was actually very real – and here with me right now. James appeared in the mirror next to me in the entrance hall as I thought deeply about the whole situation, making me jump. "Will you stop doing that?" I snapped.

"What? I am walking that is all!" he gestured.

"Appearing without any warning! I am not as used to this as George! Anyway, how are you doing that?" I then asked as I walked to the mirror and tried to look down into it and beyond.

"What, walking? I have feet!" he sarcastically replied as he lifted them one at a time to show me.

"Oh, we have a comedian! Not walking, you arse! Moving from one mirror to another!" I stated with as much sarcasm.

"Oh, this is going to be so interesting. She isn't going to let you get away with anything, you know!" George laughed as we bantered.

"I'm not sure. I can walk on this side of the mirror, like you can the rooms on your side. They are whole, and as I walk I move to another window – well, mirror to you. I see them as a window looking out into Northfield," he replied informatively.

"That must be so weird for you. I cannot imagine how frustrating it must be to be able to see your home as you left it, but not really be here!" I replied before carrying on walking.

We arrived at George's apartment and I found myself quickly looking around for a mirror. A tall one faced the island at which I sat and when James appeared in it I smiled. "I'm not sure that I will ever get used to that!" I announced.

"Oh trust me, you will. He's like an extra shadow. You just have to remember that for everyone else he isn't there!" George then announced.

"So, does this mean that I am pure of heart? That would please my mum immensely!" I then prompted George.

"Well, the spell was only to be visible to those who are. Trust me, you do not meet that many these days!" He winked at me.

George passed me a steaming mug of coffee and placed a plate of biscuits alongside. He suggested that I have one to give me a sugar kick after the adrenaline rush that I had just experienced. "So, do you have any more questions?" George then asked.

"Oh, plenty! I just don't know where to start!" I announced as I sipped the coffee.

"How about the whole 'witch' thing – was it a shock to discover? You know, to know that they exist?" James suddenly said.

"Trust you to fall for the oldest trick in the book… beauty handed to you on a plate usually suffers some consequence in all fairy tales. I actually admire the fact that the 'witch', Alice, gave you some time to reflect on you and the self-destructive person you were!" I replied honestly.

"That's a little unfair; I didn't ask to be left like this. I treated her well whilst I was with her!" James tried to justify.

"I do not think it was her intention to leave you that way for fifty years, either; I think that she maybe would have tried twenty years – long enough for everyone you knew to leave you behind. I think that she would have broken the spell then; I have a feeling that she loved you too much!"

"Well, I wish that she would have just talked to me!" James sarcastically replied.

"Would you have listened?" I asked.

"No he wouldn't have!" George then answered. James shot him a look of disapproval.

"How did you find out about her being caught and killed?" I shivered at the thought. "That must have been horrific for her to deal with!"

"She was a witch! What else was to be done?" James snapped.

"James!" George sternly replied, with the tone of a father. It made me smile. "I searched for her for twenty years. Margaret asked me to try and find a way of resolving the spell; she found it difficult to be separated from James. When Margaret died about eight years after James found himself in this situation, I carried on searching. It was only when I travelled to Yorkshire and visited many places that I found out about Alice. I didn't want to really believe it myself, but she lived in a small village near a place called Pendle Hill, and it has in its past been renowned for witchcraft and witch hunts. The poor girl wasn't even thirty-five years old; she had changed her name to Eliza, but it was confirmed that it was her and it was too late, there was only one other way now!" George sipped his coffee. He had made an extra cup and James turned around and from his side of the mirror picked up a mug that looked exactly the same, although the one in front of us still remained where it stood. George looked at me, then the mug. "It takes a while to get used to how things work. It took us years to understand," he then confirmed. I nodded in reply.

"It also took George another two years to tell me about Alice!" James then stated angrily.

"Well, how could I tell you that the easiest resolution was no more?" George shrugged.

"I find it hard to believe that in all this time, you still have not managed to convince a woman that you love her by word alone? I mean, you're handsome, have a great home and are obviously wealthy. Why are you still trapped?"

"The spell was never about that! It wasn't about James' wealth, assets or good looks. It was about self-respect, and respect for others, and above all love and loyalty. You cannot love someone if you are not loyal to them and respect them whole-heartedly!" George announced. I raised my eyebrows.

"Well, I can't argue with that!" I smiled. "You still haven't managed that?" I asked, as I looked James. He held his head low.

"I know that my behaviour was unforgiveable, and my treatment of the women I had liaisons with unforgiveable also. I have had time to think about all of the things that I should have done, but did not. I have had time that no man ever chooses to have to reflect on my actions, and I can assure you that I am truly sorry. I have now convinced myself, however, that I do not deserve to be loved by any woman, nor I to love anyone in return after what I have done. My mother was right; she always said: 'You can never love anyone until you let go of the sorrow in your heart and love yourself!' I was too busy blaming the world for the loss of my father and the loneliness of my mother, when all along I could have been the solution to a happier family, one in which my mother could have been proud of me. Trust me, when she died alone, and I could not reach her, I knew the error of my ways; but it was too late. I do not deserve a second chance!" he said with a tear in his eye.

"Well, speak for yourself!" George then said. "I want to grow old and relax and live a little, instead of watching your sorry face for eternity!" he smiled.

"Always one to bring me back down to earth George!" James replied.

I could easily see that they had a close relationship, albeit physically separated. George had almost become a second father to James, and I know that even though he did not say it, he was very grateful for his sincerity and commitment. I rubbed my face and finished my coffee and then realised I needed my bed.

"Alright, gentlemen, I really need some beauty sleep. It is four in the morning and I am exhausted. So we will talk more tomorrow at breakfast!" I announced as I stood. Both George and James stood too.

"You promise that you will not run during the night?" George asked.

"George, I think fainting is enough for one night. If I had wanted to run, I would've gone a long time ago. Besides, you have an alarm that is better than a guard dog watching my every move!" I joked as I gestured to James.

"I need sleep too!" he was quick to say.

George kissed me on the cheek and bid me goodnight, and as I turned and left the room, James also called goodnight. I held up my hand in the air without turning to acknowledge him. Maybe I would wake up tomorrow and this would all be a dream? I did laugh though as I walked away and I heard James ask George, "What the hell does she mean I'm like a guard dog?"

George simply replied, "Goodnight James."

Chapter Eight

I woke and rubbed my eyes, knowing that it was later than I had expected to sleep. As I reflected on the conversation and revelations of last night, I sat up quickly and looked around, trying to convince myself it was a dream but knowing all too well that it was not. My biggest worry now was how I could do a piece for the magazine on this. I knew for a fact that I wasn't going to be able to print the truth. Firstly, I would have to make the whole world believe what I had experienced, and then secondly – if anyone did believe me – I was going to scare everyone to death with the notion that witches and magic exist! I sighed heavily and stretched, then climbed out of bed just as my phone vibrated on the dressing table. It was John calling me.

"Morning sleepy head, it's eight forty-five, I thought that you would be on the way back to the city now!" he enquired.

"No not yet. I didn't sleep too well!" I replied despondently.

"Why? What on earth happened?" John then asked, with a tone of worry. I perked up, trying not to let him in on any idea of something being wrong.

"Nothing. It thundered, there was lightning and it

rained torrentially here last night and the combination kept me up!" I announced convincingly.

"Ah okay, I thought that something bad had happened," he confirmed, but before I could reply he then asked the question I had been dreading: "so, did you get your story?" I closed my eyes and grimaced, trying to think quickly of an acceptable answer.

"Well, there is sort of a story, but I don't think that it's front-cover material. I may have to look elsewhere!" I told him.

"That's a shame, babe. Never mind, I told you he was probably a dead end and just a lonely old fool!" he commented harshly.

"Don't say that about George. I really like him!" I snapped.

"Okay, okay. Don't get so touchy, darling. I suggest you go and ask George for a cup of coffee – I think that you need one!" he then stated to my annoyance. "I will see you tonight then?" he asked.

"Yes, see you later on!" I replied, then quickly ended the call before I said something that I would really regret.

"You seem angry! Everything alright?" a familiar voice then asked. I turned to the large mirror at the end of my bed and there stood James.

"Fine!" I quickly replied as I looked down at my pyjamas and decided that I probably wasn't looking too great. He smiled at my obvious observation. "I'm not sure if this is appropriate, James, you know, you turning up in my bedroom unannounced. I mean, I could have been undressing or something!" I informed him. He quickly realised that he had made it very awkward for me.

"Why, of course. I do apologise, Katharina. I simply came to tell you that breakfast is ready if you want to join us?" he kindly asked, as he made an attempt to turn away from me in my nightclothes. It made me smile; it wasn't like I was indecently dressed, and he had seen me the night before, but I was simply worried about him appearing whilst I had significantly less on… I felt that would be a shock to both him and me! "Please do not dress on my account. Nightclothes are acceptable; God knows George is still in his!" he then joked. "I will see you downstairs!" he ended as he marched away from the mirror and toward the door from my room. This was such a bizarre thing to get my head around.

"Thank you!" I called. "I will be there in a minute."

I quickly paid a call to the bathroom, splashed some water on my face and then brushed my teeth, before slipping on my robe and going to find George. Work was not expecting me back until after lunchtime, so I took the opportunity to quiz them some more. "Good morning Katharina, how did you sleep?" George asked as I sat at the island in his apartment.

"Is that before or after the fainting and realising that I am involved in a modern-day fairy tale that involves magic, witches and a young man trapped within a mirror?" I sarcastically replied.

"Point taken!" George nodded as he passed me a mug of coffee and a plate of freshly-made fluffy American pancakes. The smell was divine, and I knew that I was going to enjoy them immensely.

"Thank you!" I replied as I took a spoon to the thick syrup that was in front of me.

I was halfway through one pancake when I realised that they were both staring at me. I hadn't spoken between mouthfuls, so I slowed and looked at them. "I have a really good appetite!"

"You keep eating, I will keep making!" George smiled. "So now that you have had time to digest our situation a little, how do you feel about it? Is there anything further that you want ask?" he prompted.

"Well, I am sure that there will be a thousand questions and that things will keep springing to mind. One thing that I did think of; you can obviously see the main door in the entrance reflected in the mirrors, so why don't you just walk out of it? Is there not a place to go to outside of the house? Would that not release you?" I finished as I pulled another mouthful of pancake off my fork.

"I've tried. Believe me – windows *and* doors. If I get too near to them or try to step through them, I get the strongest burning sensation, like I am about to burst into flames! It really isn't pleasant and so not an option, but it has been considered many times!" James replied. I nodded.

"How about finding another witch to break the spell? They cannot all be bad!" I then stated.

"Ah, we enquired about that. Unfortunately a spell of this calibre cast by one witch cannot be broken by another! It is bound to the witch that makes the spell!" James confirmed.

"So, when she died, why did that not break the spell?" I asked as I kept eating.

"Well, we think that as the spell was cast with her

96

giving two options – one being her words alone to break the spell, or a woman's words that may have learned to love me – neither has happened, and so I am stuck here for eternity it seems!" James stated sadly.

"Never give up! That's a ridiculous attitude!" I replied.

"She's right!" George replied.

"Does no one ever seem slightly sorry for my situation?" James asked, looking at the two of us.

"Well, in fairness you got yourself into this situation!" I smiled as I carried on eating. I looked at George, who smiled, then winked at me and my remark.

"Oh this is just great, now I have two of you to keep happy, and I have to listen to your sarcasm!" James sighed. He stood and walked a little bit away. I had a small feeling of guilt.

"Hey, I'm sorry – it really must be the worst torture. To think that you have had to live for so long watching people come and go, and especially loved ones... it is actually very sad," I then stated as I looked at James.

"The worst torture ever!" George then expressed as he excused himself for a moment. I looked toward James and gave him an inquisitive look.

"George had a wife and a son. He had to watch them live and grow older, as we stayed stuck in this predicament," he gestured to his appearance. I raised my hand to my mouth.

"So he experienced them passing him in age – and eventually their demise?"

"Indeed! His son did marry and had children of his own, but how do you explain to children as they grow a situation such as ours?" he said as he sat. "He made a choice after speaking with his son to never see him again, once he realised the pain it would cause at a later date to have to let him go – and his own grandchildren. He managed to keep getting updates on how his son's family were doing, but as you can imagine it was tough. It was not an easy decision, I assure you, and I am to blame!"

"I am sure that you feel guilty about his grief, but from what you have both told me, George made the decision to be with you. He must have realised in some small way the consequences of that decision?"

"It does not make light of the matter though, Katharina. He sacrificed everything for me. I look to him as a son would to a father. I would not have survived these many years without him!" James then stated sincerely.

"Have you told him that recently?" I enquired. "I think that he would like to hear that!" James nodded.

"I never seem to have found the right time!" James put his head into his hands.

"Jeeze, you've only had over 200 years!" I sarcastically replied as I ate another delicious mouthful of pancake. I smiled at him, as a gesture that I understood him.

"Point taken!" he replied as George returned to the room.

"George, this breakfast is to die for. I haven't eaten this much – or anything this high in calories – for ages. It's heaven!"

"Another?" he asked of me, but I had to hold my hand up in defeat.

"I need to shower and dress, then come to a decision

with you before I leave about this story!" I concluded as I finished the last mouthful of coffee. "I simply do not think that the world is ready for this type of truth, believable or not!" I stood and turned to leave.

"Do you think that you will visit us again?" James then asked.

"Are you kidding me? Of course I will be back. I want to hear as much of what you have experienced over these years as possible!" I excitedly replied. I turned to find them both smiling at one another. "Oh, and for the record, your secret is safe with me – unless it's a matter of life or death that I have to tell someone!" I smiled at them both and went up the stairs with a spring in my step.

Showering was slightly worrying; I found myself trying to cover all the mirrors and anything I could find that was reflective with towels and facecloths. It was strange; if I wanted to look at my own reflection, I simply thought about that, and it was like any other everyday mirror. If I wanted to see James, I simply thought about him and there he was! Was it this simple for everyone? George had stated not; maybe because they were not open to believing such things, or pure of heart. *Pure of heart,* I smiled to myself; *my mum would love that.* I sounded like Snow White, or some other fairy tale character. These thoughts made me think about the fact that some fairy tales could be based on fact, as George had said: handsome princes and damsels in distress were a lovely thought, but wicked witches and evil stepmothers and magic? I shook my head in disbelief. "This is crazy!" I muttered to myself.

Once dressed, I returned downstairs. I left my bags in the entrance and returned to George's kitchen with my notepad. James and George were both talking and I smiled as I realised that even though the reality was very different, they were like two ordinary people discussing everyday things. I perched on a stool and George handed me another coffee. "Feeling better?" he asked.

"I think that this will take some getting used to, but I'm not running, and I think I am starting to get my head around this a little better!" I gestured to the three of us. "It's what I am going to tell my editor and John that has me worrying a little. I thought this was going to be my big story – and believe me, it's big! – but I don't think it is front-page news for the present; I would get laughed out of my job if I tried to explain this! I need another story to deter people from you whilst we sort something out!" George looked at me as I finished.

"What do you mean, 'whilst we sort something'?" he asked.

"Well, I can hardly walk away now, can I? I'm a big believer in fate, George, and something made me want to meet you. I am going to have to help you now. At least I can feel satisfied that I have done one really good deed for someone else in my life!" I sipped my coffee. "Well, that is if you do not mind me spending time with you both whilst we find someone for you, James?" I then enquired.

"No, no we don't mind at all, do we James?" George quickly stated.

"I have no reservations in you visiting us more regularly, Katharina, but I am not sure what you can do to help!" James answered with an air of authority.

"Well I can try!" I smiled as I sipped the coffee in front of me.

"That is very kind of you," George replied as he looked at James and nodded for his approval.

"Indeed, very kind! Although I am at a loss as to why you would want to!" he confirmed.

"You really don't think that there are any good people, do you? I think that you have had plenty of time to see the error of your ways, and you now believe that people have become too bitter to see the real you! Trust me, some of us do still want the better things in life and are actually nice people too. I can understand that you feel guilty and hurt and it must have been torture for both of you to lose everyone around you, but I think that it is time that we try and end this for the both of you, don't you?"

"Agreed!" George quickly stated as he looked at James.

"Unless you would rather stay this way?" I then sarcastically commented as I looked toward the mirror at him. James shook his head, indicating that he was not happy with the current situation either.

"Agreed!" he quietly announced.

"Great. That's sorted, then! Now I need to find another story to deter everyone from this one! It's going to make my editor very suspicious, so I may have to make something up about you, George, to get her to agree to move on to something else."

"Something like what?" he asked, sounding worried. I laughed at his remark.

"This could be fun!" James suddenly stated, rubbing his hands together.

"Don't worry, I promise not to be too harsh!" I smiled as I winked at James, who noted my air of playfulness.

"I really must be getting to work! I will be back soon though!" I stated. I checked that George had my number, and I told them both that I would call soon to arrange another visit.

So, with my bag packed, I decided to tell my editor that George was a little deluded and had not lived there for that long, but was the best friend of the previous owner who wanted him to be well looked after once he had departed this world. I hoped that it would be enough for my editor to leave the story for something that would be far more appropriate for the centre magazine spread. It may be a little harder trying to explain why I keep visiting the place, but I would make that up as I go along! More than anything, I hoped that like fairy tales written from the past, this story would become something similar that would be talked about in years to come. I felt like I was on the verge of discovering something life-changing; I was so excited about the whole prospect of what I had been witness to the last couple of days. I still found it hard to feel that it was the truth; it just seemed so much like a dream. It was going to be strange getting used to what I would find out from them every time I saw them.

The drive back to the centre of London was long due to the traffic, but nonetheless it gave me time to run through my new reasons for not doing this story before I got to work. I parked and, as I rode the elevator to the office floor, I sighed. I had the story of a lifetime and something that I could never have dreamt of in a million years, but I could tell no one about it!

Chapter Nine

The doors to the elevator pinged and I stepped out onto the office floor, greeted Michelle, the receptionist, and then walked to my desk. I had to try and convince all of them the truth behind my dropping the story, and I already had an idea that I could put in its place from previous research. The first person that would be a tester would be Claire, who was very excited when she saw me arriving at my desk.

"Coffee?" she asked.

"Please, long journey in!" I noted with lethargy.

"Then you can tell me all about it!" she stated as she bounced away.

"Great!" I said to myself.

"Kat, how was the visit?" I then heard Angela call. I grimaced then turned to face her.

"Not that great, unfortunately! Nothing really to write about, just a slightly deluded old guy!" I raised my eyebrows at her and shrugged my shoulders to be more convincing, but remarkably she replied easily.

"Shame, but you know this job Kat… you win some, you lose some!" she chirped as she happily then went to Mark, one of our other journalists who was doing a piece on pilots and flight crew, which had her excited enough to take the emphasis off me.

I knew that I would have to produce something good. It was my job, and one that I didn't want to lose; I loved this team and working here. As I sat and pondered over the stories considered prior to George and James, a steaming mug of coffee appeared.

"So, tell… what was it like? How was he, and what did you do?" she asked with curiosity.

"Well, he is charming and the place is amazing! We had dinner and chatted and danced in the ballroom, then I came back!" I replied.

"Is that it? What about the intriguing story?" she asked.

"There wasn't one, unfortunately; he is just a very friendly, lonely guy who was given the right to live there by the previous owner – a dear friend that didn't want to see George left on the street, so left him the estate!" I said matter-of-factly.

"Oh, well I suppose it is sweet, but not what you hoped for!" she remarked, then leant forward. "You did have fun, though? I mean, a house like that and the chance to stay there – it must have been great!"

"Oh don't get me wrong, I enjoyed the whole experience, Claire. George is the most kind and gentle man I have met in a long time. In fact, I will more than likely keep in touch with him; I did find his company stimulating in other ways and he made me laugh a lot, which no other male company has done in a long time!" I replied sincerely.

"Well good for you! I bet that he is really glad that he has met you too."

"Maybe one day I could take you to meet him?" I

replied, suddenly realising that Claire was single. First innocent suspect for finding someone for James!

"Maybe… although I am not the same placid person as yourself; you know that I am a little wilder. I may be too much for him!" she then replied.

"We need to fall back on one of our other possibilities, Claire. I think I may get in touch with Frances Holt, the lady who has set up her house to take in soldiers after their return, in a bid to give them some respite. I think it will be a good place to start!" I then concluded.

"I agree, I think that is a fabulous story; I always was drawn to that one," she confirmed. "I will get all of the details back out for you," she said efficiently as she wondered back to her desk.

I sighed with relief; for the most part, everyone seemed to have accepted my lie for now! I had work on my mind and was also wondering how in God's name I was going to try and help George and James. I had to take into account the fact that I was going to be spending more time with them, which I knew was going to be harder to explain to John, who wasn't even happy with this first visit. I placed my head in my hands and closed my eyes briefly, then took a deep breath and a large gulp of coffee and decided to take one step at a time. A few more days after 264 years was not going to make a huge amount of difference to them. I replayed the whole fairy tale in my head, then blinked and looked at my computer screen to try and focus on work. This was like living in a movie and I was a main lead now. I smiled; the thought of James' blue eyes staring at me made my stomach flip a little. *Snap out of it*, I said to myself. *You're an engaged woman*, I quickly forced myself to remember, and picked up my mouse and started clicking away.

The afternoon passed quickly. I had already spoken to Frances Holt and arranged an interview in two days' time; she seemed very keen to do a feature with our magazine, so that was all in place. I left work that day feeling slightly better that I had achieved something, and in celebration of that I decided to cook John dinner. I texted him to ask what time he would be home, only to get the following reply: 'Sorry babe, out with clients trying to close a deal. Probably be 10.30 before I am home!' I threw the phone onto the sofa at the side of where I sat. "Great!" I moaned to myself, then I shook my head – I hated him calling me babe. Darling or sweetheart maybe, but babe? Honestly, I felt like someone from a seedy bar! I decided that I couldn't be bothered to text him back; it wasn't like he asked how I was, and this was becoming a regular habit now, me eating alone. My mind wandered back to James and I reached across and retrieved my phone, picked up a notepad and pen and started to scroll through my contacts. I must have a few single girls that I know to introduce to James and George. I wrote the possibilities down and then looked at the list – four, including Claire at work. I scowled; this wasn't going to be as easy as I had first thought.

I made some pasta and sat curled up on the sofa whilst I ate, making a list of negatives and positives for each single friend that I had, and the potential compatibility between them and James. The only way to see if any of them were appropriate would be to take them to Northfield. I should speak to James first and see if he would agree to what I proposed. I looked at George's number on my mobile, and before I realised what I had done I had pressed call and he had answered.

"Katharina, good evening!" he said.

"Ah George, good evening. I just wanted to let you know that everything went well today – I think I threw them off your track and now I am hopefully doing a feature on another story that I had as a backup!"

"Wonderful news, thank you again for your help!" he sincerely replied.

"Well, don't thank me yet. My bank of single friends is not that big, George. I think that I may need another visit with you and James to discuss the way forward, so I propose meeting with you again, maybe on Friday about 6pm. I have to go and interview for the other story and I can swing by yours on the way back – it's not that far away," I suggested hopefully.

"That would be lovely, we really look forward to seeing you. Can I offer you some light refreshment on your arrival?" he kindly asked. "After all, you will have been working all day!"

"Yes, alright George, that would be lovely! I will see you both then!" I replied.

"See you on Friday. Oh, and Katharina…"

"Yes, George?"

"I really do appreciate what you are doing for us!" he quietly said.

"My pleasure, it's certainly something new for me!" I laughed as he bid me goodnight and I him.

I had slipped into my pyjamas after a long soak in the

bath. True to his word, as I was drifting off on the sofa whilst watching some series, John walked in the door at 10.40pm. He dropped his things at the island and walked across to me. "Hi babe!" he said as he kissed me on the forehead.

"Hi. Long day?" I asked.

"It was indeed, but I think that we have made some progress, so it should be plain sailing from here on in! I just want to get this deal put to bed as I have other pressing deals to sort. Not enough time in the day – you know how it is!" he answered as he pulled his tie off. "I'm just going to jump in the shower."

"Alright, I am tired so I won't be staying up long," I informed him.

He returned in his pyjama bottoms and with his chest bare. He picked my feet up, then sat and placed them on his lap. "What you watching?" he asked.

"Not paying attention – I'm too tired!" I replied.

"Oh yes, bad night's sleep. So how did it go?" he asked. I had long past worried about what he would think now. It didn't seem like anything I did really appeared on John's radar.

"There isn't really anything to tell. He is a very kind lovely older man, who is unfortunately lonely, but he has the right to stay in an amazing house!" I confirmed.

"Never mind babe, you'll find something else. So, he didn't try it on with you then?" he laughed. I sat up promptly.

"Jesus John, is that all you were bothered about? Not the fact that this is my job and it is important to me, or the fact that I was actually excited about it? No he didn't bloody try it on with me! I like him and I will tell you now that we will remain friends!" My raised voice shocked me too.

"Hell Kat, I do think you need sleep. I was only joking!" he replied.

"Well don't! I'm going to go to bed, I am not in the mood for arguing!" I informed him. In a bid to avoid too much more aggravation, I leant over and kissed him.

"I'm just going to chill for thirty minutes, I will be in soon. Have a good sleep babe!" he said with no feeling and without his eyes leaving the TV screen.

I wandered to our bedroom, shut the door and leant against it. 'Babe' – I was definitely going to have to pull him up on that word. It was starting to really annoy me. I brushed my teeth and climbed into the remarkably smaller bed. As soon as my head touched the pillow, I was dead to the world.

Thursday was fairly insignificant. I had now started the new story and had done some background work before the interview tomorrow. The day rolled on into a normal workday, and the time flew by faster than I could have hoped for. I had to admit to myself that I was looking forward to seeing James and George tomorrow; not just because the whole situation of a spell had me hooked, but they did actually seem to be very genuine, lovely people. I smiled at the prospect of spending more time with them. I rode home on the tube and whilst trying to imagine James with any one of my single friends, I almost missed my stop. When I turned the key in the apartment lock, I suddenly realised that I couldn't remember the walk from the tube; I was completely wrapped up in this fairy tale. More than anything, I was trying to imagine the whole situation of a witch being present and casting a spell. How would I ever be able to convince anyone else that this was all true? I would have to let them see James first and then explain; otherwise I was going to end up sounding like I had completely lost it. John had been home and changed into casual clothes for a business 'football match meeting' – his company had a private box. I knew that this was going to be another long and lonely night in. His note on the island made it quite clear that he was not in any rush to get home until he had closed the deal. I looked in the fridge, but decided that I couldn't be bothered cooking, so I ordered a pizza.

I felt remarkably tired again, and as I laid on the sofa hugging a cushion and mindlessly watching something on BBC 1, I hadn't realised that I had drifted off to sleep until I woke breathless and startled. I had been dreaming that I was at Northfield and I couldn't get out; I was running and running, and James was calling me. I could see George, but could never get to him, and then I smashed all the mirrors, thinking it would help James, but he simply disappeared and then George burst into a million tiny particles that all blew away in the air. I sat up and rubbed my eyes. That dream had been so vivid. I clutched the cushion tighter to my chest, calmed my breathing and realised that I really did care about helping them both and about what was going to happen to them. I looked at the clock; it was 10.15pm, so I switched the television off and put all of my notes away and decided it was bedtime. With glass of water in hand, I dozily walked to my bedroom and sank into bed, hoping that I would not have any more dreams as vivid as that one was.

Friday's tube ride to work was as expected: hot and crowded. There was nowhere to sit and then it was hard work fighting to get through everyone in the crowds. I reached the office in desperate need of a coffee. As I had arrived a little earlier I had beaten Claire, so I made her a drink, knowing that she would not be far behind me. At the usual Friday morning meeting I made a slightly poor excuse (and lie) for not getting anywhere with the intended Northfield story, but really pushed the new lead, which seemed to be taken well. I walked out of the meeting feeling relieved that for now I could carry on doing my job whilst on the side lines continuing to help George and James, knowing no one here was any the wiser. By the time I had grabbed a quick salad for lunch, it was time to go and interview Frances Holt, so I grabbed the car keys off Michelle at reception and took the spare car for the weekend.

The ride out to Mrs Holt's residence was easier than expected. She greeted me at the door and was most accommodating, giving me a wealth of knowledge about what she was trying to achieve. I was very impressed with her passion, motivation and generosity for helping returning soldiers rehabilitate back to some normality. She had a group of around four or six of them at a time, booking a multitude of activities for them as and when they felt they wanted to participate. She then helped them relearn the art of simple relaxation and talking to each other. She cooked all of the meals, did their laundry, and as her home was a large six-bedroom house with a swimming pool, there was certainly no reason to not enjoy it here. At the moment she was having a week's break and so she invited me to come back in a week's time when her new group of soldiers had then had the opportunity to settle in. She thought that I may like to get their opinion on what she was trying to achieve, which was all free of charge. After a couple of hours interviewing her, I made arrangements for the week after and asked if she would mind a photographer coming with me to take some pictures of her and the house and, if they agreed, some of the soldiers that she was trying to help. She was in agreement, and I came away feeling like the story was definitely not going to let me down in any way.

Slowly, because of the traffic, I made my way to Northfield, and as I arrived I yawned slightly. I was mentally tired today; I had achieved a lot and although I had slept well last night, I still felt tired. I closed the car door and then ran up the stairs to the cover of the entrance, as the rain had again started to fall. I pulled the bell handle and waited for George. I was surprised that he was not ready for my arrival, but then I realised that I was a little early – it was only 5.20 pm. The heavy door creaked open and George's happy smile greeted me.

"Katharina, quickly – do come in. This weather is terrible!" he announced as I skipped in through the door and past him.

"George, are you well?" I asked as he took my coat.

"Indeed. I was just organising a bite to eat for us."

"Oh lovely, I am sorry that I am a little early. I was finished with my last appointment faster than expected!" I confirmed.

"It is no problem at all. Come, let's get you a warm drink." He gestured for me to walk toward his apartment. As I neared the large mirror in the hallway with my reflection, I stood for a second and thought about James. Then, like fog had been lifted, I was no longer reflected and there he was.

"James, how are you feeling today?" I smiled as I realised that I still had the ability to see him.

"I am very well thank you, are you Katharina?" he asked of me. I looked him up and down and then smiled and continued walking.

"I am, thank you for asking!" I replied as I grinned, knowing that he had definitely made an effort for my visit. His hair was brushed and neat, and his clothes less shabby; his shirt was tucked into his breeches. He looked different and I wondered how long it must have been since he last made any effort for anyone other than George. We arrived at the apartment and I could smell beef and onions and gravy. "George, I hope you have not gone to too much trouble?" I asked. "I thought you were just making a small bite to eat – you know, light refreshment?"

"No trouble gone to, it is only some roast beef. I am going to make us hot beef sandwiches and they should be ready in about half an hour," he then informed me.

"Well it smells delicious!" I happily stated as he poured me a coffee. I perched on a chair at the island.

"One thing George has got very good at is the ability to cook!" James suddenly announced.

"Well, unfortunately I have had to, as you are unable to do anything for me!" George replied.

"Not by choice, I hate to point out!" James remarked.

"I never thought about that; anything we have on this side you can have on your side – like George's lovely cooking, or a coffee or a newspaper – but it cannot be done in reverse?" I asked inquisitively.

"I wouldn't want to eat any attempt James had at cooking!" George laughed.

"Yes, alright, laugh as much as you like! I would do it if I could, but alas I cannot!" James unhappily said. I tried not to laugh as George chuckled to himself.

"I can understand your frustration; it's terrible not to be able to do anything for yourself!" I sarcastically smiled; James shot me a look of annoyance.

"Don't you start, I have enough with George reminding me on a regular basis. Maybe we should have limited the mirrors George, then you may have felt like I was not around quite as much!" he said with irritation.

"Oh, so you had most of the mirrors put up then? There are a lot!" I remarked.

"Well, I realised when I put a long mirror in here that James could somehow come to this mirror, so we tried getting more to see if he had the ability to move all over the house. In fairness, it gives him more chances to be a part of things here!" George said sincerely.

"Maybe to his detriment!" James then stated as he smiled at George.

"I wouldn't have had it any other way, Master James!" George simply replied.

"Really, Master? I think we are long past that George – I am thirty and this is a new era!" he answered.

"Well technically you are 294 years old, so actually

you could be considered for the Guinness World Records!" I laughed.

"Not before George!" James smiled as he raised his eyebrows at him.

"Alright, alright, enough about my age. I am sure Katharina has other pressing things to discuss!" George quickly changed the subject and gestured for me to speak.

"Yes indeed, let me just get my notes." I put my coffee mug down and quickly reached into my bag. I placed my notepad on the island and then flicked to the relevant page of notes that I had made with regards to my single friends. "Okay, unfortunately my bank of single friends is not that large, but to start with I have four that I think could be possible contenders: Claire, Rachel, Kate and Lisa. It's not a lot to start with, I know, but I thought maybe if you agree, James, I could bring them over for dinner with the intention of either meeting my new friend George – or, a couple of them are rather wealthy, so there's always the prospect of selling the leasehold?" I reported.

"Well, sounds like a plan to me. What do you think, James?" George asked.

"You would be happy to introduce your friends to me, after knowing my past?" James enquired.

"That's exactly what it is – your past. Do you not feel that you have changed in any way?" I asked.

"Yes, I have changed remarkably, but still these are your friends!"

"Well two are, definitely, but two I haven't seen in a while. I think if anything, after all this time, your calmness at your situation shows strength of character, James, I would be happy for them to meet you!" I smiled.

James stopped for a minute, then looked across at George and back to me. I could tell that he may have felt slightly uncomfortable with the fact that I was almost setting him up with blind dates; after all, his last experience with a woman he didn't know very well did not end in his favour. I waited for a response and looked across at George, who shrugged at me.

"Very well! Let us start next week if you can arrange it: dinner here with whoever you think we have the best chance of a result. I will try not to be dismissive instantly," he said with caution.

"Great, okay, I will start with Claire, my work colleague. She is single, twenty-seven years old, brunette, about five foot five, very slim but lots of fun. I am sure she would love to come – she was very jealous when I told her about George!" I remarked.

"Maybe I could get her to fall in love with me!" he said sarcastically.

"That really is not going to help our situation, now is it George!" James laughed.

"Fair point. Let's eat – I need to get these sandwiches prepared, shall we just eat here?" George asked.

"Here is fine!" I replied, just as James said, "Here is good!" We both smiled that we answered at the same time.

The hot beef sandwich with onion gravy, chips and salad was truly delicious. I cannot say that I ate it in a completely ladylike way – it wasn't easy, with gravy dripping off my fingers, and with it being so damn delicious. It caused us all to laugh; I must have looked like I hadn't eaten for a week. I licked my fingers and then used my fork to finish my salad.

"George, you are really going to have to stop making such yummy food, I am seriously thinking of getting you to come and live with me! That was so, so good!" I informed him.

"It looked like it was good!" James smiled sarcastically. I threw my linen napkin at the mirror.

"You're lucky that you're behind that mirror, I would have been tempted to hit you for that remark!" I laughed.

"I would like to see you try!"

"Ooh, one day you will not be able to say that without it having some consequence!" I remarked.

"Indeed, and I like to see a good appetite on a woman. Food is to be enjoyed!" George stated.

"Thank you George!" I replied as I gathered our plates, including the one that sat at the end of the island opposite James with its sandwich still intact. I looked at it curiously.

"I know; it is strange isn't it? She made the spell completely confusing – trust me, it took us some time to work it out. Even though when we see James in the mirror and not ourselves, food and drink and other items still end up as a reality on his side of the mirror, even though it looks like a reflection, nothing in front of you changes on *this* side of the mirror. I can understand your expression – you have only had a couple of days of this, we have had 264 years! I think that you are grasping things really well!" George stated.

"I just feel like I am wrapped up in a Disney film or something!" I replied with disbelief.

"Come on, let us retire to the lounge with a drink!" George then insisted as he topped up my wine glass.

His lounge was small and cosy and, as expected, there was a mirror on every wall. I kicked off my shoes and then gestured to George that I would like to curl up in the large armchair. "May I?" He simply replied with "Please do," and as I sat I felt contently full and very, very, comfortable.

"So, you must have at least one funny story whilst you have been in this predicament that you can enlighten me with. Or, better still, some scandalous gossip from the 1700 or 1800s. I cannot begin to imagine what you must have seen and heard over the years!" I excitedly announced. Being a journalist, I have always loved a good story from any era.

George looked at James and then at me. He took a sip from his wine glass and then said, "How scandalous do you want it to be?" I raised my eyebrows at him and leaned forward slightly.

"Really? You have scandalous gossip from way back then? Oh I am so intrigued – I want to hear it all!" I remarked. James simply gestured for him to continue.

"Please do go ahead, as long as it does not include me!" James answered with sarcasm.

"Well feel free to chip in anytime!" George replied to James, and then, like the beginning of a fairy tale, he began:

"It was the year 1728…"

As the clock ticked on, and the stories continued, I gasped, laughed, and was shocked, surprised and disgusted with the stories that ensued. I had no idea that that era could have been quite so scandalous, incestuous and completely and, unbelievably, as unromantic as I ever could have imagined. I was wrapped up in their tales of debauchery, seduction, crime and lies, but at the same time utterly disappointed that the romance of all the stories and fairy tales I had fantasised about from times past, were just that – fairy tales – and the likelihood of happily ever after was a mere myth.

As George went to get us a coffee after his last tale for the evening, and I laughed with James about the stories they had told me, I looked at the time and was shocked to realise that it was now nine o'clock. I stretched from my comfortable chair and then happily took the coffee from George as he reappeared. I was fast becoming addicted to spending time with them both. I found George utterly charming – he was sincere and kind – and James, although he had once been a rogue, he appeared to be a very different person now. He did not feel worthy of anything, it seemed; he realised his mistakes and I was sure that he felt he deserved his predicament. I, however, could not help but feel sorry for him. He had missed being with his friends and family, and time had passed him by in a torturous way. I was happy that I had the ability to see him, because right there in that moment, as I looked at him in the mirror, I wanted nothing more than to help him; my new mysterious – and handsome, I might add – acquaintance.

Chapter Ten

After telling John that my appointment had run over and I had been stuck in traffic, I managed to get away with not explaining that I had spent most of the evening with George and James. The weekend involved a dinner on Saturday with work colleagues of John's and quite frankly it was hard work and very tiresome. Stocks, shares, mergers and advertisement campaigns for large clients were not my cup of tea. Nonetheless, I tried to look interested and commented on things that I could understand. All the while, my mind kept drifting back to helping James and trying to break a spell over two hundred years old. It was so hard to believe; even though I could see James, I definitely still felt like I was in a Disney movie.

By the time Monday morning had arrived, I could not wait to get to the office to see Claire, my first innocent pawn in this elaborate game of matchmaking. As I sat and turned on my computer, Angela came by my desk.

"Hey Kat, read the first draft copy of your story. Can't wait to read the finalised draft. Sounds like an amazing woman!" she commented.

"Indeed she is, I think it will bring a smile to most people's faces when they read about her completely amazing selfless acts!" I replied. She nodded and walked away as she read the paperwork she had collected from the reception.

A mug of coffee suddenly appeared on my desk with a blueberry muffin that was warm and smelt so sweet and fresh that my mouth started to salivate.

"What's this?" I asked as I gestured to the muffin.

"Well, you went out with John's work colleagues, didn't you, on Saturday? I thought that you may be in need of a pick-me-up and sugar kick after being drained and having all the fun taken out of you for a whole night!" Claire laughed as she mimicked passing out. I laughed.

"Alright, you know me far too well!"

"How was the meeting on Friday?" she then asked.

"Mrs Holt is an amazing lady –" I started, until she put her hand up to interrupt me.

"Not that meeting, silly. I know that story is in the bag. I meant the meeting afterwards – the one that you had with George?" She raised her eyebrows as she crossed her legs whilst perched on the end of my desk.

"Oh yes, I forgot that I told you I was going there! It was truly lovely; he made us a bite to eat and we chatted, laughed and had a glass of wine. In fact, we spoke about you!" I hesitantly said.

"Me? Why on earth would I enter the conversation?" she remarked curiously.

"George noted that I didn't seem to go out with any female friends very often, so he asked about my girlfriends. In fact, he has invited both of us over for dinner this week!" I replied quickly as I took a sip from my coffee mug.

"No way! Seriously? This is great, so I get to meet George too? Hell yeah, I'm up for that. When are we going?" she confidently asked. I was shocked that she had taken the suggestion so well. I mean, not every girl would probably think George was the most interesting person… although I knew differently, of course.

"How about Wednesday?" I suggested.

"Let me check my busy diary!" she sarcastically remarked as she mimed flipping through a book. "Yep, Wednesday is good for me, shall we go straight from here?"

"We can, but I will have to tell John that we have a business dinner. I don't think he will be too happy if he knows that I keep calling to see George, but I like his company. We can catch a cab there and back if you're happy with that?" I replied.

"Brilliant, wow this is so going to make my week interesting!" She clapped her hands together in delight, like it was the best offer she had received in a long time. I only hoped that James liked her and that we could help her to see him.

I telephoned George and made the arrangements, and he seemed more than happy that I had made plans so soon. I told him of things I knew that Claire did not like in terms of food and left the rest to him. I was excited to think about the prospect of James finding true love; it was something that I was going to love being a part of, even if I was watching from the side lines. I sighed; who was I kidding? I was in the middle of the biggest story of my life, unbelievable or not, and I was trying to matchmake everything I had ever dreamed about for someone else! I took a deep breath and placed the phone on the hook and went to Claire and announced that it was all in place. She was very excited, but all I could think was, *if you only knew…* I lied to John about where I was going, but Claire made sure that she rang and confirmed our fake business dinner in his presence, so that stopped any suspicions. By the time five thirty on Wednesday arrived, I had not butterflies but an accumulating tornado in my stomach. This was going to be interesting!

We arrived in the cab and as I paid I glanced at Claire, who was wearing on her face the same expression that I must have had when I first saw Northfield. "Bloody hell Kat, there's no wonder you like it here!" She scrambled out of the cab and looked up at the intricate facade. I noticed George and went toward him with a warm smile.

"George!" I happily announced as we greeted each other like old friends, with a kiss on each cheek.

"Katharina, how lovely to see you again!" he happily stated.

"Please let me introduce to you my good friend Claire!" I gestured toward her as she scurried over to us.

"George, it's a pleasure! I have heard so much about you!" she remarked.

"Really!" he raised his eyebrows at me. "All good, I hope?" He then smiled. "Claire, it is a pleasure to make your acquaintance," he then finished as he kissed the back of her hand. She giggled like a schoolgirl at the gesture.

"Thank you. This is amazing, and Kat just loves you, so, yes, all she has said about you is good!" she replied in a slightly higher than normal pitch.

I laughed and shook my head. George gestured for

us to go inside and then checked that our trip was not too long and frustrating. As we entered the main hallway, I touched Claire's arm as I knew the house would overwhelm her, as it had done with me. She spun around in disbelief at the splendour of the building. Whilst she was keenly observing the ornate ceiling, I looked across at the large mirror, saw James, who was very well-dressed, smiled at him and simply nodded to acknowledge his presence. He smiled in return, placed his hands behind his back and bowed to me, then calmly said, "Good evening, Katharina!" I smiled at this, then looked to Claire, who had quite obviously not heard anything. I did not dismiss it straight away; she was far too engrossed on opening her sensory perception to the whole atmosphere.

"Wow – *really* wow!" she then said. "I love it – I've never had the chance to see anything quite like it, but I love it!" She smiled as her mouth stayed slightly open in wonderment.

"Shall we?" George then asked as he gestured for me to walk to the dining room.

"George, are we eating in the main dining room? I would have thought that your apartment would have been adequate!" I happily noted.

"Only the best for two beautiful ladies; how often do I get the chance to cook and have your company here? It could only be the dining room, Katharina. Besides, it does not get enough use these days!" he replied. I smiled and took Claire by the arm as we walked across the hall and into the beautiful room that I had spent an evening in with George before he dropped the bombshell on me!

I was hoping that James would be able to converse with one of the friends that I had selected. So far, though, it was not looking good with Claire. *Give it time*, I said to myself in my head; after all, we had only been here for five minutes. I noted that he had followed us to the dining room and looked at Claire for a lengthy time from behind the large mirror to the left of the fireplace. George served dinner, which again was delicious. He asked Claire lots of questions, some of which involved me! We laughed and Claire talked – a lot – which she always did, as she was very exuberant. James commented many times on remarks that Claire made, which had both George and I smiling and occasionally laughing, but all the while it was obvious that Claire could not hear anything. As the evening progressed, George offered to give Claire a tour of the house, which she was more than happy to do. As they walked slightly ahead, James paced alongside me.

"She seems very nice!" he remarked, a little apprehensively.

"But…?" I queried, knowing that he had some reservations.

"She has very strange views on things, and it has to be said that she is very easily stimulated, like an over-excited schoolgirl!" he said honestly. I stopped for a minute, glanced in the mirror at him, thought about what he said and then laughed lightly.

"I can't argue with that comment, unfortunately!" I quietly whispered. He then laughed.

"She is really lovely, but I just do not see myself with her in any way!" he remarked. George heard his comment and turned to look at the two of us whilst

Claire happily chirped on. I got the feeling that he was not happy that James had already given up on her. I shrugged my shoulders at George and then quickly looked at James.

"There is always the fact that she cannot see you; it's probably best if you are not too enamoured with her!" I looked at him, but he still looked slightly disappointed. "Chin up, we're not giving up yet – we will break this spell!" I smiled confidently.

"Thank you, your support is very reassuring!" he then replied.

"So Claire, what do you think?" I asked her as we entered into the long hall with all the portraits.

"It is absolutely amazing; I can completely understand why you like to come here, Kat," she replied as she came upon the portrait of James, which quite rightly could stop anyone in their tracks. "Oh my God – who is *that*?" she asked with interest.

"That would be James Henry Aldersley – one of the owners of the house from many a year back!" George then informed her.

"Well he has definitely made my heart skip a beat. What a dish – I wish I had known him!" She seemed more than excited by his portrait.

"Be careful what you wish for, Claire!" I remarked as I looked across at James, who raised his hand in embarrassment and covered his face. He wasn't interested in Claire that much, I could tell, and so the fact that she liked his portrait amused me no end.

We returned to the dining room and helped George tidy away the plates back to his apartment, where he then made coffee. We sat and chatted and laughed, and then at nine thirty I suggested that we call a cab to return back to the city centre and home. After a while George walked Claire to the entrance hall to get her coat, I went to the bathroom before the trip back and when I exited the door James was stood waiting.

"James, gosh you startled me then. Are you alright?" I asked him.

"I'm sorry Katharina, I did not mean to startle you. I just wanted to say thank you again. Can I presume that you will arrange the next person soon? I feel like I am being very forward asking, but after seeing you more regularly and accepting your help I feel more confident in achieving a result than I have in many, many years!" he sincerely said. I walked toward him and placed my hand on the mirror;

"I will liaise with George in the coming days, and you are very welcome. I wasn't lying when I said I wanted to help you. I have a good feeling about this coming to a good conclusion, so keep trying to remain positive!" I smiled. "Besides, what girl in their right mind would not want to spend time here?" I then raised my eyebrows, which produced a small smile from him in return, just as George appeared.

"Are you alright? Your cab is here!" George asked as he looked at where my hand was placed.

"I am fine George thank you. I will be in touch before the weekend!" I replied as I walked toward George. "Thank you for a lovely evening!" I kissed him on the cheek.

"You are more than welcome; your company is

enjoyed and received more warmly than you can know!" he kindly replied.

"Well you two make sure you get some sleep! I will speak with you soon," I replied as we started to walk away, I turned to James and George. "Good night!" I smiled to him. He did his usual bow at my leaving and replied simply:

"Good night Katharina, our new and well-respected friend!"

Claire babbled all the way home, about Northfield, George and of course George's cooking. I answered her at relevant points, but was more than side tracked at James' last words before I left. As much as I wanted to help him, I did feel a little selfish that I also wanted to keep him to myself – but what good would that do him or George? When we arrived back in the city, where Claire jumped out to meet friends, I took the cab home. I was tired, and luckily John wasn't back yet, which was a godsend; it meant that I had no explaining to do. I took a quick shower and went to bed, and had the strangest dream again in which I was trapped behind a mirror. This awoke me at 3.30am, so I went to get a glass of water.

I was more than addicted to this spell, this fairy tale that was happening around me right now, and I decided to text Rachel – my twenty-six-year-old friend with whom I used to work, and occasionally still met for lunch. She was less exuberant than Claire, and more realistic, but she was also very quiet and not the best at chatting. However, she was very pretty and single and had a great career and that alone was a start. I simply asked her if she fancied dinner with a friend and me in very beautiful surroundings: no matchmaking, just dinner and a chance to catch up. I suggested Tuesday or Thursday next week, as I didn't want John to become suspicious if I was staying on late at work the same day every week. I placed my phone back on charge and returned to my bed. John was fast asleep and for a moment I stood and looked at him. I felt slightly disappointed that I could not tell him about James and George, and dismayed that as I watched him sleep I could think of nothing else but James entirely. I slipped back under the sheets and hoped that I would sleep until the alarm, which happily I did.

When Thursday arrived, I was happy to concentrate on my alternative story, which was very touching and coming along really well. I had arranged to go with the photographer on Friday and Mrs Holt was proving the easiest person to interview that I had ever had the privilege of meeting. As I sat and discussed the previous evening with Claire over lunch, my phone beeped; it was Rachel, 'Sounds interesting, you know me I always seem to have an evening to spare! Tuesday is good, so let me know where to meet and times, look forward to catching up! X'. I smiled and then quickly closed my phone as I didn't want Claire to be suspicious either!

I returned to my desk and continued drafting my story, trying to decide what photographs I wanted to include. Soldiers seemed like a good one, if they were willing for them to be taken. I re-checked with the photographer that he had the address and the day and time scheduled, and then whilst Claire was talking with one of the other journalists, I quickly called George to let him know my plans.

"George, it's Katharina. How are you both today?" I asked.

"Hello, Katharina. We are just fine thank you; we were just saying how nice it was last night; although unsuccessful, it was certainly interesting," he replied.

"Yes it was lovely, I am sorry though that there was nothing more to it than dinner!" I unhappily remarked.

"Well, not to worry – you have more friends in mind?"

"Yes indeed, that is why I am calling you. My friend Rachel has agreed to Tuesday night, if that suits?" I happily answered.

"Brilliant, gosh you are working quickly!" George confirmed with surprise.

"I thought, if it was alright with both of you that I would call again tomorrow evening on my way from the second visit to my other story?" I asked hopefully; I was fast becoming addicted to seeing them.

"That, my dear, is a wonderful idea. Can I make a small bite to eat again?" George asked me.

"Depends what you class as small, George! Honestly just a plain sandwich is fine, thank you," I replied, whilst actually salivating at the thought of George's cooking.

"Don't be so silly, young lady. After a full day at work, you need a hot meal. I am going to make us a cottage pie!" His voice seemed to almost skip with delight.

"I seriously cannot wait, George! I will see you at around five thirty or six – is that alright for you two?"

"Perfect. We would much rather eat in your company

than on our own. We look forward to seeing you then," he replied as I then bid him goodbye.

I replaced the handset back on the receiver and sat back in my chair. I loved the whole new friendship and current situation that I was in.

John had asked me to join him for drinks this evening, as he had finally closed a deal he had been working on, and all of the work colleagues involved were meeting to celebrate their hard work. I really wasn't too bothered, but thought I should make the effort at least. When it got to 5.30pm, I decided to go and touch up my make-up before I left – I didn't want to look hard worked. I brushed through my hair, pinned it up and then reapplied lipstick, thinking that was enough. As I returned to my desk, Claire appeared.

"Ooh, hot date?" she asked.

"Drinks with John and work colleagues. I'm not really in the mood for deal-clinching conversations!" I replied, slightly deflated.

"Well the work bit, boring, but the drinks, yeah! Have a couple of cocktails, then you won't care!" she happily replied.

"I think I would rather spend an evening with George than half of John's work force!" I confirmed with feeling.

"Well, I can completely understand that; he is really sweet. He's a bit like a father figure, isn't he?" she stated. I thought for a moment.

"Yes, that is kind of what he is like. Maybe that is why I get on with him so well; it isn't like I knew my father. Perhaps I am replacing him in some small way?" I replied as I packed my bag, ready to leave.

"Hey, there's nothing wrong with that! At least your real dad left you some money to have a future! Then you've met George, who could be like another father, and he has an amazing house! Spoilt, that's what I say!" she remarked as she winked at me and laughed.

"Well, George has talked to me more than my real father ever did and I haven't known him that long. As for the money my father left me... I don't really want to touch it, it is like guilt money!" I snarled.

"Hey, you never know when that rainy day is going to arrive and you may need it!" she then said, matter-of-factly.

"Yes, maybe you're right," I acquiesced. "Anyway, I need to get off – I promised I would be there for six and I have to get across town."

"Yes, go have fun!" she said as she gestured with her hands at me to leave. "I will see you tomorrow."

"Indeed, big day – photographer and me at Mrs Holt's tomorrow."

"Yep, so a couple of drinks tonight will help calm you for tomorrow! Off you go," she quipped as she turned and went to her desk to collect her things.

I left and got in the elevator. As the doors closed, I checked my hair in the shiny reflective walls. I sighed and hoped that it wouldn't be a really long night. I told myself to snap out of the doom and gloom; John was my fiancé and the fact that he had succeeded in an important deal was something to be celebrated. I walked out of the revolving door and hailed a cab – I suddenly felt like I needed that drink!

Chapter Eleven

I entered the bar, which was far noisier and busier than I had expected it to be for a Thursday night. I looked around briefly and spied Charles in the distance, so I knew that John would not be far away. As I struggled through the crowds of people, I looked across to see John, but my heart jumped into my throat and my stomach knotted. *She* was at the side of him; Nadine, the long-legged work colleague that I had noticed was spending far too much time with John. It made my blood boil even more when, as I neared them, he placed his hand at the small of her back and rested it there happily. I stood and gazed at them for a moment and then heard Charles.

"Hey Kat, you made it!" he announced very loudly. I noticed John remove his hand and sidestep Nadine toward me.

"Yeah I made it, seems like I was interrupting something though!" I replied angrily, as I turned and walked toward the bar.

"What's that supposed to mean?" John was quick to ask as he followed me.

"John, I am not blind. You standing with your hand delicately on her back like you're keeping her close, and the fact that you have mentioned her numerous times recently, does not go well together!" I answered as I ordered myself a vodka tonic.

"That's ridiculous; she is just a friend and work colleague!" he then snapped as he paid for my drink.

"Well, it looked very cosy!" I pointed out as I took a long sip of my drink.

"Come on babe, it's a good day. The company has just made a packet on this deal. Don't spoil it!" he then stated.

I quickly bit my lip; I seriously could have taken his head off for that comment. Me, spoil it? I didn't even want to come in the first place, and now wish that I hadn't. Just as I considered leaving, Charles came over to the bar.

"Great to see you Kat, you look great!" he happily said as he kissed me on the cheek.

"Thanks, Charles!" I replied. John took my heavy bag and placed it with all of their briefcases, then came and stood beside me in the growing crowd of people. As he stood there, whisky in hand and arm around my shoulders, Nadine leant over to me.

"Hello Kat, it's nice to meet you, I've heard so much about you!" she then said, which made me even madder; I wondered what the hell John had been saying.

"I bet you have!" My mumble could barely be heard in the noise around us.

"I'm sorry, what did you say?" she queried.

"Nice to meet you too!" I said with conviction as I took another swig of my drink and nodded to her. She simply smiled and turned to a guy at the side of her and continued chatting. If there was ever a moment where you wanted to be able to teleport like the Star ship

Enterprise – this was it! I would happily rather be sat at home right now!

The drinks were coming faster than I could drink them, and after the fifth I had really had enough. I turned to John and asked if he was likely to be much longer – I was hungry and it was gone nine o'clock. I wanted to prep for tomorrow and I was fast losing enthusiasm. He made the point that they were nowhere near finished yet, so I very quietly excused myself and told John that I would see him at home.

"Don't wait up!" Charles shouted sarcastically. So I replied in the same tone:

"I have no intention of doing so!" I grabbed my bag and John walked with me to the door of the bar.

"You don't mind do you babe? I shouldn't be that late!" he insisted.

"I'm really not bothered John – you enjoy. I have work to prepare for tomorrow and I am hungry. Just don't wake me up when you get back!" I asked.

"You got it!" he slurred slightly. I could tell it was going to be a long night.

As I shut the apartment door and walked to the island with Chinese takeaway, I breathed a sigh of relief. I had already gone past eating, but knew I needed something. The noodles were a delight and I ate more than expected. I poured a glass of water and sat and looked at my notes for tomorrow, but my brain had gone into an after-food meltdown! I decided to take a quick shower, get into my pyjamas and watch mindless television for twenty minutes. The decision to go to bed early was very appealing and I knew I had time in the morning at work to finish any pre-interview prep. I sunk into bed as the rain started to fall again, but it was soothing and made me think back to that night at Northfield, when the rain fell heavily and I met James for the first time. I smiled contentedly; I would be seeing him tomorrow and the thought made me very happy!

I had briefly woken at 2am when John had landed back, but drifted back into a deep sleep. Morning had arrived and I had showered, washed and dried my hair and got dressed, but John was still in an alcoholic slumber. I decided to have coffee and breakfast before I woke him, and picked up all of the clothes he had strewn across the floor first to put in the wash. I walked to the kitchen and put the coffee machine on and placed a bagel in the toaster, then picked up the washing I had heaped on the floor to put into the machine, after taking a pile of coins out of his pockets. Then I had that sinking feeling again. His navy shirt had beer stains down the front of it, and the collar had a dark smudge that I was going to have to spray with stain remover. I wasn't sure what it was, so I rubbed my thumb across it and my heart sank when dark-coloured waxy lipstick appeared on it. I marched back to the bedroom, woke John up, threw the shirt at him and then happily told him to wash his own shirt as I wasn't prepared to wash lipstick off his collar. Then I marched back out, grabbed my bag and left.

He was halfway through waking and taking in what I had said, but by then I had already left and had no intention of listening to anything that he had to say. I knew it was her, Nadine – the girl that obviously had puppy eyes for him. The way I felt right now, she could have him. I slowly made my way to work, collecting a bagel and a coffee from Starbucks. I didn't really feel like eating, but knew that I should as I may not get lunch. I slumped down into my chair at my desk and as I was early I ate the bagel whilst organising what I needed for later today. My phone had already bleeped four times and John had tried ringing me and left a voicemail, but I didn't have the patience to listen to it at the moment. Each text just said: 'Please call me, it's not what you think!' He had re-sent it due to the fact that I had not replied numerous times, but quite honestly I thought I deserved more from him.

When Claire arrived, I shuffled along to her desk and perched on the end of it.

"Oh no! I know that face! What happened?" she asked. Being a good friend, she was always observant of my emotions.

"John and that colleague of his called Nadine!" I replied despondently. She quickly sat down.

"What did he do?" she then asked, with concern.

"I met him last night, he had his hand on Nadine's back – just placed there delicately, you know!" I started to tell her.

"Ooh that's not good, where on her back?" she asked curiously.

"Small of her back!" I replied, as I placed my hand on my back to show her. She scowled as I continued: "That's not all. I left him out with all of his colleagues, as they were on a mission, and I went home. I woke up this morning, was about to put his shirt in the wash and

138

found lipstick all over his collar!" I finished as I looked at her face for some reaction.

"What?! Jesus, what was his answer for that?" she quickly asked.

"I didn't wait to find out!" I replied. "He's been trying to call and text me, but I don't want to deal with it right now!"

"Well that speaks volumes!" she remarked as I looked at her and shrugged my shoulders. "Well, let's face it; if you were over concerned that you had lost him to someone else, you would have wanted to know exactly what happened and would have definitely had contact with him in some shape or form by now. The fact that it is not really phasing you kind of indicates that you are not that bothered about it – or you have something or someone else on your mind!" she then finished.

My mind instantly went to James and George and the fact that I was presently slightly side tracked by the whole situation. Maybe I was not paying enough attention to John as I should be? But I still didn't think that not giving him one hundred percent of my attention would mean that he had to go looking elsewhere for someone else to give him that attention. I looked at Claire and sighed.

"What should I do?" I asked.

"I think that you should meet him, maybe for lunch, and get to the bottom of it?" she then replied as she took a bite of her breakfast muffin.

"Maybe you are right. I will listen to his voicemail and reply to his text. I need an answer or explanation, one way or the other. Thanks, Claire!" I replied.

I strolled back to my desk, took a deep breath and

then picked up my phone. I reluctantly listened to the voicemail in which John told me they had all gone to Barney's for a late-night pizza and where the very drunk Nadine had fallen asleep on his shoulder, hence the lipstick. I had a very low sinking feeling; I wasn't sure if it was because I believed it was the truth, or the fact that I wish he had kissed Nadine. Why did I feel like this? Regardless, I texted him back and suggested lunch at the deli in Covent Garden, to which he happily agreed.

The tube ride there gave me time to think about what I wanted to say to him. I had to give him the chance to explain, but in all honesty I was not looking forward to it. As I walked toward the deli, he had already arrived and was sat at a table outside. He had a look of worry about him and my stomach was in knots.

"Hey, hi!" he was quick to say as he stood and pulled back my chair. He kissed me on the cheek.

"Hi!" I replied rather nervously as he returned to his chair.

"So, that was a little hot-headed this morning!" he remarked at my outburst. I gritted my teeth.

"Well, what was I supposed to think, John? You were quite cosy with her when I arrived, and then the lipstick… well, you can imagine my disappointment!" I replied. He reached across and took hold of my hand.

"Honestly, nothing happened babe! She fell asleep on my shoulder in the restaurant that was all!" he replied. As I was angry anyway, I decided to confront the 'babe' nickname I had been given.

"Well, it's very convenient that your shoulder was the nearest, but why is she always so close to you? Does she not get on with anyone else at your firm? Oh, and whilst we are having an adult conversation, can you please stop calling me babe? I hate it!" I replied with conviction. John sat back in his chair.

"You don't trust me, do you? I can understand how it must have looked, but I don't know what else to say – I have explained the situation!" he said. "With regard to the 'babe' name I have given you – Jesus, Kat, I have been calling you that for ages; I can't believe you haven't said anything before now, it's only my pet name for you!" he finished.

"Well, I don't like it. It makes me feel cheap! The other thing – well, what can I say? I have to take your word that nothing has happened, but I do not like her being so close to you all the time. She definitely has puppy eyes for you!" I remarked. He burst out laughing.

"Seriously, you are jealous? I can't help being so charming that other women like me!" he then commented as he squeezed my hand. "What's happened to us lately? We seem so distant," he then asked.

"Work – that's what has happened, for both of us!" I replied.

"Hey, why don't we have a pizza and television night when we get home? I should be back by nine, how about you?" he suggested. I suddenly thought about James and George; I had to see them, and George was cooking – I did not want to miss that.

"I can't tonight – I won't be back until nine or thereabouts myself, and you know me, I will have to grab something to eat whilst on the go. I have a big interview lined up with a photographer. Maybe just chill on the sofa in front of the television later and do the pizza thing tomorrow?" I suggested in return. I was just as bad – I was lying about my whereabouts now, but I just could not tell him about this! He nodded.

"Alright, I will see you back at the apartment tonight and we will just chill. Tomorrow, we have that works dinner thing. You promised you would come!" he reminded me.

"Oh yes, sorry I had forgotten about that. It's fine though, I will still come – just keep her away from me!" I retorted as the waiter came to take our orders.

We sat and had lunch and in all fairness it was enjoyable. I felt slightly bad that I had told a white lie about eating later, but it wasn't like I was meeting anyone for anything other than being helpful. I put it to the back of my mind and decided that when the time was right I would tell him about them, but now certainly was not that time. We said goodbye and I headed back to work. I felt better that we had talked, but I still had a slight nagging feeling about Nadine. I knew she definitely liked him and I had the distinct feeling that this would not be the end of it!

As I left work to meet the photographer at Mrs Holt's residence, I felt happier that I had my work to focus on. She was ready for us when we arrived, and luckily as I pulled up the photographer was unloading his car. We entered her property to find that six new soldiers had joined her, and all of them were happy to discuss their thoughts on what she was trying to achieve. It really was inspiring to listen to how they were learning to readjust after returning from a tour of duty. Some of these soldiers were only in their twenties, and it was intriguing to see how mature they were and how dedicated they were to their country. They all agreed that trying to return to normal life was very difficult and that the opportunity Mrs Holt was offering them was life-changing to them in helping them to readjust. Even Phillip, the photographer, was engrossed in what they had to say. By the time we left at five o'clock, I had more than enough for an amazing story and looked forward to collating all the information that I had achieved. Phillip promised to have the photographs on my desk by Monday afternoon, which was fantastic, and I hoped that within the next week I would have my first story finished and ready for publishing in the next issue.

I travelled over to Northfield and smiled all the way there, knowing that I had achieved one small success today, and as I pulled up outside the front steps, the main door opened and George appeared with a larger-than-life smile.

"Good evening Katharina, how does today find you?" he politely asked.

"Good evening George. Very well indeed... you?" I returned the question.

"Yes, one cannot complain, but the day is brighter now that you have arrived!" he then remarked, I smiled at him.

"Oh George, you've not lost your charm over these many years!" I remarked as we entered the main hallway.

"Good evening Katharina," the familiar voice then said as I turned to the mirror.

"James, how are you today?" I asked him.

"Very well thank you. I trust that you are too?"

"I am very well thank you. I feel that I have achieved

my story this afternoon and everything is going to plan at the moment!" I happily announced.

"Good!" he remarked as he smiled at me.

"Shall we?" George then asked as he gestured for me to go through to his apartment.

"Yes please, because whatever you have cooked yet again smells delicious!" I replied.

We moved into the kitchen and happily sat and ate the most delicious cottage pie. It was becoming slightly addictive, letting George cook, and it was so enjoyable. James told me what they had achieved over the last couple of days; it wasn't a lot, as he could not do very much in his situation, but George had been shopping and done the usual household chores. It made me a little sad to think that this was what their life had been like since they had found themselves this way. I told them about Rachel, and the fact that she could manage Tuesday evening, so I would join them with her and see what happened there. James seemed happy that people even wanted to come, so I felt he was getting more interested in breaking the spell.

I offered to help George wash up and turned on his radio that sat neatly on the counter; Radio Two was playing classics from the sixties onwards and as we washed and dried the pots, I was delighted when my all-time favourite song started to play; 'Don't Worry Baby' by The Beach Boys.

"Oh my God I love this song!" I stated as I started to sway. "Some of these words are quite appropriate for you, James!" I then joked as the words began.

I started to sing along.

By now I was swaying around the kitchen, with

George laughing and joining in the song and James just watching us, but the next part of the song had me stood in front of the mirror, pointing at him as I sang the main title of the song.

George had now come over to me and was spinning me around the kitchen as we sang and laughed and enjoyed the song in its entirety.

"Yes, alright, I get the message! Some words are very apt, and I trust your enthusiasm in helping me out of this situation!" James remarked as both George and I laughed and thanked each other for the dance.

"Well I thoroughly enjoyed that!" George then stated as he filled the kettle with water. "Coffee?" he asked. I nodded in reply as I sat at the island. "So how is that fiancé of yours, Katharina?" he then asked out of the blue. I sighed.

"Oh don't ask, he isn't quite my favourite person at the moment!" I replied.

"How so?" James asked of me.

"A misunderstanding, apparently on my part. There is a girl that works with him called Nadine, and she is a little too close to him if you know what I mean!" I replied, slightly agitated.

"He has not dishonoured you in any way?" James then asked with concern.

"No – well, I don't think so. Lipstick on his collar is not the nicest thing to find though!" I remarked and then looked up at them. George was looking at James.

"He is a fool; does he not know a good thing when he has it?" James remarked as he stood and excused himself for a minute.

I looked at George, grimaced and then raised my shoulders.

"Shouldn't I be the one that is upset?" I asked.

"Too close to home!" George replied. When he realised I wasn't quite sure what he meant, he continued: "He had the opportunity to take any woman he chose, regardless of their husbands' or partners' feelings. He knows the error of his ways, but it infuriates him to see others making the same mistake!" he finished.

"I never thought… maybe I should go find him?" I replied as I stood.

I wandered into the main house kitchen and as I walked to the main hallway I could see him pacing and rubbing his head through one of the mirrors.

"James, are you alright?" I quietly asked. He quickly turned.

"Yes… well, actually, no – it sickens me to think that someone is hurting you. You are the only other friend I have had in a long, long time. It makes me slightly angry that my ways of the past still continue today in others!" he remarked. I suddenly felt very selfish that I hadn't thought about his feelings – and, let's face it, John had told me that nothing had happened. I walked across and placed my hand on the mirror.

"I'm sorry; I did not realise that comment would upset you, I just find it so easy to talk to you both – sometimes my mouth opens and I speak before my brain kicks into gear!" I apologised. He smiled and walked toward me, which made my stomach knot strangely.

"You have no need to apologise to me, Katharina, but please promise me something?" he asked.

"Anything!"

"If he ever upsets you again and you need some space, will you come here? We will take care of you!" he remarked. I swallowed, then smiled and nodded.

"Yes, I will come here!" I replied. "Now, will you join George and me for coffee?" I asked him hopefully.

"Of course, it would be my pleasure," he replied, and we turned and walked back to George's apartment.

I felt strangely sad to be leaving at nearly nine o'clock, but I wanted to head home and try and see John. I happily reminded them that I would be back on Tuesday and that I looked forward to that. As I drove home, I found myself thinking about James quite a lot, and how I wished it would be easier to free him from his torment than it was proving. I pulled up in the underground garage and went up to the apartment. I walked in to find John already home; he was unusually attentive, so I jumped in the shower and snuggled down on the sofa with him in my pyjamas. Maybe I had been too harsh on him and the whole George and James thing was playing on my mind. Whatever my frustrations were at the moment, if I wanted things to work with John, I had to commit more time and effort that was for sure.

Chapter Twelve

As we entered the hotel lobby where John's dinner was being held, I sucked in a large breath of air. I had to compose myself, as tonight meant facing Nadine, but I had promised to be on my best behaviour so I was definitely going to try. John held my hand as we caught the lift to the Woodcote Suite and as the lift doors opened there was a buzz amongst the accumulating people. John walked through with me following; he didn't let go of me, but shook hands with numerous people along the way until we came upon Charles and Helen.

"Hey, you made it!" Charles shouted as we neared them. Helen smiled at me.

"Did we miss anything?" John asked him.

"No, nothing!" Charles then stated with disappointment as he leaned across and kissed me on the cheek.

I couldn't help myself but I constantly kept looking around for her and hoping that she was not on our table. Helen was talking to me, but I was not listening to a word that she was saying. By the time we sat down to eat, she appeared, wearing a tight long black dress and killer heels, with her hair pinned up and make up done to perfection. She quickly said good evening to everyone and took a chair opposite me. Great! An evening having to face her was not my idea of fun. I smiled reluctantly and then the starters arrived, thank goodness.

The meal progressed from one excellent dish to another and before I knew it the dessert had arrived. I felt absolutely stuffed by the end of it, and before the coffee arrived I went to the bathroom. I returned to the table but John had disappeared, as had Nadine; I quickly looked around the room, but could not see her anywhere. Approximately ten minutes passed and then John reappeared at my side.

"Where did you get to?" I asked.

"Went to the gents and got talking to an old work colleague!" he quickly responded, then he turned to Nick at the side of him and started talking about the next big deal.

About five minutes later, Nadine sat back down. As we sipped coffee, I couldn't help but notice her smiling and staring at John, who glanced over at her a couple of times too. He then excused himself and went to talk to someone on the table across from us. I had that horrible sinking feeling again, and so as I was sat next to Helen, I decided to do a little bit of digging.

"So, the boys seem to be enjoying their drinks again tonight!" I commented.

"God, I know. You think that they would get sick of it, wouldn't you?" she remarked.

"John was in a state on Thursday night. He snored all night and stunk of alcohol!"

"Yes, Charles was no better; he fell in the door at eleven thirty and almost broke the console table in the hallway! He woke me and scared me to death," she then said. Instantly I knew that something wasn't right. John hadn't returned home until the early hours and he never stayed out when Charles had left; they always went at the same time.

"I'm not surprised, as they hadn't eaten. They should have gone for something to eat on the way home!" I then announced, knowing that John had told me that they had gone to Barney's for pizza, and I presumed that meant all of them.

"Indeed. I told Charles they were stupid for not eating!" she then said just as Charles leant over to listen to what we were talking about.

"What's that?" Charles asked.

"I was just saying to Kat that you boys never learn and should have definitely eaten on Thursday night – it may have helped soak up the alcohol," she pointed out.

I looked at Charles and his face dropped. It was all the confirmation that I needed that something more was going on with John and Nadine. He knew that I suspected something and so I decided I had nothing to lose.

"So I take it that John and Nadine had pizza at Barney's on their own then? If that's what you want to call it!" I replied sarcastically.

"Honestly Kat, I don't know what he was thinking. I know they went to eat, but I'm sure that was all!" he quickly replied.

"Don't cover for him!" I replied, shaking my head. "I am leaving – do not tell him that I have gone. Quite honestly I have just lost any reason for staying!" I stood and said goodnight to Helen.

"I'm so sorry Kat, I have no idea what is going on or what can of worms I have just opened, but I am so sorry!" she unhappily stated.

"Helen, it's fine; I already suspected anyway!" I whispered as I rubbed her shoulder in acknowledgement that I wasn't mad with her.

I hailed a cab and went back to the apartment, and was relieved that after thirty minutes John had not texted me, which meant that Charles and Helen had kept their word for now. I stood in the middle of the apartment and then let out a small scream. How could he? The lying bastard! I looked around the apartment and suddenly I didn't want to be here. I marched to the bedroom, packed a bag and collected my work bag and then went straight back outside and hailed another cab. I jumped in and then texted George hopefully.

'I have not had the best night and do not want to be anywhere near John right now – do you mind if I come and stay the night with you?'

I did not have to wait long before my phone beeped, signalling an answer.

'Absolutely no problem, you are welcome here anytime. Shall I come and pick you up?' George asked.

'That won't be necessary, I am already in a cab and on my way – I should be there in approximately twenty minutes… thank you George!' I replied, feeling relieved that I had somewhere to go to that I loved.

My phone beeped again and when I looked at the front screen it was John. I pressed the messages and read his text: 'Where are you? Charles said that you left and gave me a quick synopsis of your conversation. I can explain – I knew that you would be suspicious and so I thought it best to say nothing. We were both hungry and went together, that was all!' I slammed the phone shut and threw it on the seat. If he had been next to me right now, I would have slapped him. I was fast losing any trust that I had for him. I picked my phone back up and replied: 'I do not want to speak to you tonight John, I am staying somewhere else – I will be in touch tomorrow. The lies just keep stacking up, don't they?' I hit send and dropped the phone in my bag. He hadn't even had the courage to ring me, and that was infuriating enough. The taxi pulled up and as expected George was already walking out of the door in his overcoat. I paid for the cab, grabbed my bags and stepped out in my dinner dress. I hadn't thought to grab a coat.

"Katharina, are you alright?" he asked, like a worried father.

"I will be! Thank you so much for letting me stay tonight. I couldn't think of anywhere else I would rather be right now!" I replied honestly.

"You know that you are welcome anytime, Katharina. I am glad that you felt you could call me," George answered as he carried my bags and ushered me inside.

I entered the hallway, dropped my handbag on the chair and then put my hands on my hips and sighed.

"Katharina?" James then asked. "Are you alright?" I do not know whether it was the softness of his voice or the fact that they were just being nice to me, but I broke down in tears. "I'm going to kill him, it's obviously him!" James said, enraged.

"I do not think that Katharina needs to hear that right

now, James!" George stated as he placed his arm around me and walked me toward the kitchen. "Hot cocoa and then you can tell us everything!" he said.

By the time we reached his kitchen, I had controlled myself and calmed down. I felt very silly and wished the whole teary episode hadn't happened, but I just couldn't help it. I looked at George as he handed me a mug full of steaming cocoa. Then I looked at James, who was pacing again.

"Gosh, I seem to cause trouble wherever I go!" I replied with a slight laugh.

"What did he do?" James then asked me again. I looked at him.

"I am not one hundred percent sure, but he lied to me twice about where he was, and with who, and then tonight at dinner he disappeared for a while at the same time as Nadine and then they sat looking at each other all night... his friend confirmed to me that only the two of them stayed out on Thursday night and I have no idea what they got up to, but after I found lipstick on his collar... I just couldn't face any more lies today!" I quickly told them.

"Can I just say something?" George then asked. I nodded in response. "What a complete and utter bloody idiot he is!" He said it so sincerely that I couldn't help do anything but laugh. Then he laughed and James laughed.

"I completely agree with you, George," I laughed, and then I stopped.

"By the way, you look stunning this evening Katharina," George then stated. I looked down at my dress.

"A little over-dressed at this time of night maybe, and with panda eyes too!" I remarked as I looked at the tissue George had passed, which was covered in mascara.

"Why don't you go to your room and change into your pyjamas? I will pour us a stiff brandy; it seems that you may need one tonight!" George suggested.

The suggestion was well accepted and I carefully walked to my room and changed, then returned to George's apartment. As I neared the kitchen door I heard them again.

"You need to calm down, James. There is nothing that you can do other than support Katharina."

"Trust me, it is a damn good job that I cannot freely walk out of here right now, I think that I would seriously do that man some damage!" James said furiously.

"You are very protective, I notice?" George then stated. It was quiet for a moment.

"She is the best thing that has happened to us in a long time. She is giving up her time to help us, I do not think kindly on anyone who would upset her intentionally!" James finished. I smiled at his comment and then decided that I should walk in. As I did, James fell quiet again.

George had poured three glasses of brandy and I drank mine very quickly.

"Better?" James asked.

"I will be!" I remarked as George refilled my tumbler.

"Well as I am an old man and it is late; I am going to retire to bed. The fire is still burning in the lounge, so why don't you sit in there whilst you finish your drink? I am sure that James can keep you company. I will talk with you some more tomorrow once you have rested!" George announced. I found myself throwing my arms around George to bid him goodnight, and he hugged me in response. "Try and get some rest. Things may seem better in the morning!" he then said.

"Good night George, and thank you!" I replied sincerely as he left and went toward his bedroom. James looked at me from the kitchen mirror.

"Shall we retire to the lounge whilst we finish these?" he asked.

"Sure, that would be nice!" I replied as I walked toward the warm glow from the fire.

I slumped into the armchair and took a large sip of brandy, and then looked up at the mirror to find James just staring at me.

"What?" I asked him.

"Why do you put up with his intolerable behaviour?" he questioned.

"I wasn't willing to tonight; that is why I am here. Believe me, casting a spell right now would be a punishment fit for him, but I think I would turn him into a donkey or something!" I laughed nervously.

"An ass would be more fitting!" James replied. I laughed more.

"Yes, well I have to agree with you on that one!" I replied as I threw my head back, closed my eyes and sighed. "I think that you are better off with no relationship – look at the trouble they cause these days!" I then said as I opened my eyes to look at him.

"Trust me, you would not want this; it is hardly bearable and I would much rather fight and argue with someone physically than be in here alone!" he replied solemnly.

"I'm sorry James, of course you would. I was thinking out loud because I am angry and I spoke before taking your feelings into consideration…again!" I apologised.

"It's alright, I can understand your disappointment. I will confirm what George stated, though; that he is an absolute idiot. Why would he risk losing you for someone else? He has a very shallow character if he thinks that he can find someone better than yourself!" he sincerely stated. I blushed and then took a sip of my drink.

"Well, my judgement of him at the moment is… is… actually, I don't know what it is. I just know that I really do not like him very much at the moment. I cannot trust him – he has lied to me and we are most definitely drifting apart," I announced.

"Well, I am sorry about that. I am sorry that you have been let down by this scoundrel!" he replied honestly, but I heard a tone in his voice that made me look into his eyes, which in this light were like moonlit pools. He looked different; I could not put my finger on it, but I definitely felt like there was some kind of connection between us, which I wasn't sure I could handle right now.

"Are you really sorry?" The words came out of my mouth and as he stared at me and I him, my brain tried to tell me that I had actually asked that question and not just thought it in my head. I snapped myself back to reality and threw the last bit of brandy down my throat. "I think that I should get some rest. I feel remarkably drained now!" I informed him.

"Of course!" he replied. He stood quickly, drank his brandy and then gestured for me to leave the room. "May I see you to your room?" he then asked.

"You may!" I smiled. This was after all his home, and I had hijacked their evening.

We spoke all the way there; he asked me how my other story was coming along and asked after Claire. I knew that he was trying to change the subject for my benefit, but I welcomed the kind gesture. Once we arrived at my door, I stopped and turned to the mirror.

"James, thank you for letting me stay here. I haven't known you very long, but you welcome me like we are old friends, and right now I could not ask for anything more comforting than that!" I sincerely informed him. He smiled.

"We are friends; I feel like I have known you for many years also, and you are very welcome here anytime you feel like visiting us. I am very pleased that you felt that you could call upon us when you needed someone; it certainly makes a change for us to help you when you are so willing to help us!" he replied. I smiled at him, placed my hand briefly on the mirror and simply said:

"Goodnight James."

"Goodnight Katharina!" he replied as I closed the large door behind me.

If I said that I slept well, that would be a lie. I had strange dreams, woke in tears a couple of times and was angry when I was awake instead of sleeping. I did feel that I had a watchful eye over me on a couple of occasions, which helped me settle a little easier. I was not looking forward to confronting John today and I knew that he would want to see me at some point. I went to the bathroom and took a hot shower, and when I returned to my room in just my towel I heard a small cough – an announcement that someone was there. I turned to the mirror to find James glance briefly at me and then turn around.

"Good morning. George presumed that you may be up fairly early and so he has made breakfast, if you would care to join us," he invited.

"I would love to, just give me ten minutes!" I replied, and James nodded and wandered toward the door in the mirror. "Oh and good morning James!" I then called to him. He stopped briefly and then continued until he was gone.

Effort was not playing a big part in my appearance today: I wore jeans, t-shirt and a dash of tinted moisturiser. I did not suspect that they would mind me having breakfast with them whilst I had wet hair, so I simply tied it up loosely. As I approached the kitchen, I could hear them talking; they seemed to sound concerned with my wellbeing, which was nice to hear. As I entered, James stood and bade me good morning again, whilst George simply walked up to me and gave me a big hug. I hadn't realised until then how much I needed one.

"Good morning Katharina. How did you sleep?" he asked.

"Not as well as I would have liked!" I laughed lightly. "I am glad that I was here though, so thank you for having me."

"It was our pleasure. Would you like some pancakes

this morning? There is nothing like comfort food at times of upset!" George asked.

"I would love some, but only if you have something sweet and fattening to put on them, George. I think I need a sugar overload this morning!" I replied as I smiled.

"We can certainly help you out with that," he said as he placed jam, syrup – both maple and golden – honey and fruit compote on the island. My stomach instantly started to rumble.

"So, what are your plans today?" James then asked as he watched me pour a little of everything on the stack of pancakes that George had just placed in front of me.

"I have no idea. I suppose I need to confront him and try to decide what to do with the outcome of the many answers he could give me," I said, trying to be realistic.

"If you want to stay here for longer, you are more than welcome," James replied as I sighed heavily.

"Honestly James, I could very easily hibernate here forever! However, that is not going to resolve anything is it?" I confirmed. He shook his head as he sipped his coffee.

"Well let's not worry about that too much for now. I need to tell you both about the phone call I received yesterday from Madison Cleaver," George then said, with slight apprehension.

"The estate agent?" I asked.

"Indeed. He had someone enquire about the house – a developer, by all accounts, who wants to turn the house into apartments!" George reluctantly said.

"Absolutely not!" James said with feeling. "How on earth is that going to help us, George?"

"Well there is the slight possibility of more people seeing you!" George replied, trying not to dismiss the whole idea.

"I cannot imagine having this house broken up into pieces, George. I would rather stay like this forever than let that happen. This is my home – our home!" he finished. I could hear his upset at the thought.

"I am sorry, George, but I have to agree with James on this one. If you break this amazing house up into pieces, its whole character and ambience will be lost!" I said sincerely.

"Thank you!" James quickly snapped in response. I smiled.

"You're welcome!" I replied as James smiled back at me.

"What did you tell them?" he asked George.

"Well I said that I would think about it!"

"Well you can call them and tell them definitely not!" James snapped again.

"Alright, it was only an enquiry. I do not want to see this house broken up into numerous living spaces any more than you do. I am merely trying to understand what options we have – after over 200 years, we do not seem to be getting very far, do we?" George then said, with the authority of a father.

"Boys! Please! I do not think it is necessary to argue over this. Neither of you – or I, for that matter – want this to happen and so the answer is no, simple as. Just leave it at that!" I confirmed, then started to eat my pancakes again. I had no intention of listening to more disagreements today, but it did send a spark of an idea into my head about the money that my father had left me – my guilt money, as I called it.

Breakfast was hearty and I was more than content after my fill of everything, including three cups of tea. I sat back on the chair and watched the two of them chatting about everyday maintenance and things that needed to be addressed. In light of my current situation, it was a refreshing change to just listen and observe and not have an opinion on anything. I asked them to excuse me for a while whilst I went to brush my teeth and on returning to my bedroom I thought I had best look at my mobile, which I had set to silent last night. It made my stomach knot when I saw eight missed calls from John, and the same amount of texts begging me to talk to him and asking where I was. I sat by the window and looked across the symmetrical shrubs below my window that led to the lawn. The day was grey, but the view was still breathtaking – it had such a variety of green and gold and brown that even the very greyest of days could not look dull.

As I sat gazing out of the window, there was a knock at my door.

"Come in," I announced.

"Katharina, are you alright?" George asked as he looked at me staring through the window. I took a deep breath and held up my phone.

"I will be when I have faced the inevitable. He has tried to contact me numerous times; I still do not know how I feel about all of this!" I replied as I hugged my knees tighter to my chest. George walked across to me.

"May I?" he asked, gesturing to the space at the side of me.

"Please do!"

"Can I say something?" he asked me. I simply nodded. "I know that we have not known each other for that long, but I do feel that I am a very good judge of character. You need to stop trying to reason with what you think and what he is going to say. Firstly, you cannot possibly understand how you will react until he has had the time to explain himself; only then can you make a decision. Secondly, I have believed for a long time that at times like this we usually, deep down, somewhere inside, already know what outcome we want. It is whether you believe it is worth fighting for, and you will only know that in here!" he finished as he tapped his chest over his heart. "Our hearts are not unbreakable; they can sometimes be fragile, but they are usually sure of what they want and desire, even if the head hasn't quite listened to it yet. Just remember that whatever happens, they do heal and repair, and learn to find what they do desire, so if the outcome is not what you expect there is still hope!" he kindly finished as he placed his hand on my knee. I had a tear in my eye and composed myself for a second before sincerely replying.

"Thank you; I value our friendship more than you can know, George, even though our acquaintance has not been long. I've only just realised that recently I do not feel that I have many of the 'real' friends that I used to, that I can just sit and talk to, like I can with you. It makes me happy to know that you are here... both of you!" I replied as I took his hand and squeezed it tightly.

"Chin up, dear. I am going to leave you whilst you call your fiancé and then, if you like, I will drive you back into London and wait until you know for sure that you want to stay there," he then said. I felt very lucky that I had such a dear friend.

"Okay, I have found a little courage now. I will be down soon to let you know what I want to do!" I replied. He nodded in confirmation and smiled, then left the room.

After taking a few minutes to compose myself, I pressed the call button on my phone before I changed my mind. John had a lot to say; a lot of apologies and a very good explanation that, whether I wanted it to or not, sounded very believable. We spoke for nearly twenty minutes and then he asked me to come home so that we could discuss it further. I decided that I owed him that much. Whether I believed him or not, I could not deny that our relationship deserved the chance to try and make some sense of this. I straightened the bedding and tidied the room that I loved so much, and then I packed up my bag and took it downstairs and placed it on the chair in the hallway.

By the time I returned to the kitchen, George had made a fresh pot of tea and coffee.

"Would you like one?" he asked.

"Coffee would be great please," I replied. He placed it in front of me and then looked at me for a few seconds before saying:

"Well, how did it go? You seem remarkably calm," he then stated. I raised my eyebrows sarcastically.

"What is the point in being anything but calm until I have the complete picture and I can make a decision?" I took a sip from my mug.

"Very sensible, but do not take any nonsense. I am sure that you will be able to assess if he is telling the truth!" George replied.

I sat and sipped my coffee as I thought about the questions that I would ask John, and glanced at James a few times. He was restless and ran his hand through his hair numerous times. He had a t-shirt on today; it was black, and the sleeves strained against his muscles when he moved. I had to snap my train of thought back to what I was supposed to be focusing on when he suddenly said:

"Promise me one thing, Katharina. If you have any doubts at all, I want you to come back here," he asked with feeling. I smiled at him.

"If you are happy to have me, and I need somewhere to go, I promise I will come back," I replied.

"Good!" he replied as he stood. "Look in his eyes when he gives you the explanation – the eyes never lie!" he then said as he exited the room. I looked to George and shrugged my shoulders; James was very hard to understand sometimes.

"Did I do something wrong?" I asked George.

"No dear, nothing at all. It simply annoys him when others have relationships that they are so quick to jeopardise, when he cannot even attempt to have any!" George smiled. "Do not worry about him. He feels the same way as I – you are our friend and he does not want to see anyone hurt you!"

The thought that James cared about me as well as George was very touching and it made me smile more. I sipped my coffee slowly and carried on conversing with George, who had already decided that he was taking me back to the city. We spoke about the impending meal on Tuesday with Rachel, and George remarked on how much he hoped that it wouldn't be long until they could live a normal life. By the time I was ready to go, James had still not returned. As we wandered into the entrance hall, George shouted him quite loudly, which made me jump.

"James. I am taking Katharina back home. Are you going to say goodbye?" he asked. In no time at all, James appeared in front of me at the large mirror.

"Goodbye, Katharina. I look forward to seeing you on Tuesday," he said quickly.

"Yes, Tuesday – I look forward to seeing you as well," I replied. I stood for a second and then turned to get my bag.

"Oh and Katharina, I wish you luck – if this is what you want!" James then stated. I stopped and turned to him.

"Thank you," I replied, and then smiled before leaving.

I felt sad to be going, and all the way back to the city John was not in my thoughts as much as James was. George did make me think once or twice that he did not drive as often as was probably needed to be a confident driver, but I was grateful that it was Sunday and the traffic was relatively quieter than it was in the week. We pulled up outside my apartment block and I took a deep breath.

"Thank you, George. It was very kind of you to drive me home," I said as I looked out of the window and at the front door. "Wish me luck!" I said as I opened the door and stepped out.

"Luck, my dear, is not what you are searching for. Honesty and truth I think prevail above luck. You are a very special young lady, just remember that!" George said with sincerity. I nodded in approval and then shut the door of the car, waved and watched him pull away, then went inside. As I stepped into the elevator, my stomach started to knot... I was definitely not looking forward to this.

Chapter Thirteen

As I placed my key into the lock and turned it, John almost pounced at the door and opened it. He grabbed my bag and threw it into the apartment and then gave me the biggest hug. With my arms crushed down my side, I was glad that I didn't have to reciprocate; I was not sure yet whether I wanted to.

"Jesus Kat, where did you go? I could have explained!" he said in my ear. I pulled away from him and closed the door.

"That's just the point, John; you would not have had to explain anything to me if you had just been honest in the first place," I replied. He rubbed his head.

"I knew that you would react like this!" he said, gesturing at me.

"What did you expect? You lied to me, John!" I said with force as I pushed past him and toward the kitchen. I needed a glass of water. "I now have no idea what happened between you and Nadine!"

"Well it's as I told you – everyone left and we were hungry so we decided to go and eat! We'd had a fair bit to drink and she fell asleep on my shoulder, hence the lipstick smudge!" he then replied, slightly agitated.

I stood for a minute and looked at him and thought

about what James had said. As I asked the next question, I looked him directly in the eyes.

"So nothing happened between you and her?" I asked openly. He looked at me briefly, then looked down at my hands, which he took in his, and then looked back at me.

"No, nothing happened!" he replied. As I stood and looked at him, I felt in the pit of my stomach that he was still not being completely honest – and the fact that he could not keep constant eye contact with me was telling – but I just couldn't face ending it right here, right now, either. I swallowed hard.

"You need to tread very carefully, John. I feel very vulnerable at the moment, but I will give you the benefit of the doubt this time!" I heard myself saying.

"Ah, thanks Kat. I knew that you would understand once I explained!" he replied as he hugged me again.

I cannot say that I felt elated that my relationship hadn't just ended; I just felt deflated that I did not feel better than this. I was fast starting to question my whole relationship with John, but for the coming days I had to try. We spent the day lounging around the apartment and watching mindless television together on the sofa and John, by all accounts, was very attentive. He did not seem too keen when I eventually told him where I had spent the night, but for once I did not care; both George and James had been the support that I needed at that moment and whether John liked it or not was of no relevance to me. We had take-out and then went to bed early, as both of us had a lot on at work the next day. I hoped, as I started to fall asleep, that Monday would bring a better day, with something else to focus on for now.

Monday arrived. The tube was ridiculously busy and when I arrived at work I felt like I had already done three hours' work just fighting my way to get there! I ran a brief synopsis of my weekend by Claire, who by all accounts was not happy with John at all. She started to raise questions that I had tried to ignore and during lunch I realised that I still was not one hundred percent sure that I had done the right thing. Maybe I should have had some space for a while? I was trying to be positive and the day did get better when the photographs from the interview on Friday arrived on my desk and turned out to be amazing; the photographer had found it amusing to put some in there of me talking to the soldiers. I hated having my photograph taken and I had made this quite clear, but obviously he did not listen. I placed them all onto a board so that I could choose the best five, which was what I had been allowed for my piece. I quickly placed the ones of me back into the envelope and put them in my bag between the pages of the diary that George had kindly loaned me: they were definitely going home and out of the way of any colleagues.

After that, my day went better than expected; the first draft of my story was entirely complete. I sent it across to Angela with a note that I had the photographs and would let her see them as soon as I had chosen the ones that were right for the piece, and then kept my fingers crossed that she was happy with it. I sat back into my chair and took a sip from my water bottle as my phone bleeped; it was Rachel. I smiled, knowing that I would see her tomorrow, but when I opened the message I was disappointed to see what she had sent.

'Kat, I am so sorry but I will have to cancel tomorrow evening. I have the most amazing news… I have just been promoted and have been offered the chance of working in the New York office for a year or two. I need to have numerous meetings this week and plan as it will be happening quickly! I want to see you before I leave, so I will be in touch soon… XXXXX'

I sighed heavily; not because I wasn't pleased for her – I was happier for her more than I could express – but I felt exceptionally sorry for James and George. That was another one that I would have to cross off my list now. I replied quickly to tell her how amazing it was and not to worry. I then promptly sent Kate a text, who not only was successful and wealthy, but very down-to-earth. I hoped that she would be free soon.

I had to let George and James know the news. George had text me last night to ask if I was alright, which was very sweet. I tried to break the news gently and decided that a text was better, as I did not want to hear the disappointment in his voice. He simply replied to my lengthy text with 'Not to worry' and thanked me for trying so hard. I felt like I had let them down and so I replied again and told him that I had already sent Kate a message. It took a while for him to reply to that; I had the impression that he was not too fond of technology.

'Katharina, you seem to have enough to worry about at the moment; please do not worry yourself over us. If Kate would like to join you here for a meal soon, that is wonderful; if not, we will work something else out. Am I to assume that in light of this we will not be seeing you for a little while?' As soon as I read it, I felt a twinge of guilt. I enjoyed spending time with them far too much, but I did needed to focus on my own relationship for now and so I decided that it was better to have a week focusing on that and work. I reluctantly replied stating it was unlikely, but that I would be in touch soon.

The week slowly continued and I got the go-ahead from Angela, with a few editorial notes. I had selected the photographs and had her approval on that, so the week had resulted in some kind of achievement. John had tried to get home a little sooner on most nights and whilst I sat at home waiting for him, I tried to remain positive. It was Thursday, finally, when Kate replied to me saying that it had been far too long and she would love to meet for dinner, but she could not do it until the following Monday. I let George know straight away, but I called him this time. It made me happier than I can tell you to hear his voice and remarkably I could hear James in the background too. We caught up briefly on the week and he exclaimed that he would be glad to see us on Monday. Once I had finished arranging with George, I texted her back immediately to confirm. Knowing that Kate would be driven there by her personal driver, I decided to ask her to meet me there. Maybe the first sight of the place may make her love it more if she saw it on her own; she certainly had the money to buy into it!

The next few days passed slowly. John and I went for dinner on Saturday night, which I tried to enjoy, but I felt slightly distracted by the fact that he was acting like absolutely nothing had happened. He mentioned work and her, numerous times, without thinking. I know that we were trying to make amends, but work was not at the forefront of my mind during a supposed romantic dinner. I was finding it harder than him to just move on and forget what had happened, not to mention that I still had a nagging feeling that he was not being completely honest with me. John went off cycling with friends on Sunday; it gave me the chance to loudly play some music of my own choice. I decided to bake some brownies for tomorrow evening, then I did a face pack – all the de-fuzzing necessary when you are a woman – and took a lengthy hot bath with a glass of wine. I found it very relaxing laying in the bath with my eyes closed, but I did find my thoughts drifting off to the image of James as Taylor Swift sang 'Everything Has Changed'! I thought of the first time I saw him, his image, his words… they played around in my head whilst I listened to the song. Then I jumped and sat up in the bath. What was I doing? Did I have feelings for James that I was trying to deny? There is no doubt that I was attracted to his looks, but I didn't know him that well, even though he had told me a lot about himself. I turned and looked at my workbag that lay on the bed and remembered that I still had his mother's diary. I sipped the last of my wine, dried and got into some lounging clothes and then took out the large diary of events at Northfield.

I was engrossed in her intricate writing about all of the small details that she had thought relevant to enter. Some were entirely about James and Howard and some about the loyal staff, who she had obviously been so grateful for. I smiled when George was mentioned numerous times, particularly at keeping James out of mischief. After it reached the time of Howard's demise, she entered less regularly; her writing was decidedly shakier and it was more about herself. I had images of what she was going through and dealing with as I carried on reading, and as tears streamed down my face I was snapped back to reality when the door slammed and John marched in and went straight to the fridge.

"Hey babe what you doing?" he asked before he downed a whole pint of juice. *Okay, so we are back to that name I hate*, I instantly thought. I composed myself for a moment and then replied:

"Just reading up on some things for work," I replied, telling a small white lie.

"Cool!" he replied as he marched to the bedroom. "I'm off for a shower, fancy joining me?" he asked. I turned and looked at him, and for the first time I started to realise that we had nothing in common any more.

"No, thank you. I have just had a really hot bath. I need to read up on this!" I replied, trying to sound convincing as I lifted the book and gestured to it. He simply shrugged his shoulders and replied "Your loss!" with an attitude. This made me just stare as he walked into the bedroom and closed the door.

"Arse!" I said to myself.

The evening was quiet. I continued reading, using my envelope as a bookmark, I was finding it hard to put down the diary. It was so sad, but it gave me more information on James and how much he was loved by his mother. I looked across at John, who had been asleep for a couple of hours since eating, and due to a long cycle ride. I was happy when it was time to settle into bed, knowing that I would get to see George and James tomorrow evening. I had already told John that I was having dinner with Kate, so I had no excuses to make for being late back tomorrow evening. I slept better than expected and as Monday morning arrived, with the added benefit of some sunshine, I smiled, stretched, sighed and then started to get ready for work.

Work was genuinely going along with no hitches at the moment. I had been given another assignment in light of the fact that I had drafted and completed my other article so efficiently. Angela had asked me to cover a recent local story about a local company that was entering the London Marathon to raise money for a director who had been diagnosed with cancer. A friend of Angela's worked there and she was intrigued by the fact that the whole team of employees were so devastated, and so loved the director and his work ethics, that they had all agreed to take part. Her friend had quoted that it was 'the best place in the world to work'. Angela wanted to know why, and what his secret was! It certainly sounded inspiring and, in light of the fact that it kept anyone from asking about Northfield, I happily agreed.

My story about Mrs Holt and the soldiers was to go into the next issue, which would be going to print this week, so I was happy about that. I informed all relevant parties to watch out for it. It was five o'clock before I knew it and as I had brought something less formal to wear, I went to get changed and touch up my make-up. Claire came in whilst I was at the mirror.

"Hmmm, hot date?" she asked.

"Claire!" I snapped. "I am engaged," I reminded her.

"Yes, and I'm sure you won't mind me saying – to a

complete arse!" she remarked. I stopped applying my mascara and stared at her in the mirror. "What?" she asked. "I'm only being honest. I think that you can do far better!"

"Well, I know that we have had our ups and downs of late, but I am trying! Anyway, I am meeting my friend Kate – I haven't seen her for ages!" I confirmed. Claire simply shrugged.

"Shame, you look hot!" she smiled as she winked at me in the mirror, and we both laughed at her remark. "Can we go out on Friday night? I think that a few post-print drinks are acceptable. First of the new series of stories and all?" she then asked.

"You know what, that would be great. We haven't done that in ages!" I remarked. "Yes, let's arrange it tomorrow!"

"Great, I can feel cocktails coming on!" Claire excitedly replied.

I said goodnight and went to collect my things from my desk. I wanted to get to Northfield a good while before Kate. It was hardly fair to have her turn up before I arrived. The traffic tonight was somewhat congested, but flowed once we had left the city centre. I arrived at exactly quarter past six, which I was happy about, as I had told Kate to arrive at seven. As I saw George walking down the stairs to greet me, I felt a warm happiness. I had missed him! He generously took my workbag and suit bag and then we went inside. It was warm inside, the fires were lit and there were fresh flowers on the round table inside the door; the scent was divine.

"George, have you gone to lots of trouble?" I asked. He smiled.

"Only the very best for our only best friend!" he remarked. I had the largest smile as I turned to the large mirror, where a very dashing James stood in black trousers and a pale blue shirt, open at the neck, and with a very neat new haircut – no long shaggy style now.

"Wow, look at you!" I remarked at his appearance, which I realised I was taking far too long admiring.

"Wow yourself! It is very nice to see you again, Katharina!" he smiled.

"Thank you, I like the haircut!" I replied, as I took off my jacket; it was warmer in here than I had expected. James ran his hand through his hair.

"It took some doing, I can tell you!" George then remarked. "It's not easy, trying to cut one's hair with equipment that we've not bothered using for a long time!" he joked.

"Of course!" I grimaced. "Gosh, we take everything we do for granted. I would hate to cut my own hair!" I then finished as I ran my hand through my own.

"Wine?" George then asked.

"Why not!" I replied as we set off down to George's apartment.

"So, this Kate – is she definitely staying in the country and is she still single?" James then asked as I took a sip of wine. I held my hand up in response.

"Firstly, I am so sorry about Rachel. I had no idea that going to New York was even on the cards, so that just proves that I have not spoken to her for long enough. Kate – I do not think she would ever leave London. She is very passionate about her business here, and she is wealthy, so if she doesn't see you she may want to buy the place!" I informed them.

"Well, it really doesn't matter; it will be what it will be," George then said. "Let us just keep our fingers crossed!" he remarked as he took a sip of wine.

They asked me about work and I happily told them about the story. George asked if I had a copy that he could read, as it sounded fascinating, so I went to the hall and retrieved my workbag and returned to the kitchen. Whilst George read the draft that I had edited ready for publication, I pulled out the diary and placed it onto the worktop where I sat, then looked at James.

"You know, reading this made me really sad at times." I grimaced. "Do you know how much your mother loved you?" I asked him tentatively. George looked up from reading and glanced at James first, then me.

"Yes, I know!" he simply replied as he turned away to refill his glass. I looked across at George, who peered at me over his glasses.

"He misses her, more than he says! It was not the best of endings for them!" George whispered before James returned to his chair.

"I'm sorry, of course you know," I quickly confirmed to James. "Could I top up?" I then asked George as I pointed to the wine bottle.

"Be my guest!" he simply replied. I poured without hesitating as I realised that James had picked up his parallel copy of the diary and started to touch the pages with his mother's writing on them. I started to feel like I had put a complete dark cloud over the whole evening. So I panicked a little as James flicked through the pages and was silent. I looked up at George again; he seemed oblivious, or maybe he was ignoring him.

"This is very good!" George then stated as he finished reading and took off his glasses. He passed the draft back and I placed it onto the worktop. Then as he smiled at me and looked toward James, I scowled; why couldn't I just keep my thoughts to myself? I placed my head in my hands and almost wanted to leave, then I heard something fall to the floor.

I lifted my head and looked toward James, who was bending down to pick a brown envelope up off the floor. I looked across at it curiously and then watched as James looked in the envelope and pulled out photographs.

"May I?" he suddenly asked me. At first I was slightly confused and then it dawned on me. They were the photographs of me that the photographer had taken. I had just slid the envelope into the book to hide them at work. As I nodded, feeling that I had no choice after my inconsiderate outburst, stating the obvious, he flicked through the six or so pictures. George then realised that there was something to be looked at, and turned the diary to face him to find the same photographs on our side of this reality.

I took a very large gulp of wine, and then another, as they both looked at them and said nothing. I broke the silence.

"Yes I know, I am not very photogenic and I hate my picture being taken. So please feel free to make any comments you feel necessary, embarrassing or not!" I joked unconvincingly as I gulped more wine.

"Quite the contrary, Katharina. Why would I want to make any negative comment, when these capture you so beautifully?" James then stated as he stared at them. I swallowed hard and then looked at him. He looked at me and our eyes met. I had butterflies.

"I agree," George then confirmed. I turned my glance to him. "I cannot understand for one moment why you think that you are not photogenic, Katharina. They are beautiful and I should like to keep one, if that is acceptable. It is a nice reminder for me of my new friend, when we are unfortunate enough to not be in your company!" George then happily asked.

I was slightly taken back by the response and had no words; I simply nodded in agreement. George turned and placed it on the shelf of the dresser to the side of the oven. He smiled and then returned to check on dinner. It was quiet for a moment.

"It really does smell delicious, George!" I remarked.

"You are always so kind regarding my cooking, Katharina, unlike some others that we know!" he then gestured to James, smiling.

"Steady on George, you know full well that there are certain things that I do not like, but on the whole it is not bad!" James replied with a little sarcasm. Thank goodness things had clicked back into place. I sighed a breath of relief and sipped more wine and then looked at my watch.

"Gosh it is quarter to seven already. Is there anything that I can do to help, George?"

"No, I have everything under control!" he smiled contently.

"As always!" James then remarked. He did appreciate George so much, of that I was sure.

I helped George carry items to the dining room and just as we were nearly ready a car could be heard at the front of the house. I turned and looked at them both, and then straightened my appearance and went toward the door.

"Fingers crossed!" I then said, as I turned and looked at them both. George walked to my side so that he could also greet Kate and together we opened the door.

"Kat... bloody hell, it's been ages!" she called as she bounced up the stairs and threw her arms around me.

"Yes, it has been a long time!" I replied as I hugged her back. She looked really well. "Can I introduce you to George, our host for the evening?" I then said as I gestured to him. She quickly shook his hand and said:

"George, it's a pleasure to meet you. This is some place that you have! Trust our Kat to find a friend with a house that is from years past. One of your dreams to have something like this, isn't it Kat?" she then stated. I laughed.

"Yes, I think that I did once say that Kate!"

"Shall we?" George then asked, as he gestured for us both to go inside.

As Kate walked in the main door, she did the usual thing expected when entering Northfield: she gasped, stood still and spun around, taking in all of the surroundings: the ceiling, the staircase, the paintings. She stopped at the large mirror, stared for a moment and then suddenly said, "Oh my God!" in a very loud voice. Both George and I looked at each other in shock and hope; poor James just stood there and stared back at her.

"You can see me?" he asked, as Kate walked toward the mirror.

"I don't believe it!" she then said, as she stood staring into the mirror. George looked so surprised and hopeful that it took me a moment before I said anything.

"Kate, what is it? What do you see?" I asked as I walked to her side. I looked up at James, who looked as hopeful as George and I. There certainly was no denying that Kate was beautiful, and I was sure that James had noted it. She turned and looked at me.

"Seriously, you could have told me that I looked so dishevelled!" she then replied, as she started to re-pin her hair. I stared at her and sighed.

"What?" I then asked in amazement. "Is that it?" I asked with regret. She turned to me.

"You know me and my appearance, Kat! What else did you think I meant?" she asked. I looked at James and then laughed lightly as he rubbed his face and then sighed.

"Nothing!" I replied as I shook my head sadly. "Nothing at all, you just surprised me with your outburst!" I finished.

George had now walked over to us, and he had a large grin on his face. I knew he had thought the same as I; that Kate could see James. I suppose they were used to being let down after the amount of people that have been here over the years. Nevertheless, I was disappointed that she had not seen him. He took one look at the look on my face and simply smiled and shrugged his shoulders.

"I thought that you had cracked it then!" he said with slight sarcasm. I coughed to hide a slight snarl at his remark.

"I am sorry. I do have a tendency to overreact to little

things!" Kate then said. I smiled and turned her to face toward the dining room, then started to walk with her whilst she continued fixing her hair. Meanwhile I turned to James and scowled at him whilst I mimed, "I am trying!" He laughed and replied:

"I know, and I love the fact that you are!"

"Let us eat; you must be very hungry after a long day, Kate! Katharina tells me that you have your own business?" George then asked her as we walked through the door. He very kindly pulled out first her chair and then my own and we sat to eat. George disappeared to the kitchen to retrieve the starters as I poured some wine. Kate immediately started talking about work and what she had been up to this last six months, which believe you and me was enough for two people to achieve.

We happily started to eat and George, as ever, asked lots of questions, which gave him and James a full picture of who Kate was and what she did. The main course was delicious, and both Kate and I commented on the cooking. James commented numerous times at Kate's busy lifestyle; most notably he made me laugh when she was talking about what she wanted to do next in her busy schedule.

"It is probably best that she cannot see me, Katharina! She has absolutely no time at all in her busy schedule for breaking a spell cast by a witch!" he joked as he sipped his wine. Then he carried on, "Does she actually breathe between sentences? It is exhausting just listening to her!" he mocked. I could do nothing else but giggle slightly, because he was right in what he was saying. George, being ever the gentleman, carried on talking whilst I composed myself.

Kate was very inquisitive as to how I had become friends with George in the first place and so I had to tell another white lie and say that I had done a story on him.

"Anyway Kate, you know me. I love meeting new people, I love old houses and George has the most amazing tales of previous owners, so how can I refuse to come when he also offers to cook for my friend and me?" I happily stated.

"She always was one for loving a really good story, George. I am sure that she has told you that when we were younger she fantasised about stories of romance and fairy tales. I think that you can thank your dear mum for that Kat!" she confirmed.

"There is nothing wrong with a little bit of wishful thinking, Kate! We have all, I am sure, heard or read about things that a small part of us wishes was a story about ourselves? Katharina is simply a caring woman who believes in achieving things and fantasises a little along the way. There is nothing wrong with that; I find it endearing!" George suddenly said. I smiled at him. His words were kind and I welcomed them. Kate carried on talking, but I found myself blocking out her words as James then added:

"The fact that Katharina is living the real fairy tale fantasy has nothing to do with anything then?" he took a sip of wine. I looked at James, who was staring at me. "I know that you somehow feel obliged to help us, Katharina, but I want you to know that if you ever feel as if you have had enough, you do not have to do anything more! After all, you have your own life to live!" I scowled at him and I knew that George could tell that I was slightly angry, so he said that he would go and get our desserts. My eyes did not leave James until Kate then asked:

"Can you point me in the direction of the bathroom, Kat?"

"Please allow me to show you; I am on my way to the kitchen anyway!" George replied.

"Perfect, thank you, I will be back in a minute," she then replied as she walked out with George.

I was slightly angry with James. He knew that I wanted to help them and yet occasionally I felt like he was trying to push me away, and then other times he seemed happy for me to be there. I felt like I had more of a connection with both him and George at the moment than I did with anyone else. I hadn't felt like part of a family for a long time, particularly since my mum had passed away, and this felt like family. So I decided to tell him what I thought. I stood up and walked toward him and the mirror. He looked slightly nervous.

"I have one question for you, James. Do you really want to break this spell and get out of this situation?" I stood and stared at him.

"Of course I do!" he then replied. I held my finger up to stop him from saying anything else.

"Then stop telling me that I can leave! You may not like it, but I am not going anywhere until I help you and George – who I do care a great deal about, by the way – get out of this situation you find yourselves in. Let's face it, it is not like you have a lot of friends at the moment, is it?" I quizzed him as I stood with my hands on my hips. He looked at me with reservation.

"No. You are our only friend, it seems!" he then answered.

"As I thought! So this is how this is going to work!" I gestured at the two of us. "I am going to help you and you are going to try and help *me* just a little bit, firstly by stopping trying to get me to leave, and secondly by turning on any charm that you have left. If you continue picking at the negative points of each person that I bring here for you, you are never going to have the opportunity to break this spell! Agreed?" I finished. He hesitated for a minute, and then George reappeared and looked at the two of us – but mainly James.

"Agreed!" he then said reluctantly. "I just do not want all of us ending up not living our lives as we should be!" I felt a twinge of guilt; he was just looking after me, and I did appreciate that, but this was the biggest thing to ever happen in my life – I was going nowhere!

"I know! Even with your negativity sometimes I do still want to help you both. Let's speak of it no more!" I smiled.

"Yes, let's not speak of it anymore. I enjoy Katharina being here, so don't you dare keep commenting on her leaving us, James!" George then said as he placed dessert on the table.

"Alright, alright I get the picture," James then replied. George winked at me.

"Oh and by the way your dessert is in the kitchen!" George then announced.

"Great!" James said as he stood and left the room.

George looked across at me and smiled, and just before Kate returned to the dining room, he quickly said;

"Well said, Katharina. It makes a change from me telling him to shut up!" I laughed at his comment and then we sat back down. It has to be said that James was very quiet during dessert and coffee and I felt slightly uncomfortable when Kate asked about John. I looked across at James numerous times and he did look up just once, when I explained to Kate that Northfield was for sale. She seemed interested in that, but only briefly. It was quite clear from her earlier discussions that she was travelling the world more than ever, and so I knew that she would not want to commit to a house of this size. It was disappointing, but I also was quite relieved. I realised that I didn't want anyone else to have it – which was very selfish, but I couldn't help it. I wouldn't dare tell James and George that I felt this way though.

Kate and I continued to catch up; it was lovely to see her. George made her very welcome. As the evening grew late, Kate announced that she would have to leave as she had to be in Paris the next day by noon. Her driver had waited all night for her, and it was so apparent that she loved what she was doing. She was still single, but had, it seemed, a numerous string of men around the globe that she hooked up with when she was in each city.

I walked her to the door and we made a promise that we would catch up again very soon, as she was to be in London for two whole weeks in a few weeks' time. She offered me a lift back to the city, but I wanted to stay and help George clear away and so I declined. As she pulled away, we waved to her and she joyfully shouted "Many thanks George!" as the car slowly rolled down the driveway. I looked across at George who was, it seemed, happy, even though things had not gone to plan. We walked back inside and James stood waiting very patiently.

"Thank you for organising dinner this evening. It was unfortunate that things did not go to plan!" he then stated. I had to stop myself from laughing; his tune had most definitely changed.

"You are very welcome. My matchmaking plans do not seem to be working very well though, do they?" I then asked him.

"At least you are trying, and contrary to what you may think, I do appreciate it!" he then said. I smiled at him.

"I know that you do!" I remarked as I started my way to the dining room. "Let's clear some of these plates away, then we can have coffee before I return back home," I suggested. George happily followed along, not saying anything.

We laughed, tidied, washed the dishes and spoke about the very hectic lifestyles of my friends. It was, by all accounts, not as easy as we had first thought, and my single friends were fast running out. The last person on my list was my friend Lisa; a little older than James, but single after a failed marriage. It was worth a shot. We had coffee in George's apartment and discussed the next hopeful dinner. When it was finally eleven o'clock and my cab arrived, I was tired and left Northfield wishing that I was not; I wanted to cosy down into that large bed. I had to get back though, as I had told John that I would be home, and it was already later than I had expected.

I thanked George again for a lovely meal, and before I left I went to the mirror to speak to James.

"Good night James!" I calmly said.

"Good night Katharina!" he replied with a gentle smile.

"You know, one day I will be able to either shake your hand or give you a well-deserved hug. We will break this together!" I stated, hoping to give him some confidence and reassurance.

"I hope so!" he simply replied, and then I turned and kissed George on the cheek and ran down the stairs and into the cab to get out of the late evening drizzle.

Chapter Fourteen

I returned home to find that John had already gone to bed, but he woke briefly when I slipped under the sheets to ask if I had enjoyed my meal with Kate. I hadn't told him where we were eating, but he knew who I was with. I gave him a quick synopsis on our night's discussion and then happily drifted off to sleep.

I started the new story at work. Kate had texted to thank me for a lovely evening at a ridiculous hour this morning, so I presumed that she was on the go at the crack of dawn. Claire was dedicated to one of the other journalists today and had her work cut out, and so I had a slightly less structured day, which included information gathering, coffee drinking and daydreaming about James and George and Northfield! When a copy of Jane Austen's novel was dropped on my desk from a height, it snapped me back to reality briefly. It had been the anniversary of *Pride and Prejudice* last year, and another colleague had offered to lend it to me once she had finished it, but noted that it was 'bloody hard reading'! I smiled and looked at the front cover and then read the first couple of pages. I could not picture the Bennets and the handsome Mr Darcy… only James, his mother and a very angry but beautiful witch sprang to mind, and I found myself daydreaming again about years past, when they would have been a physical presence.

I checked my phone again. I had texted Lisa this morning, and although she was well-known for not replying for at least three or four days, I hoped for something. It was another disappointment though; I had nothing. I carried on with my day, but it had to be said that my head was not entirely focused on the work that I should have been doing. I found myself Googling 'Northfield' and 'James Henry Aldersley' and even that was not giving me any results. I sat back and sighed; I was, it seemed, completely addicted to being involved in this fairy tale. I knew that I would not be happy until things were eventually resolved. Grimly I started to picture myself finding no single appropriate woman, and me being an old woman, with James still being the way he was – it sent shivers down my spine. I had to keep fighting for them; how lovely the images that appeared in my thoughts were, of being able to sit and share a glass of wine, or a meal, or just a conversation with James sitting in front of me instead of behind a glass barrier. I smiled to myself; I wished that there were more that I could do, but I do not think Googling or looking in the yellow pages for local 'Witches for spell breaking' would be appropriate, considering the year we were in!

The next two days resulted in no reply from Lisa, even though I had texted her again twice, but I knew that she would eventually. By the time Friday arrived, I was relieved and excited that I would be having drinks with Claire tonight. John was out with work colleagues again, but he had suggested that we meet later in the evening.

Claire scowled when I mentioned this; she did not have a high opinion of John at all. We arranged to meet at Dalla Terra, in Covent Garden; Claire had a passion for red wine and good food to nibble on and always preferred to start the night with a very decent glass of wine that 'she could enjoy and remember tasting'! It was a wise decision to have a little bite to eat before we embarked on the numerous bars that I know Claire would want to visit.

The night was running along smoothly; we were, by all accounts, getting very merry but we were luckily still in control, and Claire had managed to have two drinks bought for us in two consecutive bars. She certainly knew how to wrap men around her little finger; I had forgotten how much she liked to do that. It was apparent, however, that she was definitely not suitable for James; she was far too outgoing and liked her single life far too much. As the evening passed at a remarkably fast pace, and I found myself getting worse by the minute from the alcohol, I was reminded that I was not being very attentive to the men that were giving Claire and I attention. Claire had pointed this out numerous times, and I in return had pointed out to her that I was engaged, but then I said something that I probably shouldn't:

"Anyway, I do not want to talk to these men. I have certain interests in another man and it's not John!" As soon as the words came out of my mouth, I thought about what impact this could have, but not being able to tell anyone about James and George was killing me. I did tell them that I would only tell their story if it was a matter of life or death, and at this precise moment in time, under the influence of alcohol, I did feel that I was likely to burst and die, if I didn't tell someone… and so it all spilled out.

"Excuse me?" Claire replied as she pushed the two handsome men that were trying their hardest with us to one side. "What man is this?" she asked. That was when I realised just what I had done. Firstly she would think I was going crazy, and secondly I made a promise to James and George and I knew that there was no going back now. I could tell by the look in Claire's eye that she would most likely coax an answer out of me if I did not willingly tell, so here it went:

"You know Northfield and George?" I slurred.

"Yes?" she replied, then quickly followed it up with: "God you're not in love with George, are you? I mean he's lovely, and there is the older man thing, but not that old!" I laughed at her comment and then continued:

"No, not George! The guy in the painting!" I replied as I looked at her response.

"The dish? The guy I commented on?" she happily replied.

"Yes, that's the one!"

"Kat, if you haven't noticed he's dead!" she laughed.

"What if I told you that he wasn't?" I replied as I took a sip of the cocktail in front of me. Her eyebrows raised and she looked at me as if I was slightly deranged, but she pulled up a bar stool and perched in front of me.

"Okay, now you have my attention – this sounds interesting!" she replied.

"Please try and listen to what I say with an open mind, but promise me that you will not say anything to anyone!" I asked her as I touched her hand. "It is really important to me!" I declared.

"I promise. Jesus Kat, I don't want you locking up in an institute," she laughed.

So I told her the whole story of James and George and the witch, the magic and the spell. She sat and listened and intently gasped at certain points. She did not interrupt me; she simply sucked on the straw in her drink. By the time I had finished the whole story, I felt so much better. I no longer had the feeling of self-combustion now that I had been able to tell someone what was going on. She continued to drink her cocktail for a while and then I had to break the silence.

"Well, say something!" I then commented.

"I am assimilating!" she said, then carried on drinking. I sat and tapped my fingers on my glass, waiting for her reaction. "Well, given the choice, if he were alive, I know who I would choose!" she then declared with a cheeky smile. "You may be working too hard, or going slightly crazy, but all I can say is, I would prefer James – God he looks yummy, and I bet he is a firecracker in bed! You know my feelings on John; I've never gelled with him. I am sorry, Kat, but that's the truth!" she stated as she took another suck on her straw. "Anyway, why are we discussing this? You should definitely write this down, you know – write a book. It's a fantastic story Kat!"

"Story – yes it does sound a little farfetched, doesn't it!" I replied. "I know that you do not like John all that much, and believe me recently I have had my moments with him too," I replied. She touched my hand.

"Maybe that is why you are hoping for something else?" she raised her eyebrows at me questioningly. "Look, all I am going to say is that I do not want to see you in a straightjacket, and quite honestly I do not understand what is going on with you at the moment. However, I trust your judgement and so my advice would be this: follow your heart, Kat. Our hearts very rarely let us down and, let's face it, your head is all over the place at the moment, so there's no point listening to that!" She laughed as she finished her drink. I smiled.

"Thanks Claire, at least you didn't laugh at me… anyway just out of curiosity, how the hell can you deduce that James would be a 'firecracker' in bed from simply looking at a painting?"

"With those eyes and that alluring look? Are you kidding me? God, you seriously cannot tell me you don't look at that painting, or in your case look at him directly in a mirror… in real life… and think that he would not be interesting in bed?" She ordered us a tequila shot; I think she had the strong feeling that I needed something stiffer, probably because I did sound clinically insane!

"Alright, I get the picture!" I laughed. "Please don't say anything about this to anyone. If John gets wind of it, I do not suspect that he will be all too happy!"

"I would not give that man any extra ammunition to fire at you Hun! I do not know what your feelings are toward him at the moment, and honestly I do not see it lasting – he doesn't deserve you!" she then replied sincerely. "Your secret is safe with me!" she finished as she made the gesture of crossing her heart with her finger and zipping her lips. "Now get this shot down your neck, we are moving on!"

Claire certainly knew how to have a good time. The drinks were many and unfortunately mixed, and when it was nearly ten o'clock, and I was swaying very badly, I suggested that the next bar should be where we were meeting John. Her face dropped immediately; she was not too pleased, but she also would not want me travelling home on my own. So, swaying together, we got a cab and laughed the whole way there. Just before we exited the cab, my mobile pinged – at last Lisa had replied:

'Hey Gorgeous, hope you are well? I would love to catch up with you soon, just send me some possible dates and then we can pencil it in!'

I punched the air with excitement. Thank goodness she was back in the world of technology. I replied immediately with difficulty; the screen on my phone was, I am sure, smaller than earlier, and the buttons were even smaller than that. I told her that I was out but would be in touch tomorrow and it would be dinner sometime next week, at a very nice house, with a very charming older friend! We almost fell into the wine bar that John had said he would be at, laughing and knowing all too well that we were far drunker than we had realised. We made our way to the bar.

"Don't you want to find your fiancé?" Claire asked in a very mocking tone.

"No, I am going to look around and see where he is, but I think he should come to me!" I replied. Claire smiled at me.

"Cheers to that girl. Let's see if we can spot him!" Claire announced as our cocktails appeared on the bar. She paid and then, sucking her straw, started to glance around the room. She certainly knew her drinks and wasted no time breathing in between them! "Yep, spotted him!" she then said as she pointed precariously across the room. "Holy sshhh –!" She then stopped herself and leaned into me. "Is that the bloody girl from the office?" she asked as I finally spotted him and realised that Nadine was, yet again, draped around his shoulders.

"Yep, there's a surprise!" I replied. I was upset, but knew that I was drunk. Just as I replied to Claire, he actually removed her arm and stepped away from her.

"Ooh I bet he knows you're here or about to arrive, he's worried he's too close to her… look!" Claire slurred.

"Well, I cannot be bothered with confrontation, so I am going to text him!" I announced as I pulled my phone from my bag.

"What you gonna say? Dump him, then we can go somewhere else!" she then laughed. I scowled at her again; after all, he had tried to undrape her from around his neck.

'I'm here! Can see you, but can't be bothered to fight my way there. At the bar with Claire!' I hit send and then dropped the phone back in my bag.

"Let's see how long it takes him to come find me!" I laughed, now realising just how drunk I was.

It didn't take long. He looked at his phone and gestured to his colleagues that he was looking for me. Claire suggested we hide, but I rolled my eyes at her – we weren't schoolgirls. When he eventually caught sight of us, he made his way over.

"Oh sweet Jesus here he comes!" Claire announced as she turned away slightly.

"Hey ladies, how are we?" he asked as he pecked me on the lips.

"John. Pleasure as always!" Claire suddenly said, as if she was surprised to see him. I chuckled slightly at her.

"Claire, likewise! Sounds like you two are slightly inebriated?" he then asked.

"Oh, we're not that bad!" I then stated as I ran my finger down his bottom lip to silence him, which in turn had Claire in hysterics.

"Oh Jesus, you're both completely smashed!" he then said, as we tried to stop ourselves from laughing.

"I notice that you have your other woman here?" I then stated as I pointed to Nadine. He turned and looked at her and then back at me.

"Really? Do you have to bring that up again? She was just out with her friend, that's all!" he replied.

"Convenient!" Claire whispered under her breath.

"Excuse me?" John then asked in a sterner tone.

"Coincidence!" she said slowly and loudly, then took a sip from her straw.

"Right, I suggest that we finish these drinks and then get you home!" he announced. I nodded, much to Claire's disapproval, but unless I wanted to spend all of Saturday with my head in the toilet, I knew that he was right.

Claire ended up talking to one of John's work colleagues, Ben, who I always thought was a little quiet, but sweet. She decided to get another drink with him, and John assured me that he would see her home safely, so I was happy. The cab ride home was short – most probably because I fell asleep for part of it. As we went up to our apartment, John then informed me that he had bumped into Rachel earlier in the evening. She was out celebrating with work colleagues about her new job!

"She mentioned that you had asked her to dinner at a friend's? A big old house, with amazing charm and character?" he then stated. I seemed to sober slightly and immediately.

"Oh yes, that would have been George at Northfield. He is my friend and he offered to make me and my friend dinner, but she couldn't make it!" I replied, matter-of-factly.

"Since when have you two become such good friends? I thought that you said he was ancient and he wasn't a story?" he asked.

"Well, he is getting on a bit, but he's so charming and has such amazing stories to tell!" I then said with enthusiasm as I dragged John in the door by his lapels.

"Well I don't like it! How often have you been going?" he then asked.

"Only a couple of times. It's not like I fancy him or anything!" I then said sarcastically.

"Not the bloody point and you know it! Jesus, next you'll be telling me that you want to buy the place!" he then snapped.

"Well, I just might do that! I love Northfield!" I snapped angrily whilst swaying.

"You would waste your money on that place? What about once we're married and the new apartment that we talked about?" John then asked as he threw his jacket onto the chair.

"What? I never said that I wanted a new apartment, and I certainly do not want to live in the centre of London. I've always wanted an old house with a garden, I thought you knew that!" I asked.

"I just thought that you were daydreaming. Jesus, Kat, you cannot live your life in a fantasy world!" he then snapped. "We should be aiming to move onwards and upwards, not backwards!"

"I do not see buying a house with some history moving backwards. If I want to spend *my* money on a house that *I* choose, then I will do just that!" I replied.

"Well, it's your 'guilt' money, as you call it; I suppose you may as well spend it on something pointless and useless to the both of us!" he then said as he gestured into thin air. "Anyway, you are very drunk and I believe you do not know what you are saying!" he then finished as he ushered me to our bedroom. "Bedtime for you, young lady!" he remarked.

I was happy to drift into a slumber, which my alcoholic state helped with, but I did find myself dreaming about Northfield; I had bought it and lived there and I was infinitely happy. I did wake on a couple of occasions, due to the room spinning slightly, but each time I woke I thought about the large amount of money that I had sat in my account, gaining interest every year! I had put some money that my mum left me with it, and I had a very decent-sized nest egg to dip into, should I need it. It didn't matter how much I told myself I should save the money, though; there was this nagging voice in the back of my head telling me to invest it and buy into Northfield, and the more I thought about it, the more I felt sure that I wanted to do it.

Saturday saw me shopping with John, who needed a new suit. We seemed to walk for hours around London city centre in the hustle and bustle, but the city was alive today; it was sunny with a cool breeze, which was very refreshing to walk in despite my hangover. The city was amazing; there was an abundance of things to do and see, and something interesting on every corner to stir curiosity. It still did not make me any more enamoured about living here full time, though. I loved the thought of having the city close at hand, but having the sanctuary of my own house away from the centre was far more appealing. As we walked and John did most of the talking, I made the decision to speak to Madison Cleaver on Monday, and George. As soon as I had decided to do this, I had the warmest feeling that I was doing the right thing. I smiled happily to myself as John continued to ramble on about nothing in particular, only himself, and I suddenly realised that for once in my life I was going to do something for me – something big and something that I knew would make my mum happy. I carried on licking my ice cream with a smile, listening to John, and hoping that very soon I would be a part owner of Northfield, the house of my dreams!

Chapter Fifteen

Monday arrived and I arranged a meeting with Justin Temperley of Madison Cleaver, and asked George to meet me in the city tomorrow morning to go to the appointment with me. I could hardly contain myself, I was so excited, but less so at the prospect of telling John, who I knew would not be happy. He had, however, always made a point of telling me to spend my money and it wasn't until Saturday night that I had any idea that he expected me to pay for a new apartment obviously of his choosing, and in the city. I was fast realising that John and I seemed to be heading up two different forks in the road.

Work was moving along greatly. Stories were suddenly coming thick and fast and the charity fundraising employees that I had interviewed had the best positive attitude and commitment to work that I had seen in a long time. My original story on the soldiers and Mrs Holt was in this week's issue of the magazine and when the first copy landed on my desk, I was extremely happy at the end product. Tuesday morning arrived and I met George in Knightsbridge, near Madison Cleaver. I had arranged to meet him in Harrods for coffee before we went. I knew that he would be slightly confused as to our meeting, and I had asked him not to let James know that he was meeting me. When he eventually arrived, he perched on a chair next to me.

"Thank you so much for meeting me, George. Would you like a coffee?" I asked.

"That would be lovely, thank you," he replied as I called to the girl behind the counter. He took in the view of the whole food hall, which was a sight to see. "Wow, it has been a very long time since I came here!" he then announced.

"You have been in here before, George?" I was curious about his previous visit.

"Well, I had to come to the debut of the first moving staircase in England – they advertised it so well! That was a long time ago and I recall being handed a glass of brandy at the top once we had the courage to try it first." He laughed. "Not that remarkable these days though, eh Katharina?"

"Oh I don't know George, we take things for granted so much these days. I think I would have liked to have witnessed that!" I smiled.

"So, may I ask why you wanted to meet me, and why we are seeing Madison Cleaver today?" he then asked me. I placed my cup back down and looked at him.

"Well, I have decided that there could be too much interest in Northfield if you are not careful, and I would not want the wrong type of person to become involved in doing something that we would all regret, such as tear the place down. So I have decided that I want to buy into Northfield! It is up for sale, is it not?" I enquired.

"Why yes, it is for sale as leasehold, but I was merely trying to encourage people into the house; I would never want to sell it outright. I thought we may have some luck with James?" he stated.

"I understand that, but am I correct in assuming that you need the money? It cannot be easy running the place, and I have never asked, but I do not know how you have come to survive for so many years with no income." I did not want to pry, but it had crossed my mind.

"Ah well, Margaret left all her assets in my name, and the family were never short of wealth. I have invested and saved and so on for many a year and we are still in a comfortable position. There are items in the safe that would be worth an amount, and James, God bless him, keeps telling me to sell them, but I just cannot find it in my heart to part with them. So doing something like this helps a great deal!" he finished.

"Well, would you allow me to help you? At least then we can rest assured that your secret is still safe and we are helping each other! The thought of owning – or part owning – something like Northfield has me very excited!" I informed him.

He paused for a while and took a sip of his coffee, then gently placed the cup back onto the saucer.

"I can think of no one that I would rather have share Northfield with us, and I know that James will be happy with the arrangement. I must ask though, how can you afford this?" he then asked.

"Ah well, that was my next point! I have some money left to me by my father, which quite honestly I was never going to touch, but this is an opportunity that I feel I cannot miss. I am going to add it to the money my mother left me and then kindly ask if you would reduce the sale to the amount that I have. I merely wish to protect you both from everyone else, and this is the best way that I feel I can do that!" I happily told him.

George sipped his coffee and then smiled at me; he placed his cup gently down on the saucer and then touched my hand. "I really do not care how much money that you have; as I said, I can think of no one better than yourself to buy into Northfield for as long as you wish. The respect and help that you have given both James and I to date is testament to your good nature and character. So I would be honoured to go with you and sign any documents," George then replied. I threw my arms around his neck and hugged him tightly in a bid to stop myself from dancing around the food hall. He laughed in response and then gestured for me to sit. "I have one other question. What does your fiancé think about this?" he then asked. It immediately dampened my excitement.

"I haven't told him yet, but it is my money and I will tell him soon!" I replied.

George nodded in acceptance; I think that he knew better than to get involved in any potential argument between John and I. Then we continued our conversation with the fact that I was going to bring Lisa to dinner on Thursday evening and I would tell James the news then. I hadn't quite got my head around the fact that if James did find love with another, he would undoubtedly want to stay at Northfield. I raised this with George, who told me that there was the possibility of sharing the house once James was back in the real world, or that he could sell off assets to pay me back. George had made it quite clear that he would only ever play it safe with James' inheritance, which led me to the next set of questions.

"How on earth do you live in different eras without anyone questioning you? The banks, investments – they all need identification of some description, so how do you obtain it?" I asked him.

"It is getting harder with every passing decade! Having James back would help greatly. He could live and spend his fortune how he wished and, once married, he could become part of society again!" George said hopefully.

"Because he could take the name of his wife?" I asked.

"Possibly, although I am not sure how he would feel about that. At least he would fit into society with a wife, and if children were to be involved, it would be easier still. It is quite amazing how one can do the right thing by doing the wrong thing!" he tried to explain.

We ventured to Madison Cleaver. Justin Temperley, it had to be said, looked slightly at a loss with our agreement, and as we were not about to explain it to him he simply confirmed that he would draw up the necessary documents for us to sign. Today was a very good day; I had bought the house of my dreams, which housed a very handsome man, magic and George in the most beautiful surroundings, and I could not be happier.

I had to return to work, and George and I parted ways with the promise that we would see each other on Thursday evening. Lisa had confirmed for seven o'clock and I could not wait to get there and tell James. I almost skipped to work and nothing could have made my mood heavy, until my phone beeped and it was John. I suddenly remembered that I was going to have to tell him what I had done. I had to pick the right moment and judge his mood! I opened the message from him: 'Hi Babe! Can you meet me for drinks tomorrow evening after work? Big client wants to take a few of us with partners to dinner in appreciation!' I sighed; more niceties to be done! I felt that I had no choice, so I simply replied: 'If I must!' I would pick my moment wisely and this may be it.

Tuesday rolled into Wednesday. I had taken a copy of the magazine home on Monday evening to show John my first printed story – the first of many that I hoped would be printed in this series. Unfortunately he just placed it on the table and said that he would read it soon. It wasn't quite the response that I was looking for. I made sure that I had an extra copy for James and George on Thursday night. Claire had made it clear that she was not happy about his lack of enthusiasm for my job, and when I told her that I was going for drinks again on Wednesday evening with him and his work colleagues, she shot me a look of complete disapproval. I decided that it was probably best that I told nobody of my new expensive purchase, until I had told John – just in case someone could not keep it to themselves!

Drinks with John's clients, I have to say, was not the most enticing thought, particularly when you had no idea about the subject matter. The cab pulled up outside a very expensive-looking restaurant and I nervously walked in, feeling glad that Charles spotted me and took me to John straight away. John finished his conversation and then introduced me to a mature-looking client, who I have to say was very charming and complimentary. We all sat down for dinner and, thank goodness, Nadine was at the furthest end of the table from me. I do think, looking at Charles and Helen's faces, that it was possibly manufactured that way. The meal was delicious, and John had sat directly next to his client, giving me the opportunity to speak to Dawn, who was married to Jack, another member of the team. She was a real breath of fresh air and delightful to talk to.

John's client found my career interesting and asked how hard it was in the competitive market of journalism. It was actually a refreshing change to discuss myself, and for someone else to enquire about my line of work. John commented that I had just finished the first of many new stories that had been assigned to me, which infuriated me as I knew damn well that he had not even taken the time to read it yet! The night passed relatively quickly; it was not as uninspiring as I had first assumed, and thankfully I had not had to talk to Nadine all night, although I did give her a couple of glances during the evening.

When we arrived home, I found John trying very hard to please me. He was constantly commenting on how happy he was that I had managed to converse well with his client. Nadine was not mentioned, so I did not bring her up in conversation either. Although I had seen him look at her a couple of times during dinner, I tried not to let it bother me. We retired to bed early and all in all the evening was more enjoyable than I had imagined. I slept well and hoped that this was a sign of things to come; a happier us, being able to enjoy time together in

Nadine's company. I still had not had the chance to tell John about my purchase of Northfield, which still had me smiling. I was so excited about it and the prospect of living there in the future. Hopefully he would learn to love it as much as me.

I woke up with a bounce in my step. Later I would see Lisa, who I had not seen in ages, and also George and James. I would get to tell James my news tonight, which had me both nervous and excited, but I hoped that he would be happy about the joint venture! John left and went to work; I finished breakfast and then went back to the bedroom to collect my shoes. I noticed on John's bedside table that he had left his wallet. Trying to call him whilst on the tube would be pointless, but I knew that if I got moving I could swing by John's office and then hop in a cab to my own. As last night had gone well, I decided to try and keep the momentum going by doing a good deed for him.

As I walked off the elevator and up to the reception desk where John worked, the girl there instantly recognised me and smiled.

"Hi, I need to just see John for a second!" I stated.

"Right, well he has a meeting in five minutes, but if you hurry... I think you know where his office is?" she then asked as she gestured down the hallway.

"Thank you. Yes I remember my way," I replied as I made my way down the corridor. I smiled to myself, knowing that John would be pleased that I had taken it in for him. As I approached his door, I straightened my clothes and then walked in. I did not expect to find what I did!

Nadine was sat on his desk, facing him, one leg stretched out on his chair, her foot placed between his legs and her lace-top stockings showing. They were laughing and John was sat in a very casual and relaxed, if not sexual manner. To say he looked surprised when he noticed me was an understatement. I glared at them both and then looked at his wallet in my hand. Nadine had now turned to me, stood quickly and straightened her clothing and then simply said:

"Kat, good morning. We weren't expecting you!"

"I can see that quite clearly, Nadine!" I replied sarcastically.

"Hey babe, what are you doing here?" John asked as he stood up.

I threw his wallet onto the table and looked at him.

"I thought that you may need this, but quite obviously you would have got by without it!" I replied as I looked at Nadine and then turned and walked out of the office. I scurried back along the corridor and toward the reception desk, where the girl who had kindly pointed the way to John's office now stood looking very nervously at me as I stomped back toward the elevator.

I could hear John walking quickly along behind me, and as we walked one colleague even tried to stop him to speak with him about a current client. He kindly but abruptly told him to wait as I pushed the button for the elevator. When the doors pinged open, I stepped in quickly and turned and leaned against the rail, then John stepped in before the door closed.

"Babe, where are you running to so quickly?" he asked.

"Really? You really want me to answer that? Jesus John, you seriously have no idea, do you?" I replied as I shook my head.

"Alright, I admit that must have looked a little awkward. I keep telling you, though, that there is nothing going on with Nadine and me!" he quickly stated.

"You seriously need to see this from where I am standing, because it doesn't look so innocent to me!" I sighed as I placed my hand on my forehead. I suddenly felt very hot and needed to get out of this tight space very soon.

Relief struck as the elevator stopped and the doors opened. I stepped out into the bustling lobby and John followed, placing his hand on my lower back.

"Kat, Kat – stop, please!" he spoke firmly but quietly, trying not to make a scene. I did, if only to hear more feeble excuses. "Babe, honestly there is nothing going on, I love you!" he said as he took hold of my hands.

"Yet I seem to keep catching the two of you in very close proximity together, looking far too intently at each other, don't I?" I remarked, staring directly at him. "I really need to get to work!" I then stated as I released our hands.

"Can we talk about this tonight, Kat? I think that we both need to get things off our chest – you obviously do not trust me at the moment!" he then stated.

"You are not giving me much choice, are you?" I replied with conviction. "I am out tonight, remember, with Lisa!" I then reminded him.

"Right, yeah. How about I come pick you up – where are you eating?" he then asked, and suddenly I became the guilty one.

"You don't need to do that, we will share a cab," I pointed out.

"Why, where are you going? Can you not get the tube?" he asked curiously. I decided to just tell him; I was furious anyway.

"We have been invited to dine with George at Northfield, so we will get there and back on our own!" I replied hesitantly.

"That place and him, *again*? And you have the nerve to have a go at me?" he then stated as he rubbed his mouth and strolled back and forth.

"John, he's really old and lonely. I haven't slept with him, kissed him or lounged around him with a short skirt and lace-top stockings on! He's cooking dinner and I am with my friend, so I think that you're pretty safe!" I quickly pointed out with a venomous tone. He scowled at me, and as I was on a roll of telling him what I thought, I decided to let him know the whole glorious truth. "Anyway, why wouldn't I want to spend time in *my* house, which I bought with *my* money? I love it and love being there, so if I want to go I will!" I finished and turned away, but John grabbed my hand.

"What do you mean *your* house? Jesus, Kat, you didn't go and spend all of your savings on an old house, did you?" he then asked. I turned to him.

"Yes, I did actually! You always said it was mine to do with as I pleased, and I really wanted to buy it – it's my dream house. It is old, but it's amazing and historical and I wouldn't change a thing!" I informed him.

"I know I told you to spend it how you wished, but damn it Kat I thought that you would have bought something we *both* wanted, or at least informed me of your intentions!" He was now sounding really angry, so I decided it was best to let him get rid of some steam.

"I'm sorry if you don't agree with me, John, but it was my money. You may really like it; you should come and take a look sometime!" I then stated. "Look, I have to go. I think we should talk later once we have both calmed down." I couldn't believe that I had just said that! Maybe it was due to guilt at telling him about Northfield – and maybe, in some way, I was trying to justify catching him with Nadine by telling him my secret. As I walked out of his building, though, I realised that my secret was nothing like his. I hadn't been unfaithful to him, but I was starting to get the distinct impression that he definitely had a closer relationship with Nadine than he was letting on!

Back at work, I muffled out Claire's angry words as I tried to get on; she had now decided that John was on the biggest slippery slope. I told her about my purchase, and I have to say that although she said she was happy for me, if it was what I wanted, I had the feeling that she did think I was slightly deranged. I was glad when the workday ended, but I found myself not as happy as I had hoped to be on my journey to Northfield. I hadn't even changed; I decided to do it there once I had arrived. When I walked in, George was in the kitchen and James greeted me.

"Good day at work?" he asked me. I tried to smile.

"Not the best!"

"Oh, I am sorry to hear that. George is in the kitchen!" he quickly stated, as if he did not know what to say.

I nodded and walked slowly down to the apartment, with James quietly pacing at my side. When I saw George and he turned to me, I sighed. It felt like I was at home, here with them, and the look on George's face when he saw me made me even more relieved to be back here.

"Katharina, are you well?" he enquired. I found myself walking toward him and giving him the biggest hug. On releasing him, I found both him and James looking at each other and I realised that they did not know what to make of my mood.

"I am sorry. Bad day at work, another argument with John... I am so happy to be here though!" I replied sincerely. James sighed and George replied:

"Your argument wasn't about anything too serious, I hope?" I simply looked at George, and he knew straight away. "Ahh!" he replied as he poured me a glass of red. James then crossed his arms.

"Why do I get the feeling that I am missing something here?" he asked. "Whatever your argument with that idiot was, he probably deserved it anyway!" he then finished as I took a big gulp of wine. I smiled.

"You know what? You are entirely right. I have something I need to talk to you about, but if you will excuse me, first I am going to get changed," I stated with renewed confidence. James quickly uncrossed his arms.

"Yes, of course. I will wait here to hear of what news you have to state!" he replied with slight apprehension.

I smiled at George and then skipped upstairs and freshened up in the bathroom, and then changed in my bedroom. *My bedroom* – I could say that now and mean it! My excitement came flooding back, and I changed in record time as I suddenly felt the need to urgently discuss my recent purchase with James. I skipped back down the stairs and to George's kitchen with a big smile on my face.

"Better?" George asked.

"Much!" I replied, as he nodded at me to tell James my news.

"James," I said as I stood in front of the mirror with my wine in hand. He backed off a little, looking nervous, but I continued. "So, I have some very exciting news, and I hope that you will be very happy about it, because both George and I are!" James shot a curious look at George, who simply smiled at him in return and shrugged his shoulders. "I would like to announce –"

"That you are getting married?" James quickly finished, looking dismayed.

"What?" I quickly replied with surprise. "No... why would you think that? Jesus, I can't seem to agree with the man at the moment, never mind marry him, you fool!" I laughed. James looked relieved but shocked at my response, whilst George just laughed and then said:

"Let her finish, you're always so impatient!"

"Thank you George!" I raised my glass to him. "I would like to announce that as of Tuesday this week, I am now owner – well, in part, anyway – of Northfield!" I finished as I stared at him.

James stepped back and looked at me and then George, and was very quiet for a moment.

"Speechless!" George commented. "I did not plan on that!"

"Well, say something!" I remarked.

"But how? When, and why?" he asked with surprise.

"How… because I had some money left to me by my father and mother. When… I met George on Tuesday and we went to Madison Cleaver to get the paperwork drawn up. Why… because I haven't felt like part of a family in a long time, and you both feel like family. Besides, I do not want anyone else doing anything to this house to jeopardise your chances of a normal life. This was the best way that both George and I could think of protecting you both, at the same time as creating some income for maintaining the house. George did think that you would be happy about the arrangement!" I finished, feeling that it was not going quite as I had planned. James was quiet for a minute and then spoke gently.

"You mistake my silence as disappointment at this arrangement. It is not! I am both surprised and shocked at your selfless generosity yet again, and the willingness to help protect two people who you have not known for long. You would give up your chance of having what you wish and with your money, for us?" he asked sincerely.

"That's just it, though. This is my chance of having something that I have always dreamed of – something that I want for a change – instead of doing what is expected of me. I feel very happy about this, and with regards to both of you, I may not have known you both for very long, but I feel like I have more of a connection and common ground with you than I have had with anyone else in a long time! I hope you can be as happy as me about this arrangement?" I replied with honesty and sincerity.

"Well, I for one feel like we have known you for

years, Katharina, and I could not be happier at this arrangement. So cheers!" George then said as he lifted his glass to me and looked at James for a response. James smiled and picked up his glass.

"It is my greatest pleasure, in a very long time, to have you here and know that you are to be part of Northfield on a more permanent basis. Thank you again for your kindness Katharina, and I believe that congratulations are in order!" he then finished as he raised his glass higher. I smiled.

"Cheers! Here's to happy endings!" I toasted. They both smiled.

"Happy endings!" they both replied. We all took a sip of our wine, then conversed with laughter and relief that we had something to work towards, together!

Lisa was ten minutes late but arrived with as much eagerness as was to be expected when entering such a grand house. She too gasped in awe at the beauty of the hallway and as James stood there with a huge grin on his face, I felt that nothing could surprise him now that he had received my news. She and George became acquainted and he took her coat. We hugged and she instantly started to talk and ask questions about Northfield and George and what work was like and so on… we had not had the chance to catch up in such a long time, and it was apparent that she had been very busy since we last spoke.

George told us to sit and carry on with the catching up whilst he went to get dinner, and James stood quietly, still smiling, at the both of us.

"What a fantastic room – this whole house is

amazing!" she stated as she stood and walked around the table, looking at the furniture, ornaments and mirrors. She stopped in front of where James stood, and I raised my eyebrows at him, hoping that something would transpire.

"Do you not think that the mirrors here are amazing, Lisa? What we girls would do for mirrors in our dressing areas like this!" I asked her as I walked and stood alongside her. I looked at James, who smiled at my remark.

"They are amazing!" she replied as she stepped back and looked at the whole mirror in its entirety. Then she stepped back toward it and touched it.

"I love them all; they reflect the rooms so well, amongst other things!" I commented.

"They do; I know that you have always liked older houses, Kat. This one, however, feels very special. I wonder what interesting things have happened here in the past?" she then stated. She seemed to be staring directly into James eyes, but then she looked at my reflection. "I've missed you – it's been far too long since we got together!" she said.

"It has!" I remarked, and we returned to the table to eat as George returned with his little trolley.

Dinner was delicious. Lisa and George got on well and James laughed at a lot of her comments, which was nice; for once, he was not being as negative as usual. We were happily enjoying dessert when suddenly there was some very loud knocking at the door. James jumped up and disappeared into the hallway. As George, Lisa and I stood we heard shouting.

217

"Kat, I know you're in there, let me in!"

"Oh holy crap, it's John!" I remarked to George as I walked to the hallway.

"Katharina, he sounds angry – I would suggest that you do not let him in!" James remarked.

"Kat, Kat – come on. I want to see what you've spent all your money on!" John continued to shout.

"What on earth is he talking about, Kat?" Lisa asked.

"He's a little pissed at me for spending all the money my father left me on buying this place!" I gestured to the house. Lisa raised her eyebrows.

"Wow, now I know why you like it so much. What's he so angry at? It was your money!"

"He wanted me to buy a very modern apartment in the middle of London!" I replied.

"You've never wanted that, though. Living there was only ever temporary for you!" Lisa remarked. I touched her shoulder in recognition that she knew me better than John.

"I'm going to have to face this sometime!" I remarked as I walked to the door.

"I'm not happy about this at all!" James said as he paced.

"Me neither!" George replied.

"What?" Lisa asked George; as she couldn't hear James, George's response didn't make any sense.

"I am not too happy about his tone!" George then said to Lisa.

"Trust me, Kat can stand up for herself. I don't know what John's moaning about, it was her money anyway!" Lisa finished.

I turned and looked at them all, then turned the large key and opened the door. John, who was fresher than a daisy and damp from the evening drizzle, looked not only angry, but a little shocked as he looked at George and Lisa. Maybe because he realised now that I was telling the truth.

"I am not letting you stay here if you are disrespectful to my friends or behave like a three-year-old!" I announced before he had the chance to say anything. He held his hand up as he steadied his posture.

"I wanted to see what you'd wasted your money on for myself!" he slurred and then laughed as he stepped through the door. Before I could help myself, I found that the palm of my hand had quite abruptly slapped him hard across the cheek.

The noise was louder than expected. Lisa gasped and put her hand to her mouth to try and stop herself from laughing. George stepped forward and then stopped and James stood there and applauded three times.

"Well, I hadn't expected that; remind me not to get on your bad side!" James remarked as he grinned even more.

"I said do not be disrespectful, and that meant to me too! I have not wasted my money and quite honestly the way I feel right now, John, I don't care what you think. For once I have done something for myself; whether you like it or not, that is not going to change!" I remarked. I felt strong and in control and, for the first time, able to say exactly what I thought!

George stepped back, realising that his help was not needed. Lisa controlled herself as James stood there and looked at John with his arms crossed.

"Jesus Kat, I don't think I deserved that!" John said as he looked at me.

"I do!" Lisa replied. "It's up to Kat what she buys with her money – why can't you support her decision for a change? This place is amazing."

"Lisa, always a pleasure!" John sarcastically replied as he placed his hand against his now-reddening cheek.

"I swear to God I wish I could hit this guy for myself!" James then remarked.

"Later!" George replied quietly as he gestured for us all to go into the dining room.

John looked up at the entrance hall as we walked, and even though he would never say it, I knew that he was impressed with the place. George suggested coffee, which he poured and handed to John, who sipped it slowly.

"So, do I get the grand tour then?" he asked.

"Are you going to behave?" I replied sarcastically.

"Funny! Of course I am!" he said with sarcasm.

I looked at the others and then gestured for him to walk back to the hall, and slowly I showed him each room as George, Lisa and James followed. Lisa was amazed, as I expected. When we entered the portrait gallery, he looked at the paintings and commented on most very rudely, but remarkably, when he got to James' portrait, he stopped.

"God, he's about the only sane-looking one on these walls!"

"Yeah, and absolutely the best-looking – wow, he's gorgeous!" Lisa then commented, which made me laugh slightly. John scowled at her.

We avoided George's apartment, as it was nothing to

do with the main house. As we left the last room and walked back down the stairs, John commented:

"Well, it's big, old and needs a fortune spending on re-modernising, but I reckon you could sell it and make a decent profit once you've done that."

"John, I am not selling it – I love it just as it is. As I've already said, if you don't like it the way it is, then I really have no interest in what you have to say!" I replied.

"Are you out of your mind, Kat? What did you think, that you'd just give yourself the biggest birthday present that you could find?" he then said, and I sighed as James uncrossed his arms and stepped forward.

"Excuse me; is it your birthday, Katharina?" George then asked as he touched my arm.

"Not for three weeks, George!" I replied.

"Good on ya Kat – what a brilliant present!" Lisa then announced.

"I like this girl the more she says!" James remarked at Lisa. I smiled. John was walking around, gawping at the house and murmuring to himself.

"I think I need to get him home! He needs to sober up!" I suggested to both George and Lisa, as she was sharing a cab with me – and now a very drunken John.

"Unfortunately I think that you are right. Are you not staying here?" Lisa asked. I shook my head.

"No, not yet!" I smiled.

"Well, I'm up for sleepovers when you move in!" Lisa then replied. I laughed.

"Alright, I will bear that in mind Lisa!" I remarked.

We got our things together and, with coats on, helped John out of the door and sat him on the stairs outside so he could get some fresh air until the cab arrived, which did not take long. I felt terrible that I was leaving George to tidy away, but I knew that he understood.

"Thank you for a lovely evening again, George," I stated. As Lisa gave George a hug and spoke with him, I turned and started buttoning my coat in the mirror whilst I spoke quietly to James.

"Thank you for a nice evening. I am sorry about him!" I whispered.

"No, thank you. You have made me very happy today with your news, and under the circumstances that usually is hard to do. I just hope that you do not get any trouble from him!" James replied as he gestured towards John.

"I hope not, but I think he knows how I feel!" I replied.

"I would like to think so; he has heard your mind – and your hand – tonight!" he remarked as he laughed lightly. I smirked too and then nodded in agreement. "Take care until next time, Katharina!" he said, sounding almost sentimental.

"Soon!" I whispered again as I turned to find George smiling at the two of us. Lisa was helping John to the cab.

"Everything alright?" he asked.

"Yes, I promise that I will be fine!" I replied as he kissed me on both cheeks.

"Well, now that this is your home, you can come and go as you please!" George happily stated.

"Yes indeed!" James confirmed as I walked to the door.

"Good night then!" I said before I turned and walked to the cab.

"Good night," they both replied.

Yet again as we pulled away I felt sorry to be leaving. I looked back at the facade as we rolled down the driveway and smiled. It was mine, to share with them, and right now I could not think of anything that would make me feel happier! John had now fallen asleep and was resting his head on Lisa's shoulder, much to her dismay. She pushed his head against the seat with her fingers and grimaced at him.

"I'm sorry Kat, I know you're engaged to him, but I've been in a relationship like this and I have to say... he's an arse!" she remarked.

"It has been stated by a few of my friends recently, even myself!" I replied as I looked at her. Then, without any warning, we both burst out laughing uncontrollably.

"I've had a great evening, Kat. It's been good to see you!" she said once we'd controlled ourselves.

"It has, let's do it again soon!"

"Preferably without him!" she then said as she poked John, and he grunted, which set us off laughing again.

Chapter Sixteen

O n arriving back in London, I dropped Lisa off at home and then took a very drunk (it would seem) and sleeping John home. I managed to get him to wake up in order to get into our apartment and as we entered the lounge he fell onto the sofa and started laughing.

"Did I just dream that place, or have you seriously spent all of your money on an old, dilapidated house?"

I was fast losing patience with him. I expected that he probably wouldn't remember half of what had been said tonight, so I decided to be open and truthful.

"You did not dream it! I have bought the house of my dreams. I hoped that it would be to share with you, John, but I am fast becoming disillusioned with our relationship. We seem to want different things!" I answered as I stood in front of him with my hands on my hips. He wriggled with difficulty to his feet and looked at me.

"I thought we could have chosen something together and used your money more wisely. We could have upgraded this place for something bigger!" he then said as he gestured at the apartment.

"That is exactly my point, John. That is what you want, not me! I do not want to live in the centre of London forever and with everything else challenging us at the moment, I have to admit that I was angry with you when I decided to buy the house!"

"So this is a get-mad-at-me-and-completely-piss-me-off purchase then?" he then said, with a more venomous tone.

"Well to start with I think there was a touch of that, but once I decided I did want it – and I really truly realised that it *is* what I want, John – I could not be more delighted! I wish that you could try and be happier for me about this!" I was starting to feel that John and I were heading down that slippery slope.

"I would be happy if it was something from this era! Jesus, Kat, it will cost a small fortune to put right. In its day I am sure that it was amazing, but it's a fossil for God's sake – something that you just think you want!" he snapped.

"How would you know what I want? You don't seem to have a clue any more, and you seem to want something completely different these days!" I replied with as much force.

"What are you saying?" he then asked as he moved closer and looked more seriously at me. I shrugged my shoulders at him.

"I'm not sure. I think that you have drunk too much and I have said too much. Let's talk tomorrow after some sleep!" I suggested. He raised his hands up in defeat and barged past me.

"Yeah whatever, but sleep or not – and alcohol or not – I am never going to be happy about this Kat!" he slurred. He walked into the bedroom and threw himself on the bed fully dressed and started snoring instantly.

As I stood and looked at him, I wondered how long

I had been this unhappy with him. Was it due to recent events, or had I had an underlying feeling for some time that things were not right between us? After all, it's easier, they say to carry on, rather than face any issues. I stood leaning against the doorjamb and looked at him passed out on the bed.

"Well like it or not I am keeping Northfield and the people that reside within!" I whispered to myself, and the thought made me smile.

As the day broke and I thought about the impending conversation that John and I needed to have, I cringed slightly and buried my head into my pillow. Like it or not, truths and feelings were out in the open now and I had to face it. As John snored on soundly, fully clothed, I went and had a shower, then dressed and had breakfast. After a few jobs I sat and read the newspapers and nearly an hour passed before John finally surfaced and came into the kitchen. I had called work and said I was sick. I couldn't face work today.

He got a cup of coffee, then leant on the island opposite me and took a sip before saying:

"So that was an interesting day yesterday!" I looked up at him and raised my eyebrows.

"Really? I think it was a very stressful day, but at least some truths were spoken!" I took a sip of my coffee.

"Well the only way to resolve this is for you to sell that place – then we can get back on track," he said in a casual manner.

I tried to reserve my disbelief and placed my mug on the worktop, closed and folded the newspaper, then took a deep breath and looked at him.

"Obviously nothing that I said last night has even entered into your understanding, has it? I am not selling it, John. I'm sorry, but that is my final decision!" I told him with conviction.

"Jesus Kat, has nothing I said gone into that thick head of yours? I don't want that old place, you know that!" he replied as he banged his mug onto the worktop.

"That money was mine to do with as I pleased and left by my mum and dad. You always told me to spend it how I wished, and now that I have you are not happy!"

"Well forgive me for thinking that I would have been part of your decision about how to spend it!" he then stated as he stood up straight and crossed his arms.

"That money was mine before I met you, John. If I hadn't told you about it, you would never have known that I had it!" I replied harshly.

"Oh, so now you're saying that you would keep secrets from me, and lie to me?" he insinuated. I gasped at him.

"Do not talk to me about secrets and lies – I think that you have enough to answer for with certain work colleagues!" I stated as I stood.

"Oh God, here we go again with Nadine and me! What is it with you and her?" he snapped as he took another sip of coffee.

"Do not make me out to be the bad one in this, John. You know why I am upset about your relationship with her – yesterday was just the final straw. Don't you realise how it made me feel, seeing you together in that position yesterday?" I demanded.

"God you're paranoid, she's just a really nice girl and

227

work colleague!" he then stated, but a look in his eye said differently.

"So if you came to my work and I was sat on my desk, stockings showing, with Julian, or Mark, or another male colleague between my legs, you would just brush it off and act like it was not unacceptable behaviour?" I asked curiously, and then became angrier as he laughed.

"Well that is very unlikely to happen, isn't it!" he then announced, implying that I was not worthy of any attention from any other male. I felt like crying immediately; I wanted to shout and scream at him. In that single moment he made me feel more worthless than I ever had, and as I stared at him I couldn't wish for anything more than to be as far away as possible from him.

I knew he could tell by the look on my face that he had stepped way over the line. As quickly as he said it, he raised his hand in a placatory gesture.

"That didn't quite come out the way that I meant it!" he said quietly. I turned my back to him to compose myself.

"I think you meant that, John!" I calmly said. He walked out from behind the island.

"Babe, let's just look at what options we have, shall we?" he then said as he slid his hands around my waist. I spun quickly to face him.

"No John, let's not! Right now, I do not think that you want me at all, and quite honestly I do not know whether I want to be with you!" I replied honestly. I removed his hands, stepped back and then looked at him. "I'm sorry, but I need a break from us – I'm going to stay at Northfield for a while!" I finished.

"What? What do you mean you want a break from us? You have changed so much since you started going to that place – and now that you've bought it, I'm worried about what else you may do!" he retorted with anger.

"Actually John, you're wrong – I feel like I have found myself again. This is me, like it or not!" I replied, then turned and walked to the bedroom to pack a bag.

I felt calm and not the least bit angry that I was going to be leaving John for a few days. Quite the contrary; my head felt clearer than it had in a long time. I wanted to go to Northfield, and to have that space between John and I, and that made me realise that I was obviously not happy with my current situation. I packed enough clothing for a week and then grabbed my book off my nightstand, and my computer and workbag, and then walked back into the lounge to find John pacing.

"Are you really serious? Is this what you want?" he asked.

"It is! I think that this is best for both of us at the moment!" I replied. He threw his hands up and ran them through his hair.

"Fine – go and run to your house and the old fool that lives there. When you have calmed down, I will be here, waiting to hear your apology!" he remarked. I smiled and then replied:

"In case you haven't noticed. I am calm. Yes I am going to 'my' house, but I am not running; walking will be sufficient. George may be old, but he is no fool – and don't hold your breath waiting for an apology!" I replied as I raised my eyebrows at him. He looked at me in disbelief and watched as I walked toward the door. "I will call you soon alright?" I stated as I walked through the door and went outside to hail a cab.

As the door closed I heard him quickly call back: "Yeah babe, okay, call me soon!" It was all he could say; for once he seemed a little lost for words. The cab came and as I travelled the not-too-long journey I sat and thought about John, Nadine, recent events, and our conversation. I was a little sad at the whole thing. I never thought that any relationship I entered into whole-heartedly would break down! I was sure that I was partly to blame; I had changed since meeting George and James, but I thought for the better.

The cab turned into the drive at Northfield and drove right up to the front steps. The cabbie commented on the grand facade and I smiled, knowing that it was mine. I got my bags and went up the stairs, then opened the large door. I walked in, placed my bags inside and then closed the door behind me. I could not see anyone and so I shouted: "Hello? Anyone home?" I had hardly finished speaking when James appeared. I felt relieved to see him again.

"Katharina, are you alright?" he asked as he closed the book he was reading and then looked at my bags.

"Well, I have decided that I need a break from John. I am not sure where our relationship is going, but I really don't care for him much at the moment, so I have come to spend a week here until I decide what to do – if that is alright with you and George?" I walked across and touched the mirror that James stood behind. "It's really good to see you; I am so happy to be here. You both feel like family to me, and I need that right now!" I smiled.

"You never need to ask permission to stay here, Katharina; this is your home. I am sorry that your relationship has broken down, but I am also not sorry as it means that we get to spend some time with you!" He smiled back at me and touched the mirror in the same place that I had. "Please stay… for as long as you like!"

"Stay forever!" George then said as he appeared behind me. I turned and smiled at his comment, then walked across and hugged him. I needed the comfort of feeling secure and both of them gave me that security. "Shall we take your bags to your room?" he then asked as I peeled myself off him.

"Yes, let's!" I remarked as I went to retrieve them.

"It's good that you are here, Katharina – I am sure that James is cheating at cards at the moment and you can be the decider."

"Stop being such a bad loser, George! It is merely that I am getting lots of practice!" James remarked. As they bantered all the way along the corridor to my room, with James referring to the rules in the book he was reading. I laughed lightly to myself. I loved listening to them, but more than that, I could not think of anywhere that I would rather be right now.

I unpacked and returned to George's apartment, but not before bolting the main door, which had been left unlocked. I tutted and entered into the kitchen, where they were both still arguing about who the better player was. George handed me a cup of coffee and then I remarked on the door:

"George, it worries me slightly that you are all the

way down here and you leave the front door unlocked. You need to start bolting it just in case!"

"I keep telling him that!" James agreed.

"Well, I have a good alarm should anyone come in!" George gestured at James.

"Yes, but if someone did come in, there isn't a lot I can do other than shout – and they cannot hear me! Katharina is right; we should be more careful. I cannot help you if there is any trouble, George!" James replied. I was glad that James had agreed with me. I did not want the house to be vandalised – or, worse still, for George to be injured in some way! George held his hands up in defeat.

"Alright, alright, I get the message. I will lock the door from now on. We must get you a key, Katharina; then you can come and go whenever you choose," he said.

"That would be lovely, thank you George!" I replied honestly, then took a sip of my coffee.

"You haven't seen the size of the key!" James remarked, with raised eyebrows.

We sat and chatted. They asked me about John, and I gave them a brief synopsis, but I didn't really want to talk about him. We had lunch and then I offered to cook tea – I decided that some pasta would be a nice change, and as George had minced beef in the fridge I set to making a sauce so that it could simmer slowly all afternoon. I went to the library and looked at the many books with James to keep me company. He told me of his favourite books; the ones that had scared him as a child, and the ones that he had loved. His mother read stories to him when he was little; I could tell from the look on his face that he cherished those memories. I found myself drawn to the fairy tales again and found it soothing to re-read many of the books that I had loved as a child. Some of them were written slightly differently to the modern versions of today, but the colourful pictures, leather-bound covers and print were delightful.

It brought me great pleasure just sitting and reading and laughing with James, and then George came to see what all the fun was about. We were laughing about the witch in *Sleeping Beauty* and the fact that her spell – making everyone sleep – was far fairer than the one cast upon James. It took him a short while to see the funny side, but then he laughed along with me for some time. I almost ended up with tears running down my cheeks, and as I explained why to George I started again.

"Well, you're always one to see the lighter and funnier side of things. It is lovely to hear you both laughing!" George then said as he laughed a little more.

Time flew by, I served our pasta and we sat and ate, amusing ourselves as we sucked up the long spaghetti. It was tasty and the three of us left no morsel on our plates

"That was delicious, Katharina. You can stay as long as you like if you cook like that for us!" George stated as he rubbed his tummy.

"Indeed!" James agreed. I was happy that I was appreciated and that my cooking had been enjoyed.

"It's my pleasure; I do enjoy cooking. I am just not that great at it and I never seem to have the time!" I replied.

"I think you should make time! You are very good at it!" James then stated. I smiled contentedly as I cleared the plates, then stared at them in my hand for a moment.

"Plates – that is one thing I do not understand. If you receive a real version of each meal in your side of the mirror, you must have hundreds of plates stacked up in there somewhere. What do you do with them?" I asked curiously.

"I do not know!" James replied. "I wash them and dry them and place them in the cupboard, but when I go back in the next day, there is only the original amount that I started with! It is quite perplexing!" he finished as he placed his plate in his sink.

"This is quite a complex spell, yet it seems simple enough to break!" I commented.

"Not that simple; he's still bloody stuck there, stubborn as he is!" George then answered. I laughed a little.

"I think that I have mellowed a little over the years, George, do you not agree?" James asked.

"Mellowed, yes, but managed to find someone to love you – no! I am not sure if we will ever hear those words!" George remarked.

"Thank you for your positivity George!" James then sarcastically remarked as he sat and folded his arms across his chest.

"Look boys, I know that you have had many, many years of this to endure, but I do not think that I am doing too badly. I have managed to get some potential girlfriends here for you to meet; it's just a shame that no one can see you yet. I promise that we will find you someone!" I replied as I washed up.

"I have no doubt in your ability to do anything that

you set your mind to!" James then complimented me. I turned and smiled at him.

"Why thank you James. I honestly never start anything that I know I cannot finish!" I remarked.

"Well, that's good enough for me!" George said as he started to dry the crockery. I smiled at him and he gave me a wink back.

"Shall we retire to your day room, George?" James then asked as we finished.

"Yes, we shall. I think it would be nice to sit and talk before we retire for the night," George then stated.

I curled up in my usual large armchair near the fire and James sat opposite me. George served us mugs of tea in his lounge, and I was starting to feel more relaxed than I had in some time. It then occurred to me that the last time I had felt this relaxed was when I had last been here. I asked them to continue their stories from many years ago, and they made me laugh with many of them. They had a knack in particular of describing people; they created the most vivid characters in my mind.

After nearly two hours of tales from days gone by, I could hardly keep my eyes open and suggested that I should retire; sleep was much needed. James offered to walk with me to my room, and I was becoming more used to his image accompanying me now. He stopped in the mirror beside my door.

"Are you sure that you are well, Katharina? I have not known you very long, but it seems that you are like me, and are good at hiding the truth about how you really feel!"

"You are very perceptive, James. I am merely

disappointed. I never expected to find myself in the position of having to decide about my relationship. I always daydreamed about the fact that when I entered into a relationship it would be forever and I would love that person wholeheartedly and want to spend every day with them. It seems that this is not the case; I have allowed my love of fairy tales to make me believe that!" I answered honestly.

"Maybe the problem lies in the fact that you have not met the correct person to have a relationship with that will last forever?" he replied, smiling sincerely. "Do not give up so easily on love; after all, look where my disbelief got me!" he then said as he gestured at himself.

"I haven't given up on love, James, and I am sure that you are correct. Thank you, I find it very easy to talk with you," I truthfully replied.

"And I like to converse with you!" he then said as he stepped back. "I will bid you good night; sleep well and we shall see you in the morning," he then stated as I nodded and simply said:

"Good night James, I look forward to seeing you tomorrow." I went into my room and closed the door.

Chapter Seventeen

I woke feeling refreshed and as I stretched my phone bleeped. It was a text from John: 'Hey babe, have you come to your senses yet? The bed was empty without you here last night, call me!' I sighed and threw my phone onto the bed. It didn't surprise me that he was still blaming me for this whole problem; yes, I admit that buying this house was an impulse buy, but I love it and it was mine. The whole Nadine situation, however, was entirely down to him. Even if he hadn't slept with her, his intentions showed that he wanted to, which meant that he cannot be completely happy with our relationship.

I did not want to face ringing him yet, or texting. He had spoilt my refreshed feeling this morning and that in itself irritated me. I brushed my hair and teeth, then put my slippers on and went downstairs. As I approached George's kitchen door, I could hear him talking to James.

"Well I think it is a fabulous idea, James – let's ask her. If anything it will certainly cheer her up!" George said.

"I agree, and she has saved our home and us in more ways than one. I find her company most stimulating and the more I spend time with her the more I admire her!" James then replied. I raised my eyebrows in surprise; I had not expected to hear those words.

"She is quite something, isn't she? Well, do you want to see if she is awake? I have breakfast almost finished and then we can have a day of keeping her happy!" George replied.

"Of course!" James answered.

I panicked; I knew that James would be on the move and I did not want them to think that I had been listening in on them. I turned and ran back to the hall and then turned around and walked back as if I had just come down the stairs. James suddenly appeared and I think that I startled him more than he me!

"Katharina, I was just coming to let you know that breakfast was ready!" he informed me as I stretched and let out a little yawn, trying to look like I had just woken.

"Lovely, that was good timing then wasn't it!" I remarked as he gestured for me to walk toward the kitchen.

As I walked past him, I quickly glanced at his attire. He had very simple jersey pyjamas on and his feet were bare. I smiled at the fact that he looked quite normal. I like him looking slightly dishevelled; it gave him a relaxed look. I couldn't help but say something.

"Nice pyjamas!" I commented. He blushed and checked that they were straight.

"Likewise!" he replied as I then looked down at my silk pyjamas.

"Thanks!" I smiled as I walked to George's kitchen. I glanced back at him and he was smiling too!

"Ah, we look happy this morning!" George remarked as I entered with a grin on my face.

"I was just commenting how nice James' pyjamas

were! I have to admit they were not quite as I expected," I informed him.

"One thing we have learned over the years is that the clothing is much easier to wear – in particular bed clothes. They are far more comfortable than what we used to wear, although James does still like to wear his original shirts and trousers!" George commented.

"They make me remember who I am sometimes!" James quietly commented.

"I like your original clothing, particularly the shirts – I think that we have Colin Firth to thank for that in his role as Mr Darcy!" I answered.

"Jane Austen – yes, fine novels; she was a very interesting woman by all accounts!" George then commented.

"I would have loved to have met her!" I replied.

"Never met her, but James had friends that knew her!" George replied.

"Really? Wow, I bet that you have had the possibility of knowing some amazing people!" I replied.

"The possibility, and also the reality, of knowing some *very* interesting people," James then confirmed as George placed the biggest plate of breakfast that I had ever seen in front of me.

"Gosh, thank you George, this looks delicious."

"Well, after breakfast we can take a little walk around the garden and then we can have a day of game playing. Perhaps both James and I can teach you some new games that are old games?" George then commented.

"I like the idea of that. I'm not usually very good at games!" I replied.

"Before that, James has something that he would like to propose to you!" George then said as he looked across at the mirror. I took a sip of my tea and waited to hear what he had to say. For some reason, my heart felt like it was going to pound out of my chest.

"Yes, both George and I would like you to invite your friends and colleagues for a party here at Northfield for your birthday. It is very soon, is it not?" James enquired. I looked at them both.

"Really? I don't know what to say!" I replied with excitement.

"Say yes! It would be nice to see you enjoy yourself, and for once be the centre of attention. Besides, this house has been too quiet for far too long; some music and laughter would be well received," James finished.

"I would love to. It will be amazing to have a party here – but are you sure that you can cope with the newer music and the number of people in your home?" I quizzed them.

"It will be no problem, Katharina; we have held many parties here in years gone by and we can do it again. It would be our pleasure to do this for you. Besides, this is your home too, don't forget!" George then replied.

"Alright, it's a deal then. I cannot wait! Perhaps we should discuss when and then we can make all the necessary arrangements. I do not want this to be too much trouble for you, George," I then insisted.

"We can make some decisions today and then invite your guests. I am looking forward to the house being alive again!" George remarked. I turned and looked at James.

"Thank you. It has been many years since I celebrated my birthday so elaborately!" I told him.

"Again, it is our pleasure!" James then said. "I am looking forward to it a great deal!" he then announced. George smiled and took another sip of his tea.

As I finished eating and left to get dressed, I felt happier than ever. Who would have thought that I would part own a place like this, and be holding my own party in such a place? Whilst I dressed, I started to imagine all the things I would like to do; my head swirled with possibilities. Suddenly I heard my phone beep again. It was a snap back to reality; I knew it was bound to be John, and it was. 'You have not called me yet. I think we need to speak Kat, ring me please!' I scowled as I read and decided that it would be better to call him now, then I could spend the rest of the day enjoying the company of my friends and planning my party without any interruptions. As the phone rang, I sighed. I was not looking forward to this.

"Kat, hey babe. Why didn't you call me?" John asked.

"I'm calling now. I was sleeping!" I replied.

"So, how are you feeling?" he asked.

"Not particularly bloody great John, quite honestly. The more I think about us, the more I do not see where we are going. I know that I keep bringing Nadine up, but the way you look at her with lust is not the way you look at me. I just don't think that you are happy with us anymore and this purchase of mine has highlighted this all the more!" I honestly told him. I heard him sigh.

"Alright, maybe I need to come clean and be honest. I do find Nadine attractive, and we have been working

241

together a lot recently and spending more time together. I do not know what is wrong with me, my head is telling me it's wrong –" he started, but I jumped in.

"But your nether region is telling you it's right?" I snapped.

"I know that she has feelings for me, and she keeps throwing herself at me. I am so sorry Kat, it only happened once!" he then said very quietly.

"WHAT? *What* only happened once?" I shouted.

"That night you quizzed me about – I spent some of the evening at her place. I was very drunk and it meant nothing, I swear," he then confessed. By now I was furious.

"You made me out to be jealous, unfair and suspicious, and yet I had every reason to be! I cannot believe that you would betray me like that, you complete hypocritical jerk – and you have the nerve to tell me how to spend my money! I really do not think that there is any point in talking anymore; I have nothing to say to you right now. I will come and collect my things," I confirmed as I started to cry.

"I'm sorry Kat, I really am – I never wanted this to happen, it just did!" he was quick to reply.

"This proves how little you thought of us! Please don't call me; I do not want to talk to you ever again. You have hurt me in the worst possible way and I cannot forgive you John. We are finished!" I said as I then burst into hysterical, angry tears.

As I ended the call, I turned and hurled my phone at the wall without thinking. It broke into pieces. I leant against the mirror, slid to the floor and pulled my knees up tight to my chest. I placed my head on my hands and sobbed. Well at least I knew the truth now, and I was right – I did have reasons to worry. How could he do this to me? I knew that James and George must have heard me shouting, and I did not have to wait long for confirmation.

"Katharina?" a voice behind me whispered. "Katharina?" it asked nervously again. I turned and leant my head against the mirror and found James kneeling at my level. He was concerned. "What happened?" he asked. I laughed lightly and then replied:

"Well, right now I wish that *I* was a witch, because I would turn that ex-fiancé of mine into the rat that he deserves to be!" I replied as I continued to sob.

"What has he done?" he asked me, looking angry.

"Admitted what I thought. He has been having a relationship with a work colleague – a very intimate one! I can never forgive him. I have told him that it is over!" I replied. James held his head low and sighed, then placed his hand on the mirror close to me.

"If I could I would beat the scoundrel for hurting you! He does not deserve you, Katharina; he has no right to hurt you and treat you so. I am sorry that I cannot do anything more to help you, but one day he will feel the fury of my fist – I assure you of that!" he kindly said, then shouted for George. He appeared in quick time, so I knew that he had been nearby.

Before I stood up, I placed my hand opposite his on the mirror and looked at him.

"Thank you. You are nothing but compassionate toward me, and whatever your past faults were, I only see you as you are now!" I replied as George handed me a soft cotton handkerchief and helped me to my feet. James rose up at the same time and looked sad at my misfortune; I knew it was because he was seeing first-hand how betrayal from a man affected a woman. I felt sorry for him, having to relive bad past experiences through me.

"Right young lady, let us get you downstairs. You need a stiff brandy, a coffee and a slice of chocolate cake!" George then said, as a father would to a daughter.

It made me smile; he felt slightly like a father to me, and I knew that he felt like one to James, too, which is why James was so grateful for him.

They sat and watched me as I quickly drank the brandy that was put in front of me and then I picked at the cake. I had all sorts of things running through my mind that I wished I had said to him, but I realised that I had said quite enough for now. I looked up at them both and realised that they did not know what to say, and suddenly I felt guilty.

"Gosh… I seem to be nothing but trouble. I am sorry that you had to witness that!" I said gently.

"Trouble? You certainly are not, I do not want to hear you say that about yourself! You are a bright, kind and generous young lady who we love to spend time with. That fool should have treated you with the respect and love that you deserve… he is in all honesty a complete and utter imbecile!" George then stated with force. "Good riddance I say, what an idiot!" he then carried on, before James stepped in.

"Alright George, I think you have made your point!"

he said as he looked at me and mimed 'Sorry'. "I do have to agree with you, though, which is not usual George – well said!" he then finished, and without warning I started to laugh.

They looked at me and then each other, shrugged their shoulders and then looked at me again. I stopped and bit my lip.

"I am laughing because I agree with you too! He has lost the most important thing in his life by not thinking with his brain. He is an imbecile and although this hurts and I still feel raw, maybe this is for the best?" I stated as I stood with force. "Anyway, I started this day feeling excited and happy and I will be damned if he is going to spoil it. I will make it my duty to try and go to bed feeling in a similar mood!" I finished as I swigged the last of my coffee. James jumped up and George straightened himself.

"You are, I think, the most impressive woman that I have ever met. Your strength of character is remarkable and I commend you on that!" James then stated. I smiled, and then answered:

"Well, we said that we would take a walk, did we not, George? I think a little fresh air would be recommendable right now – although I am sorry that you cannot join us, James!" I replied, trying to be brave.

"It is of no matter; I shall await your return," James simply said.

"I think that you are going to have to get used to seeing a lot more of me, boys; it looks like I may be moving in with you permanently!" I then stated. "I hope that is not a problem?" I asked hopefully. George simply smiled.

"I can think of nothing I should like more, my dear!" he replied as he gestured for us to go to the entrance hall to retrieve our coats and shoes.

As George offered his arm and we walked down the front stairs of the entrance, I took a deep breath, closed my eyes and then exhaled through my mouth.

"Better?" George asked.

"Much!" I replied. "I can sincerely say that I think that the best is yet to come. I made a wise decision investing in this house!"

"I am glad to hear it!" George replied happily.

"You are both like family to me; I have not felt that in such a long time," I stated again. George simply grabbed the hand that wrapped around his arm and squeezed it. It was reassuring.

As we walked and talked, it was soothing. Although James could not be there, I felt his presence somehow. We sat and watched the birds fight for food, as the autumnal weather made the lawn come alive with the worms they flocked for. As we returned, I noticed the most beautiful purple flower with definite markings against a high wall.

"How beautiful… iris?" I asked George.

"Indeed, *iris unguicularis var* – very distinctive, and Margaret's favourite flower during the autumnal and winter months. It seemed appropriate to keep it!" George replied.

"May I?" I asked, looking to him to give me permission to break a stem.

"Please do," he gestured.

I thought that if James could not join us outside, I

would bring the outside in for him. If this was his mother's favourite flower, he should enjoy it too. After all, he had been more than compassionate toward me and my dilemma. I carried it carefully back to the house. As we entered, James sat patiently reading in the hallway. As we took off our coats, he enquired:

"Did we enjoy our walk?"

"Indeed, it was most refreshing!" George replied.

"I enjoyed the air more than I expected to!" I smiled as I walked to the table in front of James' mirror. "I did not wish for you to miss out so I brought you this!" I then stated as I laid the iris on the table, knowing that James would be able to receive the same on his side of the mirror.

He looked at the flower and then at George, who I could not see as he was behind me. James simply looked back to the table where it lay and then at me. "My mother's favourite!" he simply said. I smiled.

"Yes, I know. One of mine also!" I replied and then I took off my coat and walked toward George's apartment.

It did not take long for them to join me, and as quickly as I had put on the kettle and placed three mugs on the island, they were busy trying to keep me happy.

"So, tea and cards then?" George asked.

"That sounds like a good idea!" James replied.

I looked at them both and then admitted that I did not know a lot of card games. They both seemed to agree that this was a good advantage for them, as they were tired of cheating each other, and with that thought we retired to the large day room in the main house and the games and teaching began!

Chapter Eighteen

J ames and George made every effort to teach me poker, euchre, gleek and quadrille for most of Saturday and Sunday. Of all of them, poker was the easiest for me to understand, and it was quick. George had the funniest poker face, which was so easy to read; James played along, but all the while it was obvious that he could read him like a book. They moved onto backgammon, chess and snakes and ladders, which of the three was my childhood favourite. I was even happier when I won that game.

Before we knew it, the grand clock in the hallway chimed one and my tummy growled. I placed my hand upon it and smiled at them both.

"Never one to lose my appetite!" I remarked.

"Glad to hear it!" George replied. "Why don't you two sit and talk while I get some sandwiches and tea?"

"Are you sure, George?" I enquired; I did not expect him to chase around after me.

"Of course, you can think about your party!" he smiled as he exited the room.

I stood and stretched, then moved toward the window and looked out across the garden.

"I do not suspect you would ever get tired of looking at this view!" I stated.

"Indeed; we are very lucky. It would be nicer, however, to be able to experience the outdoors and the fresh air; I do so miss them!" James replied. I returned to the chair opposite him.

"Of course; goodness, I did not think of that. You cannot and have not experienced being outdoors since your confinement. I am sorry, I did not think!" I replied with sadness for him.

"George brings flowers and other things indoors to satisfy my irritation – as you did yesterday – so I get some benefit at least. It is amazing how one takes things for granted though, particularly once you realise you cannot have them anymore!" he informed me.

"I cannot imagine how difficult it must have been for you both. It is very cruel and I wish it would end!" I replied.

"Well, enough of feeling sorry for us. We have a party to organise and look forward to; what theme would you like to choose?" he then changed the subject. I sat more upright.

"Well, I would love to say something from your era, but knowing most of my friends I think that black tie and ball dresses would be more appropriate. It is very exciting, though, don't you think, me having a party here with two very much older gentlemen?" I teased.

"Hey, less of the old – I am only thirty! How old will you be on your birthday anyway?" he then enquired.

"I am catching you up – it is my thirtieth birthday also!" I raised my eyebrows at him in anticipation of some sarcasm.

"Really, you are not jesting? Not only is it your birthday, but it is a special one?" He seemed more enthused than I had thought.

"I am not joking, I am to be thirty – and, it seems, single and without a chaperone!" I then laughed.

"You will have me!" George then suddenly said as he returned with a tray full of sandwiches and tea.

"George, give the poor girl a chance. I do not think she would want to be linked arm in arm with an older person such as yourself all night!" James laughed.

"Well I am available should she need me! Did I hear that it is a special birthday?" he then asked.

"Yes, she shall reach the same age as I!" James then noted.

"What is the actual date of your birthday?" George then asked.

"September twenty-third!" I answered.

"That is only some three weeks away," George replied and then as I took a bite of my sandwich it dawned on me; "It has just occurred to me that your birthday is tomorrow is it not?" I asked James.

"Yes, but I do not choose to celebrate them these days," he replied.

"Rubbish, we will and you are! I have a meeting tomorrow until five but I will organise dinner and we will have a meal in honour of your birthday, when you officially will be 294 years old – I don't think there is a cake big enough for that many candles!" I joked.

"Yes alright, very funny!" he laughed. "On the plus side for me, though, you are going to keep ageing whilst I remain thirty until freed from this prison!" he then confirmed. I stopped eating and grimaced; that had not occurred to me either.

"That is not funny in the slightest! That's no good – we must make sure we have you out of there before this time next year!" I remarked. "I better get my thinking cap back on!"

"At least you are both not as old as me!" George then said, with disappointment.

"I don't think anyone could be as old as you George!" James laughed, and George jokily threw his linen napkin at the mirror. We all laughed. "Cheeky bloody imp! I could still get you across my knee and give you a good hiding if I had to!" he laughed with us.

"That's a worrying thought George – let us leave it at that!" James then replied.

We all laughed for a while; in the grand scheme of things, it was very much needed. John was unbelievably far from my thoughts; it was probably a protective measure of my own mind, but nevertheless it made things easier to deal with.

We discussed my party for some time and at length. They agreed with the dress code and asked what band I would like – which was exciting, as I had never had a real band before – but an amazing group that played a wide variety of songs immediately sprang to mind; I had seen them play at a friend's wedding. We discussed food, and I insisted that I would arrange a caterer I knew from many functions at work – and it was my party, so I could not allow them to pay.

The day finished better than expected, and as we sat and ate dinner I worked out the timings for getting to work the next morning. It was certainly going to be a different journey from here, so to be on the safe side I allowed an hour. George offered to drive me to the nearest train station, which would take me into King's Cross; this seemed the easiest option with the rush-hour traffic, not to mention saving the cab fare. As I bid them goodnight and walked to my room, again with James for company, I felt like I was meant to be here; was meant to have met George and James. One thing was for sure; I loved being here. We laughed a little as we climbed the stairs and I carefully tried to pry an idea of something I could get James for a gift, but he refused to divulge anything he liked; I suppose because he missed the reality of everything. I stopped at my door and thanked him again.

"It has been a great day despite the circumstances, and that is because of George and yourself, so thank you!" I kindly said.

"It has been a most enjoyable day for us to just spend time with you. Not to mention letting someone else see the humour of George's poker face!" he then laughed as he placed his hands in his pockets.

"Yes, that certainly was worth seeing!" I remarked.

"I am sorry that you had to experience such sadness and anger this weekend. I assure you that things will get better… they must. I need you… *we* need you!" he then said sincerely.

"I am not going anywhere, James," I replied as I touched the mirror. "I can think of nowhere on earth that I would rather be than here with both of you, and I am sure that you are correct – things will get better!" I replied honestly. I blushed as he stared directly at me, saying nothing for a moment.

"Right, I will let you get some sleep!" he then suddenly said, as if trying to remember why he was there. I nodded and smiled.

"Good night James, sleep well!" I replied as I opened my door.

"Likewise; I guarantee it will be a brighter day tomorrow!" he concluded, and then I closed my door.

I walked into my room and took off my knitted top. At some point during the evening, George had lit the fire in my room; it was a little cooler this evening, and the house was old, so it was well received after the cold day. I finally walked across and picked up the pieces of my phone, which had landed everywhere across the floor. I placed them on the dressing table and managed to retrieve my sim card and put it in my purse. That would have to be on my list of priorities tomorrow… how can you live in this day and age without a mobile phone?

It had been a long, tiring day, but I had been able to spend time with friends in a place that was now my home. I snuggled down into my bed and as I reached across to switch off my lamp I looked around the room once more. I congratulated myself once more on the best thing I had ever bought, and then happily drifted off to sleep.

Remarkably, on waking I felt very calm and content, which I was not expecting. It was as though a great weight had been lifted off me. I had not thought much about John – although if I did it still hurt deeply – and I had slept incredibly well. *There has to be something in that!* I thought to myself. I showered, dressed, went downstairs and felt a significant bounce in my step. As I entered George's kitchen, I found that I was the first one up and ready. It was only 7.30am, so I made scrambled eggs on toast for all of us and a large pot of coffee.

George came in yawning and fastening his cardigan buttons. He seemed a little startled to find that I had cooked breakfast.

"I thought that I could smell something delicious!" he announced as he sat at the island ready to eat.

"I feel remarkably well this morning, George, and I thought it would be a nice change for me to make you breakfast!" I replied with a smile.

"Well it is well received, and I am truly glad that you feel much better," he finished saying as James appeared in the mirror, seemingly in a hurry and still fastening his jeans buttons. I raised my eyebrows.

"Good morning James!" I spoke calmly as he ran his fingers through his hair to straighten it up.

"Good morning, I am sorry that I am late for breakfast!" he then said.

"You are not late James, I am merely early!" I then informed him with a smile, as I placed our plates on the island with a mug of coffee each.

"You made breakfast?" he then asked.

"I did!" I replied happily as he sat down. Then I smiled some more. After all the clothing that I had seen James in, simple jeans and a t-shirt had not been the first thing that I would have expected him to feel comfortable in. "New clothes?" I asked as I looked across at George. James looked down at himself.

"They are quite new; I felt it may make it a little easier for you if I looked like I belonged in this era!" he remarked.

"That is very considerate!" I smiled.

"I bought those for him ages ago – I was trying to bring him up to date, but he never wanted to wear them until now!" George then replied as he looked across and winked at me. I had to bite my lip to stop myself from laughing. James ignored our remarks and sat to eat.

"So this evening, would you like me to collect you from the station that I shall be dropping you at this morning?" George asked me. I finished the sip of my coffee.

"Are you sure, George? I don't want to put you out in any way!"

"It would be my pleasure. I like to drive whenever I get the opportunity!" he then said.

"In that case, that will be lovely. Shall I text you my ETA once I know?" I replied.

"That will be difficult without a telephone!" James then reminded me. I grimaced.

"Oh yes – good point, I will have to rectify that straight away." I took another sip of coffee. "First thing on my list when I get to work. I am sure that I can get one delivered to me this morning," I finished as I placed another forkful of food into my mouth. I was remarkably hungry this morning.

We all sat, ate and chatted, then George suddenly appeared with a small wrapped gift and a card. It had completely slipped my mind this morning that it was

James' birthday. George placed them on the end of the island and stepped back as James looked at him.

"I thought that we agreed not to do presents anymore, George, particularly since I cannot reciprocate!" he simply stated.

"I know, but it was something that I thought you would appreciate, and having Katharina here recently just confirmed it," George replied.

James turned to the reflected duplicate on his side of the mirror and slowly unwrapped the present. It was a picture of some sort, and he sat and stared at it for quite some time before speaking.

"I don't know what to say, George – it's very thoughtful!" he then said. "Did you do this?" he asked.

"Yes, well… after all this time I like to keep trying my hand at different things. Something that Katharina said about bringing the outside in made me think that it would be nice for you to see this place from the outside for a change. I am glad that you like it!" George happily announced.

"Indeed I do. Now I know what you were doing in the summer when you spent so many days outside! I thought that you had taken up walking!" James replied.

"May I?" I asked George, as I pointed to the still intact present on our island.

"Please do," James then quickly said. "It is very good!"

I slowly unwrapped the paper and turned the framed picture over to see that George had painted a small watercolour of Northfield. It had been done in the height of summer. The flowers were colourful, the grass lush and green, the trees and shrubs well pruned. Northfield's rich cream old stone glowed warmly in the sunlight. It was in its entirety a true likeness, and very good for a beginner. I could tell that George was secretly pleased to have this acknowledged.

"Wow George, I'm impressed. This really is a beautiful watercolour – well done!" I replied honestly. James smiled.

"Well, a good start to the day, and it is my birthday. I am here in my home – in a manner of speaking – and with my two best friends. What could be better?" he then declared.

"Hold that thought until after dinner tonight, James – I'm not the best cook, and the day may not end as well as it started!" I joked.

"I think that you underestimate your talents, Katharina!" he replied. I blushed.

"Right, let me get my things George. I do not want to be late on my first morning of being a single, strong woman in control of her life!" I said as I jumped to my feet.

"Right – I will be with you in a jiffy, just let me get the keys!" George replied, disappearing from the kitchen.

"Oh and a very happy birthday James!" I then sincerely said. He nodded in acknowledgement.

"Thank you, Katharina. I shall look forward to seeing you on your return, and I do hope that your day is vastly better than the last two!" he remarked.

"It can't be any worse!" I sarcastically replied.

"I would like to think not!" he grimaced.

"Right, off we go!" George then said, as he ushered me out of the kitchen like I was a small child.

"Enjoy your day!" I shouted back to James.

"Likewise!" he called back, but he did not come to the hallway mirror to say goodbye.

The ride to the station was not long at all; in ten minutes we were there. George parked carefully outside the station doors and I checked my make up in the mirror, then opened the door and reached back for my bags.

"Thank you George!"

"No Katharina, thank you. I feel that we have such purpose nowadays; I have not felt that for so long!" he replied with a kind smile. It made me smile too.

"My pleasure. I will get all the groceries and I will see you here later. Once I have my phone I will text you!" I replied, then I closed the door and walked in to get my ticket. I looked back to where George, like a protective father, waited until I entered the station before making an attempt to move. I liked the gesture; it was endearing.

The train ride to King's Cross was much quieter than my usual morning tube ride. It gave me time to think about what present I could get James – and also about what on earth I was going to cook. Me and my big mouth; I was good at the simple things – stir fries, curries, anything with chips and pasta – but I did not make a good gourmet chef! I decided to pick Claire's brain once I got to work. More importantly, what on earth was I going to buy James for his birthday? As I mindlessly wandered to the tube and then to the office, thinking about presents, I was shocked when I arrived at work and dropped my bag on my desk; I couldn't actually remember the journey from King's Cross to here! I must have looked preoccupied as Claire promptly returned with a steaming mug of coffee and placed it in front of me.

"Looks like you need this!" she said as I dropped to my chair. I took a sip and then looked at her keen gaze; she was waiting for an answer.

"Strange weekend; I argued with John, left my apartment, stayed at Northfield – John rang me and admitted he'd had an affair with Nadine, I'm cooking dinner for a male friend tonight and it's his birthday and I don't know what to buy him!" I stated in a factual way. Claire's mouth dropped open.

"Bloody hell, and I thought my weekend wasn't that great! Just backtrack a second – firstly, I always told you that John was an arse; secondly, I cannot believe that he has done that to you, you should cut off his –"

"Yes, I get the picture!" I quickly intervened, holding my hand up. Not a very pleasant thought on a Monday morning. "Thirdly…?" I asked, hoping she would continue.

"Thirdly… when you bought that big old place, was that only because of the hottie you can see?" she then asked. I had forgotten that I had told her about James, in that moment when a confession seemed appropriate after alcohol consumption.

"Maybe…" I simply replied. I didn't want to get back into that discussion again.

"Birthday with a male friend? Interesting! Would he be a very much older male friend?" she then asked, making the point that she was still on the subject of James. I placed my mug on my desk.

"Look," I whispered to her. "I know that you think I am crazy, but trust me I am not. I need to buy a present

259

for a friend that hasn't had much opportunity to get out recently… something thoughtful!" I hinted, hoping that she might have a good idea. She stepped back, looked at me and then placed her hand on her chin.

"Hmmm, let me see. Not been out in a while… not in prison, I hope?" she suddenly said.

"Well, kind of. Not in the way you're thinking!" I replied as I took another sip of coffee.

"It is the hottie, isn't it?!" she then said.

"Sshhhh!" I replied. "As much as I love you for believing me, Claire, I really do not want to have to explain myself to anyone else!" I confirmed with an authoritative tone.

"Alright!" she replied quietly. "If it was me, I'd say either a bottle of champagne – to share, of course – or a picture of myself in my best underwear. That would be sure to win him over!" she laughed. I removed my bag from the desk.

"Yes, very funny, thanks for that! We do not all have the rather distasteful idea of presents that you have!" I sarcastically replied.

"Let me think about it!" she laughed as she returned to her desk.

"Oh, and before I forget, can you ring down to IT and ask if they can arrange me a replacement phone this morning? I threw mine at the wall after talking to John!" I confirmed.

"Not surprised! Of course, I will get on that straight away," she answered.

The morning went considerably well. The IT department were very efficient and had appeared with a brand new phone, put my sim card in it and sorted all the necessary stuff to get me up and running in a matter of hours. As he handed it to me, he declared that I had twelve new messages and three voicemails. I knew straight away who they were likely to be from. As I was about to open the first message, a delivery girl arrived with a huge bunch of roses and asked for me. Rachel, at the end of the office, pointed my way. Claire looked at me and raised her eyebrows. The IT guy promptly left, telling me to let him know if I had any problems, and the delivery girl walked over, put the roses on my desk and asked me to sign for them. I took the card from the outer cellophane as she left and read it. 'Babe, I am so sorry. I love you, please forgive me X.' I growled under my breath, picked up the roses and gave them to Claire.

"Please get rid of these! Do whatever you want with them – bin them, have them, whatever – as long as I do not have to look at them!" I wanted them out of my sight immediately. How dare he still call me 'babe'? If he loved me, he would not have done what he did. Claire quickly walked away with them. I flicked open my messages again.

'I'm sorry.'

'Babe, please talk to me.'

'Please… I love you.'

'I'm an idiot.'

'It meant nothing. Forgive me?'

By the time I got to the sixth message, I had had enough, so I deleted the rest. He was an idiot. He seemed to have no idea about the concept of love, and I had no intention of talking to him ever again. I sighed and took a deep breath. If the voicemails were anything like the messages, I had the strong notion that I would probably feel sick, so I deleted those as well. If there was anything important from anyone else, they could call me back and I would explain that my phone had been damaged.

I walked to the water cooler to get a cold drink and as I did so Claire walked past me. She patted me on the shoulder.

"I'm proud of you. Keep being strong, you deserve better!" she quietly said. I smiled at her and took another drink.

"What are you doing?" I asked.

"Giving this poor plant a drink – it looks like it's at death's door!" she replied as she filled the pot with fresh water. I had a sudden amazing thought for James' present.

"Claire, you're a genius!" I replied as I marched back to my desk.

"I am?" she asked with confusion, then carried on watering.

Chapter Nineteen

As I made my way to Pulbrook & Gould on Sloane Street – the best florists that I knew – it was a bit of a fight through the lunchtime rush, but I knew it would be worth it. I picked up a sandwich and a birthday card and then walked into the most beautiful shop of colour, scent and visual stimulation. It would be very easy to spend a month's salary in here; the flowers were out of this world, and some were so unusual, unlike anything that I'd seen before. I made my way to a corner that displayed plants in fine porcelain and smiled when I saw exactly what I was after. After Claire's brief spark of inspiration in the office, I had decided to get James a Bonsai tree – a little of the outdoors-indoors, and he could trim it to shape as it grew. I decided that it would be a little project for him, and the specimens they had on offer here were divine. I selected a Chinese elm, which was just like a miniature beautiful elm tree, that was a few hundred years old. It was planted in a sage green rectangular pot. Along with the Bonsai scissors they sold me, I had the present sorted.

They carefully placed it in a special carrying bag and as I headed back to work I felt happy and relieved at my choice. I knew that James would know that I had thought hard about this present, and I also knew that he would appreciate it. Claire had popped to Harrods for a special gift for her mother's birthday and so hastily I asked her to get me three luxurious-looking desserts. I was going to do fillet steak, potato wedges and salad (a hearty man's meal) and I had already picked those bits up from the trusty Marks & Spencer when I had got my lunchtime sandwich. When I arrived back at the office, I quickly ate my lunch whilst Claire showed me the lovely silk scarf that she had purchased. She said I would love the desserts, but they were tied up in a box, so I had to take her word for it. She placed them in the fridge and stuck a post-it note on my computer screen to remind me to take them.

The afternoon moved on at a steady pace, and when Claire gingerly appeared at the side of me at four o'clock, telling me that John was on the telephone, I decided that I needed to speak to him at some point. I picked up the receiver and that horrible sickly feeling came back!

"John, what do you want? You know they do not like us taking personal calls at work!" I said calmly.

"Ah, thank God Kat. You haven't replied to any of my messages! I was worried!" he replied.

"Worried about what? The fact that I cannot bring myself to speak to you, or has it suddenly dawned on you that you have lost me?"

"Please don't say that babe. I am very sorry and I want things to go back to how they were!" he said hopefully.

"Well I don't! Jesus, John, things can never be the same again! I will answer your messages when I am good and ready, but until then you need to give me some space – okay?" I said with force.

"Okay, okay. I understand you need some time to cool off!" he said flippantly.

"*Cool off*?" I said, realising that my voice was now so loud I was attracting an audience. I lowered my voice and continued; "I will never cool off from this, John. Now leave me be – I will talk to you when I stop hating you so much!" I finished and hung up. I rubbed my forehead and then reached for my mobile; I needed to let George know what time I would be back.

'I will be arriving at Bexleyheath at 6.14pm. Would that be an acceptable time to have you collect me, George? I have quite a few bags!'

I felt instantly better for knowing that I was going home to George and James. I sighed and thanked God for my new family.

Once five fifteen had arrived, I started to tidy up my desk. I knew that I had plenty of time to get to the station and my official working hours were nine to five, but it was very rare that I left on time. Claire bounced across to my desk whilst re-applying her lipstick.

"Excited about the birthday tea?" she asked inquisitively.

"Actually I am! Oh, and before I forget, I am having a birthday party at my new house soon – I hope that you will come?" I told Claire.

"Really? Ooh, how exciting. What date? I am definitely coming to that! Can you introduce me to the hottie?" she then asked.

"Claire, I have explained that I cannot make you see him. You have to see him for yourself!"

"Yeah, yeah, like some magic fairy tale, I know!" she

sarcastically replied, making hand gestures. "So when is it and what are you doing?" she asked with excitement.

"The dress code is black tie and ball gowns, and I'm having a band and caterers. I booked the caterers this afternoon, actually!" I replied. "I have printed the invitations and I will post them tomorrow after writing the envelopes tonight; it is on Saturday 22nd September."

"So organised! It's your thirtieth, isn't it?" she then enquired

"Yes it is, but I do not want a big fuss Claire!" I pointed at her meaningfully. She smiled.

"Spoilsport!" she muttered. "Can I help with anything? Decoration, organising the house, picking out your outfit?" she inquisitively asked.

"Actually, it would be really nice if you could help with all of the above!" I replied, feeling glad that she had asked. "All the female company I can get at the moment would be an absolute bonus!"

"Brilliant, just tell me when. I am definitely free this weekend," she informed me.

"Great! Well definitely Saturday then, why don't you stay over?" I asked, hoping that James and George didn't mind.

"Oh my God, I would love to! Big house, interesting stories – so you keep telling me – plus the possibility of swooning over some handsome guy… and I get to spend time with you!" she excitedly chirped.

"Well, that's settled then. Saturday it is! I must get going or I will miss my train!" I replied as I put on my coat.

"Don't forget those bloody cakes. I went to a lot of trouble carrying those!" she then reminded me.

"I am going to get them now!"

"Goodnight Kat, have a good evening!" she called as she rushed for the elevator. I waved my hand in reply and went to the kitchen to retrieve the box from the fridge.

The tube ride was unusually quiet tonight, but maybe that was because I was travelling in the opposite direction, and earlier than normal. When I walked onto the platform at King's Cross, it was a relief to get a blast of cold air, even though it was filled with diesel fumes and food smells from the nearby restaurants. I had purchased a return ticket this morning and so I simply found a seat on the train – which was a novelty – and placed my bags on the one next to me. I smiled as I looked out of the window; what a refreshing change to my usual journey home. I was looking forward to getting out of the city centre, and to being welcomed back by George to my new home.

As the train slowly pulled away from the platform, I looked at my phone. There were no more messages from John – hopefully that meant he had got the message that I had no intention of speaking to him yet. I happily placed my phone back in my bag and relaxed into the seat for the twenty-seven-minute journey to Bexleyheath. Far more enjoyable than the hot tube ride. I knew that George would be waiting, as he had replied to my earlier message simply with: 'Yes, I will be waiting. Glad to see you are back in the world of technology!' It had made me smile.

I had to stop yawning as the train pulled in; having a seat on the train was the most relaxing way of travelling. I picked up my bags and made my way out of the station toward the car park. I had no sooner walked out of the front doors than George was there, asking if he could carry my bags. It was a very strange feeling, being waited on, quite chivalrously, but I had to admit that I liked it. George chatted the whole way home and asked about my day. I told him about John telephoning me and the outcome, but he seemed glad that it was not affecting me as severely now. As we drove down the driveway of Northfield I let out a small sigh.

"Happy to be home after a long day?" George asked, smiling.

"Yes, I am! I do love it here so much," I happily replied.

As we stepped out of the car and I reached into the boot for two of the bags, George gathered the other three and prompted me to go inside. It was fast becoming dull again, as well as dark, and the promise of rain seemed inevitable. I walked in and shrugged off my coat, and suggested that I change into something more casual while George took my shopping. James was nowhere to be seen, but I was glad of this as it meant that I could hide his present for a while longer.

When I returned to George's apartment, present and card in hand, they were, as always, chatting generally about things – one of them being my party, but I had to put a stop to that, for today was not my day! I walked in with feeling.

"Right, enough about my party. Today is all about you, James, and it is your birthday so come here!" I beckoned to him as I walked to the mirror in which he stood and prompted him to come nearer. As he did so I asked him to turn his face close to the glass; I kissed his cheek – not that he would feel it, but the gesture was there. "Happy birthday!" I then announced as I turned to the island and placed his bag and card there, ready for him to receive his reflected copy. George just smiled back at me as James took a moment to straighten himself, fidgeting for a moment.

"Thank you!" he replied quietly.

"That was unexpected; I've not seen him lost for words for a long time!" George chuckled to himself.

"Look I know you said you didn't want a fuss, but I wanted to get you something. This…" I said as I touched the bag, "… took some thinking about, but I decided it would be constructive for you to have a small project that I can keep track of, and at the same time you are getting a small part of something that you have not had in a long time!" I finished as I turned to him and waited, with my hands clasped hopefully together. George had now walked to my side, he leant on the island next to me.

"This is exciting!" he announced.

"Indeed. I was not expecting presents," James simply stated as he turned and walked to his version of the present. He slowly looked into the bag, and I was happy when a very large smile appeared on his face. He reached in, carefully pulled out the bonsai elm tree and inspected it with intrigue. "This is most beautiful. It is remarkable how it is nearly an exact miniature of an actual tree – like the ones in our grounds!" he continued as he turned it.

"Well, it's a little of the outdoors indoors; you did comment that you missed being outdoors. You need to love it and look after it, and as it grows you need to trim it to shape; there are special scissors in the bag. I am expecting you to approach the task willingly as something to keep you entertained!" I advised him. He looked in the bag and retrieved the scissors, then looked at me after placing it on his worktop.

"It is the most thoughtful thing that I have received in many a year – along with the painting from yourself this morning, George. Thank you, both of you; it is indeed a good birthday!" he smiled.

"Yes well just make sure you don't kill it, boy!" George sarcastically chirped as he carried on unpacking the shopping. I looked at James and winked, then turned to George.

"George, do not think that you are getting away that easily!" I said as I pulled the bonsai out of the real bag behind me. "You, my dear friend, are going to have the pleasure of looking after its twin!" I remarked as I handed it to him. James laughed heartily.

"Spoke too soon George!" he continued. "This is now indeed a healthy competition to see who has the best tree. I cannot think of a better present at all!" he finished.

I raised my eyebrows at George, who inspected the tree and placed it on the worktop alongside the scissors. Then he turned and hugged me and kissed me on both cheeks. "Thank you, it really is beautiful. James, I accept your challenge!" he quite adamantly replied.

"Oh dear, this may end in tears I suspect!" I replied as I started to get things ready. I had seen where George put the dishes away and so I started to prepare the food whilst they both bantered away at each other humorously!

Dinner was entirely enjoyable; it was simple enough but tasty – a good mixture of the basic food groups – and we all finished everything on our plates.

"Well, that was delightful!" George said as he patted his tummy contently.

"Yes, thank you Katharina. I also enjoyed that!" James replied.

"Well, it wasn't exactly the dinner of the century, but I decided something simple was the way forward," I finished as I sipped the last drop of my wine. George reached the bottle to refill my glass as I stood and went to the fridge to get out the desserts.

The neatly tied box was quite heavy and I wondered how many desserts Claire had decided to buy. I untied it carefully after retrieving three plates and when I flicked the lid back I grimaced a little at her choice, and instantly had a vision of her laughing to herself all the way home. She had chosen three crumbly pastry desserts, filled with fresh cream and strawberries with a rich glaze, with patisserie cream in between and chocolate drizzled across the top. All in all it wouldn't have been so bad, but they were all in the shape of love hearts! Not only that, but she had got them to stick a further chocolate heart on top of the pastry, that had 'Happy Birthday' in white icing written upon them. I could kill her; hearts would not have been my choice, but it was too late now!

"Is something wrong?" George asked.

"No, not at all – I do have a confession to make though!" I replied, still grimacing. "I asked Claire to pick these up for me whilst she was in Harrods and, I have to say, they wouldn't have been my first choice – she always was one to wind me up!" I finished as I started to place them onto the plates. Both George and James looked across, and then George smiled.

"I cannot see anything wrong with that choice!" he smiled.

I gave him an 'I know you are only trying to be nice' look, but deep down I was wondering what on earth James was thinking about the whole situation. Love heart cakes on his birthday... I suppose it could have been worse, although I wasn't too sure how at that moment! I blushed a little as I placed it on the end of the island and very sheepishly said:

"Well, happy birthday then!"

He raised his eyebrows at it, then turned to his reflected copy and picked it up. He promptly pulled the chocolate heart out of the top, read the writing and ate it immediately.

"A damn good choice I say!" he then muttered, with his mouth full, and with that I let out a small sigh and walked back to my chair with relief.

We all tucked in. It seemed a shame to break into the little masterpieces, but once you had tasted one mouthful, there was no going back. They may not have been the best choice in shape, but they tasted out of this world. Once finished, we washed them down with a very lovely bottle of red that George had selected. It was the perfect end to a perfect meal. I sighed and rubbed my tummy.

"I dare not even think about how many calories were in that!" I remarked.

"Who cares?" George says. "You only live once!"

"Hmmm, and in some cases once can be a bloody long time!" I remarked as I lifted my glass to James and simply said: "Cheers."

"I am curious about something that you said, Katharina," George then stated.

"Oh, what was that?" I asked inquisitively.

"You said that your friend Claire had picked these desserts, and that she was always one to wind you up. What did you mean by that?" he continued as he licked his finger. Now I blushed even more.

"Ah, yes, well I need to make another confession!" I replied tentatively.

"This is proving to be an interesting night!" James remarked as he refilled his glass.

"Claire kind of knows about this whole situation – you know, you, James, me…" I replied, guiltily. James stopped pouring and looked at me. George folded his arms across his chest and simply replied with:

"Right, well that's interesting."

"She will not tell anyone; she is a loyal friend. I must apologise, though; I did promise that I would only tell someone about the both of you if it was a matter of life or death. Unfortunately, on the night I told her we were both a bit drunk, I was mad with John and I was telling her how happy I was when I was here at Northfield… it kind of all spilled out and I am not proud of myself for breaking my promise!" I replied with feeling.

"And how did she take it? The truth does not always make believers!" George then replied.

"Actually, she was quite open-minded and believed every word I said. She is quite miffed that she cannot see

James, though; she keeps referring to him as 'the hottie from the portrait'." I raised my eyebrows at 'the hottie' as he went a lovely shade of scarlet. George tried not to laugh.

"Ah, so now I understand the heart-shaped desserts! She was trying to make the point that you are here with two gentlemen – one that seems to be causing a bit of a stir!" George gestured to James. I had to stop myself from laughing at James' obvious embarrassment.

"Well, she couldn't see me, so I cannot do anything about that! I presume she did not know about the situation when she came to dinner?" he then asked before taking a large gulp of wine.

"No, it was some time after," I confirmed. "Maybe I should have told her before she came – it may have helped!" I questioned.

"I think if you had, she wouldn't have come at all; she would have thought you were having some kind of breakdown or were on medication, and would have laughed at the idea of witches existing!" James replied again, now sounding a little angry at my divulging his torturous situation.

"James, that's a little harsh. If she believes Katharina now, why wouldn't she then? You need to stop being so judgemental about people!" George insisted. I could see that James was irritated by my telling Claire, I partly wished I had said nothing about it.

"James, I really do apologise. I know that you trusted me to keep this secret, and I did not expect to tell Claire, but I have to say that it was a relief to tell someone this amazing story!" I replied sincerely. "I do not want to spoil your birthday!" I then finished as I looked at him hopefully.

George turned and looked at James, whose posture then mellowed a little and whose face became less angry.

"I'm sorry. I just did not expect anyone else to believe what you were telling them. If you trust her to keep this secret, then I have no reason to be worried. This may give me a better chance, should she ever visit here again!" he then said hopefully.

"Ah, that's the other thing!" I commented. "She wants to help with my party – you know, decorations, dress, and music and so on – so she is coming over on Saturday to help me, and she is going to sleep here Saturday night. I hope that is alright with you?" I asked gingerly.

"Fine with me, the more the merrier!" George chirped quite happily. "It will be lovely to have people in the house enjoying themselves."

"I do not mind. It will be an interesting exercise to see if her knowing makes a difference!" James then stated.

"Well, even if she does see you, am I correct in thinking that you thought Claire was easily enthused into the likes of a giggling schoolgirl?" George laughed.

"Hey, this is my friend we are talking about!" I protested. James laughed.

"Yes, I do think it was something along those lines! I am sorry for the comment, Katharina; it seemed quite appropriate at the time," he replied.

"Well, it could be amusing, particularly if she ends up seeing you! The doe-eyed schoolgirl may be ever

apparent, if she thinks you are 'the hottie in the portrait'."
I laughed.

"What, pray tell, do you mean by that?" James quizzed me.

"Really?" I enquired. "Well, look at you, she is right; you are very handsome, and I know that you are a very polite, caring and considerate man who is extremely easy to converse with. What's not to like?" I asked, and then realised that I had just given my honest opinion of him! I blushed, turned from the mirror and then took a sip of wine, quickly thinking what I could say to change the subject: "Right, tidy up time!" I quickly stated and stood up. Neither of them replied. I took it upon myself not to look at either of them, and made my way to the sink.

"Here, let me do that; after all, you cooked. We can leave them to drain until tomorrow," George suddenly said as he appeared at the side of me. "Surely you have something that you need to be getting on with?"

"Actually, I need to put my invitations into envelopes and send out a few texts as I don't have some addresses," I replied, feeling glad that the subject had changed entirely. I retrieved them from my bag with my address book and then glanced quickly at James. He was silently watching me, and I suddenly felt very aware that I had revealed my feelings toward him without thinking. Now I was worried that I had jeopardised our friendship, but more importantly I realised that there *was* some spark there, and a connection that I had not wanted to admit to myself. I turned away and started to write the envelopes, but the room had become somewhat quieter.

Chapter Twenty

As I sat quietly folding invitations and writing envelopes, James and George chatted about decorations they had stored from years past. George felt that they would be appropriate for my party and suggested us going to the attic to find them after I had finished my task. I could not imagine what type of decorations they would be, but I did know that they would be amazing and of the highest quality. After sealing the last envelope and sending a text invite to the remaining acquaintances that I had no addresses for, I found that my glass had been refilled and George was sat opposite me.

"Finished?" he asked hopefully.

"Yes, I have. It is quite exciting – but I thought we were not going to talk about my party today, as it is James' birthday!" I replied.

"Enough of that!" James suddenly said. "Your birthday is far more interesting to talk about, and I have had the best birthday in many a year so I cannot complain." I smiled at his comment.

"Shall we go to the attic and see what we can find?" George asked.

"Yes please, that would be lovely!" I replied as we walked out of the kitchen. George carefully placed his hand on my back to guide me through the door.

The attic door was at the end of the same corridor as my bedroom. We had not been up there before, so it was a chance to explore another part of Northfield. We climbed the creaky stairs and George turned the light on using the chain that hung from the top of the ceiling. As the dark space filled with dim light, my mouth fell open. It was filled with many boxes, and things from years past; an old rocking horse, a fort – all James' toys, I presumed. Paintings, mirrors, old travel chests, swords, a box with pistols that looked like something from a Musketeer movie, small pieces of furniture, and boxes of clothing all jostled for space. I looked at George and smiled.

"Wow – it looks like there are many memories in here?" I asked him.

"Yes, many; some good, some not. These are the things we felt we just could not part with," he replied as James appeared in one of the propped-up mirrors whilst I touched the rocking horse's mane.

"You like that?" he asked.

"I have always loved rocking horses. I never had one as a child, but horses were always present in the stories my mother told me, and like any little girl I wanted the real thing. This would have sufficed, though!" I smiled as I ran my hand along its back.

"I certainly never wanted for anything. My parents – in particular my father – used to spoil me rotten!" James remarked, looking deep in thought.

"You were very lucky that you had a father who loved you so much and would do anything for you!" I replied, wishing that my relationship with my father would have been more like that.

"I was very lucky, and I miss him more than I care to mention, but I am sorry that you never had the chance to experience the same!" James then said. I shot a look at him, wondering how he knew. Then I realised that all that time ago, when I could not see James, he had heard everything that I had said to George. I gave him a half smile.

"You have experienced more love in that one relationship than most people do in a lifetime!" I remarked. He looked solemnly at me.

"As have you, it would seem, with your mother?" he replied, and then he gave me the warmest smile.

"Yes, you are right. Maybe that's enough for one lifetime," I stated with regret. I wanted more and I wanted to give more, but I knew in my heart that was never going to be with John!

"Here we are!" George suddenly said rather loudly. It made me jump and snapped me back to reality.

I walked over to the large box that he had opened. Inside were the most amazing decorations, made from feathers and wooden beads and painted in gold and white. There were fabric bows in luxurious velvet; as I inspected them, I was amazed.

"These are beautiful, George!" I told him.

"Yes, they are. They have not been used for a couple of hundred years – actually, probably not since James' thirtieth. This is not the only box; I believe there are another two or three others with Christmas decorations," he stated as he stood to look in the box that was underneath.

"Will they do, Katharina?" James asked.

"Are you kidding? If you are happy for me to use

them, I cannot think of anything I would rather have. They are truly beautiful!" I remarked, looking at a long garland of white feathers.

"Excellent!" he replied, looking happy.

"Well, tomorrow whilst you are at work I will get them all out and then we can see what we have!" George then said. I placed my hand on his shoulder.

"Thank you very much, George. I am starting to visualise my party even more now!"

We played cards and snakes and ladders and then at 10.30pm George stood and apologised for yawning so much, but said that he needed to sleep. We bid him goodnight and then I suggested it was probably a good idea that I do the same, but James asked me if I would have one last drink with him before I retired.

"Well it is your birthday, so yes that would be lovely!" I replied as I poured myself a glass of brandy from the decanter and one for James.

"Thank you!" he replied as I placed it on the table in front of the mirror. Then I realised that I need not have done; he had a reflected copy of the decanter on his side and could have quite easily poured his own.

I sat back into the very comfortable armchair and sighed. I was so content here and loved the opportunity to just relax and be myself. I took a sip from the glass and then realised that James was very quiet.

"So James, have you had a nice day?" He quickly looked up at me from his glass.

"Yes, indeed it has been most enjoyable; mainly because I had the opportunity to spend it with you as well as George," he sincerely replied.

"Oh, you are too kind!" I joked as I took another sip, but something in the way he looked at me made me realise that he was being very serious. "I too enjoy your company more than I can say. I am very happy here!" I told him. He smiled.

"I am glad to hear that. I have not been so happy in a very long time, and I know that it is because of you, Katharina!" he smiled. I felt my face flush and my stomach danced and tied itself in knots. This was crazy; I had just ended one relationship, so how could I find myself attracted to someone else so quickly?

"I am happy to know that my company pleases you. It would be slightly inconvenient if it did not!" I remarked sarcastically. He laughed and took a sip from his glass.

"I had simply forgotten how it makes one feel to be in the company of someone other than George – the company of someone you regard so highly!" he then said. I stared into his eyes and lost myself for a moment.

"That was a very lovely thing to say!" I said quietly after a few moments. "Do you believe in fate?" I then asked him.

"Yes and no. I believe fate was not a consideration when I was left like this, but I do believe there was an amount of fate that brought you here to me – to us!" James was being very open today.

"My mother always told me that fate was something that was predetermined for all of us. I never really thought about it that much until recently, but I agree – I have a strong feeling that something guided me to you. Perhaps I am like the fairy godmother in the fairy tales?

You know, the one who helps to solve everything?" I joked.

"Nothing would please me more than that being the truth, Katharina. It would be nice to be free from this hell. I watch you every time that you are here, and I realise that I am missing living more than I have thought about in recent years," he concluded.

"I would like to be able to shake your hand, James, so let us hope that fate did bring me here, and that soon you will be living on this side of the mirror with us!" I replied truthfully. Nothing would please me more at this moment than being able to hold him and inhale the scent of his skin! He was definitely doing something to me, and I had a sudden shot of nerves; right there and then, I realised that I definitely had feelings for him, and I wanted to be with him more than I can tell you. But I couldn't tell him that, could I? John was not even remotely on my radar at the moment either, which confirmed almost one hundred percent that he was not the man for me. Fate, I concluded, had brought me to James and stopped me from making a huge mistake with John. As I looked fondly at James I felt sincerely grateful for that!

Chapter Twenty-One

Tuesday and Wednesday were not the most constructive days at work. Our photographer was ill, which had delayed the story I was working on. Claire had been assigned to one of the other journalists for the rest of the week, and that did not help me one little bit; I could have really done with her help.

On Wednesday I moved sluggishly around the office, hoping for a little bit of inspiration, but all I could think about was James and I and my party, and I kept wondering how everything was going to pan out between us.

My phone beeped with a new message; it was John. I sighed heavily and read the text, which requested that we meet. I realised that I had to confront him at some point and let him know that I had no intention of coming back. I'd felt more myself in recent days than I had in a long time. All my time with John I had been trying to be something that he expected me to be, and I completely lost myself in the process. It was nice to be me again, and I was not about to give that up so easily.

I arranged to meet John on Thursday lunchtime. I was not looking forward to it, but it needed to be done. I had received a text from Charles stating that he was shocked and surprised by John's actions, but that he was certain it was a one-off and John loved me dearly. I wondered whether John had put him up to the task, but then realised that it did not bother me either way; I had already decided that John was not the man I wanted to spend the rest of my life with. I had simply slotted into a position that he was happy with, and adjusted myself to please him at a time when I was vulnerable and needed to be close to someone. I sat at my desk and tried to think about what had made me so attracted to John in the first place, but quite honestly nothing sprang to mind. I had a clear vision of where I wanted to go and what I wanted to do now, and Northfield was a very large part of my future plan.

When I arrived back home that evening, making my own way there, I felt slight trepidation about tomorrow's lunch meeting. I had had the time to reflect during momentary lapses at work, and I know that at some point in my past I had definitely loved John, but there was no denying that we had drifted apart and that work had become our primary focus. I wasn't quite sure where it had all gone wrong, but I suspected it was not long after his proposal, when he realised the magnitude of being attached to one person for the rest of his life. I kicked off my shoes in the hallway and wandered down to the apartment, feeling instantly happier at the sound of both of my favourite men laughing. As I pushed the door open, I shrugged off my jacket and perched on the chair.

"Please can I have a glass of wine?" I pleaded as I rubbed my hands across my face.

"Bad day?" George asked.

"Long day, and quite honestly tiresome! Claire has

been assigned to another journalist for the week and I cannot seem to get my head into gear," I replied despondently.

"Is there any reason for this lack of concentration?" James enquired as George placed a large glass of red in front of me. I held up one finger, signalling him to wait, and took a large sip. It was smooth and velvety and heavenly to the taste buds. I sighed with delight.

"I had a message from John asking me to meet him. I cannot hide forever and so I have arranged to meet him tomorrow lunchtime. Not the nicest thought!" I remarked. James looked slightly agitated at my reply and George said:

"Would you like me to come with you?" I laughed a little.

"George, that's so sweet, but this is one battle that I have to conquer for myself!"

"Alright, but you know where I am if you need me!" he replied, smiling.

"Likewise!" James then stated. "Not that I can do very much!" He looked annoyed at himself.

"Boys, thank you, but I will be fine. The sooner I do this the better; then I can get on with my life."

"Cheers to that, what a good positive attitude!" George then said as he raised his glass. We chinked and then I took another large sip. "Hungry?" he then enquired.

"Starving!" I replied happily, knowing that the lovely smell radiating around the kitchen was bound to be from something delicious.

Rich steak pie with potatoes and vegetables was our

dinner tonight, and as George placed the plate in front of me my tummy rumbled loudly. I placed a hand on it.

"Gosh, my tummy loves being here as much as I do!" I remarked. They both laughed. "I think we are going to have to talk about salad, George; if I keep eating these amazing meals, I am going to grow to the size of this house!" I said as I then placed a piece of meat onto my tongue. It was delicious.

"Rubbish; I am not eating salad on a regular basis – it is not the best source of energy! Besides, it will not harm you eating such food, you have been working hard all day!" he added. I gave James a look of 'well that told me' and he laughed before continuing eating.

We had a quiet night of reading in George's lounge. It was entirely refreshing not having the television on, and instead just listening to the crackling fire. I had had a warm bath and was happy to be in my pyjamas and dressing gown, doing something I enjoyed – it was a much-needed change. I yawned heavily at ten o'clock, as I finished my book, and stood up and stretched. It still amused me that every time I moved, James stood. I was most definitely not used to the chivalrous gestures that he kept displaying, but I did love them.

"Gentlemen, I am very tired and so I am going to retire a little earlier tonight. I need my beauty sleep!" I concluded jokily.

"I doubt the latter; you are quite exquisite enough!" George kindly said as he stood and kissed me on both cheeks.

"You are far too good to me, George!" I remarked.

"May I see you to your room?" James asked. I nodded in agreement.

As we walked the long corridor to the hallway and I retrieved my shoes, I stood and looked around. "I still find it hard to believe that I partly own this place!"

"It is quite something, although a little unlived-in at the moment. Perhaps we should use some of the other rooms now that you are here? It would be nice to be able to spend more time in them; I do love George's apartment, but I miss being able to enjoy the main house," he remarked as he looked around. "So many memories!"

"You know I would love that. I have always felt very fond of the day room in which George and I first conversed; it is very opulent."

"I agree entirely. So I will speak with George and we can start retiring into that room in the evenings if you so wish?" he suggested as we walked up the stairs.

"You know, as long as George doesn't mind, or think that we are not fond of his apartment, I would really love that. I do not want to make more work for him, though!" I replied, thinking that George had enough to look after.

"I am sure that George will not mind; he has commented regularly on the lack of use of the main house. I hope one day to be able to be a part of it again," he said with sadness.

"As do I!" I simply replied as we arrived at my door. "I have had a lovely evening, so thank you!" I said as I turned the large doorknob.

"You are entirely welcome!" he replied with a large smile. "I do hope that you rest well!" he then said as I entered my room.

"How can I not, in such a magnificent room? It's more relaxing than I can tell you!" I replied with as large a smile as I could give. He simply nodded and turned to walk away.

As I got into bed and pulled the plump covers up to my chin, I let out a large sigh of contentment. I thought about my mum, and I knew that she would be so happy that I was trying to help both James and George. I was also positive that she would be proud of me for standing up to John. I missed her so dearly, but also felt like I had adopted a new family and home. It just felt so right – like it was meant to be – and I was happier than I had been in a long time. I smiled to myself and replied to a few texts – one specifically from Claire, asking if I was alright – and then I set the alarm and drifted into a most peaceful slumber.

I bounced down the stairs the next morning, feeling completely refreshed and ready to get my head into gear at work. I had deadlines, and Claire or no Claire I had to pull my socks up and get on with it. I had renewed inspiration and a fighting ambition back in me this morning, which I think was mainly to do with the fact that this was a new beginning for me – firstly by getting John to understand that I could not even begin to think about spending the rest of my life with him. I had a brief sudden thought about the fact that John had very probably been spending time consoling himself with Nadine, and I shuddered quickly and then snapped myself back to reality. Very soon it would not be my problem anymore, and I could focus my precious time on James and George entirely. I smiled and waltzed down to George's apartment, but found that he was not there as usual. I made a coffee and got myself a bowl of cereal; when James appeared, I offered to make him a coffee too, as he looked tired.

"Are you alright? It's strange not to meet George first thing in the morning!" I pointed out.

"Yes, sorry we are perfectly fine – we spent most of the night chatting!" he then replied.

"It's good that you both still talk in depth!"

"It is, but when you retire at 3.30am it's a tiring start!" he replied, straightening his shirt and then running his hands through his hair.

"Gosh, I'm so sorry – that would probably normally not happen if it wasn't for me and my trials and tribulations!" I remarked.

"Absolutely not! We talk regularly until well into the early hours – after all, what else is there to do!?" he then tried to reassure me as he rubbed his face numerous times.

I placed the coffee at the end of the counter and no sooner had I returned to my seat than the reflected copy was there waiting for him. He turned, took a long sip and then sighed.

"Coffee, it has to be said, is quite medicinal when you're tired!"

"It works for most people!" I commented as he continued to drink. "Has George decided to sleep in this morning?"

"George, I fear, would be devastated to find that we are helping ourselves this morning. He does take his role very seriously and that usually means him being in control. I do worry that he is getting weary though so a rest will do him no harm!" he kindly said.

"I love the fact that you care for him so much!" I remarked. He smiled.

"He is all I have left of my family! He *is* my family!" he then said. We both continued drinking and I ate my cereal. I felt I needed to get moving and with George not being around it made the transition a little quicker. I stood and quickly washed up my crockery, then turned and looked at James.

"Well, wish me luck! It's a busy day for me today!" I stated, trying to sound positive. He stopped for a second and then looked at me as he placed his mug back onto the island.

"Yes, I hope that you do not feel too upset about the impending meeting with your fiancé?"

"I feel quite confident that after today I will be moving forward. Fiancé, I know, will be a long-distant word! That, I feel, is a good thing!" I replied.

"Well I hope it goes well for you!" he replied.

"Me too!" I said as I stood taller and straightened my clothes. "I will see you tonight, and I hope that George feels well rested when I get home."

"I am sure that George will be back to his old self upon your return this evening," he then said as he gestured for me to walk to the hallway.

I retrieved my work things, put on my coat and then realised that George usually took me to the station. I turned and looked at James and he raised his eyebrows in question.

"I have no George to take me to the station!"

"Of course! How silly of me!" He raised his hands in acknowledgement of the obvious. "Please take the car and park it at the station; George should have no need for it today." He pointed toward the keys on the hallway table, resting in an intricate glass bowl.

"Are you sure?" I asked.

"Indeed, please do; it will make your journey easier!" He smiled.

"Okay!" I replied as I picked up the keys and simply stated, "Fingers crossed then!" I took a deep breath and then opened the main door to a brisk hard wind.

"I wish you well today!" he then called and I smiled and left before I changed my mind.

Remarkably I found a parking space with ease, and the train journey into work was hassle-free. It was a good start to the day, I felt; it was necessary to remain as calm as possible until my meeting with John, I did not want to cry, raise my voice or become anything resembling a raging woman scorned. I had decided that I wanted to rise above the hurt, torment and embarrassment and just lay down my thoughts and opinion of where our relationship lay.

Work was actually quite satisfying. I threw myself into it, most probably to keep my mind from anything else. When people in the office started moving around and putting on jackets, I realised that the inevitable had arrived – it was lunchtime – and so I stood and put on my coat, retrieved my bag and quickly told Claire where I was going. She could not have been happier; she had never had a lot of time for John. She was extremely busy and so had decided to continue working and eat on the go. I slowly made my way to the small bistro near to work that John had agreed to meet me in. At least if things got too difficult it was a short journey back to the office.

As I turned the corner and tried to breathe in and out deeply, whilst running through what I wanted to say, I peered through the window to see if John was already there. As I suspected, he was sitting at a seat near the window, looking very nervous. I felt remarkably better. I had not expected him to be so anxious; usually he was so sure of himself. It put me at ease, and as I walked through the door, I mumbled to myself: "Here goes."

Chapter Twenty-Two

"You're here!" were his first words.

"Did you expect me not to be?" I asked with annoyance. I thought that I was a more reliable person than that! He poured me a glass of water.

"I'm... I'm just surprised is all!" he then stated hesitantly.

"Well, I am here, John, so let's get this over with!" I remarked, hoping this wasn't going to take long. Three months ago, I would have fallen apart, but with renewed enthusiasm in something I believed in, it felt remarkably easy!

"What can I say? I made a huge mistake – a stupid mistake. I am an idiot and it meant nothing. However, you didn't help, did you?" he then said. I shook my head and then raised my eyebrows.

"I'm sorry, how is this my fault?" I asked, reasonably.

"Well, you're not exactly easy and then you go and buy a completely inappropriate property with all of our money. What am I supposed to think?" he said. That was it, right there, right then – I realised how shallow he was. I laughed.

"John, let me point out the obvious to you – you proposed to me; I accepted because I loved you. You proceeded to enter into a relationship with a work colleague, which in your eyes was obviously satisfactory, even though you were engaged. It is not 'our' money, it is 'my' money, and I will spend it how I choose, whether you like it or not. After your recent behaviour I really do not think that you have any say in the matter, do you?" I asked with conviction. He stuttered:

"I didn't mean to have a relationship with someone else!" he shouted. I looked around the bistro, realising that others were listening in, and beckoned for him to come closer.

"But you did, which says how little you thought about me!" I replied in a whisper. I pulled out the ring that he had given me. "This unfortunately is where I give this back to you, because quite honestly I don't want it anymore!" I then finished as I placed it on the table in front of him.

"Can't we talk about this?" he pleaded, and suddenly I felt at ease.

"No! We can't! We're done! So I wish you well, John, with Nadine or whoever else, but that's it!" I replied with confidence. He rubbed his head.

"It's your birthday next week. I'd hoped that we would spend it together!" he then said. "And did I hear you're having a party at that house you bought?"

"Northfield, John! Get used to the name because I am not selling it. Yes I am having a party there and I am sorry to say that you are not invited!" I happily said as I stood. "I really don't feel like lunch. I think we're done!" I finished as I put my coat on and started to leave. John stood up quickly.

"That's it? After nearly two years, you have nothing

else to say to me?" he asked. I tied the belt on my coat and turned to him.

"I don't think you have the right to ask me that, do you? Surely you knew this was coming? I'm not some pushover, John! Enjoy life, but I'm not coming back, so move on! I will be over to collect some more clothes this weekend, and will arrange moving anything else that is mine soon." I pushed open the bistro door and the wind that hit my face felt like a gentle pat on my cheek to say well done. I was happy and I walked away, feeling like I had achieved a great deal of self-respect.

As I walked past a wine bar I often visited, I felt the sudden need for a celebratory drink, so I entered and spoke to Hamish behind the bar and asked for a shot of his very best brandy. It was heavenly, and as they sold liquor I bought a bottle of it to take home. Celebrations were in order!

When I returned to work, Claire was eyeballing me from the conference room, which had glass walls, and I knew she was happy to see that I was not crying or upset in the slightest. At the first opportunity, she was out of that room and at my desk.

"I am so proud of you!" she said as she hugged me. "How do you know I did the right thing?" I replied.

"If you hadn't, you wouldn't look this relaxed with your situation!" she replied, raising her eyebrows at me, hopeful that she was right. I nodded.

"Yes, it went better than I expected – that's it, I am officially rid of him!" I replied. She hugged me again and jumped around a little.

"Yes!" She shot her arm in the air. "We are going to

have so much fun this weekend! Plus you get to make puppy eyes at 'the hottie'… and before you say anything, I don't even give a crap if he's real, because he sounds bloody perfect!" she then stated. We both laughed heartily.

I arrived at the station that evening with a spring in my step. I got to drive home in a lovely Range Rover, which was a treat in itself – even if the car was a little larger than I was used to. As I turned into my driveway, the house was lit and looked so inviting. I pulled up by the main steps and got out of the car, and before I knew it George was at my side.

"Katharina, I am so pleased to see you looking so happy this evening!" he said as he kissed me on both cheeks. "Can I take it from the happy look on your face that things went as well as could be expected today?" he then asked. I turned to him and passed him my heavy bag as I grabbed my handbag and shut the door, and then smiled.

"It was far better than I could have imagined and I am happy that it is over with!" I replied as I touched his arm. "Can I take it that you are feeling well-rested George?" I asked hopefully.

"Indeed I do – I am so sorry that I missed you this morning. It seems after long conversations with James on regular occasions, my body cannot distinguish between night and day sometimes!" he remarked. I smiled.

"So it would seem that we are both feeling much better then!" I replied as we happily went up the stairs and entered the house. We were busy chatting when James suddenly spoke.

"Well, this is a pleasant surprise, you are remarkably chirpier than I had anticipated!" I turned to him and smiled.

"You know James, it was easier than I expected, and I feel remarkably relieved about the whole thing!" I replied. He smiled in return.

"I am glad to hear it!" he then said as I moved closer to the mirror. I stared at him for a moment and then he smiled more, and I realised that I was just staring at him.

"I bought this as a celebratory drink. I'm sure you've tasted far better over the years, but this is really good!" I then stated as I lifted the bottle I had bought in my hand and gestured to it.

"Nothing like a good spirit!" George remarked as he appeared at the side of me.

"I agree!" I smiled. I linked arms with him and we walked toward his apartment.

"So, we are having chicken this evening. I have not done anything elaborate, so please do not expect perfection!" George confirmed.

"Everything that you do is delicious, George, and it means that I don't need to cook, so I'm more than happy – I would be satisfied with beans on toast!" I smiled back at him.

"Point taken!" he nodded.

As I poured three glasses of the fine brandy and passed one to George and placed one on the end of the island, I looked into my glass, trying to think of the appropriate toast, and then it dawned on me that it need not be complex. I looked at them both, raised my glass and simply stated: "To new beginnings!" They both looked at each other and then at me and repeated the toast, to which James added "and happier futures". I smiled in agreement at his toast and finished the rest of the brandy. I banged the glass down.

"Whoa, I needed that. I have a very strong notion that I am going to get very merry tonight!" I then informed them. James raised his eyebrows.

"Why not? I will join you... George?" he then invited.

"Well, I will try and keep up with you, but I am not promising that it will be a pretty sight!" he laughed.

"That's settled, then... you share that bottle and I will start on this one!" James then stated as he lifted up the replica bottle of brandy on his side of the mirror.

"I like this game, and I love that our bottle will last longer! It really is quite ingenious, this spell, and on the odd occasion it has its uses – as well demonstrated tonight!" I pointed out as I poured myself another glass. George looked at James.

"She does have a point! I think you would have drunk this house dry many years ago if we had to share!"

"You make me out to be some type of alcoholic, George!" James replied, slightly annoyed.

"Hey, we have had plenty of years of drinking and downed too many bottles to mention; probably more than one ship could carry. Between us – and in particular you – we haven't done too badly!" George answered, tongue in cheek.

"As much as I would like to differ with you, George, I believe there is some truth in what you are saying!" James then said.

We all laughed and talked, and I helped George get dinner ready. We were eating in the main dining room tonight, which was a thrill. The fire was ablaze and the room glowed; it was like being at a dinner party with friends of Mr Darcy, in their very opulent and grand home. The only difference was that this was *my* home! I was content with the feeling that George and James accepted me like I was family; and I was so relaxed around them. I was more than happy right now, and we talked throughout dinner, reminiscing on past things and discussing future opportunities. The wine kept flowing and I knew that I was getting merrier by the minute, but I still felt the smallest bit sad… for James. I stood and walked to his mirror after I had finished the last drop in my glass and poured the small amount left in the bottle.

"I really do wish that you could join us on this side, James!" I stated with complete sincerity. "You are, after all, the man of the house, and I am the lady of the house; it does not seem fair that you cannot participate wholly! I do hope that you can sit opposite me some day!" I then said before blushing. Those famous words 'in vino veritas' suddenly sprang to mind. "I probably should not speak my thoughts so loudly!" I then said in haste as I grimaced at myself. "I do not expect ladies of your era would have said so much?"

"It would certainly have been more interesting if they had!" he smiled. "I hope for the same someday Katharina; it does tie one's stomach into knots, only being able to watch you and George and not being a physical part of the fun and amusement! I would be more than pleased, if I was ever released from this prison, to join you, but for now just having you here with us is more than satisfactory!" he finished. I realised now that he had moved closer to the mirror and I was addicted to staring into his beautiful eyes; they made my insides somersault, which in turn made me feel a little bit nauseous (too much wine!). I raised my glass.

"To having you here with me – and George – on this side of the mirror!" I said as I took a sip from my glass. I did feel like I was swaying slightly now!

"Hear, hear!" George then suddenly said, and I turned and looked at him. He was smiling at the two of us, and then he turned back to the table. He did seem somewhat amused by something and then I realised that it was probably my inability to retain alcohol well in any volume! I took the decision to sit back down.

After dinner, we retired to the day room, where again the fire was lit. James had promised that we would use the older rooms of the house more frequently, and he was a man of his word, it seemed.

"Wow, I really do love this room!" I stated as I sprawled myself on the chaise longue in a not-very-ladylike manner. Thank goodness Jane Austen was not here to see me behaving in such a way… I do not know how she would even start a story about this fairy tale! The thought made me smile.

"I think that I will go and make some tea. That's enough for me for tonight!" George happily announced as he left the room. I sat up and immediately put my hands to my head and closed my eyes.

"Ooh, head rush! I think I may have to slow down

myself. Am I slurring my words yet?" I asked James. He laughed.

"You have been for some time. You are still understandable, though, if that makes you feel any better?"

"Oh marvellous, my first night of being single and I act like an inebriated fool!" I concluded, leaning back against the chaise longue.

"Well, fool is a little harsh; you are simply happy, Katharina. However, I prefer the word 'inebriant' to better describe you!" James then said. I opened my eyes and looked at him.

"I think that's the same thing, James! Gosh, I know how to make an impression, don't I?" I laughed.

"Hardly the same; my interpretation of the word 'inebriant' toward you would be 'intoxicating'," he then said, with such delicacy and feeling that I felt immediately sober.

What was he implying? That he found me intoxicating, as in suffocating – like being under the influence of alcohol all the time? Or intoxicating like a drug that he could not live without? I sat and looked at him and felt lost for words; he in return looked at me with reservation, waiting for a reply. I waited a minute or so before speaking.

"Well, that's nice – I think! I cannot say that I have ever been called intoxicating before. It could have many meanings, I am sure, but I will choose to take it as a compliment!" I replied. I am not sure how I managed to get those words out, as my fuzzy head returned with added force.

"I am pleased, as that was my intention!" He smiled the warmest, coyest and slightly little-boyish smile and I melted… thank goodness George returned at that moment with the tea.

"Right, tea anyone?" George asked. I raised my hand like a schoolgirl and then realised that I must look ridiculous – so I started laughing, and unfortunately for some time could not stop!

I sipped the tea and then had another cup, and then as gracefully as I could – and with every ounce of effort – I stood up, swayed a little, reached out and caught my balance on the top of the chaise longue, then realised that both of them had stood too. I pointed to them both in a drunken, roundabout way and then raised my finger up.

"I…" I declared loudly, "… am going to go to bed and get some sleep before I fall over or start drooling across the cushions."

"May we walk you?" George then asked.

"I think, should I be okay!" I replied as I moved. As I stumbled, George caught my elbow. "That didn't come out in the right order!" I chuckled. "I haven't been this drunk in ages!" I then said as I flung my arm out and caught George on the cheek, which made me laugh even more.

"Right young lady, definitely time for you to retire!" George smiled as we started walking to the hallway.

"Indeed, we do not want you to injure yourself by falling!" James then stated. As soon as he said it I felt sick; I suddenly realised that in his world no woman in their right mind would become so intoxicated in front of any man. I started to mumble.

"I am so, so, so sorry! How could I let myself get like this in your home? You must think me vulgar and rude and completely ridiculous. No woman has probably ever embarrassed herself in front of you before by drinking so much alcohol!"

"I am fast learning that any woman I knew in my era had not lived very well by not experiencing the same as gentlemen. I do not find you embarrassing, ridiculous or any of the things that you seem to think of yourself. Need I keep reminding you that this is your home too?" James kindly replied.

"Really?" I asked hopefully as we reached the corridor to my bedroom.

"Indeed, I do in fact find it – in a demonstrative way – amusing!" he then smiled, trying not to laugh. "Please George, I am sure that you agree with me?" George pulled a face and bobbed his head from side to side a couple of times.

"Yes, I have always loved women that know how to enjoy themselves, and I have to agree with James – this is quite enjoyable for us!" he concluded as we reached my door and walked into my room.

"I hate you two ganging up on me!" I joked as I mock-punched George's arm and then fell backwards onto the bed laughing. "You are not going to see me like this again!" I then said once I stopped laughing.

"Oh, I do hope we will!" James remarked as I sat up and looked into George's eyes; he was knelt before me, taking off my shoes.

"No one has removed my shoes for me before!" I sighed as I watched George. "I really do love you two like family!" I then said meaningfully as I poked George in the chest to reinforce the statement. "And I have to confess that sitting up quickly has made me feel very nauseous and the room is spinning!" I then finished as I tried to focus.

"Okay, I think it is time for you to lay down and sleep," George insisted as he pushed me onto the pillow and covered me up fully dressed. "Goodnight!" he then said. I waved my arm in the air for a second in response, and that was all I remembered until my alarm scared me nearly half to death the next morning. I woke with a hangover from hell and stuck my head under the pillow, groaning and hoping that I could stay put for the rest of the day! As I lay there, trying to determine whether my head or my stomach hurt more, I groaned and asked myself why I drank so much. A quiet voice sounded behind me.

"Dare I ask how you are feeling this morning?" James enquired. I moaned some more and then turned and sat up, looked down at myself fully clothed and realised that I probably had hair that looked like I had been dragged backwards though a hedge. Worse, I knew for sure that I had not taken off my make up the night before, so it was more than likely smeared across my face. The more I thought about last night, the more unsure I was of how I actually got to bed! I pulled my knees up and rested my head on them, sighed and then looked at James in the mirror opposite the end of my bed.

"Oh sweet Mary and Joseph, I think I have been possessed this morning!" I replied sarcastically.

"By an intoxicated demon?" he remarked, trying not

to laugh, and as soon as he said that, little snippets of conversation started to pop back into my mind.

"Ha ha, yes, I am sure that this is amusing you no end! I feel like I drank a bar dry last night!" I remarked as I threw myself back onto the bed, arms outspread, and closed my eyes. 'Intoxicated' – that word was ringing a bell in my mind. I tried to block out James' light laughter.

"I think it is safe to say that you had more than usual last night, but, as bad as you feel, it was nice for George and I to see you so relaxed and so yourself. I hope that you are still ready to start the day as a new beginning?" James then asked. I forced myself to sit back up, trying to ignore the room spinning.

"I am indeed ready to start today positively, regardless of how hungover I am. I hope that I did not say anything out of turn last night?" I replied, whilst rubbing my face, then realised that I had mascara on my hand. "Oh great, and that is probably why you are laughing – I bet I look a real sight this morning!" I sighed.

"You look very vulnerable, but I would not say that is a laughing matter – quite the contrary, I wish that I could make you feel better! I merely laugh because you make me feel happy; I love the fact that you can laugh at yourself and that you find yourself comfortable enough in our company to completely let yourself go. It is a quality that I like very much!" he said sincerely. I smiled.

"You say the sweetest things to me, James, and I love that you make me feel so relaxed here. What time is it? I need to get ready for work!" I then stated.

"I think you will find that George is on his way up with something medicinal – and breakfast I believe!" he then informed me. No sooner had he said it there was a knock at the door.

"Come in!" I shouted as I started laughing at my misconduct the night before.

"Good morning young lady, and how are we feeling this morning?" he enquired. I grimaced a little.

"Young lady? That name brings back remnants of last night! I still feel that I am slightly out of control of my body this morning due to the effects of alcohol, George!" I laughed. "And before you say anything, I must apologise to you too for any inappropriate behaviour!"

"You have no need to apologise, Katharina; you were quite in control of your faculties – with the exception of a little swaying!" he smiled.

"Oh dear, this is not sounding any better. I do find I am remembering little things now!" I shuffled back up the bed to sit up as George walked around to my side of the bed.

"Here we are; Alka-Seltzer, tea and toast!" he happily announced as he placed the tray on my legs.

"George, you are far too kind to me!" I replied as I smiled at the tidy arrangement. There was a little dish of strawberry jam and butter, two slices of toast, cut neatly and diagonally, a small teapot and milk and a small vase that held a lovely pink rose. "This looks lovely and probably what I need!" I thanked him.

"Well, I will leave you to eat and get ready, then I will take you to the station. We need to leave in an hour – I will wait downstairs for you!" he informed me as he nodded toward James and then left the room.

"Thank you George!" I shouted to him. James looked at me and then said:

"I will leave you to enjoy your breakfast!"

"No, please don't. If I'm left to my own thoughts of what happened last night, I may die of shame before you return. Can you talk to me whilst I eat? In fact..." I climbed out of bed, tied my hair loosely up out of the way and then grabbed my tray. "If I sit on the footstool at the end of my bed, surely you will be able to join me for breakfast?" I hoped as I placed the tray down opposite the mirror.

"If you are sure, I should enjoy that!" he said as we sat for a moment. I picked up a makeup wipe and proceeded to clean my face. By the time I had finished and looked across at James, I was happy to see that my tray of breakfast was now his too.

"There we go, let's eat!" I said as I buttered my toast and poured some tea. James did the same.

Although I felt slightly nauseous and my head very fuzzy and painful, the fact that James was sat there in his breeches and an open-necked flouncy white shirt, reminiscent of Colin Firth in *Pride and Predjudice*, made the whole experience far easier to endure. I had not realised before how much I found the dress code of his period so attractive, although there was the added bonus that James was wearing it! I smiled to myself.

"Something amusing you?" he asked.

"No, not at all; this whole situation is just very... well, surreal really!" I smiled.

"Oh, trust me, it gets more surreal with time!" he laughed in return. "So this weekend should be interesting; you have your friend Claire staying on Saturday, do you not?" he asked.

"Yes, I hope that is still alright with you? I do however promise that there will be no repeat performances of last night!" I honestly remarked as I raised my eyebrows.

"Shame!" he simply and very sarcastically replied before carrying on eating his toast.

"Well here goes, it's kill or cure!" Without trying to think about it I downed the Alka-Seltzer in one go. "Oh my God, that is not nice with a queasy stomach!" I did not have to look at James, who laughed out loud in between gulps of his tea. "Not funny!" I remarked.

"I am sorry to inform you that it *was* quite humorous!" he said.

"You, Mr Aldersley, are fast becoming entirely intolerable!" I replied cynically, as I stood and took a few bites of my toast whilst I paced the room, and then I gathered my underwear, dressing gown and brush. "I am going to shower and get ready now, if that is acceptable!" I stated as I sashayed out of the room while he continued to laugh at me. I liked his laugh; it was warm and deep and made him seem more human.

"Very well, I shall meet you downstairs!" he shouted after me, and I smiled all the way to the bathroom.

Chapter Twenty-Three

The feeling of a warm shower on your face when you're hungover has its own medicinal benefits. The more I thought about what I had drunk, the more I was convinced that I had not had as much as I originally thought. I was simply out of the habit, and it had gone straight to my head. Well, that and the fact that I had mixed good brandy with red wine probably didn't help. By the time I stepped out of the shower, I felt much better and remarkably refreshed. I looked at myself in the mirror; *I don't look that bad*, I thought. I dried my hair, put on my underwear and slipped on my robe. I did not need to worry about James and the mirrors when I was dressing or showering. If there was one thing that I was positive of now, it was that James was a gentleman, and I trusted him entirely.

I returned to my room, dressed for work and then took another sip of tea and took a piece of the toast with me as I went down the stairs with my bags. George was placing some more pink roses in a crystal vase on the circular table in the hallway. He looked up as I walked down the stairs toward him.

"Wow, very beautiful George!" I remarked.

"Yes, my thoughts exactly!" he replied, staring at me. This constant complimenting was something that I needed to get used to! I smiled and placed my hand on his arm as I reached him.

"Definitely an improvement on last night, I should think!" I joked with him.

"Do not be too harsh on yourself, Katharina. I am sure it is not the first time you have enjoyed one too many glasses of wine and it will certainly not be the last!" he concluded.

"Fair point! Hopefully for your sake it will not be a regular occurrence though!" I finished my toast and then picked up my bags. "Shall we?" I remarked, indicating that I was ready to go to work.

"Absolutely. Ready if you are!" He opened the front door for me.

"Have a good day Katharina. Remember – new beginnings!" James spoke softly, probably for the benefit of my head! I stopped and turned and looked at him.

"Yes, new beginnings! I hope you have an enjoyable day also!" I replied and he nodded in acknowledgement and then bowed at me as I left.

The journey on the train found me thinking about last night and I started daydreaming about James – laughing, drinking, relaxing, being concerned, and not to mention looking hot this morning; there was definitely something about the flouncy white shirt with the open neck. To say that I felt hot under the collar when thinking about him, particularly when he was dressed like that, was an understatement.

Claire was ever observant at my happy demeanour and waltzed over with a coffee. She sat there for a moment looking at me whilst I unpacked my bag and then, like a volcano, exploded.

"So? Well? You look happy this morning! Is it because you are a single lady? Got rid of the beau and moving on to hotter guys?" She would have carried on if I hadn't stopped her. I held up my hand in defeat.

"Jesus Claire, enough questions! I have a very bad headache – too much wine last night!" I informed her.

"Oops, sorry! You do look happy though!" she then whispered and smiled. "Oh my God, did you get drunk with Mr Hottie last night?" she asked. I simply nodded in response and took a sip of my coffee. "I don't believe it; you get rid of one bloke – who, in fairness, was an arse – but you do not waste any time girl! I am impressed!" She chuckled to herself.

"Claire, you know his situation, so it isn't exactly going to be the relationship of the century, is it?" I tried to convince her, rolling my eyes.

"Well… yes, there are complications, I agree…" she started to say.

"Complications? That is an understatement!" I took another sip of coffee.

"Look, the way I see it, Kat, you have an amazing new home, a personal butler-type person who looks after you, and a really hot guy to drool over – what is not to like? Apart from me not being able to see him!" she stated.

"Look, I appreciate that you believe me with the whole James thing, I really do – and it is for real, I swear – but I can imagine that I look a little bit nuts. Honestly… I do not want to get hung up on him. It isn't like I can make a physical relationship out of this, is it?" I concluded.

"Why not?" she asked. I stopped and stared at her.

"I'm sorry… do you not remember the story of how he got there and the only way he can get out?" I quizzed her.

"Yeah I remember, witch, spell, abracadabra – stuck in a mirror, can't get out, he needs to fall in love and get whoever he loves to fall in love with him… I haven't forgotten, and your point is?" she asked, emphasising her speech with her hands.

"Exactly that!" I gestured in frustration.

"Oh my God! You really cannot see it, can you?" she then asked.

"See what?" I was getting more confused as to where she was going with this.

"Either you're really dumb, or you're choosing to ignore this." She stood and folded her arms across her body, giving me a 'stop being such an idiot' stare.

"What?" I asked. "I've tried to help him, I honestly have!"

"I feel like slapping you right now. Err, what are you?" she said. I stood and looked at her.

"What?" I said again and shrugged my shoulders. She laughed at me.

"The puppy eyes this morning after spending a night with him, the big grin, and the fact that you really like him… oh, and you are after all an attractive, young, *single* woman!" she pointed out.

"Well, yes, I can't deny that it was lovely last night, and he did look hot this morning…" I daydreamed a moment before Claire snapped her fingers in my face.

"Focus!" she insisted. I shook my head at her.

"What is your point?" I asked.

"The answer to the spell, Kat, is you! You're trying to help him, but why can't it be *you* that falls in love with him, and he with you? I mean, it sounds like the foundations are already in place!" She raised her eyebrows at me.

I opened my mouth, but nothing came out; I tried to assimilate what she had just said. I gasped a couple of times and tried again, but nothing. I just looked at her.

"Oh crap, you're not going to faint are you?" she then said as I slumped back down into my chair.

"Me?" I asked again. She crouched at the side of me. My heart started racing at the thought.

"Look, you know how these fairy tales are! They are never straightforward, but you are making this far too complicated. I personally think that you are the answer, Kat – meeting them, buying that place, and the fact that you and John broke up was no coincidence. I may be wrong about a lot of things, but I do believe in fate and I do like a happy ending, so call me old-fashioned and probably a bit crazy too, but I do think you could be the one to break this spell!" she then said, grabbing my hand. "Would that be such a bad thing?" I stared at her for a minute.

"Me? You really think it is possible?" I asked her.

"Well I wouldn't say no to him if he looked anything like that painting!" she then smirked. I quickly but lightly punched her arm in response to her sarcasm.

"It just never really occurred to me that it could be *me!*" I replied.

"Well you were a little wrapped up with the arse that

was John! I think it is absolutely achievable. This weekend is going to be so much fun, I'm really excited! I feel like I am in the middle of a Disney film! What time can I come over tomorrow?" she then asked as she bounced back to her feet.

"Err, not really thought about it… I could do with getting some clothes from the apartment, so maybe we could meet and go there first?"

"Sure, that's no problem! Make sure John's there and let me know what time to meet. I'll also bring my suitcase for you to fill." She smirked for a second; "We may as well both try and take out as many members of the public on the train whilst dragging our cases!" she chuckled to herself.

"You're a little sadistic deep down, aren't you?" I noted. She shrugged her shoulders.

"May drag it into Mr Right, you never know!" she remarked without blinking.

"Thanks Claire, I appreciate it. I don't really want to go back there on my own."

"Whoa, oh yeah, roll on tomorrow. I have my fingers crossed that I am going to see a bit of eye candy in that mirror!" Claire happily stated.

"Well please don't be disappointed if you do not! Not everyone will – or can!" I reminded her.

"I know, I know, but it's something to aim for! Anyway, stop talking to me and get some work done!" she then said as she winked at me and walked away to her desk.

"Right, yes, work!" I replied as I tried to get my head back into gear, but to say that I was now distracted was an understatement.

The whole day ended up being quite constructive. We had a meeting on upcoming possibilities, which was very interesting; I finished my small piece two days ahead of my deadline. I now found that I had a new spring in my step. This definitely felt like the correct way forward; I felt positive, happy and calm, and felt butterflies every time I thought about James. Even a couple of other work colleagues asked why I was so happy, and every time I thought about it before answering, there he was, in the back of my mind.

Claire and I had lunch together and discussed what we should do this weekend, and also agreed that we both needed to go shopping for a new dress for my party. I was really looking forward to it; I had never wanted to be the centre of attention, but for my party, I really didn't care! For once I was going to put myself first! We decided that tomorrow night we would have a little bit of a dance in the ballroom – new music versus old! Wine and food were a definite, along with romantic comedy DVDs, decoration sorting... and Claire made it clear that she wanted to be involved in all discussions between James, George and I, which I thought could be quite intriguing!

By the time we returned to work, we had arranged, sorted and put the world to rights. John had texted me to say that 11am would be fine to call for some things – not before pleading with me again to stay, which I ignored. I suddenly had a newfound inspiration for not dwelling on him... that inspiration of course was James, who had more respect for me – even though I had never physically met him – than John had in the last two years we had been together!

I stopped by the stationers on the way back to work and got all three of us a new journal. New beginnings need a fresh approach, and I wanted James, George and I to start keeping a record from today and not to dwell on the past; it was easier for me as I had not been around for even a quarter of the time that they had. The train journey home was not busy; this route was definitely better than the old tube ride, and it was a Friday night, which meant that most people had stayed in the city after work. It amused me that I wasn't bothered about being out, and couldn't wait until I got home to relax and converse with my friends. I looked out of the window as the train clicked along the track and simply smiled... I was very happy.

George, as always, was waiting for me when I got off the train. He looked so friendly and was so charming and treated me like royalty, it was hard to not get slightly complacent at his attention to detail. He had already popped the umbrella up he was carrying to walk me to the car, but I did not want him to think that I expected this – after all, he had been doing this job for over two hundred years; surely he must be a little bored of it by now?

"You really don't have to do this, George!" I remarked as he opened the car door for me.

"What would that be, Katharina?" he asked innocently.

"Look after me so well – I mean. I did not live in your time and things have moved on so... I can do things for myself!" I smiled. He closed the door and walked to the driver's side.

"Yes, I realise that, but you see… I have been doing this job for most of my life and it is all I know. After all, what else is there for me to do but look after the people that live at Northfield? I do actually quite enjoy it, and it is not a bad thing to be slightly chivalrous, is it?" he smiled back.

"Oh no, not at all George… chivalry, in my opinion, is one of the many important things that we have sadly lost today. My point is that you are really good at what you do, and I do appreciate it, but I do not want you to think that I expect it!" I tried to convince him sincerely. He had started driving and waited a few seconds before replying.

"I know that, but it is my pleasure to do it!" he concluded. "That, young lady, is all that is needed to be said about the matter!" he then finished.

"Very well… oh, and thank you!" I answered honestly. He simply smiled.

As we drove home and I chatted about my day at work, most likely boring George to death, I could not adequately describe the warm and almost melting feeling that I got as we turned down the driveway. The warm light that lit the large windows made the house look alive and I could imagine how anyone from any era must feel when they arrived at Northfield.

"Does it ever get tired on the eyes?" I asked George.

"No, it does not!" he replied. "I am glad that you love it as much as I do!" he finished.

"How could you not love it?" I sighed heavily. "It is nice to be home!"

George and I got out of the car into slightly blustery

weather, but luckily the rain had stopped. The soothing quietness was a marked contrast from the city centre and as the branches creaked in the wind and the leaves rustled, I stood for a minute and did a full 360-degree turn. George watched me and then continued to the main door, opening it just as I reached the top step.

"Thank you, George."

"Ah you are back! Did you have a constructive day?" James enquired.

"I did in fact, and a very enjoyable one!" I replied.

"Even with a hangover?" he then smirked.

"Yes, alright, very funny – let's not dwell on my state this morning!" I sarcastically replied.

"As you wish! Shall we have dinner? I believe George has prepared some type of pie with military precision!" he joked.

"Really? Are you still going on about my cooking skills after this afternoon?" George commented as he took my coat and hung it in the large cloakroom.

"Sounds like you two have had fun?" I remarked.

"Well, it was fun for James – he was making fun of me simply because I was trying to make the crust of the pie neat and precise, but then I got my own back when he tried trimming his bonsai tree!" George laughed.

"There is nothing wrong with my tree sculpting, George!" James sternly replied.

"I think I need to see these attempts at both of your supposed skills!" I stated as I started to walk toward George's apartment. They continued to banter as they walked behind me, which made me very happy!

The smell in George's kitchen was yet again

delightful. His cooking was fast becoming one of the main reasons to get home in the evening; if there was one thing George had learned in all these years, it was how to cook! I entered the kitchen, looked toward the oven and then lowered the door to see how his pie looked. It was something that even Gordon Ramsay would be proud of! The pastry crust was crisscrossed with latticework and I was very impressed. I then turned to see James in the mirror, looking a little nervous. I gestured for him to move to the side so that I could see his tree. It sat in the distance on his table, so I moved closer.

"Well, go and get it!" George then said as he grabbed three wine glasses.

He returned and held up the tree, which was now a slightly different shape, but it wasn't bad.

"I was trying to make it look like the tree in the grounds that I used to climb when I was a boy, from memory of course!" he then said as I inspected it.

"Looks more like a twig now!" George then giggled.

"Oh, for the love of God George, it does not!" James sternly said again, and I could do nothing but laugh at his frustration, which in turn had George laughing – and eventually James saw the funny side.

"Well, for your first attempt at topiary, I think that it is not bad!" I tried to say without laughing.

"Thank you!" James nodded in my direction.

"Good job it keeps growing, albeit at a slow rate. I think by this time next year it should be ready to be trimmed again!" George carried on laughing.

"Well, at least I attempted to try it! You simply took

off two new shoots and you were done!" James retorted. I held my hands up at them both.

"Boys, boys, please!" I exclaimed, taking control. "I did not want to cause such negative competitive behaviour. The bonsais were for you both to enjoy; whether you choose to change its shape or leave it as it is, it's entirely up to you! I think that time will tell who has the best – let's not fall out over it now!" I concluded, smiling.

"Agreed!" James quickly snapped. I had the distinct feeling that he did not like having the mickey taken out of him, but his defensive reactions were actually quite sweet; they made him appear vulnerable and more human. Once George had stopped laughing, he spoke.

"Very well… agreed!" he said as he returned to the stove and checked on the simmering vegetables.

I tried to change the subject by giving them both their new journals, which they seemed pleased with. I then perched on a stool and took a long sip of wine, the comforting properties of which were fast becoming more appreciated. I was having the privilege of sampling the wines from Northfield's cellars and I could not deny that I was enjoying them immensely.

"Wow that is one good wine George!" I stated as I took another sip.

"Ah yes, the perfect Chateau Haut Brion Bordeaux – one of my favourites! We are, however, starting to run very low on it now! This one I believe we bought in about 1990; I dare not open many dating back before 1960 now as they are more than likely undrinkable; we sample one every now and again. I do like to keep some of the older bottles, though; James' father liked his wines and the cellar has its memories. It is nice to keep some as keepsakes," George sincerely answered.

"It is a waste in my opinion, George, but I have no say in the matter as I cannot get to your bottles, so it is irrelevant!" James stated. "We must replenish the cellar for Katharina's party if we are running low; let us make that a priority!" he then concluded.

"Oh, please allow me; I need to pay for something here!" I replied as I pulled out my laptop. I had taken the liberty of buying a dongle as George had never seen the benefit of having the internet, which I needed to sort out. I Googled the label and had to stop myself from swearing profusely when the prices appeared on my screen.

"Bloody hell!" I exclaimed in shock, then realised I had sworn, which wasn't particularly ladylike! "Oops – sorry about the language," I quickly apologised, "but do you know how much this stuff is worth?" I asked them.

"I seem to recall that it was not one of my cheaper purchases, but as we bought approximately forty-eight bottles, it worked out at a very good price. Why, is it more expensive now?" he asked innocently. I held up the bottle.

"This wine is approximately £500 per bottle – and rising!" I informed them.

"What? For a bottle of *wine*?" James asked, aghast. "That is incomprehensible!"

"Hell yes, exclusive old wine is very much a wine connoisseur and collectors' dream! You could both be sat on an absolute fortune!" I informed them.

"Well, that's very nice, but I would much rather drink it than sell it! After spending an eternity with him, it is nice to have some pleasures!" George gestured to James. James simply crossed his arms and sighed.

"You are very loose-tongued today and speaking your mind freely, George; have I upset you in some way?" James asked.

"Not at all, Master James; I simply find that Katharina brings out the truth from me!" George stated, matter-of-factly, with a sarcastic smile.

"Hey, do not bring me into your feud, boys! I love you both dearly, but I do not want to be the cause of any argument!" I was quick to reply. Then, as I took a sip of wine and realised that they were both quiet, I dissected what I had just said. *Did I just say I loved them both dearly? It was kind of tongue in cheek!* I thought to myself, and tried to quickly change the subject!

"Well, that's put an end to that then, I am not buying my friends bottles of wine that cost £500 – after many drinks they won't know the difference from a £5 bottle from Waitrose!" I joked, hoping my previous comment had gone unnoticed.

"It is your choice, Katharina; you know them better than we do. Maybe we should take a trip somewhere to purchase the things you require?" George then stated.

"Yes, I would like that – perhaps whilst Claire is here this weekend?"

"Make sure that you get what you enjoy!" James then said quietly. "It is after all your party. You are welcome to anything from the cellar, should you wish it!" he offered.

"That is really kind, thank you, but I honestly feel that your wine is far too good for them; I would rather that you enjoyed it!" I smiled.

"We will enjoy it! It is yours too, do not forget!" he concluded.

"Yes indeed. We have plenty to try yet!" George then said, and he chinked glasses with me, then remarked: "After all, only the best for someone that loves us dearly!" he grinned. I blushed and laughed nervously. I dared not look at James, but I could feel his eyes boring into me, so I stuck my head back into my laptop whilst George plated up dinner.

Chapter Twenty-Four

We had dinner in the main dining room, which was informal but lovely. We carried our plates there ourselves – even James carried his from George's kitchen – and there was an air of calm and relaxation during the meal. We laughed, talked, drank wine and discussed the coming weekend, which seemed to be causing James a bit of concern.

"What if she can see me this time?" he asked.

"That would be a good thing; it would confirm to her that I am not completely insane!" I replied.

"What if she thinks that I am intolerable?" he then suddenly asked. George and I looked at each other.

"And why would she think that?" I asked.

"You have told her how I came to be here, have you not?" he asked.

"Yes, but that is no reason for her to dislike you, James!" I pointed out.

"But the circumstances of my being here is repulsive to most women; she may have a strong opinion toward my past behaviour, which may result in a very uncomfortable weekend for you!" he then stated with apprehension.

"Are you worried that if she sees you, she may fall madly in love with you, but hate you at the same time for what you have done?" George asked as he placed his fork down. "Because, seriously, it's a little late to be worrying about that, don't you think?"

"No; that is not my concern. I have seen her before and, even though she is a good friend of yours, Katharina, I could not commit to a match with her. I honestly think that she would drive me to wish that I was back in my current situation!" he replied honestly. I laughed.

"Well, you do have a point there; she is fairly full-on… all of the time!" I remarked.

"At this moment in time, I am happy with my situation. Spending time with you both is giving me immeasurable pleasure. I simply do not want her to think that you are dedicating yourself, and your time, to some lost cause!" James then declared. I banged my fork onto my plate with some force and George stopped and looked at me.

"I have never been more certain in my life about the actions that I have taken recently; buying into Northfield, meeting you both and helping you in every way that I can was my choice! Even if Claire does see you, I can assure you that she will not say anything unpleasant to you! She knows that I hate not being able to break this spell and the affliction that it causes you both, and so the last thing she would do is confirm that torment by attacking you. If anything, she would want to help me!" I concluded. George smiled at me as I picked my fork back up. I consumed another mouthful of delicious food, James replied:

"I feel that I continue to underestimate your strength of character, and I apologise that I fail you on that point.

I am honoured and indeed blessed to have your help and understanding, and I am sorry that for a moment my own self-preservation was paramount to that of your happiness. I am sure that you are correct, and I again thank you for your unreserved generosity!" he said, sounding sorrowful, and then as I turned to reply he stood and walked from the room.

"That was a very sincere thing to say, Katharina, and I agree – we are lucky to have you here helping us," George stated.

"Where did he go? Is he always this stubborn about his predicament? I mean, I know that it is unfortunate and torturous, but his attitude is not getting him anywhere, or making him happy!" I asked.

"Oh, this is good! Trust me, in the past he was so much worse!" George replied. I placed my hand on my heart.

"I feel for him, I really do. So I promise you this, George: he will not be in there forever. I will strive until my dying day to free you both from this hell!" I said with force.

"Ambition is a very strong quality indeed! I like it!" George smiled and then raised his glass toward me.

Sometime after finishing dinner, James still had not returned, and I started to fear that he was still angry after his outburst. I excused myself from the table, informing George that I wanted to go and find him; he in return told me that the library was probably where he had retreated to. As I opened the heavy oak door and looked toward the large mirror, I could see him quietly pondering over a book. He did not hear me come in, but

I could see that he was not reading; he closed the book and placed his head in his hands. I truly felt for him; he seemed to think that nothing he said was correct and it seemed that he had lost all respect for himself. I walked over and sat on the chaise longue in front of the mirror.

"Is there anything in that book about how to stop putting yourself down?" I asked him in a sincere tone. He turned and looked at me and stood to accept my presence.

"My apologies, I did not see you enter the room!" he remarked.

"James, please sit down." I gestured to his chair. He did so and lowered his head, pretending to take an interest in the book again. "If you feel that you have wronged me in any way, please believe that you have not!"

"I cannot seem to find the right words when I am with you; I merely seem to act like I distrust you, and you must think me very rude."

"No! I do not!" I exclaimed firmly. "Gosh, I wish I could get to you right now, because quite honestly I would knock some sense into that thick skull of yours!" I retorted. He gave me a look of complete shock and that confirmed that I had his attention. "James, you seriously need to stop this self-pity and doubting yourself. Your behaviour from long ago is just that; you are not the same person – even though I didn't know you back then, I can see that – and it makes me exceptionally angry to find that you still do not believe that you have changed in all these years!" I stated. He sighed sadly, and so I continued:

"Please come back to the dining room with us; it

saddens me that you will not finish dinner with us because of whatever you think of yourself… I love your company, and I am missing the stories that you tell during our evenings together!" I smiled at him. "I cannot bear to think that you are sat in here alone, torturing yourself! I do not like it, and I will not have it, so snap out of it and get yourself back in there!" I finished. I stood and crossed my arms in a motherly way and gave him an 'I'm not going without you' look. I managed to get a half smile from him but I knew that he was going to try and stay where he was, so I stepped in again: "James, I will not take no for an answer!" I reinforced as I raised my eyebrows at him. He stood up.

"So it would seem! Yet again you teach me a valuable lesson on living, Katharina. I should be glad to accompany you back to the dining room, please forgive my pitiful attitude toward myself!" he replied. Wow – I won, I was so happy! As I turned, I clenched my fists in delight.

George was refilling glasses. He had moved our plates and brought dessert, which I was ready for. He seemed happy that I had managed to get James to return with me, and out of respect for both James and I, he did not bring the subject up once. He instead started to tell the tale of some slightly deranged woman who had dined here in 1898, when the house had been occupied for a mere year by the Williams family.

"Do you remember her, James? She looked like she had just walked off the stage – she wore the most grotesque make up – and she had a laugh that was more annoying than I care to mention, plus she conversed like some crazy, unruly heiress, wanting to tell everyone about her fortune!" George took a sip of wine and shook his head.

"Well, I can imagine that she was a sight to see!" I remarked.

"Oh, she was more than that. She was completely insane, of that I am sure! Although she was friends with the Williams, it gave me great pain and anxiety when she asked them over dinner who the young man staring at her was!" James replied. I turned and looked at him.

"What, she could see you?" I asked with interest.

"Oh yes, she could see me. Unfortunately for me, she returned many times during the following month, to gaze upon me!"

"What, and you didn't try to break the spell with her?" I asked, trying not to smile; the look on his face made it obvious that he was frightened to death of her.

"Dear God, no! Being in here was far less painful than trying anything with her!" he said, horrified, as George burst out laughing.

"It was bloody amusing though; I hardly saw James for a month. He went into hiding every time that she came; there was no way he was conversing with her on a regular basis!" he managed to say between laughing.

"Well, she was one of the scariest women that I have ever had the unfortunate pleasure of 'meeting'. Having to spend an eternity being grateful to her for breaking the spell would have killed me anyway!" James then said. George was still laughing, which in turn made me laugh.

"Alright, I get the impression that under your hard exterior hides a scared little boy... frightened of a woman indeed! I would not have thought that of you, James!" I replied, chuckling somewhat.

"You did not see her! I was completely scrupulous in my decision to hide from her. It would not have ended well in any way!" he tried to convince us. "I am glad that you find this amusing, but the last time I did not listen to my immediate instincts, look what happened to me!" he finished, gesturing to his presence behind the mirror before placing his fists onto his hips in agitation.

"Actually George, he does have a point!" I said, after controlling my laughing. "Really, was she that bad?" I asked, and both of them replied in unison:

"YES!"

We all calmed down for a while and ate the delicious chocolate fudge cake that George had made. It was one of those cakes to eat when you're down, sad, happy, in love or – in fact – in any circumstance, and it was delicious. I held my stomach in appreciation afterwards, and realised that I had eaten two servings to their one. I started to have thoughts about my weight again, but this food was far too good to give up.

"George, you spoil me completely. These delicious dinners are not going to do anything for my constitution!" I pointed out whilst patting my very full tummy.

"Oh nonsense! It is good to eat well; don't worry about your figure, it will do you no harm! We could do with fattening you up a little bit!" George replied.

"That's sweet, George, but now you are reminding me of some fairy tale or folklore about the fattening-up of people before they are eaten!" I said.

"I assume you are referring to *Hansel and Gretel*, or something of that ilk?" George replied. "I'd not thought about that, James – we should fatten her up and keep her here forever, what do you think?" he chuckled. I frowned at his response sarcastically, but James simply replied:

"Having Katharina here forever is a thought that I favour most ardently, but in regards to her figure – Katharina, you are, in my opinion, perfection indeed, and instead I would make a reference to a fairy tale such as *Snow White* or *Cinderella*," he sincerely said. I looked at George, who seemed surprised at his comment, and then I looked at James.

"Am I correct in thinking that you have just complimented me, James?"

"That would be my intention, yes!" he replied.

"Then I am flattered, thank you! I am happy to see that we have *you* back with us, not the character that was in our presence earlier!" I happily stated, smiling at him.

"You may have it on good authority that the character – or should I say fool – from earlier will not be gracing your presence again!" he informed me, before giving me the most heart-melting smile of sincerity.

"Well, I am glad to hear it!" I replied. George was quiet, and I knew that we had just had another 'moment'; then he jumped up.

"Right, let's tidy and retreat to the drawing room this evening. The fire is lit and the game board is ready. Oh, and for you, Katharina, I have had another television aerial installed, so you may now watch anything that you should wish!"

"George, you need not have done that for me! I am

very happy spending the evenings chatting with the both of you and playing cards. It is actually a refreshing change to not have the television on," I replied.

"Well, with Claire here for the weekend, I understand that it is usual for young women to watch films that are full of romantic gestures whilst drinking wine! Am I mistaken in thinking this?" George asked, and I laughed.

"No, you are quite right, George – unfortunately even today us women like to dream about the fantasy of finding the right man, in the most romantic situation! Alas, it seems that all good men, in my experience, are just that – a fantasy!" I finished sadly.

"Oh, I do not believe that, Katharina!" he replied.

"Nor I!" James also stated. I smiled at them both.

"I have not had very many positive experiences with love and romance – except in films – but I do not give up so easily!" I smiled, and then I had the most amazing idea. "I am going to bring some films tomorrow, some of my favourites – Jane Austen's *Northanger Abbey*, *Pride and Prejudice*, and also some newer ones maybe. I think that I should let you indulge in some of my fantasies!" I remarked.

"That sounds most intriguing; I have never had the desire to watch many of these films over the years. George does make me watch the news, but other than that I receive a greater satisfaction from reading," James replied.

"Well, it will be interesting to see if these films are truthful to the period that they depict. You both are from the time when Jane Austen wrote, so I expect the etiquette to be correct. The question will be whether you can stand to watch it or not!" I remarked.

"I accept your challenge, Katharina – do you, George?" James was quick to join in.

"Well, I think it should prove interesting, so yes, I am happy to join in the challenge!" he replied.

"That is settled then. I presume that you do not have a DVD player, George?" I asked.

"Oh, if you are referring to the machine in which you need to insert the small circular objects, yes, he does indeed have one; I have seen him watching many things in the past," James said.

"You have been spying on me all this time?" George asked James.

"Well I would hardly call it spying, but I do think that you need your own space, so I never like to make it apparent that I know that you indulge in these modern extravagances!" James replied.

"This will surely be a new experience for you then James?" I asked him.

"I did not say that I have not seen one before, but I have not watched fictional things on a regular basis," James informed us.

"Ah, so you have joined me on some evenings to watch my films?" George asked. "I was never entirely sure, but I am not in the least bit bothered!"

James nodded in acceptance, and I was now excited about the fact that I could quiz them both on some of my favourite films.

The evening ended well; George and I beat James at cards, and snakes and ladders. James was remarkably unfazed by this and even laughed at his defeat. It was like he had become completely nonchalant about everything, and it made me pay even more attention to him; he was more handsome when he was agreeable in every way! We had a wonderful evening, and after washing up and having coffee, I excused myself. I was tired and knew that with Claire here tomorrow, I was sure to have a late night. James offered to walk me to my room, which I happily agreed to.

"I hope that this weekend will see us having the most fun to date!" James stated. I smiled at his statement and new state of being; it suited him so much and these gestures made me like him more as every moment passed.

"I am sure that if Claire has anything to do with it, fun will be at the top of her list!" I replied. "I like seeing you so casual, not worrying about what will happen – it becomes you!" I then remarked. He – very calmly, and with a voice like melted chocolate – replied:

"Thank you, I feel that I am happier entirely because of you, Katharina. You are proving to be a very priceless addition to our lives!"

"Why thank you James! I am liking these compliments that you keep bestowing upon me more and more!" I stated as we reached my door.

"Until tomorrow then?" he asked.

"Until tomorrow!" I repeated, and as I looked at him I tried my very hardest not to swoon or look like a schoolgirl with a crush. I closed my door and leaned against it, and then wondered how long I was going to have these feelings for. He turned my stomach into a sea of butterflies and I had to admit that it was getting worse, not better. I climbed into bed happy, relaxed and still extremely full from dinner; the combination made me feel completely content, and so I drifted off to sleep easily, but not before quietly saying: "Goodnight James, I hope that you have pleasant dreams!"

The next morning, I woke up with a spring in my step. I felt completely refreshed and was looking forward to the weekend. I jumped in the shower, dressed, dried my hair quickly and then loosely pinned it up out of the way. When I arrived at George's kitchen door, I was thrilled to hear him and James laughing and talking about the delights of the coming evening. I walked in and was happy to be greeted by hot tea and bacon sandwiches, and two very amiable men. James was dressed, but was wearing one of those flouncy open necked shirts from the 1800s. I could suddenly now see all of the appeal of Mr Darcy and those other characters from the same period that many women fantasised about. I couldn't take my eyes off him for quite some time, and I knew that he had noticed this.

"So Katharina, what is the plan for today?" George suddenly asked. I took a sip of my tea;

"Well, I am going to meet Claire and then go and collect some belongings from the apartment. I can hardly keep wearing the same clothes weekly. Then we are going to grab a cab back here, or a train – so all being well I should be back by one o'clock. Does that tie in with what you both have planned?" I enquired.

"Fine with me – the sooner you are back, the better!" James replied. I smiled.

"Are you going to be alright, collecting your belongings? I do not like to think of that scoundrel upsetting you anymore than he already has!" George stated.

"Honestly, I will be fine. I have Claire with me, so I know she will be watching my back! I just want to get as much as possible, mainly clothing, and with the two of us it will be easier," I replied, trying to sound confident.

"If he causes you any pain or upset – more than he has done to date – I do not think that I will be able to contain myself, should I ever be faced with him!" James then stated.

"I hope that there will be no need for that, James; I am growing stronger every day. I do not intend to let him injure me any more than he already has and I don't think you will need to trouble yourself!" I replied, smiling at him. He waited a few moments and then simply said:

"Very well!"

George kindly took me to the train station. I had arranged to meet Claire for a coffee first; a caffeine kick seemed a good idea before facing John. We were actually ahead of schedule, but I wanted to get it over with. As we arrived at the apartment – Claire with her suitcase in tow – I took a deep breath, looked at Claire for confidence and then nervously knocked on the door.

Chapter Twenty-Five

We were greeted by a dishevelled John, who looked like he had only just woken up. It was 10.30am and very unusual for him to not be working or out running by this time.

"You're early!" he stated, quite surprised.

"I am a little, but did not want to be hanging around. Claire and I have plenty to do today," I replied.

"Well, can you give me a moment?" he then asked nervously.

"Sure!" I replied as he turned toward the bedroom door just as it opened.

"Kat, I am so sorry – I had intended not to be here when you arrived. John and I were working late on a project and so I slept over," Nadine said, suddenly walking out looking fresh from a shower.

"Yeah, I bet you did!" Claire retorted sarcastically.

"Is that my blouse?" I then asked, looking at what she was wearing. She looked down at it.

"Oh, yes, I hope that you don't mind, John said that it would be alright!" she blushed, obviously realising that it was completely inappropriate.

"Keep it! I don't want it back now!" I replied, glaring at John.

"Touché!" Claire then added.

"So, may I get my things please?" I asked rhetorically.

"Yes of course," John said, running his fingers through his hair.

"I think I should leave!" Nadine hastily said.

"I do too!" Claire confirmed.

"Don't leave on my account – I don't intend on being long!" I replied as I marched into the bedroom past them both.

I grabbed my suitcase and Claire joined me. As we started filling the cases, we could hear John and Nadine whispering. Claire gave me an 'I can't believe the jerk' look, but I tried to focus on why I was there. I heard the apartment door close and guessed that she had left. What was he thinking? He knew that I was coming this morning, and having her here was like rubbing salt in the wound. Thank goodness I had Claire with me!

"You okay?" she asked.

"I will be as soon as we get out of here!" I replied, as I threw perfumes, creams, hair products, books, and any other items that I could get into my bag. I walked across to my side table where my favourite picture of my mum sat in the antique frame that I had chosen. I smiled at it and placed it into my case carefully.

"She would be proud of you, you know!" Claire quietly said. I smiled.

"Yes, I know!" I replied just as John walked into the bedroom.

"I had hoped that we could talk, Kat!" he stated.

"There's nothing to say; you have obviously moved on. This was never going to work, John, and I simply needed that confirming, Nadine being here did that and so thank you!" I calmly replied as I threw in the rest of my underwear.

"She only stayed the night, we were working!" he tried to sound convincing.

"Is that what you call it?" Claire retorted. I grimaced at her.

"And where did she sleep?" I enquired. John quickly looked around and rubbed his head, realising there was only one place that she could have slept.

"Yes alright, point taken." I felt a small victory and smiled as I zipped up my case.

"Look John, this is for the best. You weren't happy, and neither was I, so let's just be adults about this and move on!" John nodded.

"What about the rest of your things?" he then asked as we started to wheel the cases out.

"I will arrange to collect them later – and we need to sort out the paperwork for this place. It's your responsibility now!" I pointed out. Then I grabbed Claire's arm and dragged her out of the door; I needed to get out of there. I knew it was the end, but it still hit me quite hard and I felt a little sad that I had not made this part of my life work; I hated failing.

"Hey, don't look like that! I know you; don't feel sorry for him, this was not your fault. Anyway, you've moved on to bigger and better things!" Claire tried to bolster my spirits.

"I know, I just hate failing!" I replied.

"You didn't fail, you tried – it just wasn't meant to be!" Claire replied.

"Thank you for being there!" I remarked as I pushed open the door onto the street.

"Any time, Kat, you know that! Now let's get a bloody drink. Start as we mean to go on!" she replied, pulling my arm and marching toward the nearest wine bar.

I really should have said no at 11.30 in the morning, but a glass of rosé wine seemed like the perfect solution to the stressful situation. We marched in, propped up the bags against the bar and ordered one large glass each. It was refreshing; Claire cheered me up with jokes, which was just what I needed. I felt remarkably light-headed after one glass, so before she could order another one I suggested that we get a cab home. That way we could relax and know that we did not have to go anywhere for the rest of the day. The sun had come out, and the smell of coffee mingled with the smell of the recent rain. The traffic was heavy and the people plentiful, but it was London on a Saturday, and I knew that within the hour I would be home away from all of this hustle and bustle, and that made me happier than ever.

As we pulled down the driveway of Northfield, Claire shuffled to the end of her seat and looked out at the facade.

"Wow, it really is amazing Kat. I cannot believe that you live here!" she said honestly.

"I can hardly believe it either!" I replied.

We paid and hopped out, dragging our bags, cases and everything else that we had picked up on our way. Claire had stopped to buy wine before the cab ride back; she didn't want to turn up empty-handed. I then stumbled a little, which made us laugh; that wine was fast becoming a bad decision. I pushed the main door open, and we almost fell in the door laughing.

"Good, you are back!" James suddenly stated.

"Yes, one glass of wine later and I feel very merry!" I replied, looking at him. Claire in return stared at me.

"What? Oh, you are talking to him?" she asked and then answered herself. I nodded whilst she stared at the mirror.

"James, I think that you remember Claire?" I gestured toward her, and for whatever reason she curtseyed. I simply looked at her and laughed. "What are you doing?"

"I have no bloody idea!" she laughed. "James, I cannot see you, but if you can hear me – it's nice to... err... know that you're here!" she managed to say loudly.

"Does she think me to be hard of hearing? How old does she think I am?" James asked sarcastically. I just laughed.

"What did he say?" Claire then asked.

"He wants to know how old you think he is. He's not deaf! You cannot hear him, not the other way around!" I pointed out, laughing at her. She raised her hand to her head in confusion.

"Yes of course, I must look like an idiot. This is going to take some getting used to!" she finished.

"I wouldn't use the word idiot, though, I would prefer –" James was about to finish, but just then George walked in.

"James – enough of that!" he quickly stopped him. "Claire, it is a pleasure to have you return so soon!" George kindly remarked. She almost curtseyed again, then stopped herself and looked at me.

"Thank you for having me!" was all that she said.

"I have prepared the room next to yours, Katharina; shall we take your bags upstairs?" George asked us.

It was a good idea; I should unpack before I decided that I may be doing the wrong thing, moving in here permanently. Claire helped me after she had got over the initial shock of the splendour of her room. She told me it was better than any weekend away in any house, and that even Chatsworth would struggle to improve on it. I know how she felt; this house was a sight to behold. It did indeed feel like stepping back in time, giving us a glimpse of an age unfortunately forgotten by most. I was happy to have her here; she continually talked whilst I hung and folded clothes.

"Goodness, is this how the whole weekend shall proceed? I do not think she has stopped to breathe yet! I feel that George and I will be exhausted and exasperated by the time she leaves," James explained.

I walked past her, then past the end of the bed and to the wardrobe, glowering at James. He in return raised his hands and gestured at her and said:

"Well, please – you cannot disagree with my opinion?!"

As I walked back past him to retrieve more clothes, I whispered to him:

"You said that you would be amiable. Stop it now please, she is my friend!" he raised his hands in agreement.

"I did, and I apologise. I simply came to tell you that George has made lunch!" he informed me.

I stopped Claire, left the unpacking and guided her

downstairs and toward George's apartment. James walked with us, and I caught glances of him trying to keep up with Claire's pace of speech. He shook his head at one point, which amused me – he was probably used to women from his era listening most of the time. We walked in to find plates of sandwiches and a freshly-baked Victoria sponge cake, a large pot of tea and pretty china cups and saucers set out on the island.

"George, this looks lovely, but I told you not to go to any trouble!" I told him.

"It is no trouble; what is a man to do with so much time on his hands?" George replied, smiling, as he passed a plate to each of us.

"What a delicious way to spend time!" Claire noted. "I am starting to see the appeal in living here, Kat! Do you do this regularly, George?" she asked.

"Most days; I am a very lucky lady!" I smiled in response.

"You can say that again! This is great!" Claire replied as she started to tuck into the small feast.

I placed a selection on a plate and left it on the end of the island, which caught Claire's attention. James smiled and thanked me, but then pointed out that he had a whole plate full of them on his side of the mirror, as well as a whole cake, which he was looking forward to eating. George then proceeded to explain the whole 'items reflected in the mirror, but not people or living animals' situation to Claire. Claire looked intrigued and asked many questions, and whilst they talked James spoke to me.

"How was the visit to the apartment?" he asked

sincerely. "Not too distressing, I hope?" He took a bite of sandwich whilst he waited for my response.

"It was easier having Claire there. It wasn't too bad, but it did confirm that my decision was correct!" I smiled. Claire was looking at George and me and the mirror, trying to understand how it all worked.

"I am glad to hear it; hopefully you shall not have to see him any more now?" he asked.

"I just need to sort out paperwork and collect my larger things, but I can arrange that at a later date!" I replied. "I am fine, honestly James!" I finished as Claire excused herself from George's conversation.

"You say you are alright, but that was tough, girl! It did not help that she came waltzing out of the bedroom!" Claire informed them.

"What?" George asked unhappily.

"He knew Kat was going, and he had Nadine there, who had obviously stayed the night – and to add insult to injury she had one of Kat's blouses on, with the approval of John. I tell you, Kat, I would have ripped her head off!" Claire openly pointed out. I shot her a look of disapproval.

"He allowed that woman in your presence after she caused you this upset in the first place? How dare he! The nerve of that man!" James angrily snapped as he stood and paced with his hands on his hips. I now wished that Claire had said nothing.

"James, calm down. I am fine, I promise you. It wasn't as bad as you think!" I tried to convince him.

"What is bad is that he put you in this situation in the first place – but to reinforce it with her presence, when

344

he knew that you were to call upon him, is a complete atrocity!" James was not happy, but I had to say I liked his protective instinct; it was very chivalrous.

"What is going on? Someone please tell me what James is saying!" Claire pleaded. George looked at her.

"James is not too happy about the actions of Katharina's former fiancé. He finds him selfish, arrogant and somewhat discourteous!" George informed her simply.

"That's a little polite, isn't it? I would prefer the term 'absolutely incompetent lying little bastard' actually!" she quite bluntly said. We all fell silent for a minute and stared at her before she said: "What? Come on, you all think the same, you just don't want to say it!" She took another bite of her sandwich and shrugged her shoulders and then James started to laugh. Both George and I looked at him.

"She does have a point! I am now starting to see why you two are friends; sometimes we need to hear the truth!" He laughed lightly and retook his seat at the end of the island.

"Yes, Claire has guided me so much in matters of all kinds over the years. I can firmly say that I trust her implicitly with my wellbeing!" I replied as I leaned and hugged her.

"Oh thanks Hun! I love you too!" she remarked, then pushed me away jokily. "I was the one who convinced her that helping you two was also the right thing to do – does that win me extra brownie points?" she asked, whilst looking at George and then to the mirror.

"Oh, this weekend is certainly not going to be dull, I

can see that now!" James remarked as he smiled at her. I smiled.

"James likes you!" I simply stated in reply. Claire blushed.

"Liked by a hot guy, that's fair enough!" she then said. I glared at her and she looked at me. "I just said that out loud, didn't I?" she then asked, and we all burst out laughing whilst she apologised.

After lunch, we brought out the decorations. George had taken them out and re-boxed them in room order as he saw fit, but he said the decorating was entirely my decision. We got them all out on the ballroom floor, and Claire – as I had done – gasped at how beautiful they all were. She held them up and touched the velvet bows and remarked how lucky I was to be able to use such things. We started to regroup them and wandered back and forth to see where things would fit best, with George's guidance. It was after approximately an hour of this that she decided it was time for a glass of wine and a little bit of music.

"Do you have plug sockets in here George?" she asked honestly.

"The time of no electricity and candles are long past Claire! Of course we have plug sockets!" he informed her, pointing some out.

"Brilliant. Kat, where is your iPod docking station?" she asked me.

"Oh, it will be in my bag upstairs, I don't think I have unpacked it yet!"

"No problem, I will go and retrieve it!" she happily stated as she bounced out of the room.

"I can see why you like her. I feel that my previous judgement of her was slightly cruel!" James suddenly said.

"She does take some getting used to; probably because she is so full of life and speaks her mind!" I tried to explain.

"Yes, I can say that I have witnessed that now!" he replied before saying; "Her company makes you happy, therefore I am happy!" I smiled at his remark as George appeared with a bottle of wine and four glasses.

I stood to help him and stretched my legs; sitting cross-legged on the floor did not do well for my posture. He poured a glass for us all and then placed the bottle on the ornate side table that rested against one of the walls. It looked like it had been made for this room, and George had stood the old gramophone upon it. James had walked to retrieve his glass, and when Claire returned George proposed a toast.

"To the future, to new friends and to your birthday party!" he announced happily.

"I'll drink to that!" Claire said, before taking a large gulp.

"And to our good fortune that Katharina stumbled upon us, and is now a part of our lives!" James then sincerely added. I stopped and looked at him and so did George. Claire got the gist that something had been said.

"What did I miss?" she asked.

"Another toast!" I remarked, staring at James. "That was a very sincere thing to say… thank you!" I then finished.

"What did he say?" Claire eagerly asked. "I do not like not knowing!" she then stated unhappily.

"He said; and to our good fortune that Katharina stumbled upon us and is a part of our lives!" George repeated for Claire's benefit. She stood and stared at me staring at him. I was smiling, and James was smiling too – in fact we all were.

"Okay, I am definitely drinking to that too, because she is the best friend that I've ever had!" Claire broke the quietness.

"Likewise!" George said as he lifted his glass. As George, Claire and I took a sip of wine, James simply smiled at me for a few seconds before then raising his toward me and taking a sip. I had a feeling of butterflies and nausea all mixed into one, and I questioned myself again briefly as to whether I had really fallen for him.

As I sipped my wine and walked around the ballroom, taking in all of the immaculate painting and ornate woodwork, I listened to Claire asking George who his favourite band was whilst she set up the iPod. She then quickly retracted her question, joking that he probably preferred a string quartet. George tried to sound like he had moved with the times, stating that there were singers that he had grown to like, and that he particularly favoured Frank Sinatra. She happily obliged by playing 'Fly Me to the Moon' and it humoured me to watch her ask him to dance. I stood next to the mirror in which James stood and leant against it.

"It will be lovely to have this room filled with music and dancing very soon!"

"Indeed, it has been many a year since anything of importance happened in here!" James replied.

"Are you sure that you are alright with me having this party? It seems a little unfair to you!" I remarked.

"How so? I will have you here, and to see you enjoy yourself during the celebrations will be adequate enough for me," he replied. I smiled.

"I am just sorry that I have not managed to free you yet. To have you here physically would have made me happier!" I replied honestly.

"I would have liked that, and it saddens me that I will not be able to dance with you on your birthday!" he then said, gesturing toward Claire and George, who were now in full swing and enjoying themselves. "Although I must say that I am a far better dancer than George!" he then laughed.

"Really?" I enquired as I turned to face him.

"That is so not true Katharina; do not believe a word that he tells you!" George suddenly chirped. I liked that George was always listening in to anything that James had to say; I suppose over the years he had become a resident background noise for George.

"Honestly George, you cannot disagree with my comment – you know people have always remarked on how gracefully I move to music!" James confirmed.

"Well that was a long time ago, and I suspect that you are completely out of practice now!" George replied, before explaining to Claire what the discussion was about.

I happily sniggered at the two of them. The playful banter was amusing and even Claire had plenty to say about how good George was, which George clearly loved as he swirled her around the ballroom floor. By the end of the song, Claire looked slightly dizzy and requested that she take a sip of her drink, so George asked me for the next dance – 'Come Fly With Me', which was one of my favourites and already had my foot tapping. I happily accepted. Claire stood by the mirror and sipped her drink. I snuggled in close to George and whispered my thanks to him for being so kind to Claire. He thanked me for my continued support and remarked that he could not imagine being in the house without me here now, which made me tear up slightly, and so I gripped him tighter and whispered:

"I cannot imagine not being here either!" We looked at one another and hugged like a father and daughter would.

"What am I missing here?" James suddenly asked, knowing that George and I were obviously talking about something.

"Nothing you need to worry about!" George replied as he turned and dipped me into a sweep, leaning me backwards. I saw Claire and James upside down and smiled as George stood me back up.

"God, she even looks graceful ballroom dancing too. No competition!" Claire said lightly as she threw the last bit of her wine down her throat with gusto.

"I agree!" James confirmed, which snapped me back to reality a little.

The song finished and Claire declared that it was time for some modern pop music, starting with Kylie! We decided where everything decorative was going and then re-boxed them ready for next week, and danced around trying our best to sing along – which was worse than karaoke – whilst George amusingly tried to bop along with the music.

The wine was going down pretty quickly and so I offered to get another bottle from the fridge. Claire had also brought some rosé, which was definitely hitting the spot. I felt happy, relaxed and excited. As I returned from the kitchen, I could hear Claire talking and I stopped for a second to listen.

"You know, I love Kat. She is for all intents and purposes like a sister to me, and so although I am totally up for her helping you guys, I need you to promise me something!"

"Of course, what is it that you require?" George asked.

"Don't stop her from living! She is so wrapped up in you guys. I know that she is emotionally attached to the both of you, but I don't want her to get hurt!" Claire replied.

"I would never hurt her in any way. I care for her too much!" James then stated. I swallowed hard and placed my hand on my chest.

"We care too much for her to ever allow that to happen!" George then reiterated for Claire's benefit.

"Good! That is all I needed to know, and I promise I will say nothing else about it. I mean, it is pretty cool, being involved in this whole fairy tale thing!" she then happily said. I composed myself and walked back in, raising the bottle.

"Anyone for a top-up?" I asked innocently.

"I think that would be in order for all of us!" George then replied as he tried to take the bottle from me to pour. I placed my hand on his shoulder.

"Please let me!" I smiled as Pharrell's 'Happy' started to play. "Oh I love this song!" I told them as I danced around, filling the glasses. I got to the mirror and placed the bottle on the table so that James could get his reflected copy and asked him to dance along with me. I sang as I tried to provoke James into dancing.

"These words do not make sense!" he tried saying to avoid dancing. I laughed, as did George.

"Oh come on, relax a little!" I told him as I carried on singing. Claire had now joined in and we danced along. James did try to bounce along a little, but after a while he reached for his bottle and poured himself another glass. I shook my head at him.

"This kind of dancing is going to take some getting used to!" James then said.

"I suggest that we move to my kitchen and continue this soirée whilst I prepare dinner!" George then suggested. Claire and I stopped the iPod and laughed about the last time we had a girls' night dancing! We followed along to the kitchen and took a seat at the island as George started to cook. The wine was flowing as we talked and laughed, then George asked Claire if she had any amusing stories about me – which actually worried me a little, as I knew she had plenty!

Chapter Twenty-Six

I don't know why I felt so embarrassed at my drunken moments from the past, but as Claire reeled them off, I grimaced more times than I could count whilst trying to justify everything that she was saying. I nearly choked on my dinner when she decided to tell them about the extremely cringing time I tried salsa dancing at a new club, where I proceeded to be spun and flung around the floor like a ragdoll by numerous men… and then she told them the rest:

"Oh and if you ever want to see a very sultry Kat, then you need to get her 'dirty dancing' – it is a moving, visual experience!" she chuckled as George raised his eyebrows at me.

"Really? Well I am not sure what 'dirty dancing' is exactly, but it sounds slightly suggestive!" George innocently said. I grimaced some more.

"That's obviously another film that we need to make you boys watch!" I said, trying to sound as convincing as I could.

"Well, I think it is something that I would like to see Katharina doing; it sounds very much the opposite of her character to date, and so a visual representation is most definitely needed!" James suddenly said, and I knew that he was being sarcastic to cover up my obvious embarrassment. I turned to him and pulled a face at him before throwing my napkin at the mirror.

"You are unbelievable sometimes!" I joked. Claire was quiet for a moment then she replied:

"Is James starting to get a better picture of the real you?" she asked.

"Very funny – you make me sound like some crazed, dancing psychopath, but honestly I'm not!" I pleaded to both James and George before hitting Claire jokily on the arm. "For goodness' sake Claire, you're going to scare them both to death and make them think they have made a huge mistake letting me be in their lives! I love it here, I love everything about it, so don't make them question me!" I snapped.

"Okay, okay, keep your panties on, I'm only joking with you – these guys know that!" Claire looked to George for support, knowing that I was a little annoyed as well as embarrassed.

"Of course we do!" George confirmed as he refilled our glasses before turning to James and gesturing with his head for him to say something. James looked at me.

"I do not see any problem with you enjoying yourself; dancing is as good a form as any. I have to confess that I have had my share of enjoyment in the past… probably a little too much!" he remarked, and I smiled at his honest words.

"Alright, maybe I overreacted then, just a little, but I really do not want you thinking the worst of me!" I replied calmly as I looked at James.

"I have no perception, thought, or word that would give me the slightest reason to have any doubt or disapproval toward you! I do not wish for you to ever think that I would. After everything that you have done for us and *are* doing for us, I have nothing but complete appreciation for you," James then said, and I knew that he meant every word.

"Hear hear!" Claire then suddenly said, and both George and I jumped up and stared at her. She looked up at us from her glass that she had just taken a large sip from and simply said; "What did I do now?"

"You heard that?" I asked curiously; she did not seem to realise what had just happened.

"What, the very lovely compliment? You always get all of the good stuff, don't you?" she said, very nonchalantly.

"But you heard James?" I asked again, and she nearly choked on her wine.

"Holy crap, was that James?" she then said as she stood up too. "How did I do that?" she asked with excitement.

"I don't know!" I shrugged and looked at George and then James.

"Why can't I see him though?" she then asked. I looked at the mirror and James and then her.

"You can't see him?" I asked. "He's right there!" I gestured toward him.

"Hearing but not seeing? Well, that's new for us!" George then said.

"Indeed, this is quite perplexing!" James replied.

"Ooh, you spoke again!" Claire grabbed my hands and jumped up and down. "This is so exciting, I can hear him now – wow, you were telling the truth!" she then remarked and I looked at her, a little shocked.

"What, you didn't believe me before?" I enquired.

"No, I believed you Kat – I trust everything you say – but at first it did sound a little nuts to be fair! But holy crap, it's really real!" She walked to the mirror and studied it hard.

"This makes things a little easier, I believe!" George then commented, looking at James.

"Easier, but I am not entirely sure that it will continue. I have never experienced this; there is no confirmation that it will last!" James said firmly. Claire turned and looked at George and I.

"Jeez, is he always this negative?" she asked. In unison, we replied;

"Sometimes!"

"Hey, I am here you realise! I am only being realistic, this has never happened before!" he confirmed.

"Okay, let's take this one step at a time." I took a deep breath whilst James paced. "I suggest we carry on as normal and just see what happens!" I looked for reassurance from the rest of them.

"Agreed!" they all confirmed.

We sat and filled our glasses and I changed the subject to the choice of film. *Pride and Prejudice* was my initial thought – the newer version; I didn't think that I could keep James and George's attention throughout the whole BBC version with Colin Firth. As I made a point that the best thing to do might be to put it on and try to relax a little, Claire started giggling to herself and so I just looked at her inquisitively.

"This is the best freaking weekend ever!" she simply said.

"We are glad to be of service!" James replied. Claire chuckled more and took another sip of wine.

"Well, this certainly has changed the whole outcome of the weekend!" George replied whilst I inserted the DVD and took a place next to Claire on the large and comfy sofa. We both curled up whilst James settled himself in the armchair, looking very worried about what he was about to watch, and George simply sat back and smiled.

"I am hoping that you can share some truths about this film – and it should be a reminder of how things used to be. I hope that it is not too painful though!" I then stated as it began.

"Nonsense; if anything it will be amusing to see if history has been correctly presented. Both James and I shall give our input if you have any questions!" George kindly said.

I looked across at James as Keira Knightley walked across the screen, reading her book as Elizabeth Bennet, and James shuffled on his chair, looking like he had seen a ghost. He watched the screen with complete uncertainty and turned to look at George and then me. I smiled in reassurance and nodded to let him know that it was alright, after which he settled back into his chair, picked up his glass and proceeded to watch the entire film. I only noted him taking his glance off the screen to refill his glass. Claire commented many times on the characters' dialogue, making it quite clear that she was glad the language of today was not so formal. I disagreed and told her that I thought it was chivalrous and simplistic and a lost art; James and George both noted that it was far simpler in their day, having rules in place on the expectations of etiquette. I asked about the dancing and noted the amount of staff each household had.

Claire was happily curled up alongside, leaning on me quite heavily, but I greatly appreciated that my best friend was here, with the added fact that she could at least hear James – it made my job far easier this weekend. Once the film had finished, she sighed and openly asked both George and James:

"Well, what did you think?"

"I think that in the grand scheme of things, it was a fair representation of the time!" George replied. "Jane Austen was indeed a very distinguished writer of novels."

"And very petite, from what I remember!" James then said. Claire sat up.

"You say that as if you knew her!" she asked excitedly.

"I knew *of* her; she visited here with acquaintances for a very brief time. I was in this unfortunate state and unable to meet her, but I do believe that George conversed with her – did you not?" he asked George.

"Indeed I did – she was very amiable!" he confirmed.

"Wow, that is so, so cool!" Claire replied, but I found it hard to speak. Jane Austen had been in my house at some point, and she was my all-time favourite author of romantic novels! I simply smiled and then asked them:

"You didn't tell me that before. Is there anything that you miss from that period of time?"

"Yes, I miss the letters and wax seals. Receiving correspondence from any person was a greatly anticipated treat. The smell of the wax seal, the noise once you broke it to unfold the letter, and the ink… its smell alone was delightful. The handwriting of the time was second to none, and another art now lost I fear – that is what I miss the most. It is far too easy today to pick up a piece of technology and never put pen to paper!" George sadly stated, and I had to agree. I looked at James.

"What about you, James?"

"I dearly miss the people; my father, mother and friends now lost. I agree with George that correspondence has somewhat changed and that is a shame, but I cannot argue that times have changed and society along with it. The world is very much a different place now!" he replied.

"It never occurred to me how difficult it must have been to leave people behind; I am sorry for you both for that!" Claire then said. James looked up at her.

"Thank you, your thoughts are appreciated," he replied sincerely, she smiled. Claire sighed heavily before standing.

"Well George, do you have any more wine in this place? I feel the need for more – this weekend is definitely turning out to be more than interesting!" she stated joyously.

"Yes, I'll show you where the wine cellar is and you can help yourself!" George replied as he gestured for her to follow. I stood with the empty bottle and started to make my way to the door when James stopped me with a question.

"Do you think that love can endure anything or any situation?" he candidly asked. I stopped and turned to him.

"Are you referring to the film?" I asked.

"Not entirely. I merely ask your opinion. I looked at

you during the film and you seemed moved by the plight of Elizabeth and Darcy's love!"

"My experiences toward love to date have not been very fulfilling, James, but I do think that true love can endure anything. I also understand how tormenting it can be, especially when watching something like that! I would like to hope that during my lifetime I will experience a love as true and meaningful as theirs – who wouldn't?" I replied with honesty.

"You fervently believe that that kind of love can be felt and experienced by anyone?" he then enquired. I moved closer to him and, as truthfully as I have ever been with any man, replied:

"I sincerely think so. In my opinion, life will be very hard to bear if I never get the chance to experience a love so strong, and so true that I would rather die than live without it. So in response to your question; if there was a chance of having a love like theirs, I would strongly encourage it!" I smiled, curtseyed to him for some reason and left the room.

What was I thinking? *I have truly lost my senses – or I now think that I am living in times past; why the hell did I curtsey! Great, he's bound to have found that amusing – I am trying to impress, not look irrational!* I cursed myself as I walked toward George's kitchen, and then he appeared again and so I composed myself quickly.

"I feel… that you are the most intriguing woman that I have ever met!" he said.

"You probably think that I am also slightly deranged! I didn't mean to curtsey – I think that film has melted my brain a little!" I joked.

"Ah so you did, but I didn't really notice – I was more fascinated by your feelings toward loyalty and love," he replied, which made me blush and swallow hard, hoping that I hadn't just given away my growing feelings toward him.

"Well, I think it's every girl's fantasy to wish for a love like that! Who wouldn't want that? I would give everything to have that!" I then honestly replied again, then turned away from him and cursed myself again for being so truthful. I was bound to be scaring the poor man to death.

"I find your conviction in your beliefs and your honesty at expressing them to me rather endearing," he then replied as sincerely. I stopped and looked at him.

"Thank you!" I simply said, and smiled. It wasn't as bad a response as I had expected. He gestured for me to continue walking.

"I should thank you," he then said.

"For what?" I enquired.

"Trusting me enough to be so very honest with me! I have always enjoyed conversing with you, Katharina, but the fact that you are so open with me is indeed quite flattering," he continued.

"James, I may not have known you for very long, but in my head and my heart I feel like I have known you forever! I find you easy to speak to, and I am grateful for that!" I replied. He smiled and just as we neared the main kitchen George and Claire appeared, laughing about something.

"Right, George and I have decided that it is time we indulged in some older wine, and we have to drink it once opened no matter what!" Claire announced. "I can feel a hangover coming on already!" she then finished.

I turned and looked at James, and we both grimaced slightly before he crossed his arms and then raised the suggestion: "I am all for enjoying ourselves and merrily intoxicating our systems with old wine, but should it be like strong vinegar, I feel that we all need to be accountable for any personal illnesses that it causes! George will not want to clear up the contents of anyone's stomach other than his own!" he remarked.

"Well said James; I am not great at tolerating anything expelled from other people's stomachs!" George agreed.

"I should think not, I can think of nothing worse!" I replied, cringing at the thought. "Trust you to turn this into a binge drinking night; do you realise how expensive some of these wines are?" I asked Claire.

"I dread to think, but I am going to try at least one of them!" she then replied as she ushered George to his kitchen to find a corkscrew. I looked at James.

"I am so sorry, there is no explanation for her behaviour!" I said as I rubbed my head.

"No apology necessary, she knows how to enjoy herself… obviously!" James laughed.

"Oh, I assure you she certainly knows how to do that!" I replied.

The drinks flowed – far too many in fact, where I was concerned – and Claire, in her usual boisterous way, had George dancing yet again, to pop songs that I am sure were not to his taste, but he indulged her nonetheless. James and I laughed at them and the fact that I was slurring my words, along with Claire. George and James seemed completely in control and that frustrated me a little. I went up to James and quite decisively pressed my index finger against the mirror at him.

"Do you ever consume enough alcohol to become the slightest bit inebriated?" I managed to say without slurring too much. He smiled.

"Oh believe me, I have had more than my fill, and I am sure it will cause some affliction in the morning!" he said.

"Hmmm, we shall see. At least I have managed not to completely embarrass myself this evening!" I sniggered as I started swaying.

"The evening is the worse for it, I feel!" James remarked humorously.

"Are you saying that you enjoy seeing me behaving inappropriately?" I asked with annoyance.

"I enjoy seeing you behaving so free-spiritedly! I do not wish any affliction upon you, but it does make me feel warmly toward your nature when you are so relaxed with both George and I!" he replied.

"I feel that you are one of the most kind-hearted people I have ever met, James Aldersley, and you say the nicest things! I am so glad that I met you," I said as I placed my hand against the mirror and he in turn placed his against mine. We stood and looked at each other. At first I thought it was the wine, but soon I realised that I was breathing heavily, with the sensation of an overactive bottle of champagne being opened in my stomach. I confirmed to myself right then that I had intense feelings for James and I suddenly became very aware that I felt incredibly vulnerable.

I snatched my hand back to my side, and he looked at me with slight concern. I placed my glass down on the table and then quietly said before turning away from him:

"Forgive me – I feel that the effects of this wine have allowed me to put you in an incredibly uncomfortable position. I think it is high time I retired before I make a fool of myself!" What was I thinking? Plain Katharina attached to a man with such distinguished credibility, good looks and charm? Regardless of his past, how could he ever fall in love with someone as plain as me? I did not wait long enough to hear him say:

"You do not realise how much I have hoped to see such a reaction from you!"

I forcefully marched over to George and Claire and informed them that I needed to retire before I fell over. We exchanged cheek kisses and I left the room, shouting goodnight as I walked.

I was not aware of James shadowing me, but I heard Claire say to George: "Is there more to those two than I know?"

"I fear not, but it would be a match to envy any from any novel or film that I have ever come across!" George replied.

I swallowed hard and shook my head; obviously my behaviour toward James was becoming noticeable to others too, and so James was bound to be aware. I stopped and took off my shoes before continuing up the stairs and as I turned down the corridor to my room I was aware of James' presence.

"Are you following me?" I asked, trying to sound casual.

"I merely wished to see that you arrived to your room without injury!" he replied. I smiled at his casual response, then he continued: "Katharina, I do not want you to retire without accepting a response from me to your last comment!"

"James, please don't – you have no need to make me feel better or try and resolve my obvious lack of tact. I understand that I am average and plain and I should not make gestures toward you to make you think that I am trying to attach myself to you." I grimaced in the knowledge that he felt the need to smooth things over with me, but I did not expect his response.

"My pride has often been in the way of my feelings, but your complete tenderness to my plight and your selfless endeavour to end it has indeed captured my heart. I cannot allow you to retire feeling that you have made a fool of yourself, for your complete honesty and unselfish behaviour toward me, make me think of you as nothing less than my saviour! In response to your last comment, any attachment to you – friend or otherwise – is truly my honour!" he said it with such warmth that I almost melted… it took me a while to reply.

"As always you calm my worries with your words!" I replied; he acknowledged my response by nodding once. "To know that you are not repulsed by my honesty and actions pleases me more than I can say!" I finished, then I smiled, and before I realised what I was doing I had walked to the mirror, raised myself up on my tiptoes and kissed it in the vicinity of his cheek. When I lowered my heels, I stayed where I stood for a moment, my breath condensing on the mirror, and I listened to his breathing, which was now exaggerated. I stepped back, looked at him and simply said: "Goodnight James."

"Goodnight Katharina," he replied as I opened my bedroom door. "I hope that tomorrow sees us not too afflicted by the consumption of old wine!" He smiled.

"Oh I really hope so too!" I replied.

"I shall return downstairs and see if Claire and George are ready to retire!" he then informed me before he turned to leave. I closed the door and smiled to myself. Perhaps there was a possibility of us being more than friends, if he should ever have the inclination to feel any love toward me.

I managed to get to sleep easily; the alcohol made sure of that. However at approximately 4am I woke after dreaming, sweating and thirsty. My mouth felt like a dry desert, with the aftertaste of one too many glasses of wine. I decided to go downstairs and get a glass of milk to help me get back to sleep. The house was a very different place in the dead of night; reflections from the windows and the large clock's ticking in the drawing room were more noticeable than at any other time of day. I reached George's kitchen and quietly crept in, retrieved a glass and opened the fridge door. The milk was cool and thirst-quenching and I quickly drank a glass and refilled it. I closed the door, glass in hand, and nearly jumped out of my skin.

"You are finding it difficult to sleep also?" James suddenly said.

"Jesus, I didn't see you there!" I replied as I placed my hand on my heart to slow its frenzied beating.

"I am sorry to alarm you," he quickly replied. I laughed nervously.

"It's fine, you just startled me – I wasn't expecting anyone else to be awake!" I replied as my heart rate slowed down.

"Very well," he calmly said, and we stood in silence whilst I drank my glass of milk nervously.

"I suppose we should be quiet in case we wake George?" I then said.

"He is usually a very sound sleeper!" James replied, but as he said that we heard George stirring in his room, so I gestured for James to follow me into the main house.

I felt like a teenager, creeping around the house, and unfortunately I was now wide awake. I paced the hallway, then wished that I had put on my robe as I was cold. I thought for a moment; I wanted to speak with James, but it wasn't right to be stood shivering in my pyjamas. I decided to take a plunge and ask him something that he would probably find slightly out of his social rules of etiquette, but after our earlier conversations I hoped that he would oblige.

"James, I am cold and even though I am now awake, I would prefer the comfort of my room."

"Of course, I am sorry – please go ahead!" He gestured for me to leave.

"I was hoping that you would keep me company for a while?" I then asked. He glanced at me once and then half smiled.

"I should like that, if you are entirely sure?" he replied. I nodded in response and then started my way up the stairs.

I closed my door and climbed onto my bed and under the many sheets. The warm ambient light from the lamp made me instantly relax. James looked nervous and so I started the conversation.

"So, as we are both awake I think that I should like to hear some more stories about you from your past!"

"I am sure that my past would not make you think very well of me," he replied.

"Knowing that you suffered or for that matter made others suffer slightly in your past does not stop me wanting to know more about it or you! After tonight, it occurred to me that there have probably been many times that you have been more than intoxicated from alcohol. Surely there are some interesting stories from then?" I smiled hopefully.

He was sat on the end of the reflected copy of my bed. He had his flouncy white shirt on, open at the neck, and his breeches; his hair was messy but I like that. It was arousing to say the least, but I managed to control my reaction. He pondered for a short time and then his face relaxed and he smiled.

"There have been a few moments in my past in which I thought my time was upon me," he remarked, and then proceeded to tell me about all the amusing incidents in which he had lost control of any sane reasoning – enough to do something very stupid whilst drunk. He made me laugh, which was something that I had not done with such force with a man in a long time. I tried to muffle the sound with my sheets as I worried about waking Claire numerous times. His retelling of a duel with pistols – which he had insisted upon during a fight in an ale house – had ended up with him merely injuring the other party and them calling a truce. After both parties were continually falling over on the icy ground they gave up trying to stand still long enough to shoot. That is where the pistols in the attic had come from – he took them as a token of the day, and a reminder of his stupidity. It also came to light that George had accompanied him on this duel, and it made me realise why he felt such parental responsibility for James; he had been through more challenges with him than most parents ever have to endure.

I started to feel tired again; the excitement had worn me out. As I yawned and rubbed my eyes, I gestured to myself and my obvious state of exhaustion and the fact that I could no longer stay awake. I straightened my pyjamas and then looked to James and his attire.

"Where are your pyjamas?" I asked him. He shrugged. "You know, I think if you want to move on, James, it would be a good idea to start wearing clothing of this time period more often!" I remarked.

"I should but, in all honesty. I thought that if I were to dress in clothing from my period, it would be easier for you to relate to me!" he finished.

"It would be nice to see you in a pair of jeans again!" I confirmed, smiling, and then I reached over to the lamp. "Goodnight James. Thank you for keeping me company, this has been a lovely evening!" I said, before switching off the light.

"Indeed it has!" he said in the darkness, and then I drifted off to sleep happily.

Chapter Twenty-Seven

*S*unday morning was relaxing and satisfying. George had made the biggest English breakfast that I think I had ever seen, but he insisted that it was necessary in aiding a quick recovery from the wine last night. I had to say that even though I felt unwell the night before, I woke feeling better than I could have expected. Claire was not so great! She had finished the rest of another old bottle of wine with George, and retired to bed nearly an hour after I did. Even though she ate, she complained at her rollercoaster stomach and the fact that she had a very bad headache. I passed her some paracetamol and refilled her coffee; I had had the sense to take two when I had my milk in the early hours of the morning.

I had not made any comment, but I noted that James had arrived at breakfast this morning in dark blue jeans, which sat low on his hips, and a plain black t-shirt. He looked casual and fairly relaxed, and I presumed that he had done this for my benefit after our conversation last night. I smiled at him after giving him the once-over, then took a large bite of my toast, and he simply shrugged in acknowledgement and smiled back. We seemed to have a mutual appreciation and respect for each other, and the thought of that made me exceptionally happy.

The morning proceeded slowly. After reading

yesterday's paper, I took Claire outside to show her around the grounds, during which she of course quizzed me.

"So, how long are you going to let James stay in this state?" she asked.

"Excuse me?"

"Well, it seems that he needs to make someone fall in love with him and they have to physically say that to him. What are you waiting for? It's obvious you think he's mega hot!" she then stated.

"Claire, I can't believe that you would think that!" I replied hesitantly.

"Oh come on... I mean, after John you could say that this is a bit of a whirlwind situation, but if he's as hot as that painting then I'd have had him out of there and in my bed by now!" she laughed. I pushed her in annoyance and then smiled.

"It's not as easy as that though – that's just it. I want him to love me too. I do not think that I am good enough for him, but you are right – the longer I spend here with them, the deeper my feelings for him get. I just feel that I shouldn't; I mean I have just ended one engagement!" I confirmed.

"Oh Jesus Kat, that is nothing, you could have been married five times already, but it makes no difference if you love each other! They are slightly strange circumstances, I'll give you that, and the fact that you have never physically met him is a little out of the ordinary, but... it is what it is, so make the most of it!" she said. I hugged her; she always was one for putting things into perspective. "Unless of course you free him and he either has bad breath or a small penis, then you may want to throw him back in!" she then laughed, and I couldn't help myself – I did too.

We entered the house in fits of hysterics after she announced that she thought the latter unlikely, and both James and George came to see what all the fuss was about. I had to elbow Claire to stop her from saying anything crude, but she simply stated that we were reminiscing about old times. The day was more enjoyable than I had anticipated and we went to the wine merchants to buy supplies for my party, played games, listened to music and I showed Claire the library – she was as fascinated with it as me, and we stayed in there for some time. When it came to 3pm she decided that it was time she returned home. She had errands to run before returning to work tomorrow – one of them was visiting her brother Scott, who had just started a new job; she promised she would call by to find out how he was getting on after his first week. George offered to take her to the station as he wanted to pick up a couple of newspapers and so after she had packed up we said our goodbyes. She offered to come back and help next Saturday, the day of the party, so that I was not stressing! George kindly invited her to stay for the night; he knew that I enjoyed her company. She looked at the large mirror in the hallway and said:

"Nice to hear you James!" she smirked to herself.

"A pleasure to have you stay with us, Claire!" he replied, and although she could not see him, he bowed to her. She walked up to me and hugged me and then whispered in my ear:

"His voice is to die for, so I know he's definitely hot. Get cracking, girl – I can't wait to actually see him!" She enforced this by slapping me hard on the right buttock. James and George simply raised their eyebrows at her in curiosity; hopefully they had not heard her!

The house seemed a little quieter after she had left, and I had not realised until then how tired I was. I asked James if he would like some tea.

"That would be very nice, but it does bother me that I cannot make it for you for a change!" he stated.

"That's sweet, but it's only a cup of tea!" I replied. We proceeded to sit in the day room; the view across the gardens was never tiresome and we conversed for a while before James excused himself and sat at the writing desk in the corner. As I picked up my book from the library to continue reading, he produced the journal that I had given him, along with what looked like the journal that his mother had written in. It frustrated me that I could not simply go and read what he was writing, as he dipped the quill into the inkpot and then started writing along the paper. I closed my eyes and imagined being next to him; being able to see him, smell him, touch him and see what he was writing.

It was some time later when George came back into the room and woke me up from the chaise longue, where I had fallen asleep. As my sleepy eyes opened, I looked at my half-drunk cup of tea that was now stone cold and then I sat up slightly and looked at James, who was now sat reading. George smiled at me.

"It seems we have one very tired young lady!" he remarked at my zombie-like state.

"I am sorry, how rude of me," I replied, then looked at James: "I am so sorry for falling asleep in your company!" He looked up from his book.

"I could not be prevailed upon to wake you. You looked... serene. No apology needed!" he simply said, and his gaze went back to his book.

I sat and stretched and George handed me a *Sunday Express*. I placed it at my side and reached for my cup, which I intended to clear away, but George stopped me and told me that he had made a fresh pot and I should stay put. I took a deep breath and then circled my head a few times, trying to alleviate the slight tightness in my neck. James simply watched me and so I closed my eyes and couldn't believe it when I started to imagine him massaging my neck. I opened them again quickly and steadied myself where I sat.

"Everything alright?" he asked. I felt slightly flushed, but quickly answered:

"Perfectly!" I smiled and picked up the newspaper.

George returned with the tea, which was refreshing, and we all sat and read the papers, sharing them between us. I glanced up a couple of times and was happy to find them both relaxed and quiet and simply enjoying the time to read and take in news from the world. This was fast becoming a happy scenario in my daily life, and I loved every minute of it. I noted that James had now taken to relaxing with jeans, a t-shirt and no shoes – he was barefoot – and it made him more real somehow. I excused myself before dinner and went to refresh my face; the cool water was needed, as I could not seem to snap out of this sleepy feeling. I returned downstairs feeling much better;

just brushing my hair made a difference, and I chose to pin it up for dinner. We ate – no more wine, thank goodness, and no dessert! – and then for a change watched a little television. By the time the news came on, I decided that was my cue to leave and retire to bed. James again asked if he could walk me to my room and I agreed.

"Well, this weekend has proved to be most enjoyable!" he remarked, smiling.

"Even with the complexity of Claire's character?" I asked. He laughed.

"Yes she is quite different, but I can see why you like her. She is not afraid to state her opinion, as firm as it sometimes is!" he then said.

"I have never known her to be any different. I think in some way it is for self-protection. It would be nice to see her settle down with someone!" I replied.

"I feel they would have to have a very strong character also! I would find her frustrating at times!" he said laughing.

"Well, it was simply nice to share something amazing with one of my best friends, and the fact that she could hear you was progress I thought?" I gestured to him. He nodded in agreement.

"Indeed, that has never happened before. I have the strong feeling that things are changing, I think it is for the better!" he then said hopefully.

"Well, we have next weekend to look forward to. I am really excited! I shall be shopping for my new dress soon with Claire; it is strange to think that by this time next week it will all be over!" I then commented sadly.

"Then we must ensure that we enjoy every single moment!" James said as he stopped beside my door.

"Yes, we must – and that includes you too!" I then confirmed. He smiled.

"Good night Katharina."

"Good night James!" I replied before walking into my room and closing the door.

I walked across my room and realised that all of these formalities were things that I loved; James walking me to my room, his protective instinct at my wellbeing, his complete dedication to my happiness… all things that I had craved in every relationship, and yet I had never once seen James in the flesh. I questioned if I was doing the right thing, putting myself in this situation; maybe at some point soon I would wake up in hospital after a bump to the head and realise it was all a dream! For now, I wanted to live the fairy tale, including James, George, the house, the chivalry, the magic… I was in love with everything here. I smiled, realising that Claire was right; that love that I felt did include James.

I went downstairs the next morning very happy at my new realisation that I was – however ridiculous it may seem – in love with James. In the last few days he had proved how much he meant to me, and Claire, in her usual manner, had reinforced something that I was trying to hide. Even though I felt bound to him, I did not want to say anything just yet for fear of rejection and him not returning the sentiment. After all, I had just ended an engagement, which initially made me think that I may just be trying to grab onto anyone that made me feel wanted. I made a decision for now to say nothing until I felt sure that he had feelings for me, which could be some time – it was obvious that he found it difficult to express his feelings at all. In the kitchen, he was sat yet again at the end of the island, wearing jeans and a white linen shirt that was open at the neck and had the sleeves rolled up. He stood as I entered and I smiled widely.

"Good morning!" he calmly said and gestured for me to sit. George, with apron on, produced a pile of pancakes topped with blueberries and strawberries and repeated the greeting.

"Good morning!"

"A very good morning to both of you!" I replied. I was trying not to continually grin, as it would have them enquiring after my happy persona! They looked at each other and then at me as I started to help myself.

"I trust that you rested well?" George then asked.

"George, I did indeed. I feel better than ever this morning!" I replied, with a tone of contentment. They looked at each other again.

I ate, got myself ready to go and then bid James farewell, firstly by saying it and then by yet again kissing the mirror in the vicinity of his cheek. He raised his eyebrows at George and as I walked toward George I kissed him on the cheek also.

"Shall we go?" I then asked. They both stood still for a moment, and then George jumped to attention and followed me out of the door. James said nothing, which amused me – he was probably in shock at my actions this morning.

Work was fast-moving; my new story was well under way. Angela was impressed with my seemingly new focus and input during the meeting, particularly on other colleagues' work, and everything seemed to be slotting into place. Claire eyeballed me a few times curiously whilst she took notes, and as soon as it came to lunchtime we sat to eat at the small cafe around the corner. She said nothing at first, as I took a bite of my sandwich, but then asked:

"Okay – spill the beans!! What is it with you today? You are more confident, happy, being very constructive with everyone at work and still smiling! What happened after I left yesterday?" she enquired.

"What makes you think it was to do with anything at home?" I asked, smiling like a Cheshire cat. She folded her arms and scowled at me, and I put my sandwich down. "Alright, I came to an obvious conclusion last night: I love everything at Northfield!"

"I know that!" she said, obviously expecting a more detailed answer.

"… Including James!" I then said and looked at her, hoping that she wouldn't think I was mad.

"I knew it!" she exclaimed, banging her hand on the table. "I told you I knew that look. You certainly never looked like that at John – since a long time ago, anyway! Did you tell him? Is that why you're happy? Did he come out of the mirror and give you the best night of your life?" she then said and I nearly choked on my sandwich as she took a bite of hers.

"Oh my God, is that all that you think about?" I asked.

"Pretty much!" she laughed. "So?" She gestured for me to continue.

"It was everything; we sat together reading the papers, had dinner, talked, watched some television and then he walked me to my room. He always seems to know what to say, and it makes me melt!" I concluded.

"Well, if his voice is anything to go by I can understand that! Why haven't you told him?" she asked as she took another large bite.

"I am worried that he does not feel the same way. For this to work and the spell to be broken, he needs to hear me say I love him, but I want him to tell me that he feels that way too. If I declared my love and he didn't, I do not think that I could live there any longer!" I said with dismay.

"So you would rather live like this? Not have James at all in the real world and just live in a fairy tale? Jesus, snap out of it Kat, this is meant to be!" she whispered as she leant in closer.

"I'm scared!" I replied, and in usual Claire fashion she gave me an ultimatum.

"Right – this is how it is going to work. If you do not tell him by the end of your party on Saturday night, then I will!" she stated forcefully.

"You wouldn't!" I replied with concern.

"Oh, I would! I am not watching you carry on not being as happy as you could be just because you will not say three little words!" she finished. I gulped and then took a deep breath.

"You're right; I have to tell him. He has waited long enough. I am being selfish if I do not, aren't I?"

"Yep!" she nodded in reply, but smiling.

"Maybe my party is the best time; this torture started on his thirtieth birthday and if the spell breaks it will end at mine! Do you think it was meant to happen like this?" I asked her. She sat gawping at me.

"If you had asked me a couple of weeks ago, I would have slapped you myself for going crazy, but I've experienced this and it *is real,* Kat, and it *is happening*, and until you said that I had not realised… how amazing and right this is!" She grabbed my hand. "Why shouldn't this fairy tale have a happy ending?" I smiled at her and nodded.

"Saturday night it is then! If it doesn't work out, promise me that you will get me out of there to save my embarrassment?" I declared.

"Oh this is going to work… wake up, girl! With the compliments that he has been giving you, he must have feelings for you, and one of you has to be the brave one!" she laughed. We both sat and finished our sandwiches with the feeling that things were about to change.

When I arrived home that evening, I suddenly found myself being slightly coy around him. I kept thinking about how I felt about him, and then trying to be the normal Katharina that I had been, but I kept saying silly things. I went to the bathroom before we ate dinner and told myself to get a grip. *Act normal*, I said to myself, and then I shook my head, took a deep breath and went back downstairs, but whatever I did I could not take the huge grin off my face. James and I laughed about things, taunted each other and complimented each other, and George either joined in or said nothing. They asked me about my choice of dress for the party and I confirmed that Claire and I were shopping tomorrow and Wednesday. The days were busy and I craved the evenings; I knew that Saturday would be here before I knew it, and that gave me a butterflies-in-a-tornado feeling in my stomach!

By Wednesday lunchtime I had tried on twelve dresses. I had only ever invested in one ball gown, but it was so out of date that I would probably never wear it again. I wanted something elegant, sophisticated and drop-dead gorgeous – and of course it had to make me look at least one dress size smaller. I was getting slightly disillusioned until Claire suggested that we went to Harvey Nichols, and as we walked in I sincerely wished that we hadn't! We walked into the evening dresses section and almost died and went to heaven; Donna Karan, Moschino, Alexander McQueen, Marchesa and Catherine Deane all jostled for space. Claire's eyes lit up and before I knew it we had four exceptional dresses to try on. One of them was a deep scarlet red and when Claire zipped me up and stepped back, I knew it was the one. She stood and raised her hands to her mouth and fought back a tear.

"Oh my God, you look amazing. You have to get it!" she said, and when I turned and looked in the mirror I gasped – it was amazing, and I couldn't think of anything else that I would rather have. So after trying not to fall over after glancing at the price tag – particularly when I needed to pay for the caterers, etc – I had the assistant bag up the dress and we carried it back to work. Luckily I had fairly new shoes and a bag from LK Bennett which were more than adequate to pair with the dress.

When I got off the train that evening, George looked surprised at the large dress bag that I carried with me. He immediately took it from me, placing it in the boot of the car. We jumped into the seats and then set off home.

"So shopping was constructive, it would seem?" he smiled.

"Oh George, it really is the most beautiful dress. It cost me an arm and a leg, but I want to look perfect on Saturday – as I want it to be one of the biggest days of my life, I hope!" I replied. He looked at me curiously.

"How so?" he asked, and I wondered for a minute whether I should say anything to him, then decided that he may be able to give me a better picture of how I stood with James.

"George, if I tell you something, can you keep it a secret for now?" I asked. He continued driving but looked at me twice, realising that I was serious, before saying:

"Of course. I swear that I will not breathe one word to anyone. What troubles you, Katharina?" he asked. I smiled.

"I am not troubled, George. I am more certain of something than I have ever been and it makes me very happy!" I replied.

"Well, you certainly have my undivided attention Katharina. Please do not make me wait any longer!" he replied. I took a deep breath.

"I have known for some time really, but it was only when Claire made me confront my feelings that I embraced the fact that spending time with you both has made me happier than I ever expected to feel," I started. George looked at me and realised that I was trying to say more. He reached across and squeezed my hand in reassurance and then said:

"Katharina, you know you can talk to me about anything!" he reinforced as he smiled encouragingly. I nodded, took a deep breath and said:

"I am in love with James!" I blurted it out before I changed my mind. George in turn started to laugh warmly and then squeezed my hand some more.

"Yes, I know!" he simply said. Then he controlled himself and carried on. "I realised a few days ago, but I wondered how long it would take you to confess to it! This is better news than I could have ever hoped for, and yet you seem slightly apprehensive about your confession?" he replied.

"I am worried that he will not believe me, or worse still he does not feel the same way. What if he laughs in my face and tells me that I am being ridiculous?" I asked. "I mean, I have not been too successful in my past experiences of love, have I?"

"Oh my dear, that will not happen! Anyway he has strong feelings for you, of that I am certain, and you can never compare one relationship to another! Are you planning on telling him soon?" he asked hopefully.

"Yes, at my party – it seems the right time and that is why I want it to be perfect!" I replied.

"Ah, today is the best day that I have had in a very long time. You make me extremely happy, Katharina, and I promise that I will say nothing until you have told him yourself. I feel that Saturday could be a very fulfilling day for all three of us!" George replied. "Stop worrying my dear, I know that everything will turn out the way you hope for!"

"I really hope so George, and if he does believe my feelings of love toward him, then the spell will be broken and both of you can end this torture and live your lives like everyone else!" I smiled.

"I cannot tell you how relieved that makes me feel! You were indeed sent to us from above; and quite possibly are an angel, Katharina!" he stated with emotion, and I squeezed his hand for a moment. I had not really registered how much it would mean to George to be able to live normally and grow old like anyone else. He had spent so long thinking that it would never happen, it was sure to make him a little nervous!

George smiled all the way home and I dreamed of how it would all turn out on Saturday. As we turned down the driveway I had butterflies circling my stomach and I took three deep breaths. George stopped the car and turned to me.

"Stop worrying; this is all going to fall perfectly into place and I know that James will be so very happy that you have feelings for him, as I know that he certainly does you!"

"What? Has he said something to you before?" I asked, curious that I had been mentioned.

"Many times; our conversations that last into the early hours now usually revolve around you. He cannot praise you enough in word and thought and deed. I was merely unsure that you had any feelings for him, until I saw the way that you acted at the weekend and during the week preceding that. It is good that you are able to confirm your love; I could not think of a better match for both you and James!" he finished. I sat and thought for a moment.

"I never realised that he felt that way I mean, I often wondered, but I always thought that I was not good enough to deserve someone like him!" I replied, and then George stopped me.

"Do not ever say that, Katharina! *He* does not deserve *you!*" George kindly stated. I smiled.

"How do I behave now? I am sure he will guess that something is going on!" I asked.

"We will help each other!" he replied as he climbed out of the car. I checked myself in the mirror whilst George walked around to my side of the car and opened the door.

He held out his hand to help me down from my seat and then we wandered to the back of the car to retrieve my dress and workbag. As we walked to the top of the front stairs, we simply looked at each other and nodded, and then entered the house as we always would – chatting about my day.

"Good evening!" James said happily.

"Good evening James, are you well?" I asked.

"Quite well, and you?" he enquired. I smiled and looked at George, who was laying my dress bag across a long sofa in the hallway, and then replied:

"I am very well thank you," as I started to take off my coat.

"It looks as though you have chosen your dress – I take it you had a very constructive day?" he asked.

"I have, in more ways than one!" I replied and George then shot me a look that said 'be careful or you will have to explain that further' and so I changed the subject. "I am starving tonight, shall I make dinner?" I asked as I started walking toward George's kitchen. They followed as George said: "Already done, it is in the oven!"

"Really George, you do spoil me!" I commented. He was simple in his reply.

"You deserve to be well looked after!" I smiled.

Dinner was delicious again, and it was a most enjoyable start to the evening. I caught myself swooning at James on a couple of occasions. At one point I noticed him stare at me for a long time, and then I suddenly realised that I hadn't heard a question he was asking, which was why he was looking at me for a response. George had to turn away so that he didn't show his amusement. I quickly answered, snapping myself out of the daze; and realising that George had noticed, I tried to correct my behaviour. After dinner I carried my dress bag upstairs and glanced again at the gorgeous gown that I had purchased. It was the most beautiful thing that I had ever bought – well, apart from Northfield. I changed out of my work things and then placed the dress in the wardrobe, and as I straightened the bag after hanging it James knocked lightly and then coughed.

"Yes James?" I asked as he nervously looked up at me.

"I simply came to tell you that we have made tea and retreated to the drawing room," he informed me.

"I shall join you shortly. I was just hanging up my dress!" I then replied, leaning against the wardrobe door to close it.

"It seems that you are very happy with your purchase!" he then gestured at my large smile.

"I am very happy, but there is absolutely no peeking allowed until Saturday night!" I then pointed out to him.

"I have every belief that you will be a vision on Saturday; I do not wish to spoil that image for myself by looking before then. You have my word that I will not peek at all!" he then said with a slight smile. I nodded in acknowledgement and then suggested that we join George.

I was relaxed as I had changed into my joggers before James had appeared, and as I walked barefoot down the corridor whilst talking to him, we laughed about the expectations we had of my party and the guests that would be attending. He asked if all of the women who had been here under my invitation to try and help him would be attending, and I confirmed that they would, hoping this would not make him feel anxious. He then asked how many guests in total had accepted the invitation, and I now had eighty-five that had given me a definite yes. James raised his eyebrows with surprise; maybe he had thought that I was only going to invite twenty and keep it a small affair.

"Are you sure that it is alright, me having so many?" I asked.

"Of course, you may ask whoever you wish. If you are happy I am happy!" he simply said.

By the time we reached George in the drawing room, he had poured us all tea and had a plate of freshly baked cookies beside the teapot that he handed to me as I sat. I picked up a new book that I had selected from the library and started to read. It did not matter how much I tried to focus, though, I was too distracted; I re-read the same passage about five times before I gave up and put the book down. I had glanced up at James numerous times, he was reading quietly and George had simply looked back at me twice and smiled on both occasions. I studied the room for a while and then decided to go for a walk to the long room with the portraits. I wanted to study them in greater detail; it would be the perfect opportunity to ask questions about the people they had known. I took my mug, refilled it, excused myself and wandered through the quiet house.

I walked slowly around the room, starting with the portrait of James, which had me smiling in an instant. As I walked around to the first one, which I remember being Edward Montgomery – the man who had the vision to start the build of Northfield – I looked closely at him and grimaced a little, then took a sip of my tea.

"Quite a daunting character, is he not?" James suddenly asked me. I smiled at the fact that he had come to find me, and I wondered if it was under George's instruction.

"Yes he is, he does look very frightening, but other portraits that I have seen do not often do the person any justice!" I remarked. He laughed.

"I agree. I am glad that the time of standing for portraits is no longer necessary. There are far more efficient, modern ways of capturing one's image!" he replied as I walked to the next one.

"They don't have the same impact as a painting, though, don't you feel? The fact that someone had the talent to paint it in the first place is amazing, and some of them – like this one of Mary, and of your mother Margaret – are very, very good. I love the detail of the lace on her dress and her intricate jewellery," I replied as I pointed out my favourite parts of Margaret's picture.

"Yes, well, my mother always did look elegant; I cannot deny that. She was indeed captured well in this portrait," he replied. I turned and looked at him.

"I am sorry, is this too difficult for you?" I asked as I walked to the next one.

"Not at all; I have had many years to look upon them. I have fond memories of my mother, and this painting reminds me of how I personally want to remember her!" he replied sincerely. I nodded in agreement.

When I came upon a portrait of James at the young age of four, I tried not to smirk. His face was that of a very bored child and I wondered how long it had taken to do this portrait – probably with a great deal of frustration for the artist. I chuckled to myself.

"You find this one amusing?" he asked curiously, with his arms now folded and wearing a look of annoyance.

"You look sweet really, but also very angry at being made to stand there! I imagine that this was not your favourite day in the world!"

"Yes, well my father would not let me move until the outline was finished; he made sure of that by sitting behind the artist and telling me not to move. I then had to stand three more times whilst the paint was applied – not the most constructive of days for a four-year-old, I feel!" he remarked. I laughed a little more.

"That probably explains the flushed cheeks then!" I smiled.

"Yes, alright, move on!" He gestured for me to look at the next one of the family together.

"I really love this one. You all look so happy!" I stated.

"We were, until my father died. That is a time I do not wish to recall!" he said. I decided not to dwell on it any longer, after all these years it was obviously still painful for him. I looked inquisitively at the one of him at sixteen years old, in which he looked so sad, and as he did not have anything to say about that either, I moved on again. I arrived at the one that made my pulse race… it was breathtaking and so much better than anything depicted in a film or from an Austen book.

"I really do not remember this one entirely from start to finish. I think that I was having far too much fun at the time!" he suddenly said. I could feel my cheeks flush and I quickly tried to hide it. "Are you alright?" he asked.

"I am quite alright thank you!" I replied, trying to compose myself before looking at it again.

"You seem somewhat flustered; are you unwell?" he asked again. I let out a small laugh like a schoolgirl, then stopped myself and replied:

"No, not unwell James, unless a rapid heart rate whilst looking at something you find enticing is an illness!" I happily said and then I turned and left the room. I knew that I had just said something a little too revealing, but I loved the slightly forward way of speaking and being in control.

He quickly caught up with me once I had made my way into the library.

"Enticing? You find my portrait *enticing*?" he repeated curiously. I smiled at him.

"Oh come on James, you must realise that you are handsome? The portrait merely confirms it!" I remarked. He simply raised his eyebrows at my reply and looked like he was about to say something, but then fell silent. I turned and looked at the books on the shelves.

"Is there anything in particular that you would like

to read?" he asked me instead, deliberately changing the subject.

"No, not really. I just love this room, I have always loved libraries but I never imagined that I would have one of my own. It's amazing!" I confirmed as I ran my hand along the neatly shelved spines. I almost felt like he was about to say something else when George appeared.

"Would anyone like to watch some television? I am finding that it is becoming quite addictive!" he asked.

"George, that sounds like a marvellous idea. What would you like to watch?" I asked him as I took his arm, feeling glad that he had interrupted, and we walked back to the day room.

The evening finished at a very quiet and restful pace, and when it was time for bed, James – as always – walked me to my room. I found that we could now say so much with just a look; our connection was growing and when we said goodnight, I yearned for him to be able to kiss me. Only two more days and then I hoped that a kiss would be a reality! I slept contently and happily and felt so incandescently in love, I was sure that my heart had grown three sizes!

Chapter Twenty-Eight

Thursday resulted in confirmation on timings from both the band and the caterers, who were sending waiters to serve canapés and drinks. I had never had such a big event for myself, and as I sat looking into my coffee cup, I wondered if I was biting off more than I could chew. With the party, the people and telling James how I felt, I started to feel slightly nauseous, with a panic attack approaching. As Claire turned up at my desk to drop off some papers I must have looked panic-stricken.

"Hey, what's wrong?" she asked. I pulled her closer.

"Do you think this Saturday is trying too hard? I mean it's a lot to take in – and a lot to expect, particularly from James. Oh god I feel a little ill!" I told her.

"Kat, stop this consistent worrying, would you? It's normal to be feeling a little anxious; this doesn't happen every day – in fact, scrub that, it *never* happens!" she then said.

"Not helping!" I sighed. Then she laughed and I sat and looked at her. "I cannot believe that in my state of hysteria you are laughing at me!"

"It's just made me realise how much you love this guy. It's really 'stick your fingers down your throat' sweet, surely you can see that?" she asked sarcastically. I sat for a while and smiled.

"I really do, don't I?" I then confirmed, and my fears started to dissipate a little.

"There's nothing wrong with that! It's about time you had that glow about you, and I only ever see it when you talk about him! Roll on Saturday; I really want to meet the hottie that has captured your heart!" she then finished before winking at me and then waltzing off. I smiled, took a sip from my coffee and carried on working with the biggest smile on my face, knowing that I would be fine.

Thursday turned into Friday, and the day bounced along remarkably better than I was expecting – I thought I would be stressed, worrying and not getting any work finished on time, as I had decided to take Monday off. When it came to home time, I was really excited that George and I were going to start putting up some of the decorations. When he greeted me at the station, he was stood with a huge bouquet of flowers. I looked at him curiously.

"Both James and I know that it is not your birthday until tomorrow, but we decided that the celebrations should start now!" he simply said as he took my bag and handed me the flowers. I smiled at the gesture.

"Thank you, that is really kind and I can honestly say that I have never been so spoilt!" I remarked as I inhaled the sweet smell of the flowers.

George enquired as to how my day had gone, as always, and I filled him in on what I was sure was not that interesting to him. He commented and looked remotely interested, which was good enough for me. I told him that I was glad to be taking Monday off, and hoped that it would mean spending the day entirely with both him and James, and he in return simply smiled. When we approached the driveway I sighed.

"I just love turning into this driveway and seeing our home. I thought I would get used to it, but every time it gets me right here!" I said as I gestured toward my heart.

"I know the feeling, Katharina, and I have had many a year with that same feeling!" George confirmed.

We hopped out of the car, me with my flowers and George with my bag, and we walked up the stairs whilst talking about how we would all be able to dance the night away on Saturday. I entered the front door but did not expect to see what was waiting for me. I stood motionless, flowers in hand, which were then lowered toward the floor in my absolute amazement. Every table and doorway in the hallway was filled with displays of beautiful fresh flowers, all in cream and white and green. The fresh freesias were a heavenly scent and I swallowed hard as James then asked:

"Welcome home, Katharina, I hope that you do not mind but both George and I wanted to contribute to your party; we thought this was a perfect way of doing so." I turned and looked at George.

"You both did all of this, for me?" I asked, feeling like the most important person in the world.

"Only the best for the ones that we love!" He winked at me.

"I don't know what to say!" I replied as I turned and took the sight of them in. Then I realised that George had been busy arranging decorations too! "And you have also arranged the decorations!" I remarked.

"Show her the ballroom, George!" James then said with excitement.

"There are more?" I asked. George offered his arm to me, so I placed the bouquet he had given me on the only remaining space on the table and walked with him. He rubbed my hand that was linked with his arm in a very fatherly way and I could feel myself welling up.

When we arrived at the ballroom, he pushed the doors wide open, which was the best thing to do as the impact was stunning. There were stands of more flowers all around the dance floor, and on the ornate furniture. It was a vision that even I struggled to take in. I stood with my back to them for a moment, and composed myself, but by now I had tears rolling down my face. This was a gesture that took my breath away and as I stood silently they spoke.

"So you like them? Will they suffice?" James asked hopefully. I turned to them both.

"I am sorry; my silence is not because I wish for something different. I love them, in fact I more than love them, and I cannot believe that you went to all of this trouble for me! How could you think that they would not suffice? They must have cost you a fortune!" I laughed lightly to show them that not only was I happy; I was overwhelmed. George walked across to me and handed me a very neatly folded cotton handkerchief.

"I told you that she would love them, they are from her favourite florists!" George replied as he placed an arm around me. "We were not expecting tears though!" he then laughed. I smiled as I dabbed my eyes.

"Thank you, both of you; you are making my birthday an enormously special occasion!"

"No amount of money, or the time to organise anything for you, Katharina, is the making of any trouble; we simply want you to be happy – you deserve to be happy!" James then stated as he smiled at me.

"Well, I am so happy at this moment that I feel like I may burst; I am completely overwhelmed!" I replied. I turned to George and gave him the biggest hug, and he simply rubbed my back in reassurance.

"Shall we have dinner?" he then asked.

"May I change first? Do I have time?" I asked, wanting to put on something a little nicer than my work dress.

"Of course, shall we see you in the dining room in say fifteen minutes?" George asked.

"That would be perfect!" I smiled as he gestured for me to leave the ballroom. I turned once more, took in the whole room and then turned to James and gave him the biggest smile before walking out.

I decided that as they had gone to so much trouble for me, I should wear something to dinner instead of my usual jeans. I walked into my bedroom to find more flowers in my room and I gasped, wondering how many more displays I was likely to find around the house. I refreshed myself, sorted out my now slightly smudged make up and decided to put on a little cocktail dress. It was a beautiful shade of purple and probably a little over-dressed for dinner at home – but this was no ordinary home! I felt really nice and smart and I was glad to make the effort. I slightly curled my hair and left it cascading to my shoulders and then decided that heels were in order, but nothing too high.

When I neared the dining room I could hear James and George talking; they were trying to organise what was happening tomorrow and when, and were making sure that in and amongst this entire organisation of my party, I was to have time to myself. I smiled, knowing that it would happen anyway; both Claire and I had arranged to have our hair and makeup done in the afternoon. I knew once Claire arrived at 10am it would be all go, go, go!

I tentatively walked into the dining room and gave them both a warm smile as they looked across at me. The table had been prepared with the best silverware and crystal glasses and as I walked further into the room, George put down the wine that he was serving and walked toward me.

"Katharina, you look lovely! Does she not, James?" he then prompted him.

"Indeed, you surely are a vision tonight Katharina!" he replied. I felt myself blush.

"Thank you! You have gone to so much effort for me, it seemed only fair that I reciprocate!" I remarked lightly.

George walked me to my chair and as I sat down he pushed the chair gently in, then laid a crisp napkin across my lap. The starter was already on the table; it was a medley of king prawns with a glaze drizzled across them, and a heavenly-looking mousse of some description alongside. My mouth started watering!

"George, have you been working hard in the kitchen all day again?" I asked him.

"Not today!" he simply replied. I looked at him inquisitively, just as a chef appeared in the dining room, which surprised me a little.

"Good evening, I hope that you enjoy your starters; you have king prawns in a lemon and coriander glaze and a prawn and lobster mousse with a champagne sauce. Please enjoy," he simply said and then he departed the room. I shook my head in disbelief.

"Did that just happen or did I imagine it?" I remarked, gesturing to the door.

"No trickery! I told George that he too should have a weekend off cooking, and insisted that he find a chef for the evening!" James remarked.

I looked around and noted that there were three places set at the table, with a starter on each. Then I looked back at James.

"How did you get around the third person, so that you can eat?" I asked.

"Ah, well – we simply stated that you had hoped a friend would be joining us and that even though we were not sure of their company he should still serve each course in case they do arrive! We have had many years of practice!" George replied.

"I can see that!" I concluded as I lifted my knife and fork. "Shall we?" I asked them.

"Indeed, *bon appetit!*" George joked, looking smug that he had the chance to sit and enjoy dinner for a change, with no part to play in the cooking element. I chuckled at his reply and repeated his remark.

"*Bon appetit*, and thank you so very much. You are making my birthday more meaningful as the evening progresses!" I concluded before excitedly placing the first forkful into my mouth.

"Our pleasure!" James simply stated. After that there was silence for a couple of minutes; the food was heaven itself and there was no time to converse!

The starter was followed by a delicious fillet of sea bass with a roasted red pepper sauce, along with asparagus and potatoes that were creamed to perfection. George must have taken note in our previous discussions about how much I loved fish; he was not the best at cooking it, and I liked to order it when I dined out. We had the time to talk, laugh and discuss tomorrow evening in some detail. They asked me what my plans were for the day and as we discussed the finer points of tomorrow evening, I felt very excited and nervous at the same time. George and I were laughing about the fact that he and James had decided upon a more modern dinner jacket for tomorrow evening. James did not seem too enamoured about the fact that it was not his usual dress, but it seemed that George had persuaded him to wear it, with the knowledge that if everything went to plan, he would be joining us at some point during the evening. We definitely needed him to fit in in that case! My heart skipped a beat at the thought; he already looked exceptionally handsome tonight in his modern suit, which he had removed the jacket of, but he had a waistcoat over his shirt that made him look deliciously admirable. The chef appeared again.

"May I serve dessert now?" he asked. He had already cleared the plates and we had applauded his food.

"Please do so!" George replied. He nodded in response, disappeared briefly and then returned.

"Warm chocolate fondant with white chocolate ice cream," he simply said as he placed my portion in front of me and I inhaled the warm scent of melted chocolate. "May I take this opportunity to wish you a happy birthday?" he then asked.

"Thank you, and may I thank you for a truly delicious meal. I cannot fault one aspect of it!" I replied. He nodded again in acceptance and then simply said:

"Please enjoy!"

"I really think that the dress I bought may not fit too well tomorrow night after I have eaten this!" I joked.

"Nonsense; the overall excitement during the day will have burnt this little pudding away by tomorrow evening!" George laughed.

"I really don't care actually – gosh it smells delicious!" I replied, picking up my spoon.

"It does indeed!" James agreed.

"You have picked the menu well, George – picking everything that I love!" I smiled at him. I raised my glass. "Thank you both for a lovely evening!"

"Thank you for being here!" George then said as he winked at me and raised his glass. We chinked them once and then turned to James and raised our glasses to him. He in return smiled and calmly said:

"Yes, thank you for being here. I cannot imagine Northfield without you now!" His reply was honest and sincere and as I took a sip from my glass, I had the feeling that things were going to be just fine!

I felt spoilt rotten, and the evening passed more quickly than I realised – probably because George was able to spend the whole time with me. When the clock chimed ten o'clock, the chef reappeared, explaining that there was coffee and brandy served in the drawing room, as George had requested. George asked me to excuse him a moment; it was apparent that the chef was ready to leave now. I thanked him again for such delicious food and then they disappeared back toward the main hall. I took a deep breath, feeling so contently full, and then reached for my glass.

"That has been one of the most enjoyable dinner parties that I have been to for such a very long time!" James then commented.

"It has been perfect and you are both very generous!" I remarked before taking a sip of my drink.

"I would not settle for anything but the absolute finest for you!" he then said, and I could have melted into a puddle of warm mush right there on my chair. I tried to casually swallow the wine in my mouth, and then I turned to him and smiled.

"You always say the sweetest things to me!" I replied.

"I would not say them if I did not sincerely mean them!" he then stated and he gave me the warmest and biggest body-tingling smile back and I melted again.

George returned after paying the chef, who had tidied up George's kitchen, so there was not really anything for him to do. We all retired to the drawing room and I slipped off my shoes before curling up on the chair by the fire. I really didn't want the evening to end; I was having my own little fairy tale evening right there and then. I couldn't wait for tomorrow to come! George played some music from my iPod, which he was now getting the hang of. He selected Billie Holiday – another growing favourite of his, and I always loved her voice. I took great pleasure in listening to them tell more stories from long ago; some were humorous and some quite tragic, but they were all fascinating. I knew that I would never grow tired of listening to their stories, but I was growing ever more tired, and I decided at eleven forty-five that I should get some sleep.

"I cannot thank you enough for a most enjoyable evening!" I stated as I stood to take my leave. "I do really need to get some sleep though, as tomorrow night I feel will be quite long!"

"Of course! I think that I can speak for both of us when I say that we have had an excessive amount of pleasure this evening, being able to share it with you on such a lovely occasion!" George then said as he leant forward and kissed me on the cheek.

"May I see you to your room?" James asked.

"Yes, I would like that!"

"Do not rush yourself in the morning dearest; we will make sure that you are well looked after!" George then called as I walked toward the door.

"I have no doubt in that George!" I remarked as I smiled and left for the stairs.

James walked patiently alongside me in every possible mirror, and I stopped at the first landing in the stairway and looked back at the empty hallway below.

"I really cannot wait to see how this house feels when it is filled with people having fun, and hearing music and laughter and expressing love. I am sure that it will be an entirely different experience!" I needed him to realise that I was looking forward to this more than I could possibly show him.

"It will be like times past, and a pleasure and an honour to share it with you!" he said with whole-heartedness. We arrived at my door and I turned to him.

"I have the strongest and most absolute feeling that tomorrow will definitely be a night to remember!" I said as I moved closer to the mirror, and we stood and looked into each other's eyes. I knew that if he had physically been stood in front of me right now, I would not be able to control the strong urge of desire to be kissed by him. The look in his eyes and the fact that he had to swallow hard made me feel that he had the same urge. This was all that I needed until tomorrow; I wanted the moment to be perfect, and in my head that meant that I would be wearing my new dress, and it would be my birthday and James would not be expecting a true confession of my feelings at my party. He was far too selfless to expect anything from me, and so this would be my gift to him!

I entered my room after bidding him goodnight, and climbed into bed after taking the time to carefully remove my makeup. If I was to look half decent in the morning, should they appear to surprise me, I wanted to look as good as possible when just waking! *Plenty of moisturiser before I turn another year older*, I thought; not that one night of excessive cream on my face was going to make a difference, but it was worth a try! I snuggled down into the heavy blankets and drifted off easily, dreaming about tomorrow.

My eyes opened to a pool of light streaming through the curtains; it was light and very bright and the birds were singing. I did not suspect it was late, just a very lovely morning. I reached across to my phone on the table beside me and glanced at it to find that it was only 7.00am; my natural working body clock had kicked in. I put the phone back down and rolled over and snuggled my head back into the feather pillow. It may have been my birthday, but it was far too early to wake properly and so I closed my eyes and tried to drift back off. I did not even realise that I had until there was a sudden knock at my door, and I knew that it would be George and breakfast. I sat up, slightly startled, quickly jumped out of bed and then brushed my hair before jumping back under the covers in record time, and then in an effortless voice I simply said:

"Come in!" The door creaked open and there was George, looking very happy.

"Good morning Katharina and a very happy birthday!" he said with affection.

"Thank you George. You didn't have to do this; I could have joined you in the kitchen!" I honestly replied and just as I did so James appeared.

"Absolutely not, this is our excuse to give you our undivided attention today!"

"It really isn't necessary!" I replied.

"It is imperative that you relax and do as you are told today, young lady!" George then said as he laid my breakfast tray on my lap. "Starting with you eating breakfast!"

I looked at the tray and my tummy rumbled; there was a full cooked English breakfast with wholemeal toast and tea and orange juice. I smiled and then looked at George.

"I have to say that after that large delicious meal last

night, I did not think I would be hungry this morning, but you have managed to make my taste buds tingle and my tummy rumble!" I remarked as I took a sip of juice.

"You need to eat well – you have a long day ahead of you!" George stated. I looked across at James and he was smiling at me and so I smiled back.

"I wish you a happy birthday and I hope that it brings you all that you wish for!" he then said.

"I'm certainly going to be careful what I wish for!" I remarked sarcastically. He ran his hand through his hair and laughed.

"Touché!"

"Please do be careful; I don't think that I could take another 250 years of this type of thing!" George laughed with us as he gestured at himself and James.

"We have cards and presents, and plenty of time to let you eat in peace!" James then said. I frowned.

"No, please don't leave me – I don't want to eat alone. I would much rather you both stayed here with me!" I asked. James smiled and nodded at my request.

"Very well!"

"Have you both eaten already?" I asked whilst enjoying the crispy bacon.

"We have – we wanted to make sure that you took priority today!" George then said.

"I am going to be so spoilt by the both of you today!" I grinned.

"We do not want it any other way!" James then said.

I ate and told them of years past and birthdays with my mum; it was nice to reminisce with them about parties where I was a princess, a cowgirl and a clown! It was lovely to talk about my mum and to have them listen intently. When I had finished eating, George moved my tray, and I briefly excused myself and went to the bathroom. When I returned, they both looked a little reserved and as I jumped back onto the bed they both stood.

"Ooh, this looks serious!" I remarked.

"We both have gifts for you," George said as he moved around to my side of the bed and handed me two neatly wrapped boxes.

"I do not know which to open first!" I said with excitement. George looked at James and then took the smaller box.

"Please open mine!" he said. James looked relieved.

"Alright!" I answered. As I tentatively unfastened the silk ribbon that was tied around the box, George looked a little worried.

Within the paper was a very old-looking leather box. I suddenly had the feeling that this was something very special and I didn't dare open it. Before I did, I looked at George, who nodded to confirm that I should. The little box creaked slightly when I pushed it open, and inside was a beautiful gold bracelet set with little red stones. I took it from the box and inspected it closely.

"George, I don't know what to say; this really is beautiful. Thank you so very much!" I was touched, and then he tugged at my heartstrings further:

"It was my wife's, and I cannot think of anyone I would rather see wear it than you, Katharina!" he said with such sincerity. I felt so very honoured. I looked at him and then leaned across and hugged him meaningfully.

"I love it, and will cherish it always!" I remarked. He looked slightly tearful and then he picked up the other box and passed it to me.

"This is from James!" he said. I took a deep breath to stop myself from becoming too emotional and looked over at James, who was now stood with his hands in his pockets, looking as worried as George had.

This was a much larger box. I had no idea what to expect; I had butterflies again, and my heart was beating rapidly. Once again I untied the silk ribbon, and once again a leather box lay inside the wrappings. I curled my lips in nervously and before I opened it looked across again, to James, with an anxious look. He smiled and nodded with encouragement. I took a deep breath and lifted the box lid, and felt light headed at what I saw: the most intricate and ornate necklace lay within. This was no costume jewellery but a genuine necklace of sparkling stones that were no doubt diamonds and rubies. I swallowed hard and found it difficult to find words; tears filled my eyes and then I spoke.

"I have never had such beautiful gifts bestowed upon me. I really have no words; they are more beautiful than anything I have ever seen! James, I cannot thank you enough, as mere words don't seem appropriate; are you sure about this?" I asked. This was no small gift!

"I am more than sure, and I hope that you will wear it tonight!" he said hopefully. "It was my mother's, and I too cannot think of anyone I would rather see wear it!" he then repeated, as George had said. I closed my eyes and shook my head. I was in a fairy tale; no one had ever given me anything so thoughtful and of such value; not just monetary, but sentimentally. I could only think of one thing to say:

"It would be my honour to wear them!" I sat and admired them in their boxes.

"Well, enough of the present opening for now! You have Claire arriving in forty-five minutes, and you need to get ready!" George then prompted me.

I carefully closed the boxes and placed them in the top drawer of my dresser. Then, without even worrying about how open I was being, I told them how I felt:

"I just want to say that this has been the best birthday ever. Not just because of the presents, but just being here with both of you has made today perfect already!" I smiled at them both. "It has been a long time since I've felt part of a family as you know, and you both have given me that feeling again, so the beautiful presents are just the icing on the cake," I finished nervously. They both stood quietly and so I decided to move. "For now though, I really must shower!" I then said. They both quickly moved in response.

"Yes, of course – carry on dear!" George said.

"We shall see you downstairs!" James then confirmed.

"You most certainly will!" I replied before excusing myself and going to the bathroom to catch my breath.

Chapter Twenty-Nine

As I stood in the shower with the water beating down on my face, I kept holding my breath and then blowing out in one big breath – was this really happening to me? No one had ever given me gifts like theirs, and it made me feel slightly uneasy that they were of great value – I felt like royalty and needed to calm my worries if I was going to wear them tonight. It was such a dear sentiment, them giving me something that belonged to their loved ones, and quite honestly I still wasn't sure exactly how to feel about it.

I jumped out of the shower and dried and moisturised. I had shaved in the shower – smoothness was an absolute necessity for tonight. I put my jeans and a simple white t-shirt on and strolled downstairs. George had made another pot of tea, and had stood my cards on the island; I smiled at them when I entered.

"So when Claire arrives, what would you like us to do?" George asked.

"Nothing really; Claire and I can arrange the final decorations and then we have an appointment at the hairdressers and beauticians at one o'clock, so unfortunately gents you will be on your own for a while!" I commented.

"Well we have enough to get on with!" George

finished. I looked at him; he looked slightly like a fish out of water. He was used to handling everything and it seemed to make him uncomfortable, not being able to be in control.

"Actually George, the caterers and the band may turn up before I get back, so if you wouldn't mind pointing them in the right direction?" I then asked.

"Of course, I can arrange that – no problem!" he then said, smiling and seemingly happy that he had a job to do!

We sat and drank tea and talked about possible problems, none of which were unsolvable, and so all was relaxing and calm… until Claire arrived! She bounced in through the kitchen door, shouting all the way down the corridor to the kitchen. "Where is the birthday girl?" I grimaced a little at her noise level and then turned to face her.

"Good morning!" I announced as she walked in.

"It is indeed and even better that you are now thirty and I am not yet!" she chuckled.

"Yes, alright!" I remarked with annoyance. She pushed a card and present into my hands.

"I really hope that you like it! I'm sure that you will!" she happily stated, looking at me in anticipation. I placed it on the counter.

"Tea?" I asked her, and then she realised that she had not even said good morning to the boys. She looked at me and noted that I was trying to slow her down a little.

"George!" she suddenly said. "Good morning, how are you today?" she asked, and then she looked at the mirror at the end of the island. "Cannot see you James, but if you are here – good morning to you too!" she then said.

"Good morning!" James replied. She jumped like she had just been given an electric shock.

"Ooh I've not lost it, I can still hear him!" she excitedly said and then she sat next to me whilst I shook my head at her in disbelief.

"Good morning Claire, would you like breakfast?" George then asked. She held her hand up.

"No thank you George, I have eaten already – tea would be great though!" He poured her a cup whilst I opened my card.

I tried not to show my amusement at the very funny card; it was sexually orientated, as was standard for her. I did not want to explain it to George and so I read it to myself and then placed it on the counter with the others.

"Thank you, it's very… you!" I remarked as George read our version and James read his. George tried not to laugh and James blushed but smiled. I was extremely embarrassed and so started to unwrap the gift. Claire sat fidgeting on her chair whilst rubbing her hands together; I could tell that she was excited about this present! I unwrapped it carefully and felt overwhelmed when I opened the plain box to find a Victoria Beckham handbag inside. I gasped whilst she clapped her hands together.

"Oh my God Claire, this is the bag that I said I loved!" I remarked as I pulled it from the box.

"I know! Isn't it adorable?" she replied with excitement.

"But it's too much Claire – it must have cost you a fortune!"

"Nonsense, I wanted to get it for you!" she said.

"I do really love it, I just wasn't expecting anything so, so –"

"Expensive – I know! Kat, you're my best friend. I work all the hours God sends and earn a decent wage; I live in a not-badly-priced apartment and don't really have any outgoings of measurable note, so if I want to buy you something nice for your thirtieth, then that is what I will do!" she then sincerely said, and I put the bag down and threw my arms around her.

"Thank you, it's amazing and I love it. You are the best friend anyone could ever wish for!" I smiled and she hugged me back.

"Right then ladies, let's drink this tea and get cracking!" George then announced, trying to organise us again.

We happily followed George to the ballroom and retrieved the other decorations to finish hanging and placing around the house. James kept us entertained by telling us stories of a ball that his friend had held at his estate and at which his friend had drunk so much that he ended up kissing his chosen one's mother!

"Nothing seems to have changed that much from your era to ours; men still cannot seem to work out a good thing when they have it! One drop of alcohol and it's like aliens have taken over your bodies!" Claire declared.

"I have to say, Claire, that not all men are like that, but your perception of them not realising the importance of things is quite precise!" James replied.

"Well, I know the importance to me of everyone in this room!" I then happily stated.

"Yeah, you're only saying that because I bought you a nice gift!" Claire then laughed. I stood up from the box I was leaning over and grabbed her by the arm.

"Speaking of presents – you need to see what George and James gave me!" I said as I started to drag her from the room. "Do you mind?" I then asked them both, pausing before we left.

"Please go ahead!" George gestured and I carried on at speed, dragging Claire through the hallway and to my bedroom!

I pushed her into my room, closed the door and leaned against it, looking at the mirror to check that James had not followed, and then rushed to the dressing table.

"Wait until you see these!" I remarked.

"Oh God, if you've put them in your top drawer I dread to think… I hope they've not had a trip to Ann Summers, knowing that you're on your own!" she laughed.

I turned with the boxes and glared at her.

"This is serious!" I replied and she stopped instantly. I sat beside her. "George gave me this first; it was his wife's and he wants me to have it!" I said. Claire swallowed.

"Okay, now I feel a little teary!" she said as she opened the box. "Oh that's beautiful… and really old!" she then remarked as she gently touched the bracelet. I let her inspect it for some time and then she looked at me, and with her hand on her chest sighed. "Oh bless him, that's just so sweet, and it's beautiful!" she then said.

"I know, I was touched, but then even more shocked

when James gave me this!" I replied as I handed her the other box. She looked at me as nervously as I had felt and opened the box.

"Holy crap, is that real?" she asked. I nodded.

"Yes, it is! James has asked that I wear it tonight – it was his mother's!" I then informed her. She closed the box and threw herself backward onto the bed.

"This is the best fairy tale I have ever been told about! You really need to write about this!" she said as we lay there and sighed.

"I'm starting to think that I might! I'm hoping for the happy ending to finish this story though!" I replied. She reached across and touched my arm.

"I have a feeling that tonight is going to be amazing!" she stated as she sat back up and looked at the necklace again. "Wow! You are one lucky lady!" She smiled.

We took a few moments to compose ourselves and then returned back downstairs and carried on with the decorating, singing along to the music that Claire was playing rather loudly. George made sandwiches at twelve and then we borrowed the Range Rover and drove to our hair appointment. Having our hair styled, make up done and nails manicured was relaxing and stress relieving. The girls at the salon gave us a glass of champagne, which eased our nerves. When we were on the way back to Northfield, Claire asked me how I was feeling.

"Nervous about telling him how you feel?" she asked.

"I want to tell him how I feel; I'm finding it harder to resist every moment I spend with him!" I started.

"But?" she asked.

"I'm still worried about what he might say in return. He may not like me in that way and just love me like a sister or something!" I replied. She started laughing and I looked at her – it was not the response I needed.

"You really think he wants to treat you like a sister? What with the compliments, the protective instinct and a gift like that? He's in love with you, girl!" she happily said.

"You really think?" I asked nervously.

"Hell yeah! The sooner you tell him, the better; Jesus, the anticipation is killing *me*, so God knows how you feel!" She laughed again.

"George knows!" I then admitted to her.

"What? He knows that you love him or that you are going to tell him tonight?"

"Both!" I grimaced.

"Wow, you work fast – what did he think?" she asked.

"The same as you really!" I replied.

"There you go then, and George knows him better than anyone else – I mean he's had long enough!" she remarked, and at that comment we both laughed. "You'll be fine, I'm just glad that I am here to experience it too!" she smiled.

When we arrived back at the house, the caterers were unloading their vans and the band had already got everything out and into the ballroom. Things were shaping up, and I started to get those butterflies again… the beautiful kind! George commented on how lovely we both looked, as did James, and when Claire tried to reply to him I had to remind her that no one else could hear him so it made her look a little nuts!

"This is harder than I thought!" she remarked.

"You get used to it!" George then said. "I think that we should have some champagne and relax a little!" he then suggested, gesturing for us to go through to his kitchen. The caterers were using the large kitchen, as most of the food was a chilled buffet.

George had placed chocolates on the worktop and had four champagne flutes waiting. He poured as we all chatted and enjoyed the fact that everything was under control and that no action was needed from us at this point in time. He passed a glass to both Claire and I and then looked at James, when James had his glass, he stood and raised it and cleared his throat.

"I think it only appropriate to share a toast on this special occasion. George and I have not known Katharina very long, but I think it is fair to say that neither of us have ever met such an incredibly selfless and amazing woman, and we both feel very honoured to share our home with you, and your birthday celebrations." He stopped and swallowed for a second and looked a little flushed, whilst I stared at him with the biggest smile on my face. I steadied my breathing, then he continued: "To Katharina, may your birthday bring you everything that you wish for!" He raised his glass and nodded toward me, and then the others followed the sentiment. George winked at me and then declared another toast.

"Katharina: the best thing to happen to us in a very, very long time!" George simply said.

"Yeah here's to you Kat, you're the best!" Claire said, smiling at me whilst raising her eyebrows to note the very kind toasts preceding hers. We all chinked glasses and took a sip.

"Thank you; those were kind words and I am really pleased that you are all here with me!" I raised my glass to them all. "To all of you, my very dear friends!" I toasted and we all took another sip.

As I savoured the champagne, I realised that the flutes were old and very beautiful crystal. I inspected them and then Claire realised what I was doing and looked at them too.

"These are gorgeous glasses, George!" Claire pointed out.

"A gift from a friend of my father's when he married my mother. I believe that they are French; I suppose they are very nice!" James chipped in.

"They are beautiful; you cannot buy anything like this today!" I replied.

"Never mind the glasses, let's refill them!" George then stated, as he gestured for Claire to pass hers. There was no argument from either of us!

The time passed quickly and when the clock chimed five thirty, I looked at Claire. I felt slightly light-headed and needed to finish getting ready! I wanted to take a quick dip in the bath and as my face and hair were done, this seemed the obvious choice, plus it meant that I could smother myself in moisturiser again. I asked for a glass of water and then looked at both James and George.

"I need to get ready. Perhaps we can meet for another drink before any guests arrive?" I asked them. James had already stood when I had done so.

"Of course, take as long as you need! We need to

ready ourselves also," James replied. I looked at Claire to prompt her to come with me and then before leaving said one more thing:

"I am really looking forward to tonight! This evening is going to be the start of a new chapter for all of us!" I finished. James looked slightly perplexed and looked at George, who simply smiled warmly at me. I knew as soon as I had left the room that James would be enquiring as to what George knew that he did not!

Claire and I went into my bedroom after I had started the bath running. I took my dress from the wardrobe and laid it across my bed. I couldn't wait to put it on. I had new underwear to complement the dress, and had already checked that my bag and shoes matched perfectly.

"Wow Kat, you're going to look amazing! I don't think that any guy in the house will be able to stop staring at you! This is so exciting. I brought my trusty long black ball gown – I hope that it lives up to yours!" she then finished as she laid her dress beside mine.

"Oh Claire, that is really lovely. I don't think that I have ever seen you wear that!" I commented.

"Probably not, I've only ever worn it twice; both occasions were nothing to do with work! I do love it though!" she remarked.

"I can see why you do!" I replied, touching the luxurious fabric, whilst she took out her shoes and very sparkly Swarovski clutch bag. They were just as beautiful. I placed my arm around her waist. "Isn't it fun to get dressed up?"

"Absolutely!" she laughed. "We don't do it often enough in my opinion!"

"Well, I'm just going to take a quick refreshing dip before I get into this expensive dress!" I stated, undressing and slipping into my robe.

"Watch the hair! It's a masterpiece, and there is no way I can replicate it if you get it wet!" she smiled. I nodded and wandered off to the bathroom.

It was just what I needed; a light wallow in lovely scented bubbles. I closed my eyes and tried to make myself believe that this evening had arrived already! It gave me goose bumps thinking about how James may look, and it made my skin flush just thinking about the fact that tonight, for the first time, I may feel the touch of his warm hand on my skin! I sighed deeply. To think that a few weeks ago I was living an unfulfilled life with a man that, in hindsight, I didn't really know very well at all! I thought about my mum and her words from when I was young that: "Everything happens for a reason!" and "Never stop believing in yourself!" I missed her greatly, but I knew that she would be smiling down on me, and the thought made me feel stronger. I knew that I could go through with this tonight!

After overdosing on heavenly moisturiser, I returned to my room feeling smooth and refreshed. Claire nipped out to use the bathroom and I sat on the bed and inspected the beautiful pieces of jewellery. I was slightly nervous about wearing them, in the event that I broke one of them, but I knew that the boys expected to see me wear them and that is what I intended to do. When Claire returned, we laughed and put our underwear on, commenting that we probably couldn't eat in the tight 'suck you in everywhere' pieces that we had chosen! She passed me more champagne, which George had delivered whilst I was in the bath, and we chinked glasses and sipped. It was decided that I needed it for courage – I was just slightly unsure as to how much 'courage' Claire had in mind for me! It came to the big moment; I had my shoes on, which were beautiful, and Claire helped me slip my dress on. As the fabric ran over my smooth skin, it made me hold my breath. She straightened it and then zipped me up before standing back and looking at me.

"Oh my God – you really are beautiful, do you know that?" she said. I looked in the mirror and as the dress pooled a little behind me I smiled.

"I hope he thinks so!" I remarked. She put her arm around me.

"How could he not!" she smiled. "Let's get this jewellery on you and then you can help me!" she stated, retrieving them from my dressing table.

It was almost like they had been meant to be worn with this dress. They both complemented it beautifully; they were not too overpowering, but subtly stunning! I touched the necklace that hung around my neck and then looked at Claire.

"It is so beautiful; I can't believe he gave this to me!"

"He obviously thinks you're worth it!" she replied. "Now please help me – it's 6.30 and we need to have a drink with the boys before guests start arriving!"

She was easy to dress; she had the nicest figure, with just the right amount of curves. Her dress fit her like a glove, and I had never seen her look so stunning before!

"If you do not pull tonight in that dress with one of my friends I will be gobsmacked!" I retorted. She laughed heartily and then passed me my glass with the remaining champagne.

"To us: let's hope that tonight sees us with the men we want and awake all night!" she laughed. I blushed but laughed along; she was never one to hide her thoughts! We threw the remaining liquid down our throats quickly and then turned to the mirror, put on one more coat of lip gloss and sprayed ourselves with perfume. I was about to suggest we go downstairs but she told me to wait five minutes whilst she found George and James.

"You need to make an entrance young lady! We will meet you at the bottom of the stairs!" I nodded in agreement, and then paced the room when she left, trying to stop myself from hyperventilating. I looked at my watch; it had been five minutes. I opened the bedroom door, took a deep breath and started walking along the hallway. Music was resonating from the ballroom, and I smiled at the slow melody that I was sure George had asked them to play. I turned and walked down the first flight of stairs and to the return landing, and when I looked down to the hallway, George and Claire were waiting, with James patiently stood alongside them in the mirror. I slowly walked down the stairs whilst they all beamed at me. I reached the bottom fairly elegantly, and as I neared them I stopped and did a very slow turn for them to see the whole dress. I smiled.

"How do I look?" I asked.

"You are an absolute vision, as I expected!" James replied. I looked at him and smiled the biggest smile; he had on a beautiful black dinner suit and looked immaculate.

"Likewise!" I simply replied.

"Katharina, you are more stunning than I can say!" George said as he walked to me and kissed both cheeks.

"Might I say that you too look very handsome, George!" I replied, remarking at his also immaculate dinner suit.

"Why thank you!" he said in a very spritely tone as he did a very low bow. I laughed.

"Drinks then?" I replied as we went into the ballroom, which in itself was now a vision.

"Oh yes, let's get this show on the road!" Claire quipped as she grabbed George and walked over to where one of the waiters stood with a tray of champagne flutes. I held back for a moment with James at the side of me.

"You look more beautiful than I had imagined possible!" he then said. My heart started racing!

"And you look more handsome than I ever imagined!" I replied as I looked at him. He blushed but accepted the compliment as George returned with champagne in hand. Claire was quickly learning; she returned with an extra glass and then commented on the fact that George had beat her in getting one for me, so she placed it on the furniture to the front of the mirror and winked at the mirror. James laughed lightly.

"This is going to be the most amazing night!" Claire commented as we watched the band playing a very old Frank Sinatra song. She suddenly turned to George and suggested that he should ask me for the first dance, and he agreed with no hesitation.

"It would be my pleasure; would you do me the honour, Katharina?"

"I would love to, George!" I placed my glass down and walked toward him.

His ways of old had not left him; he escorted me to the dance floor, holding his arm for me to place mine on, leaving his other hand behind his back. As we turned to face each other he bowed and I curtseyed, and then he smiled and scooped me up into a rhythmical waltz! He held me close and moved me around the floor with ease. I looked across to Claire who had moved closer to the mirror and held her glass close to her mouth. I could tell that she was saying something to James, and I danced closer with George so that I could overhear their exchange.

"She is the best woman that I know! Kind-hearted, faithful, hard-working and so much fun! You are lucky to have her here you know, James!"

"Yes I know that. She is more than I could have ever hoped for, but my situation does cause an apparent problem!"

"Well, your situation as you call it may not be a situation for much longer."

"What are you implying?"

"You'll see! Just promise me that you will not let her down!"

"I would never wish to cause her any reason to doubt me."

"Good, hold onto your stomach then, because tonight you're in for one hell of a ride!"

Claire threw the remaining champagne down her neck and then placed the glass down just as the song finished, and she walked over to where we stood.

"Don't be hogging the best-looking man here Kat, it's my turn now!" she said. I stepped back, thanked George and then gestured for her to take my place.

"Indeed, please do he is an amazing dancer!" I replied.

"Firstly I'm the *only* man here, and secondly my dancing is a little rusty – I need plenty of practice!" he laughed.

I walked back to the mirror and picked up my champagne. The evening had already started as well as I had hoped.

"You dance very elegantly!" James then remarked.

"Thank you, I hope that I can dance with you sometime soon!"

"I would like that!" He looked at the necklace. "It is more becoming on you than my mother!" he remarked. I touched it and then swallowed hard.

"That is a very kind thing to say, but I am sure that your mother looked stunning when wearing this; it has the ability to make whoever wears it dazzle!" I smiled. He nodded in reply.

As the clock in the hallway chimed seven, one of the waiters in charge came to find us in the ballroom. He stood patiently at the door and so I walked over to see what he needed.

"I believe that you have guests coming down the driveway, Miss Stuart. Would you like to greet them at the doorway or in the entrance hallway? We have waiters ready to serve champagne," he kindly asked. I turned to the others to see what they thought, and then replied:

"I think the hallway would be good; they get to see the grand entrance as I greet them, and I don't have to shiver on the doorstep in this dress!" I replied. "Could you all greet them with me?" I asked hopefully.

"Of course!" George replied and he walked behind with Claire. We all took our places for the impending evening.

Chapter Thirty

To say that people were stunned at my new home was an understatement. They all gawped and gasped with awe at the incredible house and I couldn't blame them – it was what I had done and still did! All of my friends arrived, including Rachel, Kate and Lisa; they were all in the country and I was pleased that they could all join me. I had invited people from work, and others that I had kept in touch with but not seen in a long time. Claire's brother came too, with his girlfriend, and he was nothing but charming, as always. As more guests streamed in, I wondered how many more I could possibly have invited – numbers on paper seemed fewer than actual people. As the music played and there was laughter, talking and dancing, I could see how this house must have been in George and James' time. It made my heart sing a little to see that they looked happy that the house was buzzing again.

Once it seemed that most people had arrived, and I had managed another glass of champagne, I moved to the ballroom. The band looked at me and I gave them the nod to start the more modern covers that I had asked them to play. When they started 'Locked Out of Heaven' by Bruno Mars, the floor quickly filled and it was lovely to see people dancing around in their tuxedos and ball gowns. There was a vast array of colour and as I walked and talked to people around the dance floor, James walked with me. After talking for a considerable time, I stopped and took another glass of champagne and raised my glass to Claire, who had started dancing with Rachel's brother, much to her delight! I looked at James, who had not stopped drinking champagne now that he had numerous bottles at his disposal.

"Are you enjoying yourself, Katharina?" he shouted a little to be heard over the music.

"Yes I am – it is a really lovely sight to see this room filled with people!" I smiled at him.

"You certainly have a very diverse group of friends!" he then remarked.

"Yes, I do. I like every one of them attending for such different reasons," I laughed lightly.

"I love to hear you laugh!" he then said and I blushed and took another sip of champagne. "I feel that they are very lucky to have you in their lives!" he then finished and as I turned to him he raised his glass at me and we both took a sip.

"I have had many comments from them about my necklace!" I then informed him, whilst my hand went to my neck to check that it was still there. "I still cannot believe that you gave this to me!"

"I hope it will be the first of many presents I can bestow upon you!" he then said, and as my stomach pooled with butterflies I was glad that the band interrupted me just then.

"Can we take this opportunity to ask Katharina to join us over here?" they requested. I raised my eyebrows at

427

James and he smiled and gestured for me to go. "We would like to wish Katharina a very happy thirtieth birthday. I am sure that you will all do the same! This is one of the most awesome gigs we have ever played at, this house is amazing, so thank you for asking us to play for you tonight. I believe there is a little something for you here, Katharina, and so if everyone can join me…" the lead singer finished as George appeared, carrying a cake; I sighed at his thoughtfulness as the whole room erupted on cue from the band to start singing 'Happy Birthday'! I blew out the candles and was handed a microphone. Suddenly I had an awful flashback of Bridget Jones and her speech. *Deep breath*, I thought, and then started.

"I cannot thank you all enough for taking part in my birthday celebrations at my beautiful home. The gifts were unexpected, but very much appreciated. I expect to see lots of dancing, there is a buffet to die for that will be served soon, and I definitely expect everyone to leave here more than a little merry!" I laughed. Then I raised my glass. "To friends and family!" I then toasted, looking first at Claire, who blew me a kiss, and then I smiled at George and then James. Everyone in return repeated the toast. The lead singer asked for a request from me and I thought for a minute and then asked for one song that seemed appropriate: 'Magic' by Pilot. As the band started the music, I shrugged at James and then walked across to Claire, dragging George, and we danced happily along as Claire shouted:

"Very appropriate choice!" to both George and I. I laughed and threw myself around. When a few more songs had been played and I had danced for nearly half an hour, David, the head caterer, came up to me to say that the food was ready to be served. I asked him to ask the band to announce it, as they needed a break too.

I went along in the stream of people, with Claire and George not far behind me. The dining room had been set out with a delicious buffet that lined the grand table; its set up was easy and approachable from all sides. I selected a small amount and then moved to the corner of the room, chatting with friends and explaining how I came to buy the house, which intrigued many of them. I moved around and tried to speak to as many as possible before eventually excusing myself and making my way over to George, who it seemed had attached himself to Claire whilst I was busy socialising.

"Are you alright, dear?" he asked. I blew out a large breath and shook my head. "Are you ill?" he asked with concern.

"No, just nervous!" I replied. "I need to speak with him now – I can't wait much longer. The anticipation is killing me!"

"Well, go get him then!" Claire said in her usual matter-of-fact way. George looked at her.

"I have to agree!" he simply said. I nodded and straightened my shoulders just as James appeared in the mirror behind them.

"Everything alright?" he asked and George prompted me with a small cough.

"Please may I speak with you in the library?" I asked. James looked a little nervous, but agreed instantly.

As I walked through the hallway, with James following alongside happily in the mirror, the main door suddenly burst open and John all but fell into the house. I stopped in my tracks for a moment and then headed over to him. I was then greeted by Charles, who mimed that he was sorry, and then in walked Nadine. I froze on the spot and glared at her, and then looked back at John.

"What the hell are you doing here? You weren't invited!" I pointed out.

"I tried to tell him that, Kat!" Charles quickly interjected.

"Shut up Charles!" John silenced him and looked at me. "I don't know what has gotten into you, but seriously Kat, you've lost it!" he then said, slurring slightly.

"You have the nerve to tell me that when you have brought *her* here?" I asked, and then realised that I had a small audience. "Come with me. You stay here!" I remarked, pointing at Charles and Nadine and then dragging John to the library. Claire and George followed and closed the door behind me. James was now furious and paced the room, running his hands through his hair.

"You deserve so much better than this!" James said.

"I'm starting to believe that!" I replied. John shrugged his arm free.

"Who are you talking to? Seriously, you've lost it Kat, you're going crazy! First George, then this house and spending all of your money and then you ditch me!" he remarked whilst waving his arms about.

"If he ruins this night for you I will not be held responsible for my actions!" James then said bitterly. I held my hand up to the mirror to calm him. Claire had her arms crossed and was glaring at John. George looked anxious.

With John facing me near the desk and blocking my view of James, I decided to tell him what I thought.

"You really have no idea when to give up, do you? I'm not coming back to you, John – not ever. You are the most arrogant, selfish, despicable person and I really do not know what I ever saw in you!" I remarked.

"Well said!" George stated. John glared at him.

"Everything has changed since you started coming here!" he then said. As he moved closer, I backed up.

"I love it here!" I replied as he staggered closer still.

"I think you love George!" he then laughed.

"You're right I do – he's like family to me, unlike you!" I simply stated. James now had his hands pressed up against his side of the mirror.

"So help me God, this will not end well!" he remarked, now punching the mirror.

"You are nothing without me. Who would have *you*? You're going mad and no one in their right mind would hook up with you!" John then said, which hurt. I looked toward the mirror at James, who looked as hurt as I, and then answered;

"John, stop denying what has happened; you must admit that we were not happy for a long time. I'm sorry, but I do not want to spend another minute with you. I want to be with someone who respects and understands me and, more than that, is faithful to me!" I commented calmly. James sighed and looked down, disappointed, and so I continued: "Besides, there is someone else!" I then informed him.

I could see James look up at me from the corner of my eye. George and Claire simply glanced at one another hopefully.

431

"What?" John shouted. "You've been cheating on me?" he asked, becoming even more agitated now.

"John, she would never do that. Shows how little you knew her!" Claire said in my defence.

"Shut up Claire!" he directed at her.

"Now, now young man that is no way to speak to any lady!" George replied as he stepped a little closer.

"Who is it? I want to know – tell me!" John demanded as he grabbed me by my shoulders and shook me, knocking me backwards onto the desk chair. I looked up at him and suddenly found a new confidence – I needed to get John out of my life, and I wasn't afraid to hide my feelings any more. I looked around him to the mirror – James was stood there with desire in his eyes – and then I returned my gaze to John.

"I am in love with James Henry Aldersley!" I stated with conviction, and then I smiled. George looked to the heavens, his hands in a prayer-like fashion, whereas Claire just punched the air miming a huge 'Yes'. John shook his head, and I had no time to register James' look as John came back at me bitterly.

"What? Isn't that the guy in a painting here? Jesus, you *are* crazy, do you think that you're in a fairy tale?" John shouted again. I laughed lightly – if he only knew!

Amidst all of the commotion, I hadn't noticed George walking toward the mirror. James had one hand on the mirror and one hand on his stomach and then I heard words that I had hoped for: "I am in love with you too!" he said, but then gestured that he was in pain. I tried to look beyond John, but could not see as he kept stepping in my line of sight and blocking my view.

George had stepped back and pulled Claire with him – why I was not sure – and I now had John pushing at my shoulder repetitively whilst cursing me.

"You seriously need a mental institution; I'm going to recommend that you are institutionalised as clinically insane. What you need is a good hard slap to wake you up from this!" he said with a tone that put fear into me. He stepped forward with his hand raised; I braced myself for pain and put my arms up to my face and closed my eyes, but nothing came… and then I heard him.

"That will not be necessary!" James said. He sounded close by and as I looked up at John, James was stood there behind him and had John's raised hand caught in his! John spun in disbelief.

"Who the hell are you, and where did you come from?" he asked, a little dazed.

"I would be James Henry Aldersley, and there is no way that you are laying one finger on the woman that I love as long as I draw breath!" he replied calmly but with authority. I swallowed hard and looked at George, who had his hand on his chest and seemed close to tears. James in the meantime placed John's hand behind his back and pushed him away from me. John, in quick response, turned back on James and lunged toward him, fists ready, stating: "Don't push me around!" The door creaked open and Charles and Nadine walked in just as James' fist quite rightly made contact with John's chin, knocking him backwards a couple of steps and onto his arse. I sighed in relief.

"Really?" James asked. "You keep coming at me, John; I could hit you all day after what you have done to

Katharina!" he remarked as he stepped in front of me to shield me. Nadine ran to John's side, pampering him, but he stumbled to his feet and pushed her out of the way.

"You can have her! God, I can't put up with this sham – whatever it is!" he gestured with hand movements. James dropped his fists as Charles and Nadine told John it was time to leave and ushered him to the library door.

"Oh, and John – Katharina and I will be calling to pick up her remaining items soon, as she will never be coming back – this is her home, here with me!" he then shouted after him. George covered his mouth and tried not to laugh.

"Arse!" Claire piped up as he passed her.

"Oh whatever!" He gestured to us all as he nursed his swollen and bleeding lip. "I give up – I've no idea what is going on here; she never mentioned you living here!" he mumbled to himself, looking back at James as he exited the door.

James then turned nervously to me and moved closer. He reached out his hand to help me stand and then he placed one hand on my cheek. I closed my eyes at his warm touch.

"Are you alright?" he asked with emotion. I smiled at him as I placed my hand on his.

"You're here, you're really here!" I smiled. He smiled back and lifted my hand to his lips to gently kiss it, and then he inhaled the smell of my skin. I felt slightly nauseous, light-headed and confused, but I also felt so in love as I looked into his beautiful eyes.

"I am here, thank you for believing in me!" He

breathed out heavily. "I love you Katharina Josephine Stuart!" he then smiled. "My wait has been worth it!"

"I love you too!" I simply replied, and as I did so he moved closer and scooped me up in his arms and kissed me, just as I had dreamed he would. We would have continued kissing all night if Claire hadn't broken the silence.

"Got any more of those hotties in there for me, George?" He laughed loudly at her remark.

"God I hope not, one is enough!" he replied as Claire joined in laughing.

James turned around and with my hand in his walked toward George, who simply said:

"Back in the land of the living then lad?" He almost looked ready to burst into tears, but James simply threw his arms around him and they hugged like father and son.

"I intend to make the absolute most of it George, as I hope that you will!" he simply replied and then as he stepped back he sincerely said: "Thank you for being a father and a good friend to me all these years!" George was choked up and cleared his throat before replying:

"My pleasure! I only have one word of advice – and not that he didn't deserve it – but you best not go hitting everyone you meet for the first time!" George patted him on the arm in acknowledgement. He laughed and then looked at his hand.

"Yes, but it did feel good to give that man a piece of my mind!"

Claire gave me the biggest hug.

"Jesus, that was an experience and he is hot, hot, hot!" she whispered. "You need to write about this –

seriously!" she then stated as James took my hand and pulled me back to him. He hugged me more tightly than anyone ever had and placed his head into the nape of my neck.

"It feels good to hold you. I cannot tell you how long I have wanted to do so!" I leaned back from him.

"Me too! Maybe I could have ended this sooner than I thought? This was not quite the way I had intended on telling you, but I wasn't sure how you felt about me!" I remarked.

"You captured my heart from the moment we met!" he then replied as he placed his hands on my face and leaned down, pressing his lips against mine. I surrendered to his tenderness and lost myself for a moment, before hearing Claire again.

"Hey, wait a minute – I feel slightly cheated now, I could have been the one to break the spell if we had waited a little longer!"

"I'm not going to say maybe another time Claire!" George winked at her. James rested his forehead on mine and then said:

"You have guests and a party to attend, my dear!" I nearly melted.

"This is by far the best birthday that I have ever had!" I replied honestly.

"May I have the next dance?" he asked as he smiled at me.

"Oh God, this is so not fair! Seriously? He's hot *and* a gentleman?" Claire shrugged as she started to walk toward the door. "Come on George, you are going to have to settle with me!" she gestured to him.

"That would be my pleasure, Claire!" he smiled, leading her out of the room.

As James and I followed, his hand entwined with mine, he heard the music and then grimaced a little. "Maybe not?" He looked at me apologetically. I laughed and looked at George hopefully.

"Give me a minute, I can sort that!" he replied, laughing a little and taking Claire with him.

As we left the library, I looked toward the main door where Charles and Nadine were talking sense to John, who simply stared at us. James tightened his grip on my hand. I had to make sure they left and so I looked at James, hopeful that he would let me speak with him.

"Just give me a minute?"

"Do you want me to go with you?" he asked.

"I'll be fine, I will be right back!" I smiled as he reluctantly let go of my hand.

I walked over to them and Charles was quick to apologise, and at the same time tell me how stunning I looked. The comment barely registered! John straightened himself and stood in front of me.

"I need to say I'm sorry, Kat. I would never have touched you, you know that don't you?" he asked whilst rubbing his forehead in shame. I sighed at him and shook my head.

"John – I am sorry this has ended this way, but you need to face up to the fact that you and Nadine are to blame for this. I want you to leave, all three of you – I never wanted this ill feeling but you've left me no choice!" I confessed.

"I can see that! I am sorry and I hope that you are

happy, I will regret this one day," he replied. I turned, looked across at James and smiled.

"I know that I am going to be very happy!" I simply replied, and then I gestured to the door and they knew that it was their cue to leave. I had no expectation of getting any further apology. Nadine simply mouthed 'Sorry' as she scuttled out of the door after John, and in a small way I found it amusing!

As I walked toward James with my friends watching us, he held out his hand. As I slid mine into his, it fit like a glove. He smiled at me and looked happy that I had now removed anyone that could cause any sadness and as we walked toward the ballroom, the song the band was playing changed to 'I'll Be Right Here Waiting For You' by Richard Marx. I smiled, knowing that George had a list of my requests and had chosen this song especially. I was lost in the intimacy of having James here with me and as we slow danced along with others, who were watching us intently, I inhaled the scent of his skin and wrapped my arm around his neck, pulling him closer. Whilst he hugged me tighter, he cradled the back of my head and swooped in for another kiss. Just his touch made me feel filled with love; as we swayed along, I could not be any happier.

I insisted that he ate with me, and drank champagne; just to do that together was so pleasurable. Claire, George and James and I seemed to have our own little private function going on, but I did introduce James to my friends and colleagues. Angela was definitely taken by his good looks! She swooned in front of him, which Claire found highly amusing. She did point out that she wanted details on where to find 'one of those', and I wasn't sure that I was ready to explain!

Claire was certainly not shy and she asked if she could 'borrow' James for one dance. I agreed as I wanted to dance with George. He spun me around to the band's version of Nina Simone's 'Feeling Good'. We laughed at how apt the words were, and as it came to an end, George hugged me harder than James had and whispered in my ear.

"You are our saviour! I love you for your honesty, belief in us, and your love for James!" I pulled back from him and smiled.

"I love you too George; you're definitely my family now!" I replied and then we both hugged even harder as James walked back to me and placed his hand on the small of my back.

"You are going to squeeze the air out of her if you hold her any tighter, George!" he joked.

"I am simply conveying my appreciation for Katharina!" George smiled. James tapped him on the shoulder in a friendly gesture and then turned to me, took my hand and kissed it again.

"You have guests leaving!" he pointed out. I looked at my watch; it was nearly one in the morning. I looked at him, knowing that it was coming to an end. James gestured toward my waiting guests. "Shall we?" he asked, I nodded in agreement.

Claire had definitely had an impact on Tom, Rachel's brother, and it looked like he may be staying the night. I watched him spin her around the dance floor whilst I said goodnight to leaving guests. Once everyone had gone,

James and I and Claire and Tom had a last dance on the floor alone. Just being able to hold James close to me was mind blowing. I couldn't believe he was really here! George was celebrating with more champagne, and when the band had packed up it was just us left. Knowing that people would be back to clear up in the morning, I thought about the rest of the night.

Claire pulled me to one side and declared that Tom was staying and asked if that was alright. I said it was fine – as long as they didn't keep everyone awake all night! In response she nudged me, looking at James. He was stood with one hand in his pocket, looking at me whilst talking to George.

"Don't think you need to worry about that – you're going to be awake anyway!" she laughed. I had a sudden panic attack.

"God, what if I let him down?" I asked.

"Jesus Kat, he's well out of practice; I reckon by tomorrow he will realise it's like riding a bike and will be up for much more practice!" she said as George locked up the front door. Claire kissed George and James on the cheek before hugging me once more and with her hands on my shoulders she said: "Relax and enjoy it!" As she bounced up the stairs with Tom, she stopped halfway and turned to face us. "It's really great to finally meet you James!" she happily said, and I knew that she meant it. James replied with one word:

"Likewise!"

I smiled at her remark and as I looked at James, I knew that he was more nervous than me. He was anxious and so I went to him.

"Are you alright?" I asked him. He brushed my cheek with his hand.

"I feel like I am dreaming!" he smiled. Then he kissed my cheek. "I am trying to work out how I am going to rest until tomorrow without you near me!" He gestured to Claire and the fact that it was time for bed.

"No!" I stated loudly. "I don't want to be alone – not tonight. I've only just got you; I don't want you to leave me!" I declared honestly. He sighed.

"Katharina, I'm never leaving you!" he replied as he kissed me again. Then he looked into my eyes. "But I am not sure that it would be appropriate for me to stay the night with you!" he said in his gentlemanly fashion. I swallowed and then replied:

"I respect that you feel it's inappropriate, but times have changed. Do I get a say in the matter?"

"Of course; I want you to be comfortable with any decision that you make!"

"I've never been more certain about anything. I just want to be close to you, hold you, and feel you hold me!" I said. He held me tight.

"I want to hold you and be close to you! I love you!" he stated again.

"I know, I can sense that you do!" I told him. George had now walked back over to us.

"Right you two young lovebirds, I am off to bed for the first night's sleep before the start of a new day for us!" he said with a slight slur.

"George, are you alright?" James enquired, looking at him.

"Bloody marvellous!" he said loudly whilst chuckling

441

to himself. He walked away, waving his hand at us. I laughed.

"A little merry it seems!" I remarked and then I took his hand. "Shall we?" I asked. He nodded and we climbed the stairs whilst he held me tightly around my waist.

We arrived at my room and I locked the door once we entered. James stood and looked vacantly around the room and so I walked over and faced him, standing on tiptoes to reach his lips. I kissed him and as my hand rested on his chest I could feel his heart racing.

"Your heart is pounding!" I confirmed and he simply nodded.

"I never thought that I would ever be loved again – not like this – or love anyone, or have this opportunity to…" he trailed off nervously. "It is somewhat overwhelming that someone like you would want to love me!" As he finished his sentence, I placed my finger over his lips and shushed him.

"I love you, and I never want to leave you, and I have never felt' like this about anyone. Is that not enough?" I asked. He nodded and took my hand in his.

"It has been many years since I shared the company of a woman!" he said with a worried look. "I do not want to leave you unsatisfied!" he finished. Just those words made the pit of my stomach heat up. I knew that we were going to have a lot of time to make him feel more at ease, and quite honestly the thought made me tingle.

I decided to take the first step. I was nervous too, but I unfastened my hair and let it cascade down my back. I shook my head a little and looked at him; his eyes were a pale but sharp blue and sparkled with such heat and life, never moving from mine. I pushed his jacket from his shoulders and let it drop to the floor and then unfastened his bowtie. Sliding it from his neck and then unfastening the top button of his shirt made him breathe a little more erratically, and so I pulled off my shoes and then kissed him again. He was breathing harder and his heart was racing faster.

"Hey, are you alright?" I asked him.

"I have so many emotions right now; my heart it seems does not know how to respond!" he gently said as he took a couple of deep breaths. I smiled.

"I can understand that!" I smiled and I stepped back. "Broken spell brain overload?" I then joked, trying to relax him a little.

"I am overloaded and overwhelmed at everything that has happened tonight, but more so at how beautiful you are, and how kind your heart and soul is!" he said honestly. I melted again, but felt his anxiety, and so I made a suggestion.

"James, I love you and that is all you need to think about for now. Why don't you get settled into bed and I will be with you in a moment? I think you just need to be held closely for now!" I replied. He stepped closer.

"The fact that you understand makes me love you more!" he sighed, and then kissed my hand.

"Would you unzip me so that I can undress?" I asked, turning and lifting my hair to reveal the zipper. I could feel his hands shaking, and he apologised as the zip was a little stiff.

"I am sorry!" he said as he tugged at it, but I found it endearing and so I laughed lightly.

"It's fine, you're doing great!" I replied as he managed to unfasten it to the bottom. He placed his hand around the back of my neck and kissed my shoulder. I shivered and closed my eyes. His touch was delicate and tender and warm. When he stood back up, I turned to him. "I will be back in just a minute!" I replied as I pulled my robe and my sexiest nightdress over my arm and disappeared to the bathroom.

I removed my makeup and brushed my teeth and hair, and then quickly shrugged out of my dress, laying it over the chair in the bathroom. When I returned to my bedroom and reached the door, my heart was racing and I had to stop and stand with my hands on my hips and take three deep breaths. I turned the door handle and walked in, locking it again, and was pleased to see that James was laying in bed. He looked nervous, but with his chest bare he was a vision. I shrugged out of my robe and then walked around the bed, not taking my eyes off him. He nervously sat up and I slid under the covers. I propped myself up on my elbow and then simply said, with my arms open:

"Come here!"

He shuffled across to me and as he embraced me, letting out a small breath, I moved us further down the bed, holding him close. He hugged me tightly, and whilst he held me I gently drew circles on his back. The smell of his skin and the warmth against my body was intoxicating. We lay still for some time – not speaking, just embracing – and then he lifted his head and looked at me.

"I am the luckiest man on this earth!" he simply

stated before kissing me firmly and without hesitation.

He had no need to worry. As we became more entwined beneath the sheets, he had forgotten nothing!

Chapter Thirty-One

When I woke, I was surprised to find James facing me, wide awake. He was simply staring at me. I smiled, quickly reminiscing about last night, and I knew that I blushed just a little. He reached across and touched my cheek and then I stretched.

"Good morning handsome, did you sleep well?" I asked.

"I slept for some time, but then I found my head had too many questions about what would happen next. I found comfort just watching you sleep!" he replied.

"I hope that you have not changed your mind, Mr Aldersley!" I stated with authority. He kissed me gently.

"I could never change my mind about you or how I feel! I keep looking at the mirror and wondering how to live. I am so used to being on my own, trapped in there, that I do not know where to start!" he replied nervously. I embraced him and held him tightly.

"We will figure it out together!" I replied and he squeezed me and then kissed me. He made a small murmur deep within his chest and then looked at me.

"You are going to be a danger to me, Katharina; you are more intoxicating than I imagined!" he smiled. I laughed lightly.

"I have you under my spell instead?" I joked. He laughed, rolling onto me.

"That is definitely true, and a spell I do not mind enduring for all eternity!" He kissed my forehead then jumped out of bed. The sight of his naked buttocks made me nervously look away. "You take your time and get ready, I am going to make you breakfast now that I can! I'm just going to shower, so see you downstairs soon," he stated as he pulled his trousers on and left his shirt open and walked to the door.

I threw the covers over my head when he left and giggled like a schoolgirl. This was really happening to me. James was here and I couldn't have been happier, and last night... wow... it was the best night that I had ever had! I closed my eyes and as thoughts ran through my head I must have drifted back off, as I suddenly heard talking and music and banging around the house, which startled me. I climbed out of bed and went to the bathroom to find Claire just leaving. She grabbed hold of my arms.

"Well?" she asked hopefully, looking at me for any small clue. I smiled.

"Absolutely amazing!" I simply said in return. She hugged me like I had just won the lottery, screaming and laughing.

"I knew it. God he's got everything, *and* he's great in the sack!" she laughed.

"How was your night with Tom?" I asked her.

"You know what, he's really sweet! I like him; we are going to have dinner next week!" she replied – I was shocked. A second date for Claire so quickly after the first was a big thumbs up. I touched her arm in a sisterly way.

"I'm pleased – you should give him a chance, he's a really nice guy!" She nodded and then I stepped past her. "I'm going to take a shower. James is making breakfast!" She rolled her eyes and tutted, then gestured for me to get ready.

When I arrived downstairs, the whole place was buzzing with people tidying. I walked toward the ballroom and stood just inside the doorway. It had already been cleared and my thoughts returned to the many people who had been in here last night. I stood for a moment longer and then I felt two arms wrap around my middle and pull me back into a firm chest. James held me tight and I rubbed his arms. He smelt delicious and as he kissed my neck I closed my eyes and inhaled deeply.

"I wondered where you were; I hate to be parted from you!" he said as I turned to face him. He had a white t-shirt and jeans on and fit in with everyone else. I raised my eyebrows at him.

"I like your new wardrobe!" I stated, glancing up and down at him.

"I have to become part of this era. I need to start by dressing in the correct attire!" he said, and I laughed a little.

"I think that we need to work on your vocabulary too. You still sound like something from your era!"

"Duly noted!" he replied with a huge smile. "I have made breakfast, shall we join George?" he asked.

"I would like that. How is he feeling this morning?" I enquired.

"Not as well as he did last night!" he joked. He took my hand and led me through the hallway, glancing in

448

every mirror that we passed. "This is very strange, and will take some getting used to!" he remarked. I wrapped my other hand around his arm and pulled him closer.

"You're going to be just fine!"

Breakfast was delightful, mainly because James was with us. Claire and Tom had joined us, and it felt like any other normal family morning. George was the happiest I had seen him, regardless of his sore head. James invited Claire and Tom to stay for the day, as he reminded me that I had presents to open. I was glad that he had asked. As the day was dry and somewhat sunny, after lunch, when all the tidying was done and the house was back to normal, I went for a stroll with James in the garden. There were so many things that I wanted him to see, including London, where I worked and the places that I loved. I knew this would have to be done one step at a time, though; it would be very daunting for him and I didn't want to freak him out.

The weeks passed and I had never been happier. James and George had gone with me to collect the last remaining items from John's apartment. I had taken them for dinner in London, to my favourite restaurant. James had picked me up from work numerous times via train and tube; he liked to travel on the train – he found it 'stimulating'. He had also visited the office, much to Angela's delight. I couldn't have imagined myself in any other situation now; it was hard to think that I was in such a different place this time last year.

I left work after a long day with a spring in my step. George had made the point numerous times that family was the most important thing to him and he was so happy for James and me. I also hoped that he would meet some kind-hearted lady who he could spend the rest of his life with; he had been alone for so very long. It had given me the idea of looking up George's family tree and trying to trace any long-distant relative that he may have. My search had been successful and I arrived at the train station that evening feeling excited. I was greeted by James on the platform. He always wanted to meet me as soon as he could and hugged me tightly every time I returned to him. We kissed as always; it was our first greeting to each other before we even spoke. I knew that George would be waiting outside, and so I quickly told James my plan. He was more than excited about it; he couldn't believe that in my search I had managed to trace George's family right down the line to his existing great-grandson (eighth great-grandson to be exact!), who had children of his own. I had suggested that we invite them for the day to Northfield, and remarkably they lived in Kent and so they were not too far away! It would have to be a well-devised plan, and I had the perfect way in enticing them to join us: I wrote them a letter telling them that we had been researching past descendants of Northfield and told them of their link. I offered them lunch in the main house at no cost so that we could let them know our findings. Thankfully they had agreed to visit, with all of their children, as they had been doing a family tree too.

It was our secret and when the day arrived, we were ecstatic. We had explained that we were having visitors to George, and that they were friends of mine; he had not questioned it too deeply. We all waited for their arrival.

James smiled at me and told me to explain. George looked at us with slight confusion, knowing that we were up to something. James stood beside me with his arm around my waist and prompted me to begin.

"George, I have a confession to make. The people visiting today are not my friends."

"I'm sorry, I don't understand!" George remarked.

"They are family – your family!" I replied.

"What? How?" he asked, looking a little nervous suddenly.

"Katharina wanted you to know that despite our situation your son and their subsequent sons thrived. It was all her idea!" James explained. George sat down, a little dazed.

"I never dared hope that they had carried my family along the generations. How did you find them?" he asked. I crouched in front of him.

"There are many ways to trace people now, George. It is about time that you had the chance to take a look at the amazing family you created! I hope that you are not angry; I just wanted you to meet your great grandsons!" I replied.

"*Sons*?" he asked inquisitively. I nodded.

"Ryan is your great, great, great, great, great, great, great, great-grandson." I counted along my fingers. "He is fifty years old and is married with three children – two boys and a girl!" I replied and then touched his knee in reassurance.

"I do not know what to say!" he then stated, and a tear ran down his cheek. "I never expected to ever see any person related to me by blood ever again. I am touched that you gave me such consideration!" he then said and he touched my hand. I smiled and stood up, and as I glanced out of the window I could see a car approaching.

"You best take a couple of deep breaths, George – I believe they are here!" I remarked. He stood up and straightened himself and James patted him on the shoulder to give him more reassurance.

"This is a good thing, George; your family flourished and it is good to see that after everything you have endured!" James confirmed. George nodded and then walked to me and hugged me.

"Thank you, Katharina. I never expected you to surprise me more than you already have. You are such a generous soul!" he said. I hugged him back and then took his hand.

"Come on, let's go and say hello!" I suggested as we walked to the hallway and opened the front door.

Their little boy and girl bounced out of the car and their elder son, who was eighteen, stretched as he exited the car. Ryan and his wife Sarah got out and walked to the bottom of the front steps, where we now waited. George trembled a little, but managed to say:

"Welcome, we are so pleased that you could join us today!" He reached out his hand and Ryan shook it.

"Thank you for inviting us. It was a coincidence that we have been trying to do our family tree for some time. You may be able to enlighten us a little more!" he said eagerly. George released his hand, looking at his own, and then replied:

"I hope to do just that!" He stepped across and kissed Sarah on both cheeks like a friend would.

"It's lovely to meet you!" she said. "Children, come and say hello to –" She stopped and looked at him.

"George!" he answered for her. The little boy bounced across to him.

"That's my name too!" he said, and then he reached out his hand, "I'm very pleased to meet you!" he continued and shook George's hand vigorously. It made us all laugh. They introduced us to Isabelle and Mark and we all greeted each other before walking with them into the house.

The day was better than we could have hoped for. George seemed younger somehow in their company. The children delighted us, and Ryan and Sarah were really lovely people; they loved the house and everything that George had to tell them. He had decided that maybe the truth was a little too much to take in right now, but he gave them all the other information that they asked for to help with their family tree. He was buzzing with every story he told. When it came to them leaving, he was happy when Ryan asked if it would be possible to speak with him again, should he need to. George answered by saying that they could call or visit whenever they wished. He wasn't sure what more he could tell them, but he liked the idea of keeping in touch.

George waved them off, and then hugged us both together and thanked us. I was happy that he had embraced the whole thing so well, and it was obvious that he had enjoyed every minute of it. I think that James was pleased that we had done something for George for a change. He asked if we would all like some tea, and as he started to wander away, dancing a little, James turned to me.

"Could I ask you to join me in the ballroom?" he enquired, taking hold of my hand.

"Sure!" I replied, following along.

When we entered, he walked to the table opposite the door, which now permanently had my iPod and speakers sat on top. He pressed play, and then walked back to me as a song started playing; 'Cheek to Cheek' by Fred Astaire. He held out his hand for mine, and as I willingly gave it to him, he spun me and started to move me around the floor.

"Interesting choice!" I commented.

"George likes this song; I like the words!" he said, smiling.

He was very graceful and held me tightly to him. We had practiced numerous times at dancing; James regularly waltzed me around the dance floor – something that John had never liked to do! When the song finished, he dropped me into a leaning swoop and then kissed me. It was very romantic. After taking my breath away slightly, he returned me to standing and touched my cheek.

"Katharina, I have something that I need to ask you!" he requested my complete attention.

"Anything!" I replied honestly. He put his hand into his pocket and then dropped to one knee in front of me. My heart started racing and I felt a little dizzy. He produced a very large diamond and ruby ring between his fingers and gave me a very sincere look as he then said:

"I cannot waste another moment without confirming and knowing that you are mine forever. Katharina Josephine Stuart, will you do me the incredible honour of marrying me? I promise to love you and protect you and be faithful to you for the rest of my days!" He said it with such love and conviction that I did not have to even think about the answer!

I reached down, placed my hand on his face and then replied:

"I never want to be without you, James. I love you more than words can say… yes, I will marry you!" I replied, smiling. He stood and placed the ring on my finger before scooping me up and spinning me around.

When he placed my feet firmly back on the ground, he kissed me again and then looked at my hand, which bore the ring proclaiming that I was his.

"It suits you!" he said, looking at it. "Rubies are a good choice for you, and they signify love! I can understand why my father chose it!" he quietly said. I swallowed hard.

"This was your mother's too?" I asked.

"It was. Now it is yours, and I can at last understand why my mother was so grief-stricken after losing my father. I know what a love like theirs feels like now!" he honestly replied. I threw my arms around his neck.

"I love it, it's beautiful. Nothing else could have been more perfect. Thank you!" I replied, now feeling a little emotional. James held me a moment and then with his hands on my waist he looked toward the ballroom door.

"George, it's alright, you can come in – she has agreed to be my wife!" he shouted. George's head popped around the door and then he quickly scuttled in.

"Thank goodness for that!" he said as he marched straight to me and hugged me, then kissed me on the cheek. He shook James' hand and then hugged him like a father. He looked at my hand and the ring. "It suits you well Katharina! This calls for more champagne to continue the merriment!" he said happily and he turned to retrieve some, but I had other ideas.

"Wait a minute. I'm glad that I have the two of you in here whilst you're both so happy. We need to bring you both into the modern day – just wait there a moment!" I gestured for them to not move and whilst they both shrugged at each other and looked lost, I walked across and flicked through my iPod. I found an appropriate song and pressed play: The Police's 'Every Little Thing She Does Is Magic' started playing.

I walked back toward them. "First lesson of slightly more modern dancing. Off you go boys!" I gestured to them both, then placed my hands on my hips.

"Really?" James asked. I could tell that he was a little uncomfortable at the thought.

"Please?" I asked again with puppy dog eyes.

"That is not fair, Katharina! I can refuse you nothing when you look at me in such a way!" James replied. George laughed out loud and I smiled cheekily. The chorus had now started.

They looked at each other briefly and then raised their eyebrows and started moving along with the music, doing their silliest dance moves. I laughed heartily at them and then joined in; they took it in turns to spin me and turn me, and then they both in unison kissed me at the same time, each taking a cheek. I kissed them both back, taking a moment to kiss James tenderly, then we all laughed and danced contentedly, not caring how we looked but knowing that beyond all doubt we would definitely live... happily ever after!

Acknowledgements

A *Different Reflection* – my first novel, would not have been finished without the support of so many people. I feel it is important to thank these people who, through their encouragement helped me to get this far.

Firstly at the top of my list; Thomas and Ryan my sons – you give me the inspiration daily to write and the confidence to be the best that I can be, you've brought me so much happiness and I love you both very much. You can now both read this at your leisure instead of over my shoulder!

My husband, Russell – although you have found the clicking of my keyboard irritating during the evenings, I thank you for telling me to follow my dreams, as I had nothing to lose. Hopefully this is the first of many!

Mum, my first critic. Thank you for your support and belief in me to succeed. I couldn't have done this without your motivation. Dad – I'm in your debt for allowing her to ignore you and sit and read and re-read pages on numerous evenings. Your words of wisdom are as ever appreciated. I am grateful to have you both as my parents and I consider myself to be the fortunate one.

Claire – my cherished friend who has listened to my thoughts and concerns so many times over coffee. Your friendship, laughter, intelligence and humour have kept me sane whilst getting this far. You are the kindest and most honest friend and I couldn't have done this without your continued advice and enthusiasm, not to mention keeping me fed with cake, sandwiches and hot chocolate on so many occasions.

My brother David – your advice and encouragement are always appreciated. Thank you for all of your support and invaluable advice which pushed me to take the right steps.

To all my other family and friends who believed that I could do this – you know who you are. I am lucky to have you supporting me and this journey has been a joy to share with you.

Finally, to all of my new friends at Troubador Publishing, it has been my absolute pleasure to work with you all. You have been irreplaceable in your expertise, advice, kindness and commitment and have made this whole experience and journey effortless. So my biggest thanks to Jeremy, Rosie, Amy, Aimee, Alice, Chelsea, Lauren, and the rest of the team. I look forward to working with you again.